SKY

STAR

Doug Evans

Dedicated to Jeni, who flew at age four. And Ray, who came cloud dancing with me . . .

Far from being trapped alone and frightened and so very high in the sky at my young age, I actually revelled in my aerial solitude. I wasn't a terrified child whose pilot had collapsed at the wheel of our light plane, I was an ebullient youngster soaring alone over sweeping brown plains; aloft far above the ground by choice, not misfortune. This was my airborne classroom in a boundless Heaven. No teacher could ever instil a greater love of flying than I already cherished, and no known god granted me this billion cubic miles of blue skies in which to choreograph my favourite pastime of *Cloud Dancing*.

Unfortunately, both time and the fuel inevitably run out so I reluctantly turned the plane back towards the farm, then lowered the nose and reduced the engine power.

On descent, my airspeed increased until the airflow screamed around me and I raced past puffy castles of billowing cotton cumulus clouds, then waltzed along elegant avenues of misty stratus layers. Soon I was dancing around giant lumpy bales of cumulo-nimbus before popping out beneath the flat and greyish/blue cloud base. Here is where, for a few hours each week, I skated and twirled with my majestic friends the clouds while my school mates sat in stuffy classrooms with dreams of only dancing with girls. To me, waltzing upon the Earth was not my future calling; I clearly saw my life up here in this great ballroom in the sky; a paradise where I surely belonged.

Below the cloud base, I was still singing '*Ice cream castles in the air*' when I spied our property's red soil airstrip, but as I approached to land the turbulent and snapping crosswind began tugging my aircraft sideways; trying to veer it away from the landing strip and onto rough ground. I was tense, but fortunately had sufficient piloting experience to control it and soon the wheels bounced onto the dirt runway with a thump and a puff of red dust. Pushing hard on the rudder pedals, I managed to swing the plane around before it ran off the strip's end and into menacing clumps of mulga.

Nearing the old hangar, I strained to peer over the high dashboard to make sure I didn't crash the plane, propeller first, into the rusty tin walls; then I shut the noisy engine down. Because I was only thirteen years old I was still a bit too small to see sufficiently forwards from the plane when on the ground, and it was only when I opened the side door could I confirm by how far I had cleared the hangar.

Climbing from the Cessna 172 with my head still *in the clouds*, I was startled to see a uniformed stranger approach. Horrors! An Air Safety inspector barked at me, 'You're too damn young to be flying that plane!' Stunned, but caught red-handed nonetheless, I trembled in fright – although I had known this would inevitably happen one day. He waved his shiny inspector's badge at me as he asked 'How old are you, sonny?' Lying to him, I brazenly stated that I was sixteen.

He said, 'Well, you certainly don't look that old to me. I think you should be sitting in a school classroom, not in *that* thing.' He was quite right, of course, because I was only thirteen and far too young to be flying any plane – especially by myself. I glanced around anxiously for help, but our homestead was deserted because our men were still out mustering cattle.

I'd run out of luck. The CASA flight inspectors only showed up once every few years - or so Maurice had assured me, and I'd hoped their next inspection would be when I'd turned sixteen and become legally old enough to hold at least a student pilot's licence. Too late: it was today and he was here now. He asked to see my fictional licence, which of course did not exist, then we waited in silence for Maurice the station owner to appear. When Maurice rode in on horseback, I darted behind the sheep washing shed as the inspector turned to meet him because, although bubbling with confidence in the air and endowed with immortality as we all were at that age, I felt great apprehension at this sudden patch of turbulence where I could soon be dancing to a different tune!

Maurice Bisley was a wonderful, warm and kind man. A 68-year-old widower, he'd taken me under his wing – so to speak - after my father, Herb Grant, died the previous year. We had lived on the property next door to Maurice's 50,000 hectare *Darmornie Station;* and ours was called *Wundala Station.* Dad had taught me to fly our Cessna when I was still twelve - or unofficially taught me, I should say, and I could already proudly boast 230 flying hours in the co-pilot's right-hand seat by the time he suffered his heart attack that dark night. We were the only two souls living in the old colonial homestead because my mother Alice had abruptly left us when I was just two years old. In shock from Dad's rasping breath, I rang the ambulance depot in town, then raced Dad's old jeep five kilometres through a midnight dust storm for help at Maurice's home - but upon our return it was all too late.

*

Doting Maurice wept as he embraced me at Dad's funeral three days later. 'You can't be living over there by yourself, Robbie. An orphan living alone at your age? No way. You can come and live with me and the boys. You're most welcome, you know. Your new home.'

As we exited the old stone church, a local news camera flashed at me. I was alarmed; failing to comprehend why any camera needed to be pointed at me. An intrusive voice barked a question about who would be looking after our property now. I started to mumble an unintelligible reply but Maurice tugged me away. I've never forgotten that incident, nor the sheer audacity of anyone questioning a twelve-year-old child at his father's funeral. The next day our local paper showed a cowering photo of me under the headline: *Orphan inherits Wundala estate.*

Reluctant to abandon my home but scared of being alone on an enormous property at just twelve, I had no other alternative and promptly moved next door to *Darmornie* with Maurice and his eight station hands. There were no females on that vast station north-west of Trangie in outback New South Wales - except for occasional dance nights when the 'boys' brought in partners for country dances and parties. Otherwise, it was a monastic male bastion of hard-working men – plus me, an orphaned boy with no brothers or sisters. Here, my only love was my beautiful blue and white aeroplane. It was legally mine now - or so our long-serving family solicitor, David Skillen, had assured me, along with the whole 27,000 hectares of *Wundala Station;*

the only proviso being the usual legalities that I must wait until I turned eighteen before attaining legal possession.

In the meantime I faced an interminable wait of six long years – seemingly *forever* at that age - while it was all to be held in a 'trust' they called it. It was as though no-one *trusted* me with these assets that were rightly mine - and one could hardly blame them: I was far too young and already knew where I would spend it: more aeroplanes!

After Dad's death we leased out our *Wundala* property - or my property as it now was, and managers soon took over - but not before I whisked our Cessna away on a five-mile flight to next door. Flying my first solo, I piloted the 172 over to Maurice's landing strip by myself – much to his dismay - but my superb landing produced his broad and friendly smile of relief. Exiting the plane, the gathered station hands all gawked in bemusement; then one muttered 'Is he only *twelve*? Are kids allowed to do that?' No, they're not, but I did it anyway, then smiled as the men declared my landing a *greaser,* (a very smooth touch-down).

Rural kids flying planes in Australia in those days weren't all *that* unusual. While many farmers' kids drove cars at my age, some also learned to fly their station's planes. I was one – *after* I'd first learned to drive Dad's yellow, open-topped Jeep to school and audaciously collected a few kids from farms along the way. We then zipped along the last three kilometres of public road to the old stone school house which proudly proclaimed: *Built in 1877.* Soon after this, Dad taught me to fly; just a year before he died.

Although Maurice wasn't a pilot himself, he had a dirt airstrip on his property; much like my father's. This allowed our planes and visiting crop-dusters to land and take off when required. Stooping and slightly shrunken from years of back-breaking toil in the bush, Maurice suffered back strain and arthritis - with perhaps other unmentioned ailments, but he nevertheless found it within his generous and loving heart to adopt me on the day I turned thirteen. Fancy that! Aged sixty-eight and recently widowed, Maurice took me in as his son - a mere boy of thirteen and a precocious and head-strong boy who did precisely what he desired – most of the time. Maurice's own adult sons were both over forty and living in Western Australia, but now 'lucky' old Maurice was a new Dad all over again. I still wonder how or why this man did it, but he did and I adored him - not only because I had known him all my life. In sorrow, I continued to deeply miss my own father, Herbert; but he had gone and my early world had collapsed when I was so very young.

Within a week of residence in my new home, I was actively campaigning to convince Maurice that I should be the station's resident pilot - although he'd had me slotted for far more mundane 'help around the yard.' So he didn't need this inconvenient question when he already had a large business to run, men to manage, his own health to consider and the current drought to worry about. Plus a brand new nagging son. 'You're only thirteen, Robbie,' he replied during one breakfast. 'You can't be my pilot. How on Earth can I put a thirteen-year-old on my books as a pilot?'

I lodged a begging protest. 'You don't have to *pay* me, Maurie. I don't want any money - I just love flying my plane. And I can handle that plane just like any adult pilot. I've got over 250 hours now and that's more than most eighteen-year-old commercial pilots at the airport in Dubbo. Please, Maurie. Please.'

Maurice deliberated the spectre of the Aviation authorities catching us with he being subsequently prosecuted, but I assured him he never would - even though this bold declaration was made without any knowledge of certainty at all. I argued that many farmers in Australia allowed their kids to fly before they were sixteen, so he finally muttered, 'Um, s'pose I might think about it . . . '

Just then a truck fortuitously rolled through the gates with another load of moaning cattle. Maurice rushed from the kitchen table exclaiming, 'That was due last flamin' week!'

I boldly assumed his non-answer was a *yes*, and when he'd gone I leapt for joy; running for my plane. I was Australia's youngest (unofficial) pilot and zoomed into the air for a grand celebratory sweep above our property; swooping and streaking my four-seater plane at one hundred knots over wide wheat fields that spread a blaze of yellow stubble below me and far away to the distant horizon. Then I followed up with a racing low pass over the old homestead which, when I glanced down, caused the cattle to moan and thrash around in the truck. Yippee!

2.

So, on that bleak day of our surprise air safety inspection, I'd achieved the distinction of becoming the youngest pilot ever to be caught for under-aged flying - according to the unamused inspector, Harold Roffe. His handlebar moustache twitching, Roffe informed us that residents from our town had reported me for flying. More precisely, some jealous kids from my high school had reported me to our only police officer, Sgt. Porter, who then rang CASA Air Safety in Canberra about this reckless boy-pilot who often buzzed the town. Maurice eventually avoided prosecution by immediately hiring Tyson Swain as his permanent commercial pilot, then assuring CASA that I would never do it again.

Trimmed, but certainly not grounded, from that time I flew with Tyson whenever I could successfully dodge school and therefore evade the other routine chores of growing up on a cattle and sheep station. Tall and friendly, Tyson proved to be not only an amiable person, but pliable, so I quickly learned to wrap him around my fingers as much as I dared. Now it was *almost* legal for me to fly from the left-hand (captain's) seat because Tyson was a qualified flying instructor; although technically I should have stayed in the right seat until I was sixteen and held a student pilot's licence. No chance of that!

Within a short time, Tyson informed me that I possessed an unusually gifted flair for piloting aeroplanes; and that I exhibited a confidence and maturity of *airmanship* far beyond my tender age. Over the next three years I accrued nearly 2,000 flying hours under his supervision where we did cattle mustering, property inspecting, water hole surveillance and general rural flying between towns often located hundreds of nautical miles apart and spread over the enormity of outback New South Wales. While my peers endured the daily grind of school, I can't remember if I went to school very often at all during these years and consequently received numerous bad attendance reports. Luckily for me, Maurice was usually too busy with his property management to read them. Now aged over seventy, he was still labouring hard.

Just after my sixteenth birthday I obtained my official Student Pilot licence in the mail. The local Chief Flying Instructor was amazed when I proudly showed him 2,476 hours neatly entered in my log book, and I had passed all the theory examinations long ago. The *CFI* exclaimed that I had accumulated more hours than his four other instructors combined, and that I certainly flew like it.

I desperately wanted my full Private Pilot's licence right then and there, but they made me wait a whole year until I turned seventeen and had completed the curriculum program of cross-country navigation flights that could then, finally, be officially endorsed into my shiny new Private Pilot's log book. As I'd already been navigating everywhere for years and had also provided my own plane, I whizzed through these annoyingly duplicate flights in a mere three days. Then, impatiently waiting out another full year, eventually became the *youngest* pilot in Australia to obtain a Commercial Pilot's Licence at just 18 years of age. As usual, everyone remarked on how young I was, and while Maurice was delighted and proud, my dad would have been even more elated.

Then, within a short time, Maurice's health had deteriorated to the point where he was forgetting many basic things and becoming easily confused about most. His doctor warned us of advanced Alzheimer's; about which I grieved. After researching the doom of this disease, I often pleaded to no-one in my bed at night: Why am I to lose my *second* fantastic dad and I'm still only eighteen?

At this time I was operating charter flights from Dubbo airport in their racy twin-engine Cessna three-ten. The *pocket rocket* it was called – and that's how it went: 180 knots of sheer joy! I was dancing with clouds in Heaven every day, then at night I winged back to Trangie whenever possible in my Cessna 172 to visit ailing Maurice. He was now 73 and soon to slide away into the one-way fog of Alzheimer's disease. A frail figure already, he would rapidly waste away from those years of toil on the land, and a few more months sadly saw him struggling to remember people's names, his own sons' names – and then my name. He was my adoptive dad and my only family, but at least I could fly to visit him; most other people - non-flyers – could never have contemplated these regular long journeys in the night.

My life was wonderful in so many ways, but too often it was equally marred by tragedy. I frequently wondered where my mother Alice was – long gone since I was two; but it seemed I was to never know. Understandably bitter, I often cursed anyone who could abandon their own child - especially a two-year-old. Consequently, I harboured mixed opinions of women due to this early poor example, and sincerely hoped they weren't all the same. But in any case, there were no females in my life to verify either way as I'd felt no love or affection from any woman that I could remember - not even a sister. Apart from ailing Maurice, aeroplanes were the only loves of my life, so I just hated to see him fade away because then I would have no-one.

3.

I borrowed some money against the impending handover of my estate and bought the Dubbo Aero Club's sleek Cessna three-ten which I was already charter flying; then back-leased it to them when I was off duty. On a sunny day over the Western plains, I flew a charter to Bankstown in Sydney then back to Dubbo where I had a few hours to kill. It was there, sitting on the fence outside the Dubbo air terminal, that I encountered the next great love of my life: an awesomely beautiful creation that would dominate my life and emotions for years to come. Of course it was an aeroplane; but not just any old aeroplane: it was a magnificent Fokker F28 Fellowship. A passenger jet. And to be precise, I didn't *see* it: I *heard* it first.

It was the mid-1980's and Ansett Airline's subsidiary, AEA - *Airlines of Eastern Australia*, had just introduced the Dutch-built F28 to regional services; replacing their old faithful prop-jet F-27 Friendships which had delivered decades of sturdy and trouble-free service. Now it was pure jets and no more propellers – just two huge fan jets mounted on the rear T-shaped tailplane of this beautiful, swept-wing airliner. A 65-seater aircraft, the F28 was a transport revolution to rural communities and could fly from Dubbo to Sydney in less than half an hour - a stunning mockery of the laborious six-hour road drive. But it was the sheer *noise* of this powerful flying machine that I loved instantly. Those two mighty Rolls Royce *Tay* engines certainly knew how to pump out more roaring, crackling decibels than any rock concert.

I heard the whine of a jet. I turned towards the runway and saw an F28 readying for departure; lining up on runway 05 at Dubbo. After spooling up the Tays, the Fellowship absolutely *bellowed* into life with an all-encompassing, deafening din of numbing, rolling thunder that battered the entire airfield while onlookers covered their ears as children squealed in fright. Dubbo had never heard this primeval bellow before and the townsfolk certainly pricked up their ears and gawked skywards when the streaking beast soared overhead - only to return from Sydney in slightly over an hour. I was enraptured: if there was a Hell then this was undoubtedly the Devil's roar!

On its next departure, because everyone in the district had heard it and word had quickly spread, the airport perimeter fences were crowded with excited locals eagerly waiting to be deafened again. I was already the F28's newest fan and it certainly didn't let us down when it blasted off again. In awe, I listened again to the raw, unfiltered assault of thrust unleashed upon nature; a resonating boom that crackled, rumbled and rolled across Dubbo town and district; crashing and ebbing like sonic ocean waves. I craned my neck as the jet rocketed steeply into overhead clouds and, at that very moment, clearly saw my own future riding ahead of those thunderous Tay engines. Yes, there I was, sitting proudly up the front in my shiny blue airline pilot's suit with a cap of gleaming gold braid, yet back in reality, to achieve this dream I needed to get a job with them first – quite a hurdle. I would become the youngest airline pilot in Australia if I won that lottery.

Eagerly pouring through the Air Navigation Regulations later, it seemed I would need to be twenty-one before I could fly for any airline. This was confirmed by friendly Captain George Milden the following day when I approached him at the check-in counter while his F28 jet sat on the apron at Dubbo airport.

'I've got my Senior Commercial licence, but I sure wish I was twenty-one,' I lamented to the captain after he invited me out to his plane. Inside the complex flight deck, I gazed around in total awe: this was the only office I ever wanted to work in. When he asked about my flying experience, I stated boldly, 'I've already got nearly four thousand hours and I'm only eighteen . . . '

Milden interrupted with warranted disbelief: 'How could you possibly have that many hours at eighteen? You're too young for that.' I tried to briefly explain my time-consuming story while cautiously omitting my airborne escapades of earlier years. Thankfully, I knew that ninety percent of those hours were legally flown with a licenced flying instructor.

We sat in the pilots' seats as the captain listened with interest, then he said, 'However, we certainly might need an F.O. (First Officer). You can be under twenty-one but not a captain until then - and only with *a lot of* hours like you. We've just lost six F/O's so it's a bit of a sad tale, really. Would you be interested?' My eyes popped in shock.

'Interested? Oh yes, sir! But I don't even have a jet endorsement. I've only flown the three-ten and singles . . . '

Milden smiled, 'Well buckle up young fella and we'll go for a spin.'

I squawked, 'A *spin*? In an *eff-twenty-eight*!' He wasn't joking. The captain explained that he needed to do a quick air test of the APU auxiliary power unit, and also assess the recently repaired tail-mounted air brakes on landing. His First Officer could sit behind us in the jump seat, and there would be no passengers or flight attendants on this test flight. The F/O closed the main door and soon I was in a euphoria of delight as Milden showed me the start procedures. Then we taxied slowly out towards the runway start markings - or 'piano keys' as they are called. Glancing outside, I was surprised at how high we were perched above the concrete taxiway.

'Slow down, Rob.' Milden suddenly ordered. 'You're taxying too fast. Walking pace only.' Then Milden looked seriously across at me as we lined up for take-off. 'Okay Mr Four-thousand-hours, I've got *twenty-one* thousand hours and I'm the captain, right? You have the throttles and the wheel. Advance to eighty-percent power, then full throttle when I say. Vee-one is ninety-five knots. Any failures during the roll and I take over immediately. Got it?'

I simply couldn't believe this magic as I nervously pushed those small throttle levers forward, yet a wry smile escaped me as I imagined the deafening roar from behind us as we accelerated down that runway; blasting out a swirling haze of hot exhaust. Unfortunately, up the front in our soundproof flight deck, we could barely hear those mighty jets so far behind us, but I knew that the whole of the Dubbo district most certainly could. Here today, I possibly became the youngest Australian pilot ever to take-off a Fokker F28 Fellowship jet. It was only a ten-minute flight, but the best moments of my life.

However, after literally coming back to Earth and receiving Captain Milden's approval of my (reasonable) landing, I soon discovered that not everyone was in love with these noisy Fellowships. My newest love affair was already being challenged in a barrage of fiery noise complaints that began arriving at regional newspapers, radio and TV stations. Farmers stated that their livestock were being spooked by the great noisy bird overhead, while mothers living near the airport claimed their children couldn't get to sleep after our thunderous evening departures. Others just seemed to invent numerous reasons to complain until trending criticism soon overtook general acceptance.

However, somewhat hypocritically, every local eagerly desired to travel on the 'new jet' and to marvel at flying to Sydney in 28 lightning-fast minutes. At such times, the takeoff noise was suddenly of no concern to those on board while everyone outside would just have to cover their ears and suffer. Seeking opinions around town, I often winced as I listened to complaints about something that I adored to the point of reverence; a sound that I often dallied around the airport until 8pm just to hear.

In the meantime, I'd flown the three-ten down to Sydney where I completed an F28/jet endorsement course in record time. Captain George Milden had been right: AEA was haemorrhaging both first officers *and* captains as the company was apparently in financial difficulties. So I was hired within one crazy week where, just as sensible pilots were abandoning the sinking ship, I was enthusiastically leaping in! Blindly, I didn't heed the hints and ignored the blatantly obvious; I just wanted to fly that wonderful thing - and did. Very soon we were reduced to just three planes and only ten pilots, but I simply didn't care. While many say that love is blind, they also sing *Love hurts!*

And very soon it was going to hurt a great deal as these became desperate times for our beleaguered regional airline which now struggled with minimal staff to keep the shrinking fleet aloft. Worse, the parent company, Ansett, was beset with its own structural woes while it battled its giant domestic competitor, Qantas.

Not caring which way the coins might eventually fall, I leapt into the co-pilot's vacancies via a rare and fortunate loophole in the Air Navigation Regulations – as Capt. Milden had indicated: being under twenty-one but with so many hours, I could fly under a special dispensation as a first officer only, but definitely not in the capacity of a captain. So, armed with only wishful thinking, I naively expected the company's chronic problems to magically resolve themselves in the 2½-year period until I at last turned twenty-one.

They didn't, and the planes themselves didn't help, either. The wonderful F28's, although modern and much faster than any previous regional planes, were also quite expensive to run – apart from being excessively noisy. These detractions only compounded the company's grim prospects, which were being valiantly propped up by short-term bridging loans and other dubious finance designed to plug the gaping holes in our budget. Blissfully ignorant, I didn't concern myself at all with the future (who does at eighteen?), and just revelled in the daily joys of flying this great bird of the sky.

And with youthful exuberance, I usually smiled to myself *cop that!* upon each decibel-shattering takeoff.

4.

Bored and lonely, I was in coastal Coffs Harbour one evening; camped in a motel and staring at the local TV news. As with most of our other destinations, there had been some protests within this lovely town about 'airport jet noise,' so a few local shoppers in the streets were asked to air their views on the news. Irritated, I was about to switch it off when an exceptionally pretty young woman holding a child was asked to speak. She said she lived in an old house on the very perimeter of the airport at Coffs. Often when our jet departed on a calm night - and especially at 7.45pm on our last departure to Sydney via Casino – our jet blast literally blew her back fence so hard that it rattled and sometimes collapsed.

I'd heard plenty of wild claims lately, including cows going off their milk, so I was wary of placing too much credence in her words - until she broke into tears: 'I'm a single mother and my baby screams every time that dreadful plane roars away. My life is just so hard at the moment and the last thing I need at night is children who I can't settle down. Then last night . . . ' but they suddenly cut her off there by heartlessly screened an ad.

Apart from beauty, something about this young woman struck me. Ten seconds on the TV and I liked her already. Quickly, I jotted down her name from the screen and wished Mrs Cristina Avey was a single person I'd met socially and not a housebound mother being upset by our plane that disturbed her so much. For the first time I felt somewhat embarrassed and guilty about my joys of 'blasting the locals' on take-off with our deafening Rolls Royce engines. Many residents simply didn't like it and the engines were, without doubt, unacceptably loud in those days before jet engine 'hush kits' arrived and reduced aircraft jet noise by over fifty percent.

In guilty indecision, I looked up the lady's name in the local phone book and wondered if I should call her to smooth things over. But what could I possibly say? Don't worry about it? Find another place to live? Or, they're not really *that* noisy. Anything except: *I love that sound!*

Nervously, I called her and explained that I was a pilot who flew that *noisy jet* and that I'd felt acutely guilty after seeing her news appearance. I wondered if I could call around for a few minutes to apologise. She replied with anger, 'You're the pilot of that horrible *thing*? I don't even want to *speak* to you, let alone meet you!' With a crash she hung up on me, so I instantly resolved to in future keep my nose right out of company affairs - in which I wasn't an official spokesperson, anyway. So I was quite disappointed in my failed mission of diplomacy, but at least I'd tried.

Then, in the morning, my room phone rang. It was the same woman. Cristina had phoned AEA to ask my motel's name, and here she was! She apologised profusely for her 'rudeness' and explained that her husband had walked out on them a year ago leaving her life in turmoil, and now the evening crescendo of decibels from our departing planes became the last straw. We chatted further, with the end result seeing me getting a taxi to her old Housing Commission house next to the airport.

Fatefully, I tapped on her door and called out, 'Maintenance! I'm here to fix your fence.' I was attired in a brand new pilot's blue suit which glittered with three gold stripes on the arms while the distinctive peaked cap glowed with aviation authority. While some stewardesses had told me I was quite handsome, I hoped I looked my professional best for 'Mrs Cristina Avey', the battling Mum who hated jets - and me.

The door flung open and I was greeted by three tiny and smiling faces. Yikes! She had more than just that one baby I'd seen on the TV. But the Cristina who'd yelled and said she never wanted to meet me was radiantly beautiful and smiled a wonderful greeting, explaining she was 'So sorry for her remarks - but please come in.' I detected a waft of perfume. Had the hassled housewife dressed up just for me? We sat down and she remarked in surprise, 'Gee, you're so young, Rob - and good looking. I mean, I was expecting a much older man with gray hair; you know, like you see those pilots on TV ads. They all look like middle-aged accountants in a uniform.'

On the lounge I was instantly attacked by three friendly little mites, crawling over me and tugging at my uniform. They weren't dirty, but seemed poorly dressed – almost in rags.

A four-year-old smiled beautifully and asked, 'Can I play with your funny hat?'

I answered nervously. 'Ah, I suppose so. What's your name, sweetie?'

'Ith Mandy,' she lisped, then proceeded to merrily rip the gold braid from around its peak while her mother made coffee. Next, she went after the gold coat buttons!

We sat together and sipped coffee while Cristina apologised again for her remarks on the phone. 'I was just so *angry* after watching myself on the news. Did you notice how they cut me off? I was trying to explain how the girls had just dozed off as the jet took off last night, then they all woke up bawling from the noise. It'd been a bad week and that was about all I could take. But they cut that part out. And then you rang . . . '

Nervous with women, I blundered, 'You know Cris, I've never had any female in my whole life who loved me, let alone one who *hated* me!' Damn it, this was an ill-placed and stupid thing to say, but she just laughed - unsure if I was joking, I suppose. Then we swapped stories of our lives. In explanation of my strange statement, I related my tale of becoming an orphan at twelve. I had no mother or sister, and no girlfriends at school because I was too fascinated and involved with aeroplanes. My present awkwardness wasn't helped by having attended only one high school formal where I struggled through just one dance.

Another coffee heard Cristina relating how she'd had three children before her 'Tony' had walked out. I was quite angered but not surprised that some men could abandon their own wife and children because I'd been abandoned myself. It was hardly unique in history. Now this nice lady was in her early twenties and a deserted mother of three girls; her life was probably ruined already. I gulped in sadness for the three little tykes playing beside me: what on Earth would become of them?

Trying to overlook *that* subject, I talked of my farming upbringing, then Cristina chatted about becoming pregnant at just seventeen and promptly losing her modelling career. I gazed at her: she was lovely enough to be a model, that was certain, and I could envisage that bouncy blond hair, laughing eyes and enticing smile on a magazine cover - although with three young ones in tow, few offers would beckon now. We strolled down her back yard as the little ones buzzed around my trouser legs. Poor little darlings; they seemed overjoyed to suddenly have a man here, just as I knew how it felt to be without a mother. As my Dad and Maurice had been the exact opposite of Cristina's deserting man, I despised this Tony person already and I had never met him! I tossed him into my sin bin along with my own runaway mother; consigned to somewhere far away.

We leant over the decrepit paling fence and surveyed the adjacent airport: the runway start point seemed barely 200 metres from her house; just past the local racetrack. The noise onslaught must be deafening. I cringed.

Cristina pointed. 'I don't mind those smaller planes like that one over there, but we couldn't rent anywhere else after Tony left. It was okay for a while - until the jets started coming. Then the papers said the jet services might increase . . . I just cried when I read that.' I thought, surely they wouldn't *increase* flights while we were going broke? This was just a media fabrication, but, unsure, I avoided getting into that. I again rued my callous uncaring as I recalled my immature grins on take-off: *'Cop that!'*

'Those damn noisy jets!' I grinned and shook my fist at the airport, then we both laughed together with the kids as they shook their tiny fists in imitation. With difficulty, I shamefully admitted to Cris how I'd absolutely adored that powerful noise from the F28 when I first heard it, but now felt embarrassed and guilty – conveniently failing to mention 'cop that', of course.

Cris flashed a radiant smile and said, 'I told a tiny fib too; the fence doesn't really blow over from the jets, it's already falling by itself.

Anyway, you definitely don't look like a middle-aged accountant; you look more like a high school movie star. Ah, how old are you Rob?' Just as I told her I was eighteen, little Amanda tugged at my trousers and squeaked: 'Are you going to be our new Daddy?' Cris flushed red as the child repeated, 'Well, are you?'

'Ah, not today mate,' I answered flippantly and rather rudely; quite unsure how to speak to children because I never had. But my heart froze as I saw a flash of deep disappointment on the child's face that told me I'd blundered yet again. I was just another big, useless, betraying man who might raise their hopes then let them down again. It pained me to see a sad tear run down her cheek. 'Mandy, that's enough!' her mother ordered, but I patted their tiny heads and said in confusion: 'She's lovely. They're all so sweet . . . but I'd better go now.'

Now why did I say that, either? I'd never made so many gaffes in one day! I had all day to myself and wasn't on duty until 6.45pm; one hour before our evening departure. I probably could have stayed there much longer but felt strangely out of place and out of (rational) words. So I said, 'Thanks for the coffee, Cris. Can I call in next time I'm staying here? We're in Coffs six times a week, but only for half an hour. I stay overnight just once a week.'

Cris smiled, 'Yes, please. I still can't believe how young you are - for a noisy airline pilot, I mean.' We agreed to keep in contact. Despite her grief, she was fun while I was dumb.

That night I accelerated the big jet along runway 01 at Coffs - instead of rolling the opposite way on runway 19 and blasting her home. I performed an early right turn out to sea, moving our deafening sound print well away from the lonely single mum's old house next to the airport perimeter. On the flight deck, I hoped she'd noticed us flying away almost silently - for a change. Down below, three little angelic faces were hopefully staring with their nice mum at our blinking strobe lights above a moonlit ocean as we eventually turned left then set course onto 345 degrees magnetic for Casino.

5.

The next month I turned nineteen, just when old Maurice's condition worsened in his nursing home in Trangie. Similarly deteriorating was our small airline as it floundered under the burden of unsustainable loans that might rupture at any time. Trying to ignore these negatives, and failing to mention that my romantic visits might be terminated very soon, I went out with Cris once a week in seaside Coffs Harbour; dancing, dining and sometimes beaching with her three girls who now adored me as much as I did them. In many ways these kids were much like me, I supposed: they'd suddenly found themselves fatherless at a very young age, just as I'd grown up and never known any mother or other woman in my life at all. Kids? I knew nothing about them but decided upon the simple formula that if I was nice to them, they should be nice in return. And they were. Here were three delightful little girls who jumped all over me and crushed me on the beach sand. At home, they raced around the house showing off to me, squealing out high pitched decibels then insisting I kiss them goodnight.

'Hey princesses,' I whispered one bedtime. 'Not so much of that loud squealing next time, eh? You're worse than that old F28.' They asked what was that. 'That noisy big plane that I drive.'

Amanda, now five, whispered, 'Mummy used to hate that big thing, but now she likes it. But don't tell her I said that, will you?' Amanda, Olivia and Emily the baby; aged five, three and one. I loved them all. They could be the family I'd never had. I'd only known two nice Dads - plus rough farming men, dirty ranch hands, smelly cattle – and aeroplanes. There was nothing feminine amidst that life and I can barely remember any females at our properties except for the occasional dances and a few vague memories of Maurice's wife before she'd passed away.

So here was I, nineteen years old, reputedly handsome and free as a bird if I wished. There were plenty of available ladies in Sydney and indeed everywhere I flew. Other pilots told me that at night, vibrant

Coffs Harbour was packed with pretty young women like my Cristina – many of them single. I could be a real Roger the Lodger had I chosen such a life: roar into town briefly, then off again at 400 knots before anyone could catch me! Instead, I spent my free time with this single mother and her three little angels who crawled over me, dribbled on me and thought I was their new Dad. Was I?

I was happily enjoying a family life I'd never known. But then the three angels were soon to become four, as Cris had dramatically announced on one of my flying visits. She was pregnant. Her contraception had failed her and she wasn't sure why. This was now a whole new situation that I tried to absorb as my mind swirled, so we celebrated with ball games on picturesque Park Beach next to Coffs Creek. Here I taught the *youngies* how to play cricket with a tiny plastic bat while Cris, also learning, was stunned but happy with her news. The kids merrily chased the ball as the overhead seagulls raucously soared and swooped - perhaps cawing *We can fly better than you!*

Having a rest and while nursing baby Emily, I decided that the examples of kindness and humanity shown to me by Maurice Bisley was obviously the only decent future path for me to tread, and I could no more take off and fly away from these four lovely females - and soon to be a fifth, than I could fly to the Moon in an F28 with silent engines! I owed this to Maurice who was slipping away from life and I owed it to my father who most certainly would have approved. If I walked away from all this now I would never overcome the horror I would see in Cristina's tears nor ease the pain in those little broken hearts. So, Rob Grant, just don't whinge any more about having no females in your life: this can be your answer: Yes or no?

'Let's play more cricket!' With the plastic bat I whacked the rubber ball and cute little Mandy ran backwards on the sand to attempt her very first catch. We all laughed as she tripped into the tiny waves. I ran to pick her up. Covered in sand and water, her little face never stopped smiling. Then I made my firm decision: instant family; just add one more. Stir for a while, have more fun, and presto! We were head-over-heels in love, so I whispered to Cris 'Let's get married – now.' But before she could answer, big-ears Mandy - soaking wet, heard me and blabbed it out for all and sundry to hear:

'They're getting married! Rob's going to be our new Daddy! I knew it!' It was too late to change my mind now because even one-year-old Emily cheered.

Within a few months we were married in Sydney and settled in there; my home base city. At our tiny wedding I certainly had no shortage of flower girls: Amanda 5, Olivia 4, and Emily 2. I had never known such happy children or such smiling and intelligent little people who had already become devoted to me. And Cris, of course, adored her handsome *pilot man* – as she called me. I was nearly twenty and she was three years older than me, but we were made for each other.

Then with dizzying speed, it seemed, a fifth female popped into our world. Yes, *another* girl. We lovingly called her Celia. She smiled with Barbie Doll good looks on her first day of life, while it seemed I was being amply compensated by the gods for a youth devoid of any females. Now it was raining girls and I was hopelessly but cheerfully outnumbered.

6.

The new baby was barely a month old when our *AEA* airline finally collapsed from the strain of strangling debt. Overnight, I went from being a dazzling and glamorous *Fly Boy* to an unemployed suburban father of four with six mouths to feed – counting my own. I was grounded and this was suddenly serious business. Despite Cristina working part-time in a supermarket, Child Care fees instantly gobbled her wages while Child Allowance support barely fed us as I searched desperately for another flying job. Compounding these difficulties, the parent company of Ansett Airlines didn't offer to hire any of us AEA boys because they were struggling with their own troubles and staff cuts. Neither did Qantas want me because they already had too many pilots.

I could keep flying my own charter plane out of Bankstown in Sydney's west - and did, but it paid a miserable net amount after my grandiose airline salary. There, most hours of my days were spent sitting around and growing desperate; waiting for a charter to somewhere – anywhere. Good days then bad days. At least my life was never dull; it always seemed to be highs peaks and low troughs. Roller coaster dramas of tragedy followed by grand times - then despair again.

Of course, I could always sell my twin-engine Cessna three-ten, but does a baker sell his bakery or a tradesman sell his tools? And so these were my darkest hours while my little Girl Guides troop of angels blissfully thought their exciting new life with a brand new dad was a magical fairyland of wonder.

It was time for drastic action. But what? After a tip-off, I attended a meeting at Sydney airport held by AEA's official receivers. They had been appointed to administer the final death cuts by selling off all the remaining assets of our collapsed airline. Buildings and other tangibles quickly vaporised and now, sadly, the three remaining F28 jets were to go, ungraciously, under the hammer.

The first two, VH-FKM and VH-FKY, were soon sold to foreign interests for the ridiculously throw-away prices of $1.1 million and $1.3 million respectively. The remaining jet, my favourite from *that* Dubbo introduction, VH-FKE, was offered for bids, but there were none. I was stunned, but the plane was getting old and had 37,000 airframe hours - although the engines were only halfway through their lives, meaning they'd been overhauled at some stage. Sadly, my beloved icon was passed in; unwanted and unloved by anyone but me.

I was distressed and felt a lump in my throat. Wasn't that magnificent machine worth anything at all? A 66-seat passenger jet of no value to anyone? Through the terminal windows I could see poor FKE sitting forlornly out on the apron in drizzling rain, its life in the skies expired. Grounded forever, it was useless, except as imminent scrap metal. Once king of the skies - to me anyway, now it faced an ignominious dismantling and being reduced to scrap.

With only minutes remaining I had a sudden and desperate idea and, with pounding heart, rushed over to the table of administrators and receiving accountants. Could I bid for it, please? I had some collateral in my property and two aeroplanes. I could possibly rake up some bailout funds. One accountant told me they were almost desperate to get rid of 'that old thing' in order to pay out the airline's creditors, and would accept almost any offer. 'Any offer?' I repeated.

'What would you have in mind?' he queried.

I took a very deep breath and, scarcely believing my own words, eventually muttered, 'Ah, I could maybe come up with about $275,000 from borrowing against my property out west. Sorry, I know that's crazy, but it's the best I could ever do. I don't want to sell this property and leave nothing for the rest of my life because I'm only twenty. I know these planes are worth over a million each but you indicated the creditors were desperate, didn't you. So just how really anxious are they?'

As I was wearing jeans and a T-shirt, the bespectacled receiver peered down his long nose as though I were some young hippie off the streets selling bongs. 'Two seventy five?' he mocked me. '*Ridiculous*!

But, I am required to submit any and all offers to the committee and will let you know tomorrow - or the next day.'

He didn't like me, that was certain. Then he sneered, 'Anyway, what on Earth would you *do* with the damned thing?' Perhaps he envisaged me holding love-ins in the smoke-filled cabin; flowers painted on the walls and bodies everywhere chanting 'Hare Krishna!'

'Ah, fly it,' was my hesitant and quite uncertain answer. But where, I asked myself? How? As a charter plane? At the moment I couldn't find enough customers for my six-seat Cessna three-ten at Bankstown, let alone fill up a 65-seat passenger jet. And apart from anything else, the jet needed *two* pilots to fly it. That meant someone else I'd have to pay while I couldn't even pay myself. And until I was twenty-one that *someone* would have to be a qualified captain. Aargh! It was all too frightening and I walked out, secure in the knowledge that no-one ever bought an airliner for a quarter of a million dollars. I'd never hear from them again, that was certain. On my way home I nervously sung that old song: *Fools rush in where angels fear to tread.*

At home, I kept my exciting news from my family – and my deep misgivings, but early the next morning the surly accountant phoned. 'You can have the aircraft for the sum offered. The owners squealed but had no choice, really. You must now proceed with the paperwork, and your bid is, of course, subject to your obtaining the relevant finance.'

Then, at auctioneer's speed, he rattled off the fine print. 'The aviation authorities have warned me that you cannot operate this aircraft on regular public transport services. You may operate charter flights only under the appropriate charter licences and permissions. You must obtain suitable parking arrangements for the aircraft. You cannot operate it whilst it remains in its present colour scheme of AEA Airlines of Eastern Australia. It must be repainted appropriately. It must be certified . . . ' I don't think I heard the rest and dropped the phone in shock. Oh Hell, I'd really done it now. Was I completely crazy? Perhaps I was suffering altitude sickness? I was ecstatic but despondent. Over the Moon yet clouded in despair.

Cris had a doctors' appointment that morning, so as she was still asleep I left home early and drove to the airport confused: perhaps to simply stare at the jet for a while. Then in the afternoon I spied a newspaper headline: *'Kid buys big jet for quarter million!'* I was amazed. How did the media know this? And I wasn't a kid, I was twenty; but they often say what they like, don't they?

Gathering all my strength and nerve, I went home to announce this most monumental and Earth-shattering decision to my wonderful wife and young family. I shuddered again to think what Cris - or indeed any wife anywhere – could or would possibly say to this startling news, while also trying hard to think of any other young unemployed man with a wife and four kids who, instead of buying a few bags of groceries, bought a jet airliner instead? None rushed to mind.

Perhaps I'd casually stroll in at home and Cris might smile and say: 'Did you see the news? Some stupid kid bought a big jet for a quarter of a million dollars! Have you ever heard anything so crazy?'

But no heights of anticipation could have ever guessed the *actual* reaction I received, nor could any fortune teller in a thousand years have foretold what hit me upon arrival at home that dark and rainy evening. My beaming smile had no impact on Cris's frightful demeanour as I walked through the door . . . 'You'll never guess what I did today,' I started out.

Startled, I gaped at her ashen face. 'Ah, what's wrong, love?'

She burst into tears and said, 'I've got breast cancer. They can't help me. I just found out . . . '

'My god!' I yelped in total horror. 'Hells bells! Ah, are you serious? The doctors must be wrong . . . surely . . . ' As I cuddled her, our three eldest girls raced joyously into the room chanting 'Hi Daddy!' just as their stricken mother sobbed, 'Would anyone joke about this?'

'About what?' beamed little Mandy. 'What did you do today, Daddy? Tell us all!'

Bewildered, I muttered, 'Ah, I bought a big jet. I'm that crazy kid.' An horrendous and bewildering hour later, the phone rang and I learned that my wonderful adoptive father, Maurice, had passed away in Warren hospital, in western New South Wales. In my crazy life, it never seemed to rain, but poured. Outside, the rain became torrential.

*

Three days later and still in continuous rain, we boarded my twin-engined Cessna at Bankstown for the ninety-minute flight to Maurice's funeral in Warren. The kids were beside themselves with excitement at their first plane ride, while Cris and I, deeply depressed and with ghostly faces, glared out at the pouring rain and dark skies blanketing Sydney; the choking gloom adding to a terrible shadow of death. The Grim Reaper had descended all around us, it seemed.

We took off and flew straight into the gray clouds and heavy rain. 'It's not fair,' protested little Olivia from the last row of seats where the baby slept, 'we can't see anything out the windows!' Amanda protested that we weren't moving at all and wanted to know why.

Nearing Katoomba and climbing through 7,000 feet, we suddenly broke through the cloud tops to reveal blue and sunny skies above white layers of strato-cumulus clouds which clung to the Blue Mountains below. This certainly pleased the girls and they gawked excitedly at their first sight of clouds *below* them. Beside me, Cris sat in silence, her once beautiful face now drawn and puckered and almost ugly with fear. The baby slept and the kids chattered as we flew on; over Bathurst, Wellington, Dubbo, my property at Trangie - and finally to Warren.

Upon arrival, my distressed Cristina understandably couldn't face a funeral, and stayed in a motel with the girls while I attended the service for Maurice. There were over seven hundred people in attendance; a shining tribute to this extraordinary person's life. I was invited to speak but remained silent and shaken. I just couldn't front any group, even though I desired to. I was faced with another funeral even worse than this - and soon; much too soon. This really *was* a horror movie.

Within weeks, the girls now understood that their mother would soon be going away for a very long time. 'Like our first daddy?' asked Mandy.

'Ah, kind of . . . ' I floundered. Cristina's prognosis was bleak, the doctors assured me. Was I now to be the youngest father of four to become a single father? A widower at twenty? I supposed there might be other such fathers in Australia to claim the title, but it certainly felt like I was a solo flyer here. Was my life in some kind of fast-forward time warp where every damn thing happened to me whilst so young? Daily, Cris and I plunged to the very depths of despair, bottomed out, then still had nowhere to go but down. The woman I loved cried incessantly as her cancer treatments failed to respond. I would be left with three of her girls, plus baby Celia who belonged to us both. Or more accurately, they would all be soon in my care alone – and so would a certain large jet that sat by itself behind a blast fence at Sydney airport, waiting for its new owner.

*

The next week, my very *unfavourite* receiving accountant barked into my earpiece. 'Mr Grant, all this paperwork and Bill of Sale *must* be completed by this Thursday at the very latest. Are you there, Mr Grant?' I told him that my father had just died and that my beautiful young wife was dying of cancer. I told him I had four little kids to worry about. I told him . . .

Uncaring, he replied coldly, 'Yes, but the wheels of business must roll on.' Apparently these wheels stop for no man, child, funeral or indeed anything. 'Thursday, Mr Grant,' were his final callous words.

I could handle the high pressure of flying a large jet, and I actually enjoyed a house full of squawking kids, but this was all simply too damned much! I had taken a reckless financial gamble of a lifetime, one that probably no other sensible person of my age would ever contemplate. I'd also taken on a wife with her instant family: like instant coffee, she often joked – and now it was all crashing down like some nightmarish fiery plane crash. I had no other family for support, no adults to console me. The kids still needed to be fed, then they wanted me to play and entertain them. They, like all children, would also expect birthday and Christmas presents and other little surprises which would unfortunately now be on hold as I arrogantly proceeded with my extravagantly ridiculous and superfluous purchase at the airport.

And I needed to visit my brave but wasted Cristina, now dying in hospital, as often as possible. I needed to explain all this to the kids and get them through it - somehow. Then I had to be bright and cheery as I set up a new charter business and attracted customers while my wife was dying. And while Olivia was starting her first school. While Amanda suffered nightmares. While the baby cried and while Emily battled the mumps. What the heck had I done? Two years ago I'd been a single, glamorous *fly boy*. Now, tripping over nappies and immersed over my head in nightmares all day, I felt anything but glamorous. Horribly, my girls persistently demanded to know why their Mummy was dying.

What do you say?

7.

As I watched the coffin slide behind a red curtain, I felt like I'd been hit by a truck. I couldn't breathe. My entire future and life's aspirations had collapsed. My ashen face must have looked like Hell on a stick because a little voice below me whispered 'Don't worry Daddy. We'll look after you.' We'd just attended Cristina's small funeral service where my three brave little soldiers had sat beside me, teary eyed, while I nursed baby Celia on my lap. In a trance, I'd heard none of the words that were spoken during the service.

In stark contrast to Maurice's funeral, this was an embarrassingly small service indeed, with only a few attendees. Cristina's estranged mother Elsie had been too ill in New Zealand to attend - or so she claimed. And Cris's sister Suzie was also far too busy: she'd phoned from backpacking holidays in Europe to say she was very sorry but she couldn't attend. Cris's father, Fred Parsons, came over from NZ. He was a strange and silent man who couldn't even be bothered shaking hands when we met. This was the first time I'd met Cris's father – *after* his daughter was dead! They'd ignored our small wedding and posted a single cheap card, and they only visited the hospital once during Cris's terminal illness - after making sure I wasn't there at the time.

After her casket had gone forever, the only words I spoke to Fred were spiked with anger. 'Gee, thanks for all your help and support, Fred.' He said nothing, just turned and walked away. I saw no tears on his callous face. No consolations or offers whatsoever were forthcoming then, or in the years ahead, to assist in any way with these three children who were Cristina's. His own grandchildren. The Parsons' were inhuman: no wonder Cris had told me dark tales about her estranged family and turbulent upbringing. I watched him stride from the funeral home. He hadn't even spoken to the girls.

Lastly, the kids' natural father, Tony Avey, completed the roll-call of non-attendees on this day – true to form. Only a few aviation friends of ours had been present, but essentially it was woeful. Pitiful. Disgraceful. So, in my lowest hours, my little mate who firmly gripped my hand was right: these precious young girls were now all I had, and I *would* look after them, and they me. We walked outside into gloomy rain where I stood motionless, getting soaked. I'd known Cristina for barely three years and now she'd gone. It felt like a week.

'Hey Mandy, my little friend,' I looked down at her through tears, 'we'll be okay. You're the big boss lady in this family now. Did you know that?'

'Wow!' she exclaimed. 'Am I *really*?' At home later, I told her that even though she was not quite seven years old she should be able to help her sisters get dressed and ready for each day. She could feed the baby her formula. She could teach them to tidy their up their rooms and she could help me around the home with various household chores. Thankfully, over the following weeks and months she rose and just *did it*. Mandy was an exceptionally intelligent little person who easily adapted to the tasks I taught her; often volunteering for more. Ha, nearly seven years old but acts like seventeen sometimes!

Despite my intense grieving, our little household needed to be *heads up* urgently. So sometimes we might play a little game where I'd say: 'See those piles of dirty clothes on the floor? If we don't pick them up, then who might?' Then we'd all raise our hands together and chant "*The Fairies?* No, *we* have to! Why? Because no-one else will!" So it's possible to invent some fun out of odd chores like picking up piles of things; but they often caught me teary-eyed and silent. Thankfully, the girls' childhood defences mostly ran stronger than mine because we'd have fallen in a heap if all of us had sat around weeping and wailing.

Gradually a workable system developed. Olivia was a quiet girl who dutifully followed her big sister's mature examples, so little Emmie simply followed *them*, sheeplike. Baby Celia had just turned two and these days wouldn't stop talking. She waddled behind the others and I laughingly called them 'Brown's cows.' She'd never know her mother but they were the best kids in the world and I suppose I wasn't a bad Dad after all, considering I'd never had a family situation to pass on from observation. So I was randomly inventing policy on the run while hoping we'd survive – somehow.

In business, the big plane was finally all mine. Bought for a song. No-one in my aviation circles could believe the price I'd paid, and many derided my foolhardy plans to charter it out.

'You'll never make a damn cent out of that bucket of old Dutch bolts,' a fellow pilot declared. 'You'll be broke in a month.' 'A week, you mean,' laughed another. 'And how will you afford to even *start* those bloody great engines?' It was far more likely they were right than wrong, because the jet was already costing me $2,000 a month in parking charges at Sydney airport before its owner could even contemplate pressing those *Start* switches. But my detractors had all overlooked a few pertinent facts: I'd already owned and operated two charter aircraft and thoroughly knew the inns and outs of all the associated procedures, licences and maintenance. Also, this jet had been inspected mechanically and was certified as airworthy for a few good years yet.

For myself, while teenage boys my age had been scratching their pimples and gawking at girls at school, I'd already amassed a hefty four thousand hours' flying experience. I'd been flying regularly since I was thirteen while most other pilots had started at 17, 18 or older. So I was re-entering the air charter business where I'd already spent three years, while they'd only worked for others as salaried pilots. Also, I hoped for an immense dose of good luck along the way – for a change.

But first, my old plane had to be painted. I'd be glad to see the last of those garish dark red and green colours of AEA. I needed a striking new look, plus an appealing name for my fledgling company. At Sydney airport, I knew some aircraft painters at Qantas who'd do the job after hours for only $7,500 – a bargain basement price even for those days. But what on Earth would I call my new aerial circus? It had to be good.

The answer fell from the sky. One pleasant afternoon, the kids were throwing toys around the yard as I sat nearby, cloud gazing. It was my birthday and I was wildly celebrating it as a housebound widower with four kids. I gave little Celia her baby's bottle as Emmie toddled around, following the others. 'Hey girls,' I called out. 'You know my big new aeroplane? What colour should I paint it?'

Straight away Mandy replied, 'Just like this . . . '

At first I didn't grasp the significance of her answer, but followed her arm as she threw a tiny plastic plane into the air. The little glider zoomed and looped, then gently touched down into the sand pit beside Emily. 'Bring it over here, mate,' I asked her. 'Let me have a look.' I held the toy – after removing it from her mouth; it nearly fitted into my palm. I'd never noticed it before. It must have been jumbled away in their toy box. The little plane was painted in red, white and blue, deep and vibrant colours, and had streaks of sparkling silver stars flying back towards the tail. Hmm, a full-sized plane would look rather striking like that.

'I like its colour scheme very much. And those pretty stars too,' I said to the girls.

Mandy said, 'That's what colour you have to paint your big new aeroplane. Okay?'

'Yes, I might just do that. And what should I call it, kids?'

'You're silly Daddy,' Mandy laughed. 'You call it what it already says on the side: *Sky Star*. See?' She hurled it back into the air and they all raced after it. This time it soared gracefully - right around our yard in fact, then made a perfect touch-down on the grass. *Sky Star*, I thought. What a hell of a great name that would be!

Once again I turned the little model in my hands; peering at its tiny painted words: *Sky Star*. My future had been right here all the time; hiding in a toy box. Or diving from the clouds.

*

At the airport, I showed the tiny Chinese-made model plane to the Qantas painters, then made it fly a few metres. 'Flies too!' one of them laughed. I retrieved it and held it up for them: 'See? Just like this, guys – with the shooting stars and all. Then we paint a giant word **SKY** near the front of the plane, then the other huge word **STAR** half-way back.

Of course, on the starboard side the words are reversed. What do you think?' (It should be said that these were the days well before the Qantas subsidiary *Jet Star* was created.)

The men's faces enthused at this pretty toy plane. They could already envisage such an eye-catching livery on a full-sized aircraft as, after all, this is what they did for a living every day. In those days, this was how they pre-planned many paint jobs – from a model such as this. 'Yep, should look fantastic!' one man smiled, then they all indicated approval. 'Way better than Qantas's drab old colour scheme. Great idea, Rob. Excellent name too.' In honesty, I reluctantly admitted that my seven-year-old had brought it to my attention.

'Should put her on the staff, then,' they all smiled.

'I will soon,' was my sincere reply. 'She'll be the General Manager one day. I'll be just a pilot.'

As they walked away, another of them yelled back across the giant hangar, 'Bloody Sky Star, eh? What a ripper! I'll book seats for me and my girlfriend on the first flight, for sure - even though I get *el cheapo's* on Qantas all the time.' 'Me too,' added another.

Oh well, I thought, there's a few seats sold already. I only need to sell the other 60 or so – on *every* flight, and I'm laughing all the way to the bank. Should be easy. Then again, these might be the only seats I ever sell, and my high-flying dreams might quickly become known as *Mothball Airlines.* Worried, I could picture the news headlines already:
Nose dive! Kid loses a quarter million in a month!

8.

The girls and I were playing Junior Monopoly. I was proudly observing how quickly Miss Amanda, the leader of my little Girl Guides troop, was learning the essence of finance with the play money. Actually, she was on the verge of beating me and taking all my toy houses when I asked, 'So troops, when my big aeroplane is painted like that little toy plane of ours, how should I get people to want a ride in it? Remember, they have to pay some money for a flight, just like this game where we all have to pay money to buy a toy house.'

Quickly, Amanda said 'Let's buy some more toy planes like that one and give them away for kids to take home. Then they can show their Mums and Dads and they'll want to pay for a ride in a real one.'

'Hmm, that's brilliant,' I smiled proudly. 'I tell you what: I'll send away to China for a big box of those toy planes and we'll try it. So, does anyone know where China is?' Emmie said it was just down the road where we had dinner one night and where I made her try eating with chopsticks. Olivia chirped in and said 'No, it's under our back yard if we dig down far enough.' Amanda reckoned they were all silly because China is far away where they make all the toys in the world. Baby Celia, my precious daughter with Cristina, just sucked her thumb and giggled at everything.

But kids' short attention spans can produce a sudden change of subject, as Emily suddenly asked, 'Dad. Where do little babies come from?' Looking serious, I said it was like that big bin with all the coloured Lotto balls inside, and where someone digs down and pulls out a few winning numbers. Only this game is called *Baby Lotto* where Mummy and I dug down and pulled out a . . . yuk! An ugly baby called Celia!'

They squealed happily as Amanda charitably decided, 'Sometimes you're funny, Daddy.'

Meanwhile, her bright and insightful business suggestion had certainly set me thinking. In two weeks the big F28 was due out of the paint shop hangar where the boys were painting it in their spare time.

Then it needed to be generating immediate revenue from somewhere. I was financially stretched, as could be expected, and each day that the GTB (great thirsty beast) sat on the apron unused would be costing me dearly. While the jet's on-going costs were guaranteed to keep me awake and in a cold sweat at night, the spectre of a failed venture was unacceptable to me. This was a huge financial gamble - my first ever, but at the moment I was struggling to beat my own kid at Junior Monopoly, let alone possess the expertise to run an air charter company at a profit.

Soon we received a large box of toy planes identical to that first one. Then we bought a sticker-making machine to add *'Your Barrier Reef Jet Charter Flights NOW. Ph Free call 1300 . . . '* It seemed to take *forever* to stick them all on, but five little pairs of eager hands hard at work eventually saw it done. Even smiley little Celia stuck a few on. Next, I urgently needed staff to man our company as I certainly couldn't be captain, co-pilot, hostie, engineer, office lady, check-in clerk and cleaner all at once. We also required some serious advertising for our proposed flights to the Reef. Regretfully in those pre-internet days, we faced mostly laborious manual promotions.

*

I called a company meeting to be held at my old rented house - simply because we had no office or premises like any 'normal' company. Not yet, anyway. First to arrive was Ken Tolman, a fellow pilot of mine with whom I'd flown a few times on the AEA jets before their demise. Ken was – or had been, an F28 captain, but was now on stand-down like me. Desperately looking for any flying work, he nonetheless seemed rather wary of joining a charter firm that possessed just one aircraft. However, it was better than no work at all, I reminded him.

'So, how many seats have we sold so far, Rob?' was Ken's first question on arrival.

My answer of 'Well, *none* to be precise, Ken,' made his eyebrows shoot up. 'But after we hand out all these toy planes to kids we'll be okay.' He seemed about to turn and leave, but I bribed him with coffee to stay. Ken was only thirty, but already sported tufts of gray hair – always an appropriate look for a captain because it implied experience and competence. Perhaps I also needed a touch of gray – along with mountains of luck . . .

David Skillen was another new starter in our fledgling company. He had been our family solicitor at Trangie and had processed my father's estate and then Maurice's a few years later. A wonderful 60-year-old family friend with an MBA degree, semi-retired and now moved to Sydney, I asked Dave to be our 'General Manager and Legal Officer.' Upon arrival, Dave laughed 'Shouldn't be too much workload involved there, eh Robbie? With one plane, a handful of employees and a bunch of kids with toys, I think I can handle that.' I told him that when we became bigger than Qantas he'd have plenty of work on his plate - *and* I could afford to pay him, too.

Just then, the Girl Guides troop marched in with plates of fairy cakes and chocolate crackles. 'Let me guess,' smiled Ken Tolman. 'These are our stewardesses and when they've eventually turned forty you'll pay them too. But aren't they a bit ah, youngish, just at the moment?'

'Slightly,' I assured him. 'But I was flying planes at twelve and everyone kept saying that was too young. Anyway, please let me introduce our promotional team: Amanda, Olivia, Emily and little Celia.' The promo team smiled proudly and bowed, but Ken Tolman looked annoyed when the baby dribbled on his shiny black shoes.

Next to arrive was 37-year-old Marie Westcott, a staff manager who nervously tapped on the door. She'd answered my newspaper ad and I quickly took a liking to her. I asked her to be my Chief of Staff – plus, in the interim, check-in clerk, office lady and general dogsbody. She was accompanied by two younger women, Laura and Gail, who had been former hosties with us – also needing work. Aviation safety regulations required that we carried a minimum of two cabin crew, or stewardesses, on every flight.

Incredulous, Ken asked, 'Is this it, then? The whole damn company?' I said there was a man named Peter arriving later who would be our licenced ground engineer. He would liaise with Qantas for our routine maintenance - which would be chokingly expensive, no doubt.

'Would you like a chocolate crackle?' little Olivia asked Captain Ken in her tiny voice.

'I think a bottle of *Black Label* might be better!' he rudely laughed at her.

'Do you like planes, Mister?' Amanda smiled at the tall captain. 'You can play with this little toy one here if you like.'

'Not just at the moment,' he smirked. 'I think I need a Scotch.' The girls stared quizzically at the captain who always seemed to have a slight sneer on his face.

Saved by the bell, I left our company's first meeting to answer the phone in the kitchen. Thankfully, it was a man who wanted to book three seats on our debut charter flight to Airlie Beach in North Queensland. I was amazed. The kids had been busy at school already, handing out our promotional toy planes: those pretty red, white and blue plastic gliders decorated with the shower of stars streaking towards the rear. They'd also obtained permission to hand them out after school in local shopping centres and after-school-care venues accompanied by our friendly housekeeper and hired nanny, Alicia McNeil – also present this day.

As the men chatted and the women commenced what were to be lasting friendships, I excitedly wrote down our first three bookings. Back in the living room, I waved the paper in the air. 'I have an important announcement to make,' just as David Skillen was laughing:

'I think we can avoid bankruptcy for about two days – three at the most.'

With precision timing, Amanda piped up: 'Daddy went bank-rupp last night in Junior Monopoly. Didn't you Dad?' The room erupted with howls of laughter as I attempted to excuse my slight mistake...'

Dave said, 'Perhaps I should file a motion *before* the first flight, instead of after. Is the committee agreed?'

'Ah, shuddup!' I laughed. 'Listen all, I just took our first three bookings for next week's maiden flight. How about that?' The girls chorused 'Yippee' as my board of directors looked quite surprised. 'Only sixty to go and we're airborne,' quipped Ken, failing to see anything positive.

My new Chief of Staff, Marie Westcott, asked, 'And what will be your actual position in the company, Rob?'

I detailed my role. 'I'm the owner and founder of the company. The CEO. And when I'm a billionaire airline mogul like Richard Branson, you'll all be queuing up for my autograph!'

Ken Tolman remarked, 'Might be waiting a while for that,' just as little Emmie asked 'Can we have more fairy bread, please? It's all gone.'

The CEO joked, 'Can't afford big jets and fairy bread too, little lady.' The Board of Directors agreed. Austerity measures were already in place, so more fairy bread was simply out of the question.

*

We men sat on the back veranda and sipped a beer – after I had magically found some more fairy bread inside. Dave Skillen commiserated; *'Four kids*, Rob! Four little kids without any mother? And you're only twenty-two.'

'I'll handle it – somehow,' I assured him. 'I have to. But yes, three are Cris's and the baby is ours together. Well, they're all mine now, aren't they? Dave, remember when Dad died and you handled our estate? You put the assets in trust for me until I turned eighteen. Everyone told me that twelve was too young to run a cattle station by myself and of course they were right. Then, luckily, Maurice took me in. But I was still too young to fly a plane by myself and too young to drive Dad's Jeep. Too young for this and too young for that. In defiance, I managed to achieve most of what I aspired to, anyway. Ken was twenty-nine when he first became an F28 captain, while I was his occasional F.O. at just nineteen – and at the time I owned two light planes as well. So things often seem to occur in fast-forward for me.

Then I met Cristina . . . and she was gone after only three short years. The best woman in the world. But she left four little mouths to feed, Dave, and I'm their father now so it's all up to me.'

With little interest in kids being fed, Ken Tolman interrupted, 'Yes, but now you've got those two enormous Tay engines to feed as well, Rob. Remember how many litres of Jet-A1 those bloody great beasts gulp every hour? Three thousand, that's how many.'

I hadn't finished my little speech, so I said, 'I don't like to think about that just now, Ken. Anyway, I made my decision to marry Cris knowing full well she already had three great kids. I loved them from the start, guys, and I naturally assumed that Cris and I would be married forever.'

I paused to wipe a sad tear, then continued. 'But then our tribe became *four* girls. Motherless, those four little angels are now totally dependent on me alone because, unfortunately, Cris's family in New Zealand have completely wiped their own daughter's children. Can you believe that? Before that, the girls' first father, having fled up north, did the same! A double whammy! I despise people like that because that's what my own mother did. In stark contrast, my Dad was wonderful then Maurice was even greater. They never abandoned anyone in their lives or retreated from their responsibilities – and I wasn't even Maurice's son until he adopted me.'

'Poor old Maurice,' smiled Dave. 'No wonder he went mad with you as his son.'

'I'll drink to that!' agreed Ken, gulping a hearty swig.

'Funny, guys. But what I'm trying to say is this: last month I was a mostly unemployed pilot – although I have assets in my two light planes and my *Wundala* homestead. If this charter venture fails I'll dispense with my *Wundala* managers and move back to Trangie with my girls. Try my hand at ranching. I know a little bit about it even if I don't really enjoy it. Maurice and Dad taught me some of it - when I wasn't out flying. So the point is: there's just about *nil* cash flow here at the moment, but if we somehow manage to succeed one day, then I intend to buy more planes and apply for registration as an airline.'

We rejoined the women where I announced, 'This company will be called *Sky Star* and nothing else. I'll be the owner but it will be run by Dave co-jointly with me. That is, with a positive approach, and none of this: It can't be done because I'm too young. Or because I've got four kids. Or because the price of jet fuel is going up. Or because of any other weak excuse for failure. Do you ladies and gents agree? If not, I'll need to find another board of senior managers right now – at the very start.' They all nodded.

'Lastly, I owe this to my new family to at least try. My two fathers showed me grand examples in life and I see it as my duty to theirs and Cristina's memories to pass that legacy on to my children. But we run it our way, ladies and gents, or not at all. And FKE is getting re-registered as VH-CZG, by the way.'

Ken remarked, 'Charlie Zulu Golf? Why?'

'Cristina Zelda Grant. The rest of the (eventual) fleet will have *our* initials.' Just then, the kitchen phone rang again. I called out, 'Amanda, can you answer that phone, please?'

'I've already got it!' a tiny voice screeched back. Then, 'Dad! A lady wants to buy two tickets for our flight.'

'Write it down,' I yelled back, as Ken and Dave's eyebrows arched again. Ken whispered to the solicitor, 'I don't think I quite *believe* this. Do you, Dave?'

David laughed, 'Pass me that toy plane, Ken. Maybe we can get one of the kids to show us how to fly it.'

Airline Captain Ken Tolman said sternly, 'You'll need the boss's permission first, Dave. I can assure you of that.'

After playing with model aeroplanes in the back yard later, and letting kids teach us how to fly them, we adjourned inside for coffee with the womenfolk. Laura and Gail asked about hostesses uniforms for our new venture.

I took a position straight away: 'Please ladies, no dowdy, drab, or 1950's business suits like many airlines seem to have. These first charter flights are flying to beachside holiday destinations, not to a conference of women company directors in freezing Chicago. While I know nothing about women's fashions, may I suggest colourful beach attire, sandals and some garlands in the hair? Imagine you're going to Waikiki for the day. Remember, they're *charter* flights.'

Given direction, the womenfolk started chatting excitedly about what might be worn. My part-time and sometimes live-in child minder, Alicia McNeil, had once studied fashion design so she happily joined in. My kids, as usual, also stuck their little noses in to join the lively discussion, but when Mandy proposed we give away free Barbie dolls to girls on the plane, I caught Ken's derisive scowl.

As I admitted to my fledgling airline's recruits how we'd either sink or swim after just one month in the air charter business because that was the limit of my tiny floating funds, another audacious thought crept into my mind. It was crazy of course, but so, probably, was I.

The room was noisy, but so far things were proceeding on course. Ken called out over the women's chattering, 'Hey Rob, how much did you steal that plane for, again?'

'Two seventy five.'

'You should be arrested.'

'I know.'

*

Not arrested, but I was certainly *distracted* after they'd all left. To be viable, we needed a heck of a lot more than those five seats sold. And on nearly every flight. I called over to Amanda, my smiling eldest girl. 'Hey Mandy. Do you remember when we went to Luna Park that time? Remember that fun ride like a small Ferris wheel that had little aeroplanes going around? It had little two-seat wooden planes with tiny wings poking out. Yes, ours was the purple one, that's right. And remember how I could hardly squeeze inside so my legs stuck out the sides? Yes, that was so funny. And how it jerked and bumped around? I was sure it was going to fall apart - but you loved it.'

She said, 'Yes I did, Daddy. Are we going again one day?'

'Tomorrow, I told her. Soon as it opens in the morning.' No child ever argued against that, I'm sure.

I had a friend, Kevin Paye, who worked for Ansett. An amateur but eager camera buff, he sometimes filmed TV commercials as a part-time hobby for a small extra income. I asked if he'd meet me at Luna Park in the morning to do some quick filming, for which I'd pay him $2,500. He jumped at the chance, then asked, 'Why Luna Park?' I replied, 'I'm going flying. With my little girl.'

9.

I felt like a complete idiot, and probably was. I'd arrived by ferry at Sydney's famous Luna Park with my friend Kevin and my little mate Mandy. The Harbour Bridge towered beside us. I was attired in a (borrowed) royal blue airline captain's uniform with glittering gold buttons and braid, four gold stripes on the arms, the cap of authority slightly tilted and dark sunnies across my face. I looked a million dollars, yet we were about to climb into a rickety old Ferris wheel, a dangerous-looking mechanical contraption with cramped box compartments that were supposed to be mini aeroplanes. On the outside, the faded paintwork displayed beaming clown's faces – much like this clown in his airline suit, I suppose – and there were a few coloured stars painted on the sides. Barely discernible, 'Flight to the Stars' was stencilled on each tiny door.

As Kevin adjusted his camera gear, I paid the young attendant for two tickets. The boy possibly thought I was some actor who was part of the show and stared curiously. 'My friend wants to film us,' I smiled at the boy who simply shrugged a *whatever* gesture. Hardly unique; everyone around us held up cameras as hordes of eager five-year-olds leapt into their little planes. I said to the attendant, 'When you start it, I'd like you to make it jerk on take-off. Like it did the last time I was here. And make it jerky the whole way around, okay? I'll give you fifty dollars if you can do that for me.' The kid rolled his eyes skywards and I wondered what *he* was thinking. But money talks, and fifty was fifty. I handed him the cash, then we commenced boarding our flight to the stars.

Following Mandy, I clambered awkwardly into the wooden plane, almost tripping over one wooden wing, then crash-landed like last time with my legs dangling outside. Bemused parents stared, while kids probably thought that I looked 'funny'- as in *ridiculous*. Sitting beside Amanda, I admired her youthful beauty with her blond hair bunched up into Alicia's pink ribbon arrangement that complimented her cuteness in a lovely new summer dress.

I waited grimly for the lift-off as Kevin dutifully peered through his huge lenses, his body leaning precariously over the flimsy safety railing. 'Don't miss it please, Kev,' I yelled. He asked what was going to happen; I said 'You'll see.' I saw the boy yank hard on the lever in his wooden control box as Mandy flashed her most wonderful smile. And then, to piercing, tinny music – we were up, up and away!

As the Ferris wheel jerked upwards with an abrupt lurch, I flicked my pilot's hat to slide half-way down my face. My expression froze in a frightened freeze-frame of terror as I gripped our little steering wheel with panic – wrenching it from side to side. Around the circle we flew, jerking and bumping as all the kids squealed with glee. At the top of the arc, Mandy shouted her prepared lines 'Come on Dad. Let's fly to the stars!' I looked over at her in fright, while onlookers were probably bemused.

A few orbits of the stars saw us eventually clunk to a halt at the bottom. Mandy leapt out and flashed another endearing smile, then curtsied at Kevin's camera while I wriggled free in a daze, straightened my apparel from disarray, then staggered upright. Right below Kevin's dangling boom mike, Mandy said, 'Come on Daddy, don't be silly. Let's go for another flight to the stars!' Reluctantly I staggered after her as she tugged my hand, then Kevin called *'Cut!'* to no-one in particular.

The following morning, the Sky Star board came together in my lounge room – although not altogether happily. We were glued to Kevin Paye's small monitor screen which was showing the first edit of our ad. Most faces around me were quite solemn, and soon Ken Tolman moaned, 'It's bloody *ridiculous*, Rob. You absolutely MUST be joking . . . aren't you? We're sunk! Sunk like the *Titanic* before we've even started the engines.'

My Mandy, who'd been so proud of her starring efforts so far, was absolutely horrified at these remarks and stormed from the room in tears – an action that would have great ramifications in years to come. Meanwhile, the women, who comprised the remainder of my air charter company were simply too polite or embarrassed to say anything, so I prodded Marie, my Chief of Staff. 'Marie?'

'I'm sorry Robbie,' she said. 'But it's just . . . a bit *silly* - and corny, I suppose. You can't go on Sydney TV doing that, surely?' My two cabin stewardesses remained mute – probably because they'd just realised they were out of work again before they'd even started.

With sarcasm, I asked, 'Anyone else love it too?' Olivia queried 'What's the matter? What's wrong with it, Dad?'

As Kevin the camera man adjusted dials, Peter, my new maintenance manager finally remarked, 'Sorry, I don't get it either.'

I stood up, 'All right everybody, listen up now. All you doomsayers can stop cringing on the floor and weeping and wailing. That was just the first half of the ad . . . '

'The first half?' someone asked.

'Yes, the *first* half. We do the rest of it this afternoon at the airport. Our shiny new Fokker Fellowship has just rolled out of the Qantas paint hangar this morning and we're all going out to see it. *That's* when we film the next thirty seconds of our ad.'

*

Two hours later, outside a Qantas hangar, everyone gasped with enthusiastic approval. Stunning, that's what it was. We all gawked up at VH-CZG, absolutely resplendent in its majestic new colour scheme of rich red, royal blue and thin white stripes. It was emblazoned with streaking white stars flying towards the high T-tail at the rear. 'Look, there's Mummy's face!' shrieked Olivia, pointing up. 'Where? Let me see,' yelled Emily. Below the pilot's cockpit windows was a small painting of my Cristina's beautiful face. The cursive script under it said: '*Lady Cristina the Sky Star*' - the name of our flagship, and painted in huge gold font near the front door was **SKY,** and towards the rear was **STAR.**

'Goodness me, that looks quite fantastic!' exclaimed David Skillen, our general manager. Even Captain Ken Tolman seemed impressed: 'Never thought it would come out quite like that. And to think what it looked like before . . . '

I tried to claim fame for designing this inspiring creation, but Mandy squawked, 'You big fibber, Dad. I told you to do it like this.'

Attracting attention, several maintenance men and a few security people gathered around, admiring in awe. A Qantas 747 was parked nearby - much larger than our smaller F28. Its First Officer walked past and smiled, 'Never seen a plane look as good as *that* before - nowhere in the world. Better than our colours.'

I waved thanks to him, then grabbed Mandy's hand and said to our cameraman, 'Come on Kevin, up the stairs. We've got more filming to do.'

Inside the cockpit, I explained to Kevin exactly what he must do. He slowly panned the complex display of dials, instruments and levers, then filmed me in the captain's left-hand seat just as I looked at Mandy and spoke in my most captain-like deep voice, 'Are we ready for take-off, co-pilot?' Then Kevin went back down the stairs and out onto the apron to set up his tripod. Taking deep breaths, Mandy and I rehearsed once again; then on Kevin's thumbs-up cue, we opened both pilot's side windows. Mandy leaned half-way out her co-pilot's window, looked at the camera far below, and with a wonderful smile, shouted and waved, 'Yes Dad. Let's go for a charter flight to the stars!' Then I leant out my side window just above Cristina's face, and shouted 'Roger. Let's fly Sky Star!'

Most people watching later should catch on immediately. 'See kids?' viewers might hopefully exclaim after watching the entire sixty-second ad: 'That funny clown was just pretending to be silly; but he really *is* a pilot. Let's go for a holiday with them.' In the first part I looked awkward, frightened and very unpilot-like. Viewers would laugh at my clown-like behaviour and pretence of a pilot. In the second half it turned out I actually *was* a real airline pilot in a *real* jet! While any dressed-up actors could have played the first piece, it would be quite unlikely they'd be permitted to complete the filming in any *real* airliner - especially with a child leaning from the flight deck window while nearing a runway for take-off. Almost as unlikely would be her own father leaning from the other side. Kevin had cleverly shot it so it would appear we were taxying out near the main runway at

Sydney airport and about to blast off to the stars, while other aircraft were later edited in to take off into the background sky behind us.

I now held much more confidence that our message would get through. Adults would understand that no little eight-year-old would be actually flying a plane. It was all fun and innocent, but quite unique. We walked to our cars in contented silence, everyone to their thoughts. Captain Ken, who only recently had bayed that we were 'sunk like the *Titanic*,' finally conceded, 'Gee, that might just work, you know.'

Dave Skillen agreed, 'Are those dollar signs before my eyes, or am I seeing stars?'

As we left, Amanda skipped along with her sisters and boasted 'Told you!' as they insisted that Mandy was going to be a movie star. Ken agreed, 'Lucky girl. Now you'll be a star!' - but she completely ignored him.

Facing the true judgement of reality, the ad would soon endure a trial by fire of public scrutiny, so I wondered if farming rather than starring might be looming as my next brilliant career. We'd soon know if the news announced one day:

Ferris wheel pilot hits rock bottom. Heads west.

10.

While Kevin Paye hawked his way around Sydney trying to place our advertisement with TV networks, the passage of each passing day saw me developing many self doubts about my audacity and wild assumption that the public would have even the slightest interest in this banal TV commercial – as it sometimes appeared to be. Losing confidence, I had a bad case of imminent stage fright. Maybe Ken Tolman was right: it *was* to some extent embarrassing and I was starting to dread ever seeing the thing screening in my own lounge room. But then again, was it much worse than what was already on the box? I began closely scrutinising other adverts for the first time, and sometimes couldn't believe how trite they were. Their developers might also cringe in shame when viewing some of their own ads:

'Coldrush Toothpaste: You'll be astonished.' Oh really? I'd never seen anyone becoming ecstatic when brushing their teeth. 'The new Holden Zoom will make you leap for joy.' Sure. 'Winklewagger's Dog Food: He'll love you forever.' And will he send you thankyou notes, too? It was enough to send you barking mad, while at least our silly ad was slightly humorous. So I might be the worst slapstick clown ever to attempt acting, or my daughter might be unappealing in her very first advertisement, but perhaps someone, somewhere out there, might at least get a giggle from it.

And hopefully some folks might take heed of our overdubbed words stressing 'Charter flights: It's your choice when and where we go. It's not a scheduled flight on a timetable; it's *your* flight!' And just maybe our plane's striking and glamorous appearance might inspire travellers to hop on board with us, have a quick weekend break on the Barrier Reef, then be back at work by Monday morning? At least our product couldn't possibly be worse than Wongledangle's Dog Food – or whatever it was. Could it?

Then, after Kevin had successfully managed to place our ad, and while nervously waiting for it to appear on TV, we managed to sell seven more seats for our first flight. This made twelve bookings so far -

mostly from those toy planes being handed out. This proved that some people were obviously attracted by our promotion and the enticing brochure accompanying it. But that still left 49 vacant seats. If that's all we sold I would still have to depart as advertised then suffer a huge loss on the whole deal. This would force such a grave re-assessment of our position that I'd have to pay off quite a few people then promptly shut it all down. A flight to nowhere.

Or I could always do a runner from town, hoping to disappear off the radar screen at a great rate of knots. Oh no, I can see Dad and Maurice wagging their fingers at me. That won't ever happen ladies and gentlemen, so rest in peace.

*

In November 1992, our one-minute ad finally appeared on Sydney TV Channel-7, just after 7.30 pm. I peered nervously through my fingers and cringed low in the lounge, then, upon sighting that crazy Ferris wheel jerking around, my four girls all shrieked with joy like a cage full of budgies. Leaping out from the screen in its stark clarity, I decided that our advertisement wasn't all *that* bad after all, so now it was right out of my hands and into those of the viewing public. We might be lucky: many TV ads didn't inspire or simply didn't work, while many wasted a great deal more than our tiny investment of $2,500 and lasted for just a few showings. Time would tell.

My happy girls went to bed soon after this first viewing, all cuddling baby Celia. As I kissed her goodnight, Amanda's face beamed how she was so excited about going to school the next day. She'd already boasted to her class about her TV ad, and had previously tried to explain the whole scenario to them. Unfortunately, the kids didn't quite grasp its essence. It was hard to fully describe what would happen in sixty short seconds on TV. Some kids probably thought her Dad sounded crazy, and could be technically correct there.

At 10pm I checked with Marie Westcott; her *1800* booking line number hadn't rung – so I went to bed none the wiser. Oh well, at least I'd tried.

It hadn't rung, but the hotline *did* ring her home at 10:15 when I was asleep. Then again at 10:35, then numerous times during the night. Marie called me excitedly at 5am to say that quite a few people had thoroughly enjoyed our little ad and wanted to book with us - maybe not on our very first flight, but soon. Many women thought little Mandy was quite cute and adorable, while some men said I was 'a *jerk* – but funny.' Some callers asked if I really was a pilot, and some asked if the girl was my real daughter. Yes, yes, Marie answered. And, satisfying to me, even more intending travellers liked the basic idea of a 'charter' flight where they had a voice in at least *some* of the itinerary, as opposed to the stiffly regulated timetables offered by the airlines. Lastly, everyone complemented us on our stunningly colourful Fokker Fellowship: our Sky Star flagship with its soaring emblem *Lady Cristina the Sky Star*. Who is she, they all asked? We'll tell you on board. See you then.

At midday, Dave Skillen rang me. 'I've just seen it. It brought tears to my eyes. I was so proud, Rob. Has there been any feedback yet?'

I told him, 'Positive feedback. Lots of bookings. You ain't seen nothin' yet, Dave!'

Then Kevin Paye called, 'This thing is going off the wall, Rob. Channel Seven wants to run it three times in the evening, plus once in the kids' afternoon slot. I can't believe it. I've never had this much success before!'

That afternoon, Captain Ken called to ask: 'Are we full up yet?' I told him we were, and had overflowed to two more flights so far. Then Amanda rushed in from school; they had recorded the ad and replayed it three times in class. The whole school had cheered her and laughed at her funny Dad. Everyone asked if he really was the pilot of that big red, white and blue jet with the stars all over it. And was she really a pilot, too? Amanda smiled, 'Well, sort of . . . '

Then someone threw one of our little plastic planes; it streaked around the classroom with thirty laughing pilots chasing it. Sky Star was airborne!

11.

After nearly a year of nursing quiet confidence, our TV advertisement won the Network Advertising Agency's *second* prize for top TV ad of the year. Genuinely pleased, I awarded myself with the triumphant fist of victory. Not a bad effort, I smiled, for a complete amateur like myself on his first attempt, and with a daughter who was also in her first acting role. And all done with an amateur camera-man/film maker using dated equipment.

At our cramped but newly painted terminal building in the former *AEA - Airlines of Eastern Australia* premises, our now well-known ad was running repeatedly on our overhead monitors. 'And to think,' I lamented to my very contented General Manager, 'that first place went to a damned dog food commercial, for Heaven's sake! I like dogs, but here was Rover with his snout slobbering in a bowl while some clucking housewife crows: "He just loves it - and he tells me so!" Then right on cue, Rover goes "Woof!" '

Dave interrupted, 'But Robbie, you must allow for the possibility that Rover has more intelligence than that clown at Luna Park.'

I conceded, 'There *is* a slight possibility, I suppose. But raising our conversation somewhat above dog food, how is the ship of state floating?'

Dave explained that, for a company with only about a year in the game, we were proceeding remarkably well indeed. We had conducted numerous charter flights throughout Queensland's tropical Barrier Reef islands; plus a few to beautiful Lord Howe Island and a few more to Darwin. We had also begun popular safari-type journeys to Weipa in far north Queensland and Gove in the Northern Territory where we joined up with Barramundi fishing ventures. Importantly, passengers loved our concept of travelling when it suited *them* – within reason of course, and not being restricted by the rigid imposition of airline schedules. Also, we weren't competing with Qantas or Ansett - although they probably kept a wary eye on us. Had we started regular flights with identical routes and times to theirs, we'd quickly be breaching the spirit of the provisos of 'charter'.

*

Our prosperous Sky Star company was enjoying quite respectable cash flow revenues even though, right from the very start, I resisted seeking any bank finance unless unavoidable. My motto was always that if we can't afford it, we don't do it. So, naturally, we may have grown slower than others who were mortgaged to the hilt, but were unique in that we were proudly the only air charter company in Australia (in those days) to operate an airline-sized aircraft. While many others flew small business jets and piston twins with seats for just 8 to 14 passengers, our great advantage was that we needed only two pilots to carry over *sixty* people. The smaller types needed to pay wages for many times that number of pilots per the equivalent passengers. Adversely, those thirsty Rolls Royce engines gulped fuel ferociously; so - *win some, lose some* was the name of the game.

Airborne, I was pilot number one on our seniority list. This was because I'd been our first pilot. Ken Tolman was number two, even though he was a captain and our chief pilot. And we now had five other pilots who had joined us. Flying our mighty F28, *Charlie Zulu Golf,* was not only a pleasure but a valuable stepping stone for young pilots to 'driving the big stuff' and eventually attaining an airline position. We knew that their employment visit with us would be transitory – a few years at the most - if we ourselves didn't soon become an airline, but in the meantime it was all fun and rewarding. Soon, more F28's would hopefully be arriving to join our modest 'fleet' so I faced the small problem of how the heck I was going to pay for them! Enjoying myself was my first priority; after all, I was still attempting to recover from the loss of my wonderful wife while coping with the raising of those four little darlings.

I had always admired our Captain Ken as a friend and a fine pilot. Our first captain, he took his position very conscientiously. Only 31 years old but with a mature greyed-hair look, Ken and I flew together almost daily. I sat mostly in the right-hand co-pilot's seat of the F28 until Ken could make time one day to train me for my *command* rating: i.e. the captain's licence. Our camaraderie was mostly genial, but we often worked under pressure: such as conducting instrument approaches prior to landing in difficult weather conditions – and this necessitated very professional teamwork, or CRM (cockpit resource management) from both pilots. 'Flying blind', laymen call it. Other times, as on perfect sunny days on a flight to the islands, I liked to skylark around a bit while Ken definitely didn't. I secretly called him Captain Serious, while I'm not sure if he had a nickname for me.

'Ah, good morning girls and boys, ladies and gents, cats and dogs,' I started our pre-take-off P.A. announcement one day. 'Rob Grant here, up at the pointy end of the ship; sitting beside a rather worried-looking Captain Ken Tolman. We'd like to welcome you all aboard our fun charter flight today as we prepare for take-off towards the south and over Botany Bay. We're hoping for a fine and smooth flight, but anything could happen, I suppose, because this will be the very first flight either of us has made. '

Ken jerked an angry face across at me, wagging a finger, 'Now, none of that, Rob!'

'Why?'

'It's stupid. It's unprofessional. And I'm the captain so I say *don't!*'

I countered, 'But I'm the owner and I say yes.'

He replied, 'You'll frighten the socks off some people saying crazy stuff like that - which isn't funny anyway. No professional pilots ever say that . . . '

We taxied the jet along taxiway *Bravo* and towards Sydney's runway 16-Left. Amongst our chanting rituals of cockpit checks, I said 'You're talking about *airline* flights Ken. Those stuffy, staid and boring flights in travelling coffins where everyone has about as much fun as a funeral party. Do this, do that, but don't do anything else. And if you smoke, sneeze or dare to enjoy yourself - you'll be shot! We've flown airlines before, but this is a *charter*, Ken, remember? A privately chartered flight. We're supposed to be casual and having fun.'

'We'll continue this conversation airborne, Rob,' Captain Tolman sternly assured me as we completed the pre-take-off dialogue of the lengthy and complex checklist.

Then, still believing my actions were harmless, I returned to my PA microphone and continued where I'd left off: 'Sorry about that folks. Our captain actually *has* flown before. I believe his last time was in the Second World War. Anyway, we're now cleared for take-off by Air Traffic Control on runway 16-left, so here we go. Talk to you again soon when I come down the aisle to entertain you with my ukulele because we can't afford any in-flight entertainment.'

Somewhat as expected, our captain was rather quiet as we became airborne and turned left over the water. Bringing the undercarriage and flaps up, we then climbed steeply over Botany Bay then Sydney's Eastern suburbs, tracking the plane to intercept a VOR radio beacon that would guide us towards the next one at West Maitland. Then we'd cruise north to Casino in northern NSW, and further on to Proserpine near Airlie Beach in Queensland.

Upon reaching our cruising altitude of 31,000 feet, Ken grumbled as he reduced the throttle power to cruise mode. 'World War Two, eh? Not funny, Rob.'

'Have you heard my ukulele?'

'You haven't got one.'

'I know.'

'Your behaviour is ridiculous.'

'That's what you said about my TV ad. *Ridiculous*, remember?

'Geez Rob, I just expect a professional approach from all my First Officers. Charter or not. It's hardly too much to ask, is it? Some passengers are extremely nervous about flying. You know that. You mustn't frighten them. They're trapped in this thing and are relying on us for their very lives. They can't just get out and walk. Under the regulations I could have you stood down, you know.'

'But most passengers have a sense of humour, Ken.'

'Jee-zuss!' hissed Captain Ken. This wasn't going well at all - and we faced years more of flying together, not just these three hours today.

'Tell you what,' I offered, standing up. 'I'll go for a walk down the back for a while and ask those poor sheep trapped down there what they think of it all. Okay?'

'Sure. Don't fall out a window or anything,' sneered the captain.

Before leaving the flight deck I reminded him, 'Check oxygen mask on.' Embarrassed, he'd overlooked this vital requirement that must be followed whenever one pilot leaves the flight deck. If the cabin suffers a sudden depressurisation, the remaining pilot can't be left alone struggling for breath: he's got too much else to do. Ken donned his overhead mask as I left him to stew with all his friends, then I proceeded to wend my merry way rearwards towards, hopefully, more agreeable and friendly territory. I think the half-time score at this stage was one-all.

Passing row #13, I smiled a cheerio at two charming elderly ladies who were sitting together. 'Are you our captain?' one asked. And before I could answer, the other one said, 'But you look so *young*.'

Now where had I heard that before? I smiled again, 'No, I'm the other one with the ukulele. Ah, I was wondering, ladies . . . '

The woman next to the window interrupted, 'Are you in the movies or something? I've seen you before. Now what was the name of that one we saw last week, Dorie?'

I gave a hint: 'TV.'

'A TV show? A quiz show, was it? No, there was a pretty little girl. Oh yes, that's it. That ad on TV. The one for this charter company, of course. That crazy pilot on a merry-go-round was you! Wasn't it just so funny!'

'It was a Ferris wheel, actually. At Luna Park.' Other nearby passengers joined in the merriment as they too recognised me. Hmm, I briefly wondered if our captain would appreciate us actually *enjoying* ourselves down here. But what the heck; we were here to have fun - supposedly.

I chatted further to the ladies, then they asked again about the 'delightful young girl' in our advertisement. I told them she was my daughter, and I also had three others who were younger. Doris exclaimed 'Oh, their mother must be so proud!' To their shocked faces, I explained sadly that she had died last year; then we talked about the prevalence of breast cancer these days – which was really the *last* thing I wanted to discuss.

I added, 'But I have a nice lady who looks after them, so they're doing quite well in life, in school and mostly everywhere. The little one is only two, though.' The dear ladies oohed and aahed and commiserated then started relating their own families' stories, but I really had to leave them – I had fifty-three other folk to talk to. Before moving further aft, I asked a group of passengers, 'By the way, did I frighten any of you with my silly announcement about us never having flown before? If I did then I really do apologise. It was merely for fun.'

'Not at all,' assured another lady at window-side, and they all nodded general agreement. I told them our captain wasn't pleased with my flippant announcements, and someone said, 'Oh, he's probably just an old grump. Anyway, *we* laughed when you said it. Others did too.'

I was about to explain that Ken was only around thirty, when a man behind us laughed, 'Me and Jenny were terrified. So can we have our money back?' Someone else yelled 'Where's your ukulele, mate?' To laughter, I was forced to admit that I can play nothing but the fool, then made my introductions to the rest of our passengers while slowly making my way further towards the aft end of the aircraft where our friendly flight attendants, Gail and Laura, were busy in the galley preparing food and beverages for the midday meal service.

'Could you take the Boss a cuppa, please Gail,' I asked her. 'I think he needs one.'

She smiled, 'I thought *you* were the Boss Man?'

I replied, 'You tell *him* that.'

On my return forwards, a man said he appreciated a pilot coming down the aisle and introducing themself, because: 'You never see that on airline flights any more. Only in the *old days*.' I neared the two ladies in row #13 and they turned to give me encouragement, 'You look after those wonderful girls, won't you now.' Then Doris whispered to her friend, 'He's so *young* looking, isn't he?' and Mrs Window Seat added, 'And handsome, too!'

But before I could count all the tickets on myself, and as if Ken Tolman was spying on my enjoyment with the passengers, an urgent cabin chime sounded *Dinnnng-Donnnng!* followed by Ken's crisp command: 'The First Officer will report to the flight deck, thank you.' Hastening my step, I was soon back in my 'office' which I found was, shockingly, half full of gray, wispy smoke!

Astonished and gasping, I saw Ken breathing deeply into his oxygen mask. I urgently snatched my own. Ken was manipulating the control wheel and thrust levers as I leapt into my seat to reach for the slide-out Fire/Emergency check lists. We began a rapid chanting of the items on the list as Ken disconnected the auto-pilot and commenced an emergency descent from our flight level, designated as *three-one-zero.*

Any fire in the air is like a fire at sea: serious trouble. Just the *smell* of smoke can herald great danger and must be presumed as a fire somewhere until proven otherwise. I spun around in my seat and tore open the circuit breaker panel door behind me to quickly locate the culprit from amongst the 540 on display. A popped breaker was emitting some nasty-looking curls of smoke. It should have automatically popped open, but had jammed half way out and over-heated. I shut off its unessential circuit then observed the smoke as it was slowly sucked out the cabin vents. I then inserted a spare fuse/breaker and monitored its behaviour. It was fine.

Ken was magnificent in this emergency – as exemplified by his whole flying. Cool and calm, precise and diligent. He followed the rule book to the letter. After a few minutes, he asked if it was my opinion that the faulty circuit breaker had been the sole cause of the smoke, and was it now under control? I replied 'definitely' to both, so Ken cancelled his emergency descent request and assured ATC that all was okay again. 'Ops normal', as pilots say. While we had survived our first in-flight crisis, I mused about leaving the flight deck in future to chat with passengers.

Once stabilized in cruise mode again, I carefully asked Ken what he thought about this matter. He replied, 'Well, we have to leave the deck for toilet breaks, don't we? And to stretch our legs on long trips.

So I've no objections to short breaks. It was just co-incidence how that occurred while you were gone. Gail said that most people were appreciating your friendly visit to the cabin. It was fun, they said. But on a normal airline flight they sometimes felt like prisoners where they never even *saw* the men from up front who were controlling their safety and ultimate destiny. It was all so stuffy and regulated, they said. Like being in a school classroom.'

'In short, Rob, I can see some value in your congenial PR exercises. *Not*, mind you, that last trip when you went down the aisle in swimmers, goggles and snorkel . . . '

I'd been telling the passengers, "In the unlikely event that we have to swim back to shore . . ." but Ken droned on, 'So while we are just flying charters I'm going to be slightly more tolerant from now on. I was trained in a rigid cockpit environment by a strict old captain and it's hard to shake off that regimentation overnight.'

Phew, Ken's demeanour had certainly moderated, but was unlikely to last for long. Cheekily, I asked, 'Well, if I can't wear goggles or snorkels in the cabin, what about a bikini?' He forced a crooked grin as we continued winging our merry way north with me anticipating two pleasurable days of sailing around the Barrier Reef islands with our friendly passengers. Meanwhile, I became concerned about an elderly lady called Doris – or maybe her friend – who might be seeking a handsome *younger* man to entertain her? My daughter Amanda would say, 'Don't be silly, Dad,' but I was being serious for a change.

*

I was greeted at my front door by my four biggest fans in pigtails. They hurled themselves at me. It was like being strangled by a quartet of junior boa constrictors. As I handed them bags of presents from Hamilton Island I said, 'Guess what girls? Our plane had a bit of a fire in it on Saturday . . . '

Ripping parcels open, Emmie asked, 'Did it go down and crash?' No, I assured them. I'd put the fire out. I'd been away for two days and it hurt to know how much they missed me. Thank goodness for Alicia, my ever-patient nanny.

Despite my enthusiastic welcome and a few grabbing matches over various new dolls, I noticed Amanda crying. 'Now, what's the matter with my little Amanda? What's happened darling?'

She sobbed, 'Yesterday Mrs McNeil said you're not my real Daddy. But she said you're Celia's Daddy. Why? So who's Olivia's and Emmie's Daddy? It's not fair if Celia is your girl and I'm not.'

Oh God, this was worse than a cockpit fire at 31,000 feet - or the wrath of Captain Tolman. We all sat in a circle on the lounge room floor amidst a small mountain of presents as I tried to explain our family setup – which *was* somewhat complicated, I must admit.

Alicia McNeil was red-faced with embarrassment: 'I only answered truthfully when one of them asked just who was this Tony man who had left them. I'm so sorry, Mr Grant.' Amanda had mostly forgotten about her natural father Tony, and was now fairly confused about the whole *father* issue. Tony had left them before she was four, making me the real winner in the end but clouding the matter for them. Anyway, I carefully explained about Cristina and I getting married, then having one more child who was Celia. I assured them I loved them all equally – which I most certainly did – but their mummy was never coming back so they were stuck with silly old me.

Olivia interrupted, 'So, haven't Mandy and Emmie and me got any *real* parents but Celia has?' Then Amanda stomped her little foot and repeated with hands angrily on hips, 'It's not fair!'

A similarly confused Emmie chimed in with 'So, our other Daddy ran away and our Mummy died away. But I thought *you* were our proper Daddy until Mrs McNeil said it was that other man?' I glanced to Alicia for urgent guidance, but she stared at the curtains while little Celia sat on my knee and sucked her thumb – possibly taking it all in.

I winced. 'Heck, girls. What have you lot been talking about while I'm gone? Can't you just play games and have fun? Now listen up here: I'm the Dad of you all because I married your Mum, okay? But before that, your lovely Mum had you three biggest girls when she was with your first Dad, Tony. Okay? But he went away one day - maybe because he couldn't cope with kids – I don't know. Then one day I came flying in the kitchen window . . . ' They all laughed as I zoomed my arms like wings. 'Then another day, after me and Mum got married, our little darling Celia bounced into the world and we all went *Oh nooooo!!*' This was really funny, too.

I continued in a frown, 'But some people get sick sometimes, and some of them die. It's horrible, I know, but no doctors could help Mummy get better. After she had gone from us, I was the only person left in the world who cared for you and loved you all. Someone had to feed you little devils and change your yucky nappies. I was your *real* Daddy then. Remember, a real Dad is a man who *acts* like a Dad and tries to always be there in your lives for you. Now we all have to continue living our lives together as a family. Mandy said that this wasn't fair and in some ways it isn't, but real life is not Disneyland, unfortunately. So we just have to make the best of our lives, don't we? If you still like Mrs McNeil minding you and you love me as your real Daddy, then we'll all be just fine. Anyone who doesn't understand that please raise your right hand.' No-one did - but Alicia McNeil tried to hide some tears.

Kids can be resilient. When tough times arrive, many of them simply accept adversity and tackle it in their stride. After all, to do otherwise is often not an option. So, by a show of hands I was voted the most popular Daddy in the house, then we adjourned for dinner. Amanda was showing her nice smile again, so the others followed suit. But life can certainly be hard, as I knew first hand: I'd lost my mother at two and my father at twelve - then my second dad at twenty.

In the kitchen, I gave Alicia an extra thousand dollars for her last few days, stating that I wished I could spare more. She was still upset, but I assured her we all thought the world of her – which we did. After she left, I gawked in my wallet to discover I had no money left for food for the next four days! While the old Greek man next door thought I was fabulously rich after I once showed him a photo of our jet, I was in fact stony broke and we faced more packaged airline meals for the time being.

So the girls had seemed content with my 'family' explanations and were all sound asleep by 7.30 – leaving me to face yet another long night alone with the shadows and with nothing much else to do except ponder how, yes, I'd solved that mini crisis all right.

Then, in the morning, I suddenly had only three daughters instead of four - because one had vanished!

12.

In great alarm and with trembling fear, I shook the three youngest ones awake as I gawked again at Amanda's empty bed. 'Where's Amanda, girls? Where *is* she?' I frantically searched the house and yard but my precious Mandy was nowhere to be found. It was 7.30 and I was due to leave soon for the airport and a return charter flight to Essendon in Melbourne. I quickly rang Marie Westcott and informed her that one of my girls was missing and to 'Find another pilot!' - then banged the phone down.

I knew Mandy had been upset for a while last night, but I couldn't believe any eight-year-old would run away like this. How dangerous could this be! For a pilot trained not to panic in emergencies, I was surely panicking now. I threw the kids into my rusty station wagon and we raced off down our street, hoping to spy her playing nearby. Or maybe just riding her little pink *Razer* scooter along the footpath. I yelled to a woman walking to the bus stop, 'Have you seen a little girl?' She shook her head and I roared away. I would give my search just ten minutes at the most, then call the police. God, I hadn't realised just how much I loved that beautiful child until she'd gone. My final vision of her last night had been of her contented smile. Maybe she awoke this morning confused again, then went for a solo walk somewhere - out into the big wild world by her tiny self . . .

At the end of our road was a small tree-filled park; much of it overgrown with weeds. A quick scan revealed nothing, so I spun the car around and was about to race back home to call the police when Emmie yelled out: 'There she is! See? Sitting on the swings.' I spied a tiny figure alone in shadows at the very rear of the park. Screeching to a halt, I bounded from the car and ran over to my lonely angel. She was sulking and teary-eyed, rocking slowly on the swings while still in her pyjamas. She didn't look up as I sat on the swing beside her, so I regained my breath and waited for her to talk first. Innocently, the other three came running over and started happily playing on the nearby slippery dip as though their sister was often found alone in a park.

It seemed I would have to be the first to speak. 'Hiya kiddo,' I whispered. 'Whatcha doin' here all by your little self?' Silence.

'Do you know who I am?'

'S'pose.'

'I'm the man who loves you because I am your *real* daddy. Your only dad. Did you know that?'

She shrugged. 'I s'pose.'

'I'm the one who pays for all your presents and food and clothes and . . . *everything* in your life.' Silence greeted this weak failure to unravel her confused and defiant stance. Santa Claus already bought her many of these things and she didn't need a patronising man bragging about an obligation for which I had volunteered.

Hmm, I'm not doing too well here, but I stumbled along: 'And I made us a big happy family again, even though your lovely Mummy went away. Did you know that some other men might not have wanted you three little devils then, but I did?'

'No.' This made her think.

'So you mustn't run away again my little friend, because then you'll be just like your first daddy Tony who ran away from everything, won't you? You can't run away from things in life just because they sometimes get hard. You must learn to face up to your problems so you can be *better* than that Tony guy; not the same. Do you understand, mate?'

She gripped my hand. 'Yep. Sorry, Daddy.' I'd made the point: your first father ran away from his responsibilities so don't lower yourself to *that* standard. Then she whispered, 'So, didn't he love us?'

Glancing up, I scanned the clouds for answers that didn't appear. 'Ah, I just don't know, my little sweetie. I've never met the man. Mum and Tony were only young and some young men simply can't handle a family situation . . . you know, babies and all that stuff . . . '

'But you were young, too. You told me . . . ' she countered quite correctly.

'Umm, we are all different, mate. Hey, remember us on that crazy ride at Luna Park? Wasn't that fun? Would your other dad have done that with you? Did he take you anywhere? You told me I was the best dad in the world that day, didn't you?'

'Yep.'

'So how about we go back and get ready for school now? You have to be the big boss lady of my aeroplane business one day, so you've got to learn all your schoolwork first. Come on Mandy, don't be silly.'

We both laughed at that line from our advert, then she softly revealed her thoughts as I gripped her hand: 'Daddy, it made me cry when Mrs McNeil told us that because you're my step-Daddy then Celia will only ever be our *half* sister. But I don't want a half, I want a *whole* sister because I love her.'

I laughed. 'Well, I don't much like the bottom half when her nappies are yukky, but I love *all* of her anyway. A sister is what you girls make it, mate. Some full sisters or brothers don't like each other, while other step-sisters and half-sisters become the greatest of friends. Come on Mandy, growing up is a puzzle sometimes and many things are hard to understand, but you'll get there one day for sure. And you mustn't ever do this again because there's some bad people out here in the world. I've told you this before, okay?'

'Yeesss, Daddy.' The other three thought this event had been great fun and wanted to keep playing in the park all day. But life beckoned from near and far. We each had our routines to attend, both young and old. Little Celia had to be taken to pre-school as soon as Alicia McNeil arrived, and the other three to school.

And I was late for work . . . oh no, I'd cancelled my duty as a pilot for today. I would instead work on the other minor problem I faced at the moment: how to raise three million dollars for three more F28 jets. The vague shape of an idea slowly emerged into view as I picked up Mandy and watched my three other children skip innocently to the car.

Phew, that was easy.

13.

I located an aviation entrepreneur in the Philippines named Ferdinand Diego. He'd advertised three Fokker F28 jets for sale together in an aviation trade magazine; the total asking price was approximately three million US dollars. I'd known that I'd never find another plane like CZG for the bargain basement price of $275,000 again, so this deal was at least worth investigating. But first I needed to consult our trusty legal officer and General Manager David Skillen about offloading my property out west; my *Wundala* homestead station.

Even though I'd vowed to retain the station forever, I'd always suspected that a rural farming life was not for me. It would be hard to sell Dad's hard-worked property that he'd generously bequeathed to me, but lacking any intrinsic interest in the whole farming concept left me with either a property tied up for life – therefore a permanent yet unwanted liability of sorts, or a handy asset to sell now and pursue my grand goals in the turbulent skies of the aviation world. A prudent person would continue tending to his sheep and cattle, working contentedly under the blazing sun with a mighty vista of brown fields rolling before his eyes. Dad and Maurice had both lived such lives on properties side-by-side and I'm sure they had both desired and expected that I would follow suit. But I wasn't nearly that sensible: I was in my early twenties and in my dreams I never saw a farm, but always glimpsed a clear blue sky.

In Dave Skillen's office, I sucked a deep breath and said, 'Dave, you say that times are good on rural properties just now. This drought is over and values are up for a change. Now about this Philippine deal: I won't borrow from the banks, so I've decided I want to sell *Wundala*. How much do you think I might get for it?'

Skillen raised his grey eyebrows with consternation. 'Robbie, it would probably fetch around the two million mark today, but I most strongly advise you to forget it. If you pour it all into aviation it could easily vanish straight down the drain. It was Juan Trippe, the famous Director of Pan Am Airways, who once said, 'No-one ever made money from aviation.' He should know: it went broke.'

I responded, 'That was after forty years, Dave. Yes, aviation has its turbulence like any business, but you're the head of this aviation company: are you proposing we forego all our hard work and great progress now when we've only just started? We need more planes and I'm forging ahead – right or wrong. I'd also like you to kick in that half million super payout that you're sitting on and have never touched. I'm in a sound financial position just now. We showed $1.2 million profit in our first eighteen months. That's remarkably good for a tiny charter company, and much of it was generated by that one TV ad that cost me a paltry $2,500. Anyway, I seem to have a mild touch of entrepreneurial flair, wouldn't you agree? And while I'm not quite Richard Branson, I'm doing comparatively well for my age. We've got nine pilots now and we can't keep paying nine pilots to fly just one charter aircraft. So I'm going into RPT Regular Public Transport airline flying as soon as we can. To do that we'll need three or four planes - preferably four. Might even keep Captain Grumpy happy for a while.'

Dave replied, 'If possible. Anyway Robbie, my training has always been to borrow from banks and slowly prosper from there. Both your father and Maurice did exactly that. Also, you're a single parent with four little mouths to feed. What will you do if you lose the lot gambling on aviation?'

'If it all fails I'll go flying for an airline somewhere in the world as a salaried pilot. What I love doing. Then I can proudly say to myself that at least I gave it a go. But what if we're successful here, Dave? We could make millions! We might step right into Ansett's shoes one day soon because of the unique aviation scenario currently in this country.'

Dave warned that he'd been a mere country solicitor, one who'd processed our family's estate, but was now, at the age of sixty, being asked to risk his entire retirement future and 'embark upon murky waters indeed.'

'Cockies' droppings!' I exclaimed. 'What murky waters? Go back to the droughts in dusty Trangie, then. They recur every seven years. There's no murky water there. Sit in that musky little office and waste away shuffling land valuation certificates. This is your chance of a lifetime, Dave. We could make millions over the next five to ten years before you finally retire. We are approaching a golden milestone for aviation in Australia and here we are, poised with an infrastructure already in place and a bubbling zeal to absolutely *leap* into that exciting future. We could become number two to Qantas. By the way, how much interest are you getting on your term deposits just now?' Dave thought it was about 6½ percent.

I declared, 'I'll get you four hundred percent because I know how to avoid most of Ansett's mistakes.'

'How?'

'By not borrowing money, Dave. The epitaph: "*He was strangled by debt*" will *not* be chiselled onto my tombstone! I don't care how many other businesses borrow, only to go bust. I won't be doing it. I've borrowed once only – to get up and running – but no more. One hike in interest rates plus another hike in jet fuel – then whoompah! This world is addicted to borrowing and debt. I'm not. This is my only plan now: to sell *Wundala* and sink most of it into Sky Star. Are you in or out? With me or not?'

After a few days of deep deliberation, he was in! Plunging the lot on a dodgy horse called *Murky Waters*. Soon after, I sold my beloved rural station for almost two million dollars, as David had correctly anticipated, and within days of the cheque clearing I was on the phone to Mr Ferdy Diego in the sunny Philippines. He was to be my waking introduction to the Asian system of bartering - of which I knew nothing while he was apparently a master. David Skillen's hair seemed to turn a further shade of gray when I happily informed him that he'd be accompanying me to the Philippines to oversee the purchase of our new fleet additions - along with my new private secretary, Amanda Grant, aged eight.

At night, I told Amanda that we'd be going overseas together for a short two-week holiday to look at some other planes to buy. She was back to her loveable self again, having skipped past her mild hiccups of doubts and wonderings which are customary when growing up – and perfectly understandable after losing her mother at a young age. So I was once again Dad number-one and we were the greatest of mates because she was my number-one friend.

Now that she was nearly nine and an exceptionally intelligent young person, I saw the need for Mandy's further knowledge and education of our world; an irreplaceable substitute for the routine humdrum of everyday school lessons. Also accompanying us would be Paul Harland, a new First Officer flying with us, and Peter Woods, our maintenance chief, or L.A.M.E. licenced aircraft maintenance engineer. This was our attack team; ready to strike if and when I found any suitable aircraft to purchase. We would sign the documents, leap over the mountains of red tape and paperwork associated with exporting and importing an aircraft, then fly the first one home. Then we'd go back again when necessary to collect the others. Within a few months we should have a fleet of F28's painted up in Sky Star's strikingly splendid colour scheme, and our new RPT airline would be ready to take wings and soar skywards.

*

Flying as passengers for a change, we were soon on our way. We flew above beautiful cumulus clouds through a deep blue sky, then on into a dark and starry night. We were cruising north towards the 7,100 tropical islands of the Philippines; flying on Philippine Air. Amanda was agog at the in-flight movies and music available on our 747, while Paul and Peter were enjoying long chats. David swallowed pills and nodded off the whole way, (I hadn't known until now that he was nervous about flying). Sitting alone, my head was buried in books. Paperback books.

In my local library, I'd recently found several books about conducting business in Asia and flicked through them cursorily. But there was nothing really *on-topic* with what I was seeking. Then, in a second-hand book store near home, by sheer chance I bumped an old paperback to the floor. Picking it up, I glanced at the title: 'Doing business in Asia: a riotous list of Do's & Don'ts for the unwary novice.'

This could be precisely what I sought, and once on our way, I burrowed into it as the others relaxed and enjoyed their flight. The book wasn't exactly a best-seller, nevertheless it held a few vital tips that I could possibly employ with Mr Ferdy Diego – and perhaps any others. Reading keenly, the analogies were mildly amusing, I suppose, but the main messages I was able to glean were these:

1. When doing business in Asia, nothing is as it seems 2. In a deal, it is vital that the Asian person is allowed to think that he has won the deal (oh, okay) 3. It is essential that the Asian person does not lose what is called *face.* 'Face' can represent their whole life, existence or career – and particularly their public reputation. Asians who lose *face* sometimes commit suicide from the shame (faceless persons?) 4. The Asian will always ask for double the expected price. Obviously, therefore, the real price is usually about half the asking price. 5. We sometimes perceive Asians as suspicious and devious; but they see us exactly the same. The winner will be the person who is *perceived* as the less devious – even though he may not be. (What could possibly be clearer than that?)

Okay, I kind-of got the picture and was duly prepared to do battle with the allegedly devious enemy. But first, Amanda and I spent a delightful three days in sparkling Puerto Galera on the island of Mindoro, while the three men stayed in Manila where Peter Woods met our Mr Diego. On arrival, they went straight to the three unused F28's which were parked in a yard; retired from their long service with Luzon Island Air.

Meanwhile, on our tropical island of picture-postcard beauty, I quickly got to know my Mandy much better without the distractions of the other three girls constantly chattering. It became a special bonding time for us both. I was deeply grateful to have this little person as a loving step-daughter and on this short holiday we became friends for life. And while I purposely didn't mention her fleeing to the park in her pyjamas *that* recent morning, she refrained from pining over her mother or dissecting our current family arrangements.

Here in paradise, we paddled and raced our canoes around the sparkling blue lagoon as Mandy shrieked in delight, then we often floated over to the sunken bar for an iced milkshake before snorkelling above the colourful coral to observe the myriad of flashing fish that zoomed around us. At night we both stayed up late, enjoying rhythmic Filipino music and dancing in the sand beside the beach bars, while I artfully dodged several rather overt offers from smiling local ladies when my daughter wasn't within earshot.

Within a few days, Mandy had acquired a tropical brown tan; so with her blond hair tied in pink and red flowers, and wearing a white beach dress bought for only ten dollars, she was as pretty as a picture and the very image of her mother. Others thought so, too. In an alleyway, a toothless old man offered to pay me a hundred dollars if I would cut off and sell her long blond ponytail to him. Mandy looked aghast as I politely declined this startling offer. Back at our beachside bungalow, the friendly *Mamasan* laughed and said, 'He sells the hair to make wigs. He has no other money. This is Asia, yes.'

We were seeing real poverty for the first time. Everyone here works in menial tasks or operates some kind of 'scheme' because there is no social security network. I paid a boy to take $100 to the old man, then steered us well clear of that dark alleyway for the remainder of our stay until we took the fast outrigger back to the bustling port of Batangas. Then we caught an inter-island ferry across Manila Bay to where, I hoped, success awaited our exciting mission.

On the ferry, we noticed a group of Filipino school children gazing over the rails. Mandy queried how none of the girls had blond hair like her. She was amazed when I told her that no girls or boys – or indeed anyone at all in Asia had blond hair, and this was why she'd been the star attraction on our island where the women had just *adored* my little blondie and the old man sought her hair.

At Manila airport we checked into the local Hilton Hotel. Here I hired a nursemaid and a security guard for just a few dollars. They would oversee my daughter playing all day in the hotel's huge pool. Looking around, security guards seemed to be everywhere in the Philippines. I saw armed guards standing outside most shops, banks, hotels and public places. Shotguns, machine guns, handguns – they abound throughout this nation of a hundred million mostly poor, but very friendly people. It's just the way things are, I was often told.

*

Ferdinand Diego was a large and swarthy Filipino businessman aged about fifty, I supposed. He sported a handlebar moustache that twirled up at the ends, and wore a huge and expensive black suit. A white bow-tie highlighted his black shimmering hair which was so greased with lotion that it shone under lights. At first glance, Ferdy looked like your friendly Mafia hit man, but he assured me he'd 'been involved in aviation all his life.' I was enthused to meet him, but he quickly asked when our 'big Boss Man' would be coming? I advised him that I was actually the 'big Boss' and he would be dealing with *me*. Ferdy laughed loudly because he laughed a lot; this time he roared noisily at my joke - then promptly ignored me, turning to greet Dave Skillen as he arrived, then to shout him a drink at the bar.

Dave immediately insisted to our client that I really *was* the owner of the firm, while he himself held the honourable position of General Manager. It was actually me who pulled the strings, paid the money, and did the final deal, he said. In reply, Ferdy apologised so profusely that I became alarmed for his white bow-tie which was doused with spilt cocktails as its owner waved his giant arms around the bar like palm fronds in a monsoonal hurricane. I didn't know what he said, but it sounded significant. Perhaps he'd assumed I was some lowly assistant, or maybe Dave's secretary. But certainly not the 'Big Boss Man.'

Sitting down, our Ferdy was certainly a friendly and enthusiastic dealer in aviation matters as he tirelessly elaborated his family's *expertise* in the airline business. These lengthy exposés were lubricated by even more beverages to produce ever-incremental *elasticisings* of the truth. Likewise, several cocktails and beers splashed down our throats as Ferdy spared no expense on the tab. These lubrications were followed by a magnificent feast which we certainly enjoyed. I let Dave endure most of the garrulous sales pitch which spluttered out like a Gatling gun as our moustachioed friend continued, for unfathomable reasons, to ignore me - despite his previous apologies.

So, amidst our host's ranting while quaffing great dollops of food into his mouth and over his handlebars, I managed to quietly ascertain that: (a) he wasn't the owner or the seller of the planes after all; but a middle-man – an agent, and (b) the actual owner was apparently his cousin, who was, somewhat suspiciously, unavailable this evening. Hmm . . .

As time wore on, I eventually tired of the game and interrupted Ferdy's monologues with a softly spoken question: 'What would be your commission on a deal of three million?' His startled eyes told me that he thought I was the greatest fool he'd ever met because I was prepared to pay his asking price without even haggling once, but they also revealed that I knew he wasn't the seller; and for him, this was a rather disquieting development at this delicate stage.

He hesitated – for once. 'Er, there is no commission. I do this for my cousin, you see. A family matter of great pride, you see. Family members would not dare charge each other commissions in the Philippines, you see.'

No, I did not see at all. Yet I told him how impressed I was with my very first forage into doing business in Asia, and also that we could possibly learn some fine family traditions from 'your great people.' Our smiling Godfather was now looking wary, but possibly pleased with his general progress so far. In celebration, he continued splashing the wine bottle at us while Dave and I pretended to become merrily drunk. In truth, I'd had my tiny quota and secretly poured most of my drinks into the pot plant beside my chair. I assumed Dave had his own arrangements.

As time and the exaggerations dragged on, our garrulous host offered to show us later the 'exciting nightlife of Manila that you would never dream possible' – and all on his tab, of course. Feigning interest, I laughingly asked him about my chances of getting a nice blonde for the night. His eyes lit up as he assured me that *anything* was possible for us: his wonderful new friends. A blond? Anything.

'But how can a Filipino dancing lady be blond?' I asked innocently.

'Well, it is a wig, of course. You see?' Yes, this time I most certainly did *see!*

Winking at Dave, I quickly changed the subject and said to our host, 'Mr Diego, my engineer has finished inspecting the three Fokkers' airframes. He reports that they are in an acceptable condition - commensurate with their age and flying hours, that is.'

'Er, yes.'

'So, if you can so easily obtain for me a blonde in Manila, can you also get me six Rolls Royce Tay engines which work, because the ones on your planes are mostly out of hours?' As Ferdy spilt champagne over the bow tie again, I was relying on Peter Woods' advice not to trust the engine log books because they appeared to be 'manipulated.' The airframe certifications, however, should be okay because they'd been forced to obtain that routine maintenance in Singapore – a location of impeccable credentials. So, the old jet engines were virtually past their use-by dates while their log books silently failed to mention this. Perturbed by strange logbook entries, Peter's discreet enquiries around Manila airport's businesses had revealed that Ferdy's agency was mostly reputable, but they were desperate to get rid of the three Luzon Island jets 'at any price.' And in order to avoid losing 'face', the deal must be done *immediately.*

Getting no answer on the engines' acquisition question, I suddenly stood up at the table and, like a magician whipping a rabbit from a hat, thrust a cheque out to Ferdy and said, 'Thank you very much for the wonderful dinner and your generous hospitality, Mr Diego. Here is a cheque for one million U.S. dollars. We do not want your out-of-hours engines, but we'll take your planes without them. You have exactly sixty seconds to agree to this offer or Mr Skillen and I are walking out and you will not see us again.'

Dave's eyes bulged at me, as if to say 'We are?' as Diego's black moustache was twitching as though it were alive. 'But . . . but . . . the planes without engines? It is unheard of. You must take the engines, yes? My cousin will be shocked. What can I tell him? Only *one* million, Mr Grant? This is a little crazy, yes?'

I answered, 'Yes, and I'm the crazy cabin steward boy - as you seem to think. But we could always report this small matter of advertising expired engines for sale to the Philippines authorities, yes? In the meantime, I'm not quite sure what you can explain to your *cousin,* but I really hope you will not lose any face in this matter. So it would be far better, would it not, to hand him this cheque for one million dollars than to explain to him that you didn't get a cheque for anything at all?'

The answer was a pleading, 'But – but - no engines? What can you do without these engines?'

I smiled and declared, 'That will be my concern. Your sixty seconds are up, Ferdy. Do you want this one million dollars – or not?' He hesitated for a single second, then his hand shot out like the exhaust flames from an afterburner and grabbed the cheque. As we merrily bade him a fond *goodnight,* he thrust it into his wallet.

In the lobby, Dave Skillen ran a hand across his sweating brow. 'God, Robbie, I don't quite know what to say except ask the same question: how can you buy them without any engines?' He'd always called me Robbie, a habit since I was a young boy when Dave had been like a pleasant uncle to me. But no-one called me Robert, and no-one *ever* called me Bob.

I told him, 'Fokker in Holland is going broke. It's all over the trade magazines. They won't be making the F28's or anything else again. I rang them and asked about buying six Tays. They said sure, they've got plenty sitting around there and I could have them for peanuts - a fire sale - almost. They'll simply ship them here from Amsterdam in crates, then Peter can supervise their fitting. In a month or so they'll be completed and we'll ready to zoom off to Australia. We're going home tomorrow, then Paul and I will come back to take possession of the first plane when it's ready. So I end up paying only $1½ million in total - including the engines from Holland, for three planes that were originally offered for three million. Simple really – although I'm hoping Mr Diego doesn't lose too much face with his family.'

Dave argued, 'But that cheque? You can't draw that without my signature or without all the relevant documents signed, for Heaven's sake! The Bills of Sale? You can't . . . heck, I don't think I'll ever quite understand you, Robbie.'

Deadpan, I said, 'It was a dud cheque. Worthless piece of paper. I wrote "I.O.U. $1M" on it. But we'll certainly pay the money by wire transfer as soon as they . . . his cousin, that is, signs the planes over. They'll probably honour my offer, because, after all, who else offered them a cool million tonight? And if they don't, we'll simply search elsewhere.'

Dave Skillen shook his head and laughed, 'Let's go to a night club. I feel like getting drunk for the first time in ages.'

'You won't find a blonde,' I assured him. 'Unless you run into Mr Diego, of course. In which case, say 'hi' to his cousin for me. No, I'm going back to my room, Dave. I've got a daughter to look after.'

*

It was therefore slightly surprising when, upon reaching my hotel room, very tired but pleased with myself, I was barred from entry by a young and stern security guard who looked about the same age as me. I'd forgotten. He was the one I'd hired earlier and was resplendent in a shining black uniform that was adorned with more glittering badges and medals than that of a Russian general. His large silver shotgun was poking menacingly at me, and it was certainly for real. Still on duty and conscientiously doing his job, the guard insisted on identification from me before allowing entry. I did so, then thanked him profusely for his dedication in guarding my daughter who was hopefully sound asleep inside with the nursemaid, who was also minding her.

'She is lovely young lady,' Pedro announced, standing bolt upright to attention. 'I guard her with my very life. Even at the pool I stand there all day with my shotgun. I am ready at all times. Any kidnap and it is *Bang Bang!*'

Wonderful, except that I hoped he was a straight shooter. Then he continued: 'And today she show me tape of your TV advertisement. This is very funny and I laugh very much.'

Well, what a nice fellow, I thought – unless he happened to be shooting you, of course. I thanked him and laughed, 'Here's a small thankyou for your loyal service, Pedro.' His eyebrows shot up at the sight of the three one-hundred-dollar bills I handed him. He was speechless, but I shrugged and stated that my daughter's safety was worth much more than that.

I asked if he was married. He said no, he was very poor so he couldn't afford such a *luxury*. Then he boasted that he would one day tell his grandchildren about this three-hundred-dollar tip. As an afterthought, I said I'd be back on business in a few weeks and, if he so wished, might sponsor him to Australia and permanent employment in the security section of our new airline. Or perhaps as a cabin steward.

He thanked me profusely, then I asked, 'Just one little favour please, Pedro.'

'Yes sir?'

'Please stop pointing that thing in my face.'

'Most definitely and certainly, sir!' With military precision, he lowered arms and stomped at ease.

In the morning I told Mandy we'd be going home the next day, and that I'd be returning to this great country in a few weeks because of a slight delay to our program. She pleaded to come back with me then, but I argued that school beckoned. 'But Dad, you said seeing the world is lots more important than silly old school,' she countered with the truth. Unable to invent a suitable excuse because I had many other matters to digest and resolve, I replied, 'We'll see.'

We left Peter Woods in Manila to face the wrath, if any, of our friend Ferdinand Diego, and to supervise the preparation of the jets for the installation of their (almost) new engines when they arrived from Holland. Apparently he encountered no difficulties from Moustachioed Man - I was later told, and we'd even generated some grudging respect in airport circles for 'playing the game' as it has always been in Asia. Ferdy's corny act was simply par for the course;

his feigned indignation was all part of a script because they'd only ever expected to get about one million or so from the deal.

So long as you don't appear to lose face . . .

As for our latest acquisitions: I was confident the jets would serve us well for some years to come because, upon their arrival in Sydney, they'd undergo thorough inspections before the granting of Australian airworthiness and registration certifications.

Once home again, my other three sweeties were suffering from - in order of ascending age: toothaches, headaches, and a cold. I gave them great sympathy and cuddles, but somehow suspected they just wanted to stay home with me for a day or two.

14.

In Australia, my little company was progressing with very pleasing growth rates; regularly striding forwards in an arena where we seemed to have *lucked* upon fertile opportunities – as occasional observers remarked.

But *luck* was a word that often irked me. It was bandied about rather too much whenever our overall progress and my success was discussed. More pointedly, it referred to my apparent *luck* when I jumped into the gap of AEA's bankruptcy to start my own charter firm which then became an RPT airline company - both of which eventually succeeded. In truth it was gutsy good timing and daring, not luck, where I managed to purchase my first large jet for the ridiculous sum of just over a quarter of a million dollars when no-one else dared bid for it. Then came three more jets from overseas for a total of only $A1.7 million – after adding almost new engines. This was achieved only after I'd burrowed into my personal estate then raided Dave Skillen's retirement nest. 'Don't worry Dave,' I'd assured him. 'I've bet it all on the red, white and blue.' His face flushed red each time I said this.

Without such spins of the wheel, I could have remained on my inherited property west of Trangie and simply farmed; then my position after thirty or forty years would have been static. I would have eked out a farmer's income in an unchanging and often drought-stricken rural dustbowl - to me, a permanency of drudgery. Instead, I aimed for the sky and eventually made it. I took risks, yes, but carefully calculated steps – not gambles.

And if I did indeed inherit a tidy sum (for the 1980's), was I the *only* person in Australia to ever inherit a family estate? Most other such (urban) beneficiaries buy a house: a totally non-productive item that earns no income and employs no-one. Also, I didn't see it as much luck to have lost my mother at two and my father and sole parent at twelve. So it wasn't a fluke that I magically turned a rural station into an airline, it was because my life's interests lay in flying planes and not herding cattle; in chasing my dreams skywards instead of along country trails. While farming life suits many and I greatly admire those involved, it just wasn't for me.

In honesty, I *was* blessed with some good fortune along the way because, unlike me, many other orphaned children have been left without a cent. And it was certainly providential when Mandy suggested the exciting name and vibrant colour scheme for our airline. But the see-saw of life's fortunes also saw me married to a wonderful woman at twenty then quickly become a widower soon after. While I was blessed with three of her children plus one of our own, it's a challenge to sit at home most nights with four little kids to feed and entertain while also attempting to build a large business. This translated into an almost zero social life while-ever my four children needed me – which was just about all the time.

In the evenings, my visitors became few and far between because most of them were young single pilots who lived in a permanent mode of party mania; unattached guys with a glamorous job and excess money to burn. I could have pursued an excitingly similar course in my life but was home instead, playing kids' games like hide-and-seek, reading bedtime stories and performing the role of *two* parents every night.

But when Cristina died, my resolve simply doubled: her kids simply *couldn't* be let down twice in their lives. I saw no other path to follow. I wasn't Captain Marvellous, just their Dad. It was often tough but I wouldn't have traded places with anyone.

*

Speaking of trading: now it was time to put some of my young ladies to work. Our charter network so far covered some regional routes plus a few capital city runs each week when required. We also flew charters for mining crews to Western Australia, and oil rig crews to various jobs anywhere in Australia. Our smaller F28's could usually land and take-off on shorter airport runways than the heavier Boeings of Qantas and Ansett, so for some time we blended into the Australian aviation framework without too many problems and with more than a modicum of success.

But becoming an airline was a whole new scenario. We needed new advertising for our proposed 'Sky Star' airline. Initially we would offer almost no competition for Qantas or Ansett because, at the moment, we only possessed four planes while Qantas had 170 and Ansett 138. But to operate scheduled services we needed many more passengers to fill many more planes. Having just four planes now was almost a joke, and such a small number was in no way an aerial fleet. I scoured the world markets for suitable used aircraft while deliberating the advertising attack we'd certainly need.

In seeking the necessary customer volumes, I remembered that Amanda's pretty face was still quite well-known from the TV ad that had been periodically aired in various towns and cities for two years, so it was time to utilise our previous promotional successes and put her to work again. I suggested to Dave Skillen that we erect cardboard larger-than-life photos of Amanda and her sister Olivia in our small terminal building, and also on a number on billboards beside country highways. They could be the faces of Sky Star. Dave, however, preferred adult models to children.

'Once was enough,' he said. 'We need shots of handsome pilots with glamorous flight attendants. Adults want to see them because adults buy our tickets.'

'They saw a kid at Luna Park and still bought tickets,' I argued.

Dave held more than a passing interest in our financial fortunes because I'd talked him into parting with most of his half-million dollars in retirement superannuation and to hand it all over to me: Captain *Fly-by-Night*. Ha! We'd certainly needed his injection of funds after the 'Philippine affair' when I'd convinced him to kiss goodbye to his hard-earned retirement package and toss it all into the perilous world of aviation, in which, as he'd lectured me, Juan Trippe had warned that no-one ever made any money. Regardless of Senor Trippe's assertions - which Sir Richard Branson would wish to dispute today, much of

Dave's funding had paid for our six near-new Rolls Royce jet engines - and no engines equals no go!

So, with such *vested* interests, Dave was now our chief penny pincher and ship's Purser who was often diametrically opposed to the wild schemes and excesses of myself. This fine balancing act often brought us partial agreement, but sometimes generated small wars which I liked to win. We needed to be different from the other airlines and I saw youth-orientated promotions as vital to our public image, while Dave still saw them as largely unnecessary wastes that should be avoided. But if ten year olds travelled with us now and enjoyed it, wouldn't many of them, the travelling public of the very near future, remain loyal to us then? I considered that he was missing the whole point which was to consolidate our future customer base now; while he possibly envisaged little after his approaching retirement.

Dave had been a small-town solicitor in a dusty little office for over thirty years and often acted like, well, a small-town solicitor in a dusty little office. In such environments people were usually mired in their traditional rural ways, and country youngsters were expected to follow suit without question. As a result, Dave was quite content to have us toddle along forever with four planes, a dozen pilots and thirty other staff, while I saw little point in marking time when there was still plenty more business out there waiting to be snatched. At our peril, giants like Qantas would probably regard a new competitor with only four aircraft much like a dog would dismiss one more flea on its back.

Gearing up for launch day, a modelling agency in the city produced about fifty great shots of my two promotion mascots for Sky Star Airlines. This all occurred in the same week that our final applications to operate a public transport airline were, at last, approved in Canberra. Apparently I was deemed a 'fit and proper person' - albeit Australia's youngest, to hold an Air Operator's Certificate and to conduct scheduled Regular Public Transport RPT services – although I didn't feel quite so *fit and proper* after we'd climbed over that nightmarish mountain of red tape and government paperwork; a gasping ascent I described as 'slightly higher than Mount Everest.'

Amanda and Olivia, now aged eleven and ten and who looked almost like identical twins, were both to star in our new promotions. Olivia was the same height as Mandy now and, according to the agency, it was quite handy, promotion-wise, to hint that they were twins. At our check-in area in Sydney, I unveiled the billboards of the two girls that would be placed prominently for all passengers to see.

As Dave Skillen scratched his head, Marie Westcott, my Chief of Staff asked, 'Rob, do you intend to just *stand* these signs over there at the counters? I don't quite follow. They're just photos of two smiling kids, but what do they achieve? What is it about? Shouldn't the girls be, ah, saying something on the signs?' She looked at Dave who raised his eyebrows, hands out-stretched as if to say: 'Don't ask me, I'm only the General Manager.'

I answered, 'We start the promo tomorrow morning. I'm not flying, so I'll be working right here. Marie, can you get me a CSO's uniform, please. I'm commencing my training tomorrow morning – in case you didn't know.' Marie laughed that she never knew what I would be doing next, while Dave asked if someone could please explain.

I said to them, 'I believe in learning all aspects of this company that I lead. Therefore I think I should start with a day or two of work experience at the check-in counter, followed by some *famil* in the engineering department another day – and maybe with the tea lady the next. I might even try your job for a day, Dave.'

He sighed, 'Heaven forbid! You'd buy roller coasters at theme parks - or buy the whole theme park.'

So, early the next morning, into my dressy CSO's red and blue striped coat I merrily slipped. My daughters were perplexed as they'd expected the blue captain's uniform that I wore every day. Emmie asked, 'Aren't you the captain any more, Daddy?'

'Nope,' I said, stern faced. 'I've been demoted to check-in clerk because I crashed all our planes.'

'He's fibbing!' yelped little Celia as the other girls giggled and admired my new attire.

*

Well, I hadn't *really* crashed any planes – yet – but it was true that I'd finally become a captain. Chief Pilot Ken Tolman had performed my final check flight as we returned from Darwin on one of our last charter flights. Under stringent examination, I'd occupied the captain's left-hand seat - or command seat, and he in the right. Being the strict and stern Ken that he was, he'd warned me in advance not to expect any favouritism from him 'just because you're the company's owner.' I assured him that I never expected an easy check ride, and that I wanted to pass the rating on my own merits. 'And no stupid announcements either!' he added, wagging *that* finger – and meant it.

The testing was rigorous as Ken introduced numerous simulated system and engine failures, then a make-believe hijacking situation with a crazed passenger threatening our flight. These were all scenarios with which, as a pilot-in-command, I needed to be thoroughly conversant as it was entirely possible that they might occur one day and everyone on board would be depending on my training, expertise and wisdom. Finally, he drilled me on the carriage of firearms and explosives, plus the lengthy requirements of company policy on over a hundred critical matters. These were easy to pass because I wrote them!

After landing on runway *34-right* at Sydney and exiting left via one of the high-speed taxiways, Ken told me, 'You should be fine, Rob. But no ukuleles, okay?' I agreed – for the interim, and was highly pleased to have finally achieved my dream. Also, I wouldn't have to fly with Ken again except for annual check-flights, because no regular flight required two captains. I'd have my own first officers to intimidate from now on, and might even do a few humorous Captain Tolman impersonations along the way.

Upon shutdown, I glanced across at him; two captains together. His arms were folded in a triumphant sort of gesture. He never seemed to smile, but always wore that arrogant sneer as though he'd graciously handed me a gift from the very kindness of his soul.

15.

'Good morning, everyone!' I sparkled my very best smile at the four Customer Service check-in ladies as I slipped behind the cramped counter to join them.

'My God!' whispered one. 'Isn't that Mr Grant?'

'Yes it *is* Mr Grant,' answered another. 'What are *you* doing here, sir? *And* in a CSO jacket?' Many staff had barely seen their reclusive company owner before - except in magazine photos.

'Ladies,' I grinned 'I believe that I should learn to work in every section of the company, not just mine, don't you agree? We pilots need to understand the check-in procedures, along with engineering aspects, clerical, and all the rest. Now, I've never checked-in a customer in my life so I'd like to do a day's training with you ladies, starting right now. Also, it's our first big day of airline travel, as we all know, so a bit of extra help shouldn't go astray.' Fortunately, I could spare myself from the flying roster for this day because, on balance, I considered promotions to fill future seats more necessary today than me being in the air.

Settling into a booth, I asked Marie Westcott to instruct me on the reservations computer, customer processing, luggage check-in, and ticketing and boarding passes. These were still the 'old days' of *plane tickets*. Then I worked beside Margaret Steele, attempting to pay attention. Very soon, our terminal's front doors would be opening and we would know if the past few weeks of running our TV ad again had been successful or not. I'd bowed to expert advice and run the old ad again, while our media man, Kevin Paye, had modified it to announce that we were now operating scheduled airline services to Tamworth in northern NSW, then on to Brisbane, then returning to Sydney via Coffs Harbour. Further routes would be initiated over the next few weeks. It was a modest start, carefully designed not to upset our big competitors through stealing their thunder or by operating parallel services on lucrative routes.

Just before opening, I asked a porter to wheel our new billboards into place: one on each side of our check-in booths. The women asked 'Is that one your daughters from the ad? Or are they both your girls? They look like twins. Aren't they so pretty?' Then: 'But what do we do?'

'Leave it to me,' I assured them, just as our doors swung open to greet our very first airline flyers - if any.

With disappointment, we faced no great surge of humanity swamping inside. A mere trickle had arrived, not a rush, and it became, at first, no more than small queues of five persons checking in to five booths, and none at the sales counter. Although we'd taken ninety phone bookings so far, I'd been hoping for many more eager travellers to arrive *off the street* because here we were offering half-price tickets to anywhere to celebrate our first week of airline operations. But they had to be purchased here at the airport. (These days it would simply be a 'cheap fares sale' on the internet.)

I blundered through my first check-in, facing a gruff man, then almost checked his bags through to the wrong destination until Margaret corrected me. Great start! Meanwhile, the placards of two smiling girls beside him failed to attract his attention.

Under Margaret Steel's supervision, I checked through a dozen more customers who straggled in the doors and out of the rain. Then a charming elderly lady fronted up – I always seemed to impress the older ones – and handed me her ticket. She remarked 'Goodness me, you look just like that man in my favourite TV ad . . . but he was a pilot. And these lovely girls here . . . ah, is this one from the ad? We all love that ad back at the retirement village.'

Beaming, I answered, 'Actually madam, I *am* that pilot, but I'm doing promotions today. And they're *both* my daughters. This one is Amanda, the girl in the ad, and the other one is her sister, Olivia. And because you recognised the girls you've just won a free flight to anywhere of your choosing on Sky Star's network – which we're expanding very soon. Congratulations!' Margaret Steele's surprised faced seemed to say 'She has?' as the other check-in women all turned in surprise. Just look at this: the new check-in clerk is handing out free tickets to anywhere on his *first day*. Well, he *is* the company's owner.

The passenger was amazed. 'But it's already half price. What do I have to do, then?' I explained that it was our pleasure on our big debut day as an airline and she'd become our very first competition winner! We'd either refund the cost of her ticket today by posting her a cheque, or she could ring a special number to reserve a free flight for another day — once we started flying to our new destinations. Fortunately, the woman had a son in Brisbane so she opted for a Brisbane flight with her win.

As the day progressed, I changed into a pilot's uniform and chatted to several more travellers who won my competition by recognising either me or my girls on the billboards. I later explained to Marie and Margaret that over the coming months they'd be giving away five hundred free flight tickets in the promotion. Marie queried 'Five hundred? Plus the half-price tickets? We might end up with more freebies onboard than paying customers.'

I replied 'I hope so. That's the idea.'

My illustrious career as a CSO quickly came to an end in the afternoon because I was rostered to fly. But before escaping skywards, I had to face the flak guns of our esteemed General Manager. 'Five hundred free tickets!' he barked as I entered his office. 'I only authorised the half-price offer for one week; not this too. And just who pays for it all?'

I told Dave that I would be paying for it. I'd allowed $50,000 from one of my floating funds, plus other amounts from our advertising budget. It would not affect his personal investment, I assured him. Relieved, he asked, 'So how do you propose to recoup these amounts, Robbie?'

'Recoup? I won't. But future business is my long-term aim.' I explained that our lady winner would certainly boast to everyone where she lived about winning a free air ticket on an airline. Plus, she'd be sure to tell her family and friends. They would spread the story, and so would our other winners. Still, I suppose it was a fairly mild promotion where only time would be the ultimate judge.

But I *do* listen to the advice of others. As Marie and Margaret had suggested, I soon had the billboards amended so that the girls were now saying *'Don't be silly. Let's fly Sky Star!'* It wasn't exactly Logie-winning script writing, yet for some reason these innocent placards at our Sydney terminal slowly took off, so to speak – even though I received feedback that some customers might be insulted by children telling them not to be silly. Harrumph to that! Only miserable old grouches would, I supposed. *Fun* people wouldn't.

Consequently, our promotions slowly infiltrated their way around the community while our senior pilots were in the sky, eagerly plotting and surveying our new interstate air routes. Down on the ground, full-sized highway billboards faced busy highways. Eventually we determined that most passengers checking in were smart, not silly, and soon grasped the idea of making sure to remark on our billboard girls then winning a free flight of their choice. One comedian grinned: 'Geez, what ugly kids! Do I get a freebie too?' He sure did.

Happily, we were soon selling lots of tickets while giving away many more in freebies. It was no money-making bonanza, but over our first three months of airline travel we notched up a very impressive ticket growth rate of 3.5% per month, compared to Qantas' 1.1%, and struggling Ansett's minus 0.3%. After just one year, I noted a very respectable return of $302,000 in ticket sales after deducting my initial outlay of $50,000. As I had expected no returns at all from this promotion and had allowed for a loss, this was certainly a surprise windfall.

So my girls' winning smiles became the proud public faces of Sky Star, beaming out in numerous air terminals around Australia, and from the huge highway billboards and the pages of numerous newspaper and magazine ads.

*

Most of our company's progressive gains in popularity emanated from my insistence on running a *fun* air service, as opposed to the often regimented tedium of our competitors whose conventions and attitudes, I believed, originated in the early days of air travel when passengers were always attired in their finest suits, dresses and hairstyles as though they were dining out at special occasions and gala events. Appropriate for those times, of course, but hardly relevant in the more relaxed fashions of the nineteen-nineties. But back then, along with elegant dress went impeccable on-board manners and the almost God-like worship of the aircraft's captain and his immaculately uniformed officers and hostesses; a traditional flow-on, no doubt, from the early days of cruising on the grand ocean liners where passengers waltzed to hundred-piece orchestras, dined with Stirling silver cutlery, then strolled the promenade decks.

Now air travel in the late 20th century had become more akin to a bus ride: anyone could hop aboard and behave themselves for a couple of hours - or they should. Yet while the formal dressing up and rituals were now well in the past, today's travellers were still enduring aviation laws being repeatedly recited at them as though they were children, and while feeling the cold and unfriendly glares of an authoritarian cabin crew.

Many passengers find it irritating to hear the endless lectures about alleged radiation from mobile phones and laptops. These devices don't operate on the same frequencies as aircraft instruments, yet ever since they appeared airlines have been berating passengers with dire warnings about their in-flight hazards; failing to mention, however, that the use of such devices in peoples' cars somehow *never* interferes with their vehicles' electronic systems. Or in their boats, caravans, offices or homes.

Do our TV's, fridges or microwaves go haywire when we use our laptops at home? Or do packed commuter buses and trains ever crash from laptops and phones' electromagnetic output? Lightning strikes cause far more damage to electronics around the world every year than any small devices we may use in planes, and no air crash has yet been attributed to such devices.

Nevertheless, at Sky Star's inception, these dire warnings were still permeating air travel as though they were based on established fact. They actually overlooked the truism that airliners are wired electronically by expert electronic engineers, not amateur electricians with a screwdriver. Even our cars are fitted with special radio frequency shielding to help suppress engine noises in the radio, while aircraft are fitted with expensive and vastly more effective shielding looms and protective systems for this exact purpose – particularly within the navigation equipment bay in the nose cone. And if, as blared over the P.A., your little device may still affect your plane during the take-off or landing, why does it not, then, send you careening wildly off course during all those other hours in the cruise period? And why does a plane's vast and powerful array of electronic equipment never interfere with its passengers' gadgets in return? (Just recently, I noted with satisfaction that the world's airlines are finally about to relax many of these needless electronic restrictions.)

Back then in the nineties, we deftly managed to comply with all these safety regulations and warnings without going to excesses like teachers lecturing a class. A relaxed and pleasant flight was the desired objective of my cheerful airline where there were no regulations against having fun with guitars, ukuleles or mouth organs to entertain us all – if people so desired. On a steady pathway to success in the skies, Sky Star became known as a popular and fun airline as we methodically expanded our network, while a portion of our victory was certainly attributable to a few smiling kids who had launched it all with a tiny plastic toy.

16.

When I first heard about working from home via the internet's new marvels of technology, I was instantly enamoured with this revolutionary idea and quickly became a devoted early enthusiast. Yet I was surprised that so many city workers still laboured from their suburbs to their daily work grind via creeping traffic jams, then endured long hours interred in the usual regimentation of the office/factory hierarchy. Not for me; within a month of researching the concept I'd walked away from my Sydney airport office, bought a picturesque rural hobby farm out near the Blue Mountains' foothills, and enrolled my girls in local schools. Almost overnight I'd become wired up for the newest technology of the nineties; leaving most of my Sky Star associates surprised. Or bewildered, as in the case of David Skillen, my dedicated General Manager who could not easily grasp this new concept of working but *not* coming to work.

To complement this system, my discovery of video conferencing was a dazzling concept that I deemed essential. We conducted some trials and Dave quickly opposed it, suggesting that, as the video picture was a quite hazy and my voice sounded almost ghost-like, perhaps we should just abandon it.

'No we won't,' I told him. In those days before Skype and other internet wizardry to follow, video conferencing was somewhat rudimentary, but it worked well enough and therefore suited me admirably because I could spend far more time at home with my four children on our delightful hobby farm while enduring much less tedium in stuffy offices discussing the ins and outs of management and accounting *torture* – as I called it.

So I just did it, and within this new arrangement I was soon perceived as somewhat of a ghost figure in the company – like my screen image; a Howard Hughes who hid in the background away from the coal face while still pulling the financial strings and retaining ultimate control. So, as my physical presence became less necessary,

Dave and I graduated from working in adjoining offices to only catching occasional glimpses of each other.

Nevertheless, I greatly admired him. Dave and I had been acquaintances since my birth. He was forty years my senior and had been our friendly family solicitor in Trangie and great friend of my father, Herb Grant, when I arrived into the world at *Wundala* Station. Later, Dave had been quite sorrowful when my mother, Alice Grant, had fled *Wundala* and left her husband and two-year-old child behind in a barren and male-only farmhouse – an embarrassing social stigma for any farmer. Dave helped out where he could and, for the next ten years until I was twelve, helplessly observed his friend Herb slowly wane into wasted health; an aimless farmer now mechanically performing once-loved daily chores by rote; partially assisted by his semi-enthusiastic young son; a son whose eyes were constantly gazing skywards at droning planes.

Of course, neither Dave nor I ever imagined that one day we'd be running our own *airline,* with he, Dave, as our General Manager, and me as the owner. Nor would Dave have envisaged us communicating via the ghostly flickering images and hollow echoes of video conferencing. Yet within Sky Star, Dave became the solid rudder of our Ship of State while I was the crazy helmsman - defying every storm. I'm sure he considered me to be a brash and ostentatious company owner while I often wondered if perhaps these opposites would blend to produce a magic formula for success?

17.

We were in the process of upgrading our fleet of Fokkers to 160-seat Boeing 737's. As much as I worshipped my beloved Fokker Fellowships, their days were finally ending. We'd run them ceaselessly for over five years and now their useful working hours were approaching their *final departure,* so to speak. Meanwhile, our first leased 737 was now on the line after Paul Harland and I had ferried it from Rio de Janeiro in Brazil. It was quickly painted in Sky Star's stunning livery, with others soon to follow. In quick succession, three Fellowships were reluctantly sold to the Indonesian military; leaving just one remaining. De-licenced from RPT use, I could still use it privately and legally for a while yet, but not publicly with any airline.

And I'd intentionally hoarded some spare fuel to use privately. A few years earlier I'd indulged in what airlines call *fuel hedging.* Basically, an airline may contract to purchase a year's jet fuel in advance at a certain agreed price. This price remains fixed for the whole year's batch. The company, in effect, *bets* on the price of jet fuel on the world market, (hoping it doesn't fall). But if, during the year, world oil prices do fall below the agreed batch price, then the company has overpaid - *vast* amounts in some cases. Conversely, should world fuel prices rise above our pre-purchased *hedged* price, we can be way in front of others; smiling at our cheap fuel bills. Not normally a betting person, I was nevertheless attracted to the possibilities of saving millions through fuel hedging, while Qantas and other Australian operators often shied away from it (in those days).

From such adventurous chance, my first few years of playing this game of *Jet Monopoly* saw our Sky Star company save several million dollars on fuel bills which rocketed upwards for others. This naturally generated greater operating profit margins which in turn led to cheaper ticket prices – *not* more money in my pockets. Then greater profits compounded again from more bookings on the cheap airfare merry-go-round while I quietly squirreled away some fuel for myself.

So, with an idle F28 jet sitting dejectedly in a hangar, plus a few thousand litres of cheap Jet A-1 fuel, I organised a short break from my regular flying duties. Then it was: Let's go flying, kids! In our own private airliner - but without telling snoopy old Mr Skillen.

With cancer remaining such an acute memory in our family, at my own expense my girls and I flew fifty sick children from a Sydney hospital on a *Magical Mystery Tour* in our soon-to-be-retired F28. Accompanied by four devoted nurses and two of my *hosties,* we bussed them to the airport, then it was *all aboard*! As many of these little unfortunates had never even been near a real plane, they were all agog with delight as myself and First Officer Paul Harland started those noisy Tay engines then taxied out for take-off.

The kids had been told we were going for a joy flight around the Sydney area, but after take-off we set course to the north-east, out over a shimmering blue Pacific Ocean and on track to beautiful Lord Howe Island. En-route at 29,000 feet, we presented our smiling guests with baskets of brightly coloured sweets and goodies; and gift boxes packed with hidden chocolate crackles and toys. Popular music from their favourite TV shows echoed through the plane as singing, dancing and plays were held in the aisles. Every child who asked, was walked – or wheeled, up to the flight deck where the nice Mr Harland let each one take a quick turn sitting in his pilot's seat. Surrounded by walls of instruments, dials and levers, most cockpit visitors become speechless; with these little battlers it was also a mixture of astonished delight. They all wanted to grip the *steering wheel,* and one sickly boy asked could he lean out the window 'like your girl did on TV.' I apologised and told him it was unfortunately a bit cold and windy out there to do that, while I shuddered to consider his frightful future.

And today's charming hostesses on our *Magical Mystery* flight were my entertaining and smiling daughters: Amanda and Olivia of TV and billboard fame, with Emily and Celia. They were now aged 14, 13, 11 and 9. And an extremely proud Dad I most certainly was on this day. The girls were under strict instructions that this was to be the sick childrens' very special day where everything possible was to be done for them. Our family's personal enjoyment was irrelevant because the lives of our precious youngsters on board today were immeasurably more frail than any of ours - and could be significantly shorter.

My girls cheerfully rose to the occasion. Costumed as the Disney characters Snow White, Cinderella and their helpers, they performed an enthusiastic exhibition of dance and song to wonderful overhead music. I felt sure that no plane's interior had ever seen anything quite like it, heard such a crazy din, or held so many smiling young faces while streamers and balloons and paper planes helped to fill the cabin with joy. I laughed to Paul that when all those kids squealed together, it would have been enough shrill noise to send our Captain Tolman into an instant spiral dive!

After an hour of party fun, we landed on Lord Howe Island's short runway *one-zero* that runs towards the picture-postcard tropical lagoon. As I jammed on the brakes just before the runway's end, I said over the P.A. 'Oops, sorry kids! We nearly plopped right into that blue lagoon just there. Mustn't frighten the fish because we're all going to feed them their lunch soon?' The laughter of happy little voices from behind us was my reply.

Lord Howe Island is often described as one of the most beautiful islands in the world. Amazingly, the atoll has the most southerly coral in the world, exceeding in natural beauty most Barrier Reef islands which lie much further north. Here, the towering Mt. Gower hovers over an exotic blue lagoon, while blossoming and verdant heritage-protected vegetation runs riot among outlandish jungles of flowers throughout the island's eleven-kilometre length.

To our excited passengers, temporarily escaped from a frightening hospital sick bed, it was as though they were on another planet; a magical land of teeming tropical botany housing choirs of chirping birds amongst quilts of gardens flush with lavender-scented shrubs. This was a luxuriant paradise where a sky-blue tidal lagoon swarmed with flashing schools of multi-coloured fish which, at feeding time, literally ate right from the childrens' hands. I'm sure our very special guests became the heroes of Lord Howe Island that day and at departure time, together with many of the island's residents and tourists, we all sang of hope and blessings for their clouded futures.

On our evening arrival back at Sydney, we orbited the twinkling lights of the famous harbour-side Opera House and Harbour Bridge. When queried by Air Traffic Control how long we intended to 'obstruct the main approach path to runway 16?' I answered that my very sick children on board would wish to stay up here forever - if they could, but fifteen more minutes would be appreciated, thankyou. We were quickly re-cleared to remain in a left-hand holding pattern over the Harbour Bridge and City at 1,500 feet 'for as long as operationally required', and that 'other air traffic would be diverted around us.' To the sounds of the song *Starry, Starry, Night* I advised the kids to look at the sparkling lights of Sydney, then radioed ATC, 'Charlie Zulu Golf, fifty unwell kids just yelled out "thankyou!" '

Eventually, after landing towards the south, the Tower controller apologised for any unacceptable remarks he may have made earlier, and asked me to pass on the Tower's very best wishes to our children.

As we taxied below the Tower's all-seeing windows, I radioed to those inside, 'They're all smiling and waving at you!' In return, we saw several hands wave back from behind the tinted glass while friendly coloured guidance lights flashed at us.

*

I was badly overdue for some holidays, and after wangling a few more days off work I calculated we had more of my bonus fuel remaining, so I planned another little aerial expedition with my girls for the next weekend. This time it would be just us five, one *very* big rock, and some strange publicity.

While most kids couldn't imagine in their wildest dreams riding in their Dad's private jet, mine considered it almost *normal* to hop aboard the family F28 jet; a 60+seater airliner. Sometimes we simply went interstate shopping. Or to a beach on the Barrier Reef. In the early part of their lives they'd done it quite tough, so now I was determined to give them whatever joy I could. All I wished for in return was that they'd become decent and respectable adult citizens while tragically, growing up *at all* would be the forlorn hope of our hospitalised friends from last week.

This next flight however, instead of my girls being the star hostesses on board who could boast about their father being the captain, we were flying alone. Apart from Paul Harland, my co-pilot on the flight deck, the girls had the run of the entire airliner to themselves. When planning the trip at home, I'd asked 'Where should we go for our three days away, girls?' Emmie suggested we throw darts at our board with a map of Australia stuck to it. The last time we'd done this, the dart plonked into the ocean off Western Australia, so this time we hoped for a *drier* result. After drawing straws, Olivia threw first and her little dart landed smack in the middle of Australia. 'Bull's-eye!' we all chorused. Celia rushed to the chart, 'Alice Springs,' she read slowly.

'No it's not, Celie.' corrected Amanda. 'That was close, but it says Ayers Rock – Uluru.' 'What's that?' voices asked, so I explained that the Aboriginal word for Ayers Rock was Uluru. One of them complained that going to see a rock would be *boring*, but the others yelled 'Let's go!'

So we did. Now we were flying over the 'Dead Heart' of Australia, with Paul and I gazing down at the never-ending parallel lines of red and dusty sand dunes which roll towards the indefinite horizon in dry waves of desolation and cover almost half the Australian continent. Down the back and with the whole plane to themselves, the girls played air hostess games and continually ran the length of the aisle in noisy screeches. It sounded like an entire aviary of cockatiels.

Eventually we prepared for our descent after establishing our precise position over the Alice Springs radio navigation aids. Making a small twenty degrees turn to port, we tracked the plane outbound from the Alice Springs VOR beacon direct to Uluru, now a distant red speck appearing out of that timeless desert of emptiness. I barked into the intercom, 'All cabin personnel return to their seats for landing or you'll be thrown out the window!' Then, peering intently past *The Rock*, I shivered to imagine the fate of any aircraft that might overshoot its navigation to vanish beyond it and into the yawning red vacuum of the Gibson Desert; blistered by millennia of blazing sun and scorching wind. Out there, where my mind could scarcely fathom that endless *nothing*, people had somehow eked out a silent existence for perhaps sixty thousand years. Unknown to anywhere else on Earth, they were surely the loneliest societies of all time.

Soon it was all action on the flight deck for our *top-of-descent* checks, as eager little Celia joined us up front to occupy the jump seat and watch the landing from behind us. With a headset on, I let her transmit my pre-written arrival report over the radio. Paul selected VHF frequency 126.9 MHz, then her little voice called:

'Ayers Rock Radio, Charlie Zulu Golf, eight-zero DME on descent inbound to The Rock for landing. Left flight level two five zero. Received Foxtrot.' The Air Radio operator sounded somewhat surprised but pleased to hear a young girl calling him from a jet, and replied with additional landing data along with advice of other air traffic in the area.

'What's he saying?' she asked.

I told her, 'Just say Charlie Zulu Golf, roger.' She did, but probably wondered who Roger was . . .

In the pioneering days of old, camel trains usually took a tortuous week or so to traverse those last eighty gruelling nautical miles across the searing desert, but at our groundspeed of 265 knots we raced the same distance in a slippery eighteen minutes! On arrival, while watching for conflicting light planes and sightseeing helicopters in the vicinity, we flew a graceful arc over the giant and ancient rock of Uluru, then conducted a few lower orbits while the kids peered from the windows and gawked at this enormous stone slab squatting near *The Olgas* - a nearby range of bizarre sandstone upthrusts in the otherwise vast and flat desert.

I spoke into the PA handset to the gawkers behind us, 'First person who can remember the correct geological name for *The Rock* wins a prize.' Paul grinned, 'Ah, a sandstone monolith?' Emmie guessed, 'A giant red rock?' From down the back, Amanda grabbed the intercom phone and replied, 'It's called an *Inselberg* - I looked it up after we threw that dart.'

'Mandy's right,' I announced. 'It's an Inselberg. So she gets first drive of our little golf buggy.' To shouts of 'It's not fair, I wanna be first!' our happy adventuring entourage flew a wide left-hand circuit of Uluru aerodrome, then I called 'Flaps thirty, thanks Paul. Gear down.' We'd hydraulically extended the wings' trailing edge flaps which give extra lift at lower speeds while also creating more air drag to slow us down further. The 'gear' was our undercarriage – six wheels attached on three bogies - which then touched down onto the red-dusted, but bitumen, runway *31* at Uluru.

After parking, we climbed stairs up to the small *Air Radio* tower above the airport Fire Station, and chatted with John, the friendly Air Radio officer. He shook Celia's hand and told her she sounded very professional over the radio. Then he asked, 'But where are all your passengers, Celia?'

John's smile widened in surprise when she casually replied with honesty, 'Oh, there aren't any. We just came away on a family trip for a few days. Sometimes we go to the Barrier Reef or Lord Howe Island - stuff like that. Oh, once we went to Melbourne for shopping but I couldn't find anything I liked.' John's eyes sparkled as if to exclaim, 'Rich little girl. Rich and lucky family, indeed!' As he would know, many aviators fly to *The Rock*. Annually, lots of small private and charter planes journey across the Outback to the 'Inselberg' - but it is most unlikely that any private flights would be large jets like ours with only six people on board.

Upon leaving, I tried to assure John that those other flights Celia had mentioned held paying passengers, while the Lord Howe trip was a charity flight for sick children. But I'm not sure if he was listening, because now Mandy was boasting to him how she'd soon be driving our electric golf cart around The Rock. 'What golf cart?' he asked, amazed. Mandy said 'The one that Paul's dragging down our air-stairs, see?' Then she surprisingly whispered, 'He's so handsome!' We all looked out at the parking apron to laugh aloud at Paul's furious efforts as a baggage boy, wrestling a shiny red and blue cart down the plane's stairs. It was a golf cart with *Sky Star* written on it and with coloured stars flying towards the back. On its front beamed a beautiful smiling face with the name: *Cristina*.

*

In the morning we lounged around the lovely pool and bar area of our resort, enjoying breakfast while perched on submerged stools. The girls, copying some other kids, gobbled their bowls of fruit compote then fell crazily backwards into the water. Meanwhile, our *royal* arrival had apparently attracted attention from various interested parties; the local media being one. A nice-looking red-haired woman swam up next to the four sisters and began chatting. I barely noticed as Paul and I talked with the resort managers and a few aviation personnel who were staying there. When I next looked, the woman was gone.

After a morning in the pool, we toured the famous *Ayers Rock*; climbing to its peak via the chain rails then stumbling back down. Later, our little golf cart was offloaded from a ute so we could drive it slowly around the tourist walking tracks. That evening it was wining, dining and song with fun games and videos for the kids in the playroom. Mandy happily occupied herself by chatting with some eager teenage boys. I'll need to keep an eye on her, I lectured myself. What a little stunner she's going to be – or already was.

The next day when I collected the morning newspapers from outside our door, I was quite stunned to read, amongst them, the headline on the local one-page Ayers Rock news sheet:

Flamboyant billionaire and his girls roar into The Rock in private jetliner! Hugh Hefner, perhaps?'

Since starting Sky Star I'd usually been wary of any media - except when I need to produce official advertising, and felt that this exaggerated headline needed some correction, or explaining - if possible. So, on my best possible manners, I located the newsletter's tiny office just down the road and spoke to the same woman journalist who'd been the person chatting to my girls in the pool. While I respected the fact that she was merely writing for a very small-scale news sheet, it turned out that she could, if she wished, syndicate the story by fax to the Fairfax newspapers, which can then be carried by other media outlets around the country.

'Cynthia,' I said to her as we sipped coffee, 'I must point out that I'm not a billionaire by a long shot. Yes, we did *roar* into The Rock, but we had this one old plane in the hangar being unused, so I *borrowed* it for a few days – as I occasionally do. But basically I'm just a single father of four who has struggled hard to get ahead. And flamboyant? I don't quite agree with you printing those inferences of me.'

The smiling but no-nonsense reporter answered, 'Mr Grant, several people have told me, your daughters included, that you often zoom away in that huge jet of yours for private weekends to islands on the Barrier Reef, interstate day trips for shopping, and now out here to The Rock. Is that not flamboyant? Where else does the flamboyant playboy zoom off to, Rob? Or is it Hugh?'

I appreciate humour, but this had misfired. 'Gee Cynthia, talk about gross exaggeration. Hugh bloody Hefner! Hugh Hefner owns a DC-9 which is *twice* the size of my jet and he sells . . . '

'They all look the same to me.'

I continued, 'He sells girlie magazines and flies around with his Playboy Bunnies. I'm a widower and brought my daughters away for a few days' break which is my own personal business and not for the press. The other trips were chartered flights or, in the case of the Lord Howe Island day excursion, was a charity flight that I funded myself to give a day out to a group of very sick children. But Hugh Hefner peddles *sex magazines* and I don't appreciate your inference that my daughters are in any way akin to Playboy Bunnies. They're only children.'

Cynthia replied snobbishly, 'Is it not all that much different? We've all seen how you regularly use your daughters to publicly promote your airline on TV, in magazines, at airports and on roadside billboards – I saw one last week near Alice Springs. They are portrayed as attractive and engaging. Children are constantly used in today's advertising promotions. However, I didn't realise at first that your oldest one was only fourteen; I thought she was about eighteen and someone else in your party.'

'One of the Bunnies, eh?' I was annoyed. 'Flamboyant billionaire with his girls? Yes, you're trying to drum up local gossip here at The Rock – fair enough; but then you might on-sell this provocative piece of . . . trashy *rubbish* to syndicates where it could end up anywhere. This article's slant is quite inappropriate for a small community newsletter, and highly inaccurate for the national press because of my position. Don't you agree, Cynthia?'

The journalist replied, 'Look Mr Grant, I wasn't inferring or *slanting* anything. I get hot phone tips from my spy at the airport about anything interesting that comes in to land. I was told a rich guy in a huge private jet had just landed and several pretty girls disembarked with him. My headline was printed quickly – long before I met your girls in the pool. When I did, they were quite interesting and I loved talking to them, if briefly . . . and I could see they were just kids. Anyway, at the earlier time of writing it seemed a catchy angle to punch out: rich guy in his big jet. It's just my job, although I'm sorry about the Hefner comparison.'

We debated for a short while, then decided to drop the whole issue due to a mutual agreement that we'd only just met and were already overheated and over-reacting. Surprisingly, Cynthia offered to withhold the article from national syndication if I accompanied her to dinner that night. Shocked, I'd been considering threatening her with legal action but decided this was a far more wise and civil approach to resolving the issue. Besides, the red-haired Cynthia was very pleasant looking and harboured no ill intent towards us. She had worked for the Fairfax press in Sydney and this was just a short working holiday to The Rock. In Sydney they were putting staff off so this was a chance to consider her options.

That afternoon, I wondered if this lady might come in handy at our company as a media liaison officer or somesuch, instead of us being at loggerheads. It was far preferable to have the media onside than ranged against us, and as our kindly General Manager was certainly no

PR entrepreneur dripping with panache, that left just me to handle the media at the moment and I was no better!

Cooling our heels that night with an excellent dinner and wine, I sat with Cynthia and the girls in the Uluru Resort's *Outback Brasserie*. Just as I was about to mention my interest in Cynthia coming on side with us, from across the table young Emily suddenly decided to ask: 'When are you two getting married, Daddy?' The other girls giggled crazily as I spluttered and came up with a dozen sound reasons why not – including that we'd only just met. 'But, *Dad*,' Olivia chimed in seriously, 'when do we get another mum again?'

Clang! That would be enough to drive any intending suitor straight around Ayers Rock and off into the wilderness of the *Never-Never*. Fortunately, Cynthia Nilsen just laughed politely.

18.

At our picturesque hobby farm near the foothills of the Blue Mountains, my instant family worked, lived and played as a team to maintain a successful family unit despite the glaring void of having no leading lady in the house. Although not alone in this predicament, it had been many years since I'd been married to my lovely Cristina, and it seemed *eons* since I'd engaged in any sort of a social life with women. However, while I enjoyed a few offers from eager aspirants - some of them genuine and a few not so, romantic success continued to elude me. Meanwhile, my four girls were rapidly growing into young adults who often pushed me about 'hitching up' again: an enjoyment in which I seemed to have not the slightest spare moment or luck. After all, I was an airline captain *plus* a company CEO, and my hobby was being sole parent to four atomic bombs on roller skates.

I once overheard Amanda whispering on the phone: 'He's such a great Dad, but he's about as romantic as a cactus bush!' In retaliation, I snuck a cactus plant onto the toilet seat in her bathroom. My attached note said: "But Captain Cactus married the prettiest girl in Coffs Harbour!"

In my spare time - if any, I attempted to manage our little ten-acre hobby farm which had ducks, geese, chickens, dogs and a gray horse named *Sky*. My tiny two-seat Gazelle aircraft was hangared in the rear shed. I'd mown a rough airstrip for it to take off. It only required a mere 300 metres to become airborne and we sometimes enjoyed scenic flights around the local farms, towards the distant Blue Mountains, or along the sandstone canyons of the Hawkesbury River. I attempted to teach all the girls to fly, and while they mostly displayed basic competence in controlling the little plane, Olivia showed the least aptitude while Celia was the most enthused . . . we are all different. When not flying, the girls raced their ATV bikes over the paddocks or we jet skied together along the river.

So, in stark contrast to my youth, Captain Cactus wallowed in an elegant sufficiency of female company these days – totally unlike the silent emptiness of *Wundala* station when my father was out in the fields. Even when Dad had been home, the old stone ranch house often felt like a creepy museum of shadows where no feminine touches graced our tomb-like house. No fragrance of flowers or scent of perfumes ever wafted through our lonely homestead, and no dresses hung from the clothes lines outside. Worse, I had never seen a single photograph of my mother adorning the gray stone walls and to this day still don't know what she looked like. Such was this all-male environment where I'd grown to acclimatise in an almost monastic existence; whereas now, with all these cheery and chatty females surrounding me, the void of barrenness had partially vanished.

However, no parent of four youngsters can ever profess to having perfect kids. Mine were normal - I hoped - but never perfect. Girls are only human and can be catty, sulky, moody or mean. Yet I seemed to be fortunately blessed with four young ladies who were (most of the time) inured with an instinctive respect towards each other. This respect complemented a sisterly love that had been cultivated within the depths of hardship and tragedy. So, apart from the normal ups and downs of any family, I treasured this nice family I'd been blessed with; one which was usually full of laughter and merriment.

19.

Apart from full-time airline flying, Paul and I often dashed overseas to take delivery of each new Boeing 737. Most of these we leased for twelve months or so, then elected for the option to buy. I revered these fantastic machines: the world's best-selling airliners with over forty thousand sold, as a farmer would cherish cash crops that were enriched with leaves of gold. Our Boeing model-500's were 160 seaters and their global popularity soon enabled our own profits to soar skywards like the very planes themselves.

My overall strategy concerning aircraft types was to never embark upon the same perilous path of Ansett Airlines. Towards the end of the 1990's, Ansett were not only beset with difficulties of swollen debt, but burdened by the foolish blunder of operating too many different types of planes at once. This managerial bungle often meant that flight crews might be unable to operate certain flights because they weren't endorsed and licenced to fly that aircraft type. Also, cabin crews were often expected to operate unfamiliar cabin systems, while some maintenance personnel weren't trained and licenced to service *all* their planes and sometimes the right tools weren't always available.

To us in Sky Star, this was an entirely preventable predicament and, quite often, a deeply embarrassing dilemma for them. Instances occurred where Ansett pilots walked past departure gates where an aircraft was ready to go – perhaps a 747 or 767, but couldn't fly it because their licences only covered 737's or Fokker 50's, for example. An announcement would then state that the flight was delayed or cancelled due to lack of pilots, often causing waiting passengers to ask: 'But what's wrong with those pilots over there?'

I was determined to avoid such a basic trap, so we farmed out our ageing F28's – except for CZG, and gradually replaced them all with Boeing 737's. After long negotiations, the year 2000 saw us conveniently win a few coveted landing slots at Melbourne, Adelaide and Brisbane during peak hours. We added these to our existing Tamworth, Gold Coast, Cairns, Townsville, Mackay and Hobart routes to produce an impressive east coast timetable that nicely complemented Qantas and the others; rather than competed against them. By the following year, we were operating to most capital cities in Australia. This was an attainment beyond my expectations and which filled me with pride.

As I often discussed with Dave Skillen, my other resolute formula for success was to never run the business on debt and borrowings - except for unavoidable short-term bridging and leasing arrangements. This policy slowed our modest growth but gave me comfort and sleep at night. I felt we were on track – but to where?

*

One afternoon, Celia phoned to say that a stray dog had killed one of our geese, and could I please come home early. 'Okay sweetie.' I sighed with tiredness. 'But I have to fly to Malaysia tomorrow to bring another plane back. Ah, which goose was it?'

'Captain Ken.'

I almost grinned. 'Oh no. How sad.'

She pleaded. 'Can't you go away another day? We're going to bury him tomorrow.'

'No. We'll do it tonight when I get home. How's your sisters?'

'They're having a fight.'

'What about?'

'Someone set fire to the chocolate cake in the oven. Then the horse walked into the house.'

'To put the fire out? Glad everything's normal. I'll be home soon, my dear.'

'Love you Daddy.'

'Yeah, I love me too.'

'You're funny, Dad. A little bit, anyway . . . '

Once at home, my sparring girls had cooked a delightful roast dinner which we finished off with a strawberry chocolate cake that I had brought home. Then in the chilly dark outside, we conducted an impromptu funeral service for our recently departed goose, Captain Ken.

Later, I asked Mandy to have a small chat with me before bed time. In the morning I'd be off to Kuala Lumpur on Malaysian Airlines to take delivery of yet another leased Boeing 737, then fly it home with Paul. The girls were very familiar with their Dad being away from home, and these days – most of the time - seemed mature enough to operate a responsible family unit headed by fifteen-year-old Mandy and backed up by our own local Neighbourhood Watch of friendly hobby farmers surrounding us. 'But no fighting while I'm away – okay?'

'Yeesss Dad!' they all assured me. I knew that today's minor scrap was rare but inevitable in any home. In fairness, they only ever squabbled amongst themselves over the most minor of issues. As a tightly-knit and proud family unit, my four girls possessed inherited character traits that underlay my regular sermons about strong family values and sticking up for each other. Publicly, they were viewed by many peers as those tough and loyal Grant girls, and Amanda had often chewed out and fought both girls and boys who dared aggravate any of her sisters. Most of them had been afraid to retaliate.

Back inside, I settled on our sunken lounge with Mandy and said, 'Hey kiddo, remember that morning when you ran away from home to that park?'

'Oh god, Dad. That was just *so* embarrassing - and dumb! I'm sorry.'

'It was very risky, but I understood your distress. I mean, you were questioning our family structure, which was natural for anyone who was only eight. But you got it into your silly head that I wasn't your father anymore and so you just took off – like a jumbo jet!'

'Dad, I know you're my step-Dad but I'm the luckiest daughter in the world because I've got the best *actual* Dad ever. A true father is someone who *acts* like a real Dad by doing everything for his kids. I was just confused . . . '

This certainly made *actual Dad* feel grand. 'It's just part of growing up, mate. You looked so lonely and vulnerable sitting on that little swing all by yourself in your pyjamas. Gee I loved you then – and now. I would have died if I hadn't found you.' Mandy gave me a nice cuddle. She was now a tall girl with striking good looks who bore little resemblance to that small girl on the swings with two front teeth missing.

She asked what I wanted to discuss. 'Okay. That confused little girl is now a big mature girl with a strong head. So now I want to ask how you honestly believe your schooling and business studies are going? You seem to be quite keen and diligent with your business course at TAFE. Is that where you might want to make your future? In business?'

'Yes. I love it. I want to leave school soon and become one of Mr Skillen's secretaries, then who knows after that?'

I told her, 'Well, these days poor old Dave seems to have had his fill of worrying about our company. We started out with just one jet, but it's grown to its present size and I'm not sure he's coping well. He's nearly seventy now and has turned his small retirement packet into a much larger one because of what we've achieved together, so I want to give him a cheque soon for two million dollars then send him packing. Off to buy his dream boat and go fishing. Consequently, I'd like you to forget about your secretarial aspirations and work towards becoming our new General Manager of Sky Star one day.'

Mandy yelped, 'What! I can't be that at fifteen, can I? The General Manager? Dad, are you crazy?'

'I said *one day*. Listen mate: when I was thirteen I was flying planes every day with Tyson Swain. I had to be propped up on cushions so I could peer over the Cessna's high dashboard, but I was flying nonetheless. I also drove cars to school and around our town at twelve. Then, at your age of fifteen I was aerial mustering cattle and doing aerial inspections of Maurice's *Darmornie Station* and other properties too. When I passed my private pilot's licence flight test on my seventeenth birthday, I already had 3,176 hours in my pilot's log book. Many pilots twenty years old don't have anything like that amount of hours and experience - in fact most of them only have about 250. Some of these hours may have been unofficial, but the experience was certainly real and invaluable.'

'So all through those times and events, people always warned me that I was too young to be doing these things. But I believed in myself and was mature and smart enough to cope with scenarios that other teens had never dreamed of - let alone done. Then when I was only twenty – as you know - I bought an airliner - our *Lady Cristina the Sky Star.* This time absolutely everyone just *knew* I was too young to own that. I couldn't even fly the damn thing as a captain so I had to hire Mr Tolman. But we got it off the ground and matters eventually worked out for me – after I'd employed some foresight, knowledge and training.'

'Then we made that great TV ad together at Luna Park with Kevin Paye, and, once again, people decried my efforts as being stupid, hopeless and corny. Some said no-one would ever fly on our charter flights if I acted like a silly goat on a Ferris wheel with a kid. Others said I'd be in trouble for letting a child lean from the pilot's window of a passenger jet. And who would ever get on a plane with an eight-year-old at the controls, anyway?' Mandy laughed as she recalled those fun days and how she became quite a little celebrity at school because of our TV ad.

We laughed, then I continued. 'So while we had our knockers, detractors and doubters, we also captivated thousands of others who simply got the message, supported us and queued up to travel with us. First on charters, then on RPT. Now we've turned my tiny one-plane outfit into a medium-sized airline and I'm picking up our twelfth 737 tomorrow. So, I'll need the right person to run this show. It won't be me because I don't ever aspire to be managerial - I'm a pilot forever, and old Dave's looking rather run-down now and getting grumpier each day. He's fulfilled his contractual obligations to me many times over, and was originally retiring from the Trangie district when he was sixty, until I talked him into becoming my GM. So now he's done *ten* extra years' work for me, for which I'm eternally grateful.'

'And that leaves a gaping hole at the top, Miss Mandy. And remember that you were the person at the age of only eight who first suggested the appealing name for our airline, so who else should deserve the top spot?' She smiled, but with a very pensive look; contemplating the enormity of it all.

I continued, 'You're coming first in your year at almost everything you do at school. You finish your business diploma at the end of this year and I'm sure you'll be first in that, too. I don't see any need for you to complete year twelve at high school studying Shakespeare and algebra, which are irrelevancies to your goals. I want you to sit in Mr Skillen's office for the next six months and train to be our General Manager. You'll be classified as an associate director, because you can't legally become a company director under the age of eighteen.'

'After six months I'm hoping you can take the unofficial reins - but I'll appoint an interim GM to stay on until you're eighteen. That's over two years from now. So, if I could achieve all those other things when I was apparently so very young, you might too. Are you up for the challenge? Can you do it, Mandy?'

Mandy flashed her very best smile, as she'd done so long ago for a camera, then laughed – although entirely unsure. 'Don't be silly, Dad. Let's go!'

20.

I was sipping coffee latté in Bondi Junction with Cynthia Nilsen of *Ayers Rock* fame. She smiled at me, 'Well Rob, I once had the distinct impression that you didn't like me, even though we later dined together at The Rock. But when the boss man of Sky Star calls me for a luncheon date, how could I possibly resist?'

'Because I've got a proposition for you,' I grinned, enjoying her attractive face and flowing red hair.

'Here? In public?' she laughed.

'Yes. Since I last saw you at *The Rock*, I've managed to read a few of your articles and stories: Women's' Weekly, Fairfax Press, those things. I got the impression that you're not entirely enamoured with journalism and the media in general – even though you work for them. Even faintly cynical, eh? So this interests me. I liked your style when you wrote that article about the Royal Family and how they all endure the same media harassment as suffered by Princess Diana. I'm not quite royalty, but I must admit to my wariness of some of the media and this explains my usual reluctance to discuss hardly anything with them. In the few interviews I've ever granted them, they often twisted and distorted my words to suit their own rather suspect rationales, and they rarely portrayed me or my airline in any true light - even when I presented them with genuine facts. In other words, I sometimes don't trust them, but I, like all other businesses hoping to succeed, unfortunately *need* them from time to time.'

'Therefore, I require a public relations officer who knows the whole media game. Someone who understands how to handle them competently in public debating arenas and press conferences - but always with the best interests of our company foremost, of course.'

Cynthia interrupted. 'Suspect rationales? Like those billionaire playboy and Hugh Hefner lines? The media just fulfil a role and I play along . . . but are you sure you'd want *me*?'

I said, 'Why not? You explained that you were having a short working holiday at The Rock. You did leave relief at the local newsletter office in return for some accommodation and meals at the resort. You apologised for your behaviour with that racy headline, and you withdrew your story from further circulation. I was impressed by that.'

Cynthia replied, 'I was having a slightly rough time after my separation from Jim in Sydney. I went out west to chill out, as they say. And you can't get any further away from things than at *The Rock*, can you? But absolutely nothing ever happened out there to write about except tumbleweeds blowing across the road, until you waltzed in with your big fancy jet plane. My tip-off and hot local gossip said you were a handsome billionaire accompanied by several girls – so I took some wild guesses and just wrote the thing. The Hefner comparison struck me immediately, but it was only after publishing that someone else warned me these 'Bunnies' looked fairly young and could be your daughters.'

I enjoyed watching her talk. Heaven forbid: was I contemplating conspiring with the enemy as she continued? 'Daughters? I was alarmed and did some quick research, then went to the pool and found your lovely family there. I've felt embarrassed about the whole silly mess ever since. It was irresponsible journalism to write a headline for possible syndication without having ever met you or checked on my facts. I should know better than that. It never occurred to me that you might have four daughters and actually be a widower. Sorry. Anyway, I published a correction the day after you'd gone which stated what a nice guy you really were – but a confirmed bachelor - unfortunately. Ha!'

I laughed with her. 'Fair enough, Cynthia. So, I was wondering if you'd be interested in becoming Sky Star's first Public Relations Officer? If so, I might be a nice guy, as you say, but I can get angry sometimes and need a strong and skilled media handler to keep the Rottweilers off me from time to time. I am an airline captain and I need to concentrate primarily on that. I don't wish to be assailed by headline-seeking journo's before or after flights. Instead of catchy, negative or unresearched comments, I'd like to read in my newspapers some positive and accurate information fed from you to the Press.

Information that promotes our airline, protects our airline, and produces more profits for us through you giving the public favourable publicity whenever possible.'

Cynthia nodded while I continued: 'And especially in times of crisis, you'll need to open the batting for the defence. It's always possible that we could have a crash one day – Heaven forbid - and it will be you who has to front up to the *Rotties.* Many crashes aren't the fault of the airline: stormy weather for instance, so you'll need a fast course in basic aviation technicalities in order to make credible explanations to lay questioners and paint us in the right light. From now on it will be *you* who squares off to the cameras and their phalanx of microphones.'

Cynthia responded, 'I'm very flattered, Rob, and I really do thank you. I'd love to do it. It would be a complete role reversal for me: battling the media. But to be honest, I have studied PR but haven't worked in it – yet.'

I said, 'In America, the White House Press Secretary is usually a former journalist. They have to be, otherwise how else would the President cope with complex dealings amongst journalists every day; especially in times of crisis? Also, I am aware that you've studied PR because I read it in your public précis, but I heard you've just been laid off by Fairfax because they're cutting down on staff – again. Lastly, you're the only journo I know. So, it's fortunate you wrote that news-sheet headline or I would never have come marching down to your little office to yell at you.' We both laughed as Cynthia suggested a possible headline that she could write:

Billionaire Playboy Attacks Innocent Journalist - then Hires Her!

'Good one! I like it.' I laughed again. 'Oh, and one last thing: if you start with us you'll soon need to cultivate the media into accepting our new General Manager-in-training, because our present GM's getting on in years and is about to retire – although he doesn't know it yet.'

'He doesn't know it yet?' she repeated.

'No, because when he finds out who his replacement is going to be, he might get something of a shock.'

'Why? Who's the new guy?'

'*He* is a *she*. My oldest daughter, Amanda. You saw her at the pool. And *she* hasn't even finished school yet.'

Cynthia glanced around, perplexed - like Dave Skillen often does. She said, 'Gee, isn't she a bit too, ah, *young* to run an airline?'

I smiled, 'You know, Cynthia, I seem to have heard that line somewhere before. Let's have another coffee and I'll tell you the abbreviated story of my life. Or the long version, if you like . . . '

She asked, 'Firstly Rob, when do you think you'd like me to start? I certainly don't have much work at the moment.'

'Two minutes ago! After we leave here, think of all the negative comments and derision we might face concerning the training of a teenager to lead us one day but who's not quite sixteen yet. Then devise a plan to promote her to the public over the next two years and defeat all those journo's who love to seize on juicy headlines and run with them. They'll be your friendly adversaries now, remember.'

She agreed. 'True. Many of them are my friends from work and university. Hmm, sure sounds like an exciting challenge. Ah, do I also get paid for this job, Rob?'

'You already have,' I grinned. 'I just bought you two coffees!'

21.

A knock on our colonial farmhouse door revealed the esteemed presence of the General Manager of Sky Star Airlines, Mr David Skillen. My youngest girls, Emmie and Celia welcomed him on his first visit to our little hobby farm near the foothills of the Blue Mountains. The girls had donned new dresses, set nice hairstyles and had even sneakily applied some of Amanda's makeup.

Almost grown up but still kids, they beamed their best smiles for the gray-haired man who arrived with a bottle of wine and a bouquet of yellow flowers. 'I, ah, didn't quite know what to bring tonight,' Dave stammered. 'Not sure what young people like for . . . ah, it's a pleasure to see you little ladies again, anyway. Last time you two were only *this* high, and now you're, well . . . '

Emmie beamed, 'We're as tall as you now!' And they were. Olivia walked in with her rehearsed words: 'Welcome to our home, Mr Skillen. We hoped you'd come to visit us one day.' Dave sat on our sunken beige lounge and smiled with delight at the three girls who sat opposite him. Being childless, he stumbled for conversation. So did they. A silence began.

To break the ice, Dave explained that he'd been married for a short time many years ago, and then, after realising he wasn't the marriage type, they'd parted ways. That was why he had no children of his own. He'd busied himself instead with studying law, and eventually became a junior partner in a law firm in Dubbo. Then he moved around the western NSW districts to finally settle in Trangie where he operated a lone, roaming, law practice covering many hundreds of square kilometres. He became the district locum. Within this vast and lonely beat, he'd done conveyancing work for Herb Grant at his *Wundala* station. I was Herb's son.

When Dave touched upon the history of Alice, my long-departed mother, Celia, looking sad, asked him, 'Didn't our Daddy have a Mummy? We don't either. We lost our mother so long ago that I can't even remember her because I was just a baby.'

Now conversing more comfortably, Dave replied, 'I'm so very sorry, my dears. I heard your mother was a wonderful person. And her lovely face, of course, was emblazoned on our very first aircraft. Yes, I think your Dad was only about two when his mother left home and never returned – to Herbert's eternal shame. Then he died when your Dad was only twelve; perhaps from a broken heart. This was very distressing for many locals; none more than me. I'd been quite close friends with Herb Grant and Maurice Bisley on the property next door - so I felt very sorry for Herb's young boy who was suddenly orphaned. But almost immediately Maurice volunteered to adopt young Robbie. In our district this was widely acknowledged as an extraordinarily kind gesture. People were amazed when I proudly processed the adoption papers. Now look how extremely well your Dad has done since that day.'

'Did someone mention my name?' I walked into the room smiling. 'Glad to see you finally made it here at last, Dave. I've invited you here many times, but . . . '

He laughed. 'No time. I've got a pilot/CEO who I rarely see but still manages to drive me crazy with mad schemes then simply zooms off! I spend half my time fixing up his mess or gazing at a ghost on a screen.'

The girls laughed as I replied, 'Ghost riders in the sky. Here one minute - then gone the next.'

Family talk forgotten, Dave replied, 'Really? Well I can't keep up with all these pilots and planes we've got now. What is it? Thirteen planes and thirty-six pilots? Have you seen our wages bill lately?'

'It's twelve planes, Dave. The thirteenth gets here next month. But let's not talk shop; can someone open this wine, please? And bring out a vase for the flowers, please.' Olivia and Celia jumped away to fill crystal glasses just as Amanda entered the room. She looked tall and graceful; a wonderful young woman of fashion, and hard to believe she was only fifteen.

Amanda smiled, 'It's lovely to see you again, Mr Skillen.'

'Well, who have we here?' asked Dave in amazement.

I said, 'Remember the girl on the Ferris wheel? And the one with her sister on all our posters?'

The elderly man wrinkled his brow, 'But, but, you can't be Amanda . . . can you? Of course, how silly am I? I'm just . . . gabberflasted. Ah, I mean flabbergasted. I see those wonderful posters every day around the terminal, but now you're just so . . . ah . . . tall.'

Not really; Dave was short. I said, 'Dave, my little housemaids are signalling for us to go to the dining room. Shall we?'

We rose as the younger girls whispered behind me, 'He said he's feeling *gabber-something*. What's that?'

'I don't know. I hope he's not feeling sick.' 'Me too,' concurred the other.

But David Skillen *was* looking sick - as suggested. His face often showed an ashen pallor, then sometimes flushed an ugly red. To me, he looked his full seventy years and with blood pressure problems and perhaps other maladies as well.

At the table Dave asked the girls: 'How is school, girls? What's your favourite subject? Do you like your teachers?' Amanda told him instead that they were all interested in rap music, MTV and boys – but not necessarily in that order. Dave replied that he didn't think he'd ever heard MTV, and what did they sing? When Emmie said it stood for *Music-TV*, Dave replied that he only ever watched *The Fishing Show*, 'because that's all I ever get time for!' We all laughed.

We dined till nearly nine pm, then I announced, 'Okay girls; homework and things in your rooms, please. Emmie's turn to load the dishwasher. Thanks everyone who helped prepare this meal. Say goodnight to Mr Skillen. And Mandy, please stay with us for a while.'

Dave stood up as they rose, saying 'Ladies, it's been a great pleasure. What wonderful, polite and charming young daughters you have, Robbie.'

'You've haven't seen their rooms, then. Or heard them fight,' I smiled. The three girls scampered down the hall after planting goodnight pecks on Dave's cheek. His face flushed red with joy. As I wondered when was the last occasion a pretty female had kissed him, we resumed our fireside chat in the sunken lounge. Mandy sat facing us.

'Dave,' I started, 'when is your seventieth birthday?'

'A few months. Why?'

'Remember when we started out? I was a fresh-faced adventurous kid nearly forty years younger than you. I needed an older, stabilising influence to manage my airline dreams while you just wanted to retire in Sydney and go fishing. I talked you into parting with your retirement money and convinced you to forget your fishing. I got you back into stuffy offices, buried you in paperwork and loaded you with pressure and tension and corporate problems.'

Dave nodded as I continued. 'Well, I appreciate every damn thing you've done for me. You've been a lion of strength throughout our good times and hard times. Through thick and thin. We certainly failed to agree on many things, but you'll agree we usually compromised to drive the company towards today's highly successful standing.'

'Now I want you to start bowing out Dave. Your race with us has been admirable, but inevitably it must come to an end. I see you as needing a lengthy rest in retirement; plus a really good check-up at the doctor's. Now, when you arrived tonight, it was less than two minutes before you started complaining about our wages bill and the number of planes and pilots we have. Your complexion reddened as you said it, Dave. That worried me. You desperately need to let go; to take it easy; to hand over the reins one day quite soon. I think it's relevant that while pilots are forced to retire at sixty-five, you've done five years more than that. Six months, Dave. That's when I'll give you this cheque for two million dollars.' I handed a small paper to him.

He glanced at it then laughed. 'That's not a cheque. It's a blank piece of paper!'

'Just like my infamous 'Manila' cheque, eh? But in six months it'll be real enough, Dave. Your retirement investment has quadrupled. Four hundred percent over ten years. Not bad, don't you agree? You can buy the boat of your dreams and pay off that delightful waterside shack of yours at Middle Harbour; then tour the world and have a wonderful retired life. What do you say?'

He took some time to answer. 'Hmm, six months. Is this an assassination plot on the GM?'

119

'Yes Dave. You've done a superb job and I thank you. Now the time is up.'

Dave asked, 'Then who'll replace me? Hmm, you've already chosen someone to take over, haven't you? Well, let me say this: I don't want any young jerk messing around in my position and sending our company down the chute. Wearing jeans and earphones to work. I've seen those modern-day executives poncing around Martin Place in the city. They get their hair styled in women's salons and read *Metro Man* magazine. Is that who you've got lined up to replace me, Robbie? Someone like that? Come on, what's his name, then?'

As he was about to drain his wine glass, I stared Dave directly in the face and whispered, 'She's sitting right across from you.'

22.

My new and attractive employee, Cynthia Nilsen, was understandably nervous when I called her into my cramped airport office behind the engineering hangar. Her first few weeks at Sky Star had been a steep learning process where she was initiated into the depths of our company policy, instructed in basic aviation and airline procedures and coached by paid actors in the pressures of confronting multiple media questions. Luckily, her exceptional debating skills from high school had placed her in good stead for contesting duels of questioning and riposte. Now she was about to hone her skills at being the *questionee* instead of the *questioner*, and it was time for her first trial by fire. A media conference was about to begin.

She sat down and sighed, 'It's been hard work, but I'm loving it, Rob. I never realised how easy it was to be a cynical reporter and put people down without evidence or fear of reprisals. Now I know how people like Lindy Chamberlain felt because I'm suddenly in the business of defending myself and this company in whatever events may transpire in the future. Meanwhile, you know that the media will probably still write whatever they like - even after we issue plausible denials of their assertions.'

'Yep, that's why I hired you,' I agreed. 'Now comes your first true test, Cynth. Have a look at this before you go out there to face them.' I passed her today's *Melbourne Sun* with its Page One headline:

Schoolgirl Airlines! Sky Star's biggest blunder as Rob Grant anoints his teenage daughter as boss

Cynthia nodded knowingly. Showing her honesty, she said, 'I know how you must feel Rob, but I probably would have written much the same header. This will sell thousands more copies than if they'd simply admitted what a great idea it was. And, of course, everyone will believe them. But how did this get out so soon?'

'Leaks. That's how everything gets out. It happens in companies and governments every day. Trusted information, classified secrets – it gets leaked one way or another. I'd rather hoped this wouldn't, but it was wishful thinking. So your job now is to front the pack and deliver the message that the whole essence of their story is exaggerated and that Mandy is merely in training for the next 2½ years. If she's eventually successful in following Dave's fine example, she *might* become our General Manager. And, in any case, how would they know that it's a blunder already?'

Cynthia said, 'They *don't* know, but it sells news copy. People read it quickly and agree: yep, that's a blunder. Then they turn to the footy scores.'

I sighed in frustration. 'But I'm not selling dodgy cars in a back lane. I need the public to trust us in the air with their very lives, so this type of scurrilous assertion needs to be stomped on now. Also, please stress that I'm not completely crazy and that an interim manager will be running the show for some time yet.'

She smiled, 'I'll issue a statement denying you're crazy, okay?'

I laughed. 'And try to inform everyone that we are a young airline with young ideas, so that's why we're using *young* people. Without insulting Qantas and the others, stress that we intend to introduce our own new modes and comforts of air travel, plus many internet-based innovations - now that the Net is here for good. Mandy is already compiling her own thoughts and plans for the company's future and they include no more 'clunky old air tickets' - as she says. Travellers will be able to book their own flights from home via the Net.'

This was the era when we novices were still learning about the internet's basics, while a few amongst us were already envisaging the *big* picture in advance.

'So, just touch upon these ideas, Cynth. Don't elaborate too much because we haven't even developed these systems yet – as you know. Anyway, the hounds are clamouring for answers in the conference room right now. I told them that our PR Manager would be only too pleased to speak to them in a Q&A for about ten minutes. Oh, and don't forget to mention the words *storm in a teacup,* because that's what this is. Good luck soldier.'

My hesitant PR Manager gulped nervously, then rose and departed for the battle front. Nice lady, I thought, and a pity she's about to be sacrificed in her first trial by fire. The words 'cannon fodder' sprung to mind. Still, that's why I hired her. Cowardly, I ducked out a side door, through the hangar, and drove off towards the sanctuary of home.

*

I sat with Mandy and the girls, watching the evening news now breaking in Sydney and elsewhere. It was obviously what they call a slow news week in the world because our story was the very first item: and what frantic media beat-up! My plan to launch Mandy as our new General Manager once she'd reached eighteen and become suitably trained and up to speed, was being castigated by barking reporters as my new PR Manager fronted an onslaught of questions.

'Ms Nilsen,' one reporter yelled. 'Isn't it an outrage that Sky Star proposes to appoint a *teenager* to head the company? And isn't Mr Grant's daughter still under sixteen? Will air travel still be safe?'

Cynthia replied in her slightly upper class tone, 'We're saying that *adults* will run our company, as they always have done, and as they always will. No children will ever be in charge of Sky Star.'

'But you haven't answered the question, Ms Nilsen.'

Suddenly enjoying herself, Cynthia replied, 'Three questions, by my count. Any leaked information you received is merely part of the story, which is: a daughter of Mr Grant, who is still under sixteen, will next year complement her business diploma by working as an understudy for our retiring General Manager, Mr Skillen. Following his departure, she will continue her *associate* studies with an interim General Manager – soon to be announced. Upon attaining the age of eighteen she *may* then become employed as the General Manager of Sky Star - subject to various and strenuous suitability criteria being met. Ms Grant has already indicated her desires, should she attain the position, to introduce whole new concepts of modern-day air travel that should find strong acceptance with younger travellers as well as our regular clientele.

'But Ms Nilsen!' the shouts persisted. 'Is Mr Grant available for comment? After all, it *is* his daughter.'

'Mr Grant, as you know, is one of our captains. At the moment he's away on a flight.'

'But he's always away and *always* not available! When will he be back? What about his daughter? Can we speak to her?'

Cynthia said, 'You can when she's eighteen and our General Manager.'

The first reporter persisted. 'So, *will* the skies be safe then?'

This was to be Cynthia's finest moment. 'Australia has always had the world's safest skies – unlike Europe and North America which often endure heavy air traffic in adverse weather conditions. Here, we are usually blessed with an excellent flying environment where the only storms are like this one: in a teacup! Good evening all – and thank you.' She trooped from the stage; head held high in triumph.

'Phew,' I whistled to the kids. 'They'll *hate* her now! She sounded like that red haired quiz madam on *Weakest Link*. Anyway, I thought she was fantastic. Exactly what we want.' Nonetheless, Amanda complained unhappily that she was suddenly headline news everywhere. And worse, perhaps as a measure of their displeasure, the next day another biting newspaper headline squawked:

*No more Ferris wheels for her: Rich kid will get an **airline** for her eighteenth!*

After shaking my head at that, I rang Cynthia to congratulate her brave stand and excellent tactics, then added 'Your brevity was blinding. Your sarcasm no worse than their headlines. I loved it! But you'll never stop them, Cynth. We both know she's not *getting* an airline handed to her; she's being offered management of it. Don't forget; the young people of Mandy's generation are a large and potent force these days. They'll be voting soon at eighteen then travelling by air. I'm willing to bet that many of them would much prefer to fly with an outfit run by an attractive and fashionable young woman than one run by stuffy old toads in gray suits and ties – but don't quote me on that, please.'

Cynthia certainly sounded pleased with her debut performance, so I continued, 'Now, let's outpace them whenever we can. How about you get onto your Women's Weekly contacts and offer them some free fashion shots of Mandy – very decent, very appropriate – but definitely showing the latest trendy gear that the young women of today are wearing - whatever that may be. Her image will easily outshine and outsell those old airline men. This should appeal firstly to women, then to young men so they fly with us too. Let's outsmart all the negativity, just as we did long ago at Luna Park. Anyway, a great start, Cynth. You fired a few good broadsides across their bows and made them duck for cover . . . until the next round, anyway.'

Passing her high school gates the next morning, Mandy was snapped by a jostle of media photographers. This was quite to our advantage, especially when a TV background news program showed comparison photos between the bubbly Amanda Grant and the board of directors of a well-known airline: all grim old men with balding heads and dark suits. Debate raged for a while, then deflated after everyone, it seemed, had voiced their opinions on the various merits of old versus young, and aged experience versus fresh and trendy ideas. On talk-back radio, many callers favoured new directions in aviation in regards to in-flight entertainment, ticketless check-ins and internet reservations – some just visions on the near horizon back then in the 1990's. And lastly, any publicity is usually good publicity – we hoped.

The next month's issue of Women's Weekly magazine showed two fashionable photos of Amanda on page eight. Pleasingly, this tasteful feature was introduced:

Heading for the top? Sky Star's Amanda Grant steps out in style

23.

Meanwhile, I still had a regular daytime job called flying aeroplanes. I was a captain, but it's not always quite as routine as commonly believed. I was being flight tested by Captain Ken Tolman, our Chief Pilot, under a regulation whereby all captains need their performance checked regularly. This must be done by a pilot more senior than them: usually the Chief Pilot, or sometimes the Chief Pilot of another airline. I was due this day so Ken had replaced my rostered First Officer with himself in order to conduct my test.

I was running through our pre-flight check lists in one of our Boeing 737s at Brisbane airport. We had just commenced taxying out for take-off on our 9am service to Melbourne. I was in the captain's left-hand seat and Ken was the check captain occupying the right. Disconnecting from our push-back tug, I was starting both engines and reciting the check list to him:

'Generators: on. Probe heat: on. Anti-ice: not required. Isolation valve: auto. Engine Start switches: cont. Recall: checked. Auto brakes: RTO . . . '

After taxying for some distance towards the runway 01 threshold, we heard: *Chime!* The cabin Purser was calling on the intercom phone. I answered. 'Captain speaking.' The Purser explained that our gate team had radioed them to say that a Mr Ho Lin and his assistant had arrived – very late, at our departure gate. He was demanding that we return to the aerobridge to take him on board. I replied that we usually strove to leave the gate on time and that we rarely taxied back in to pick up anyone. And, to be harsh, passengers should always leave their home/hotel/office a little earlier than needed in order to be punctual for any flight. The purser acknowledged our routine policy, but stated that Mr Lin was the Chairman of the Shenzhen Orient Bank of Hong Kong. He claimed that he and many of his employees regularly travelled with us. They'd been delayed by heavy Brisbane traffic and needed to travel to an urgent meeting with our Reserve Bank Governors in Melbourne. Lin had indicated that if we refused to return for him, he'd ensure all his employees flew by Qantas in the future.

After consideration, I turned to Ken, 'Ah, Ken, I think it won't hurt to go back to the ramp and get these two. Bloody pests, but they're good for business by the sound of it.'

But Ken Tolman, not in the best of moods, was totally against the idea. He glared at me. 'No we damn-well won't! They should have been here on time like everyone else has to. I don't care who he is!'

I reasoned, 'But Ken, let's be a bit flexible here. It'll cost us about ten minutes – fifteen at most. He's got an important meeting.'

Tolman was infuriated. 'But how many of the other 154 people on board who bothered to get here on time have also got meetings, appointments and other important reasons to get to Melbourne? You're the captain under supervision and it's your call, but I warn you Rob: you wrote most of these company policy manuals yourself and now you want to break your own rules just for some big-knob Asian banker.'

Touching the toe brake pedals, I'd halted temporarily on the taxiway to conduct this slightly heated debate. I was about to ask the Control Tower could we turn around at the next turning bay, when they asked why we'd stopped. So, having just lost our place in the take-off queue anyway, I made the decision to go back for the businessmen and requested a clearance to return to the gate.

Ken hissed angrily. *'Jesus!* Now you've bloody STOPPED! Just who the *hell* told you to stop?'

I replied, 'I'm going back to the gate, Ken. It's just a small delay for our other passengers. I'll explain it to them - if you give me the chance, and everyone should be happy. Gee Ken, brighten up, please.'

He fired back at me: 'I'm the check captain, Rob, remember? You might own the damn airline but I'm still in charge of this flight. First you stop on an active taxiway and disrupt their take-off sequencing, *then* you return to the gate for two late passengers. Well, it's on your head, mate. I'm not approving that.'

This was slightly ridiculous because any delay and subsequent loss of revenue would ultimately come out of *my* pocket, not his. I was suddenly very disappointed with this whole debacle. A captain can make such a decision and any check captain should go along with it – unless, of course, the decision threatens the safety of the flight in any way. To me it was no *big deal*, but my angry check captain was trying to score points, I thought, and I doubted if he would have acted similarly had he been checking anyone else.

After returning, we hurriedly embarked the late Mr Ho Lin and his smiling assistant - both deeply grateful, then took off for Melbourne exactly thirteen minutes late. It was certainly a quiet journey on the flight deck once airborne, so I busied myself with the navigation then gazed down at the endless layers of strato-cumulus cloud tops that slowly passed far below. Softly, and with some cheek, I whistled *Happy Days Are Here Again* while Ken sat beside me stony-faced as though the end of the world was nigh. Reflecting upon the touchy matter in hand, I considered it to be of minor insignificance and believed that most passengers would hardly be inconvenienced arriving fifteen minutes late at *any* destination. It happened from time to time anyway – storms, for example, and I'd never stood at the doorway to smile goodbye to our exiting passengers and been abused for being late.

I liked to make compromises when in charge of a flight. I considered the diplomacy of fair business all round was an admirable policy for my airline to adopt. Our business passengers were on *business*, just as we were, and our business was of no more vital significance than theirs. Noble ideals indeed, but in his only words during the flight, an unrepentant Ken Tolman assured me that when he said 'No we damn-well won't!' he damn-well *meant* it! and I should have obeyed him. Where the real truth lay was debatable: both of us were right in our own ways, while both could also be considered not quite so right.

In Melbourne, Ken left us in a huff to conduct a check on another captain heading to Adelaide. But before abruptly disembarking, his unfriendly tone remarked, 'I'm not passing you, Rob. I warned you. You'll have a red dot next to your name on the board. How will that look, Mr Number One?'

*

Indeed. The dreaded pilots' flight proficiency board at our Sydney crew room soon showed a glaring red dot next to *my name*; the name of pilot number one: Capt. R. GRANT. FAILED. It was quite an embarrassment to me, but a stark wake-up call for any pilot to contemplate that if I could fail a check, then *they* most certainly could. And after two failed checks, anyone could be dismissed from the flight line. But never before had Captain Grant's name sported a nasty red dot beside it. Whispers and gossip quickly spread:

'Did you see the board? Grant failed his check. Oh really? Hard to believe, but Tolman failed him. Must be brave to do that. But Grant could fire *him* first . . . ah, couldn't he? I'm not sure. But *would* he? Hmm, very interesting.'

Upon later reflection, I considered that I'd received the raw end of the deal and tried to explain myself in the pilot's lounge. It was quite a lively discussion. Some pilots agreed with my stance, while a few captains politely reminded me of my own policies – as Ken had done – and said they'd have kept going. It was a toss-up over who was right and who was wrong.

Paul Harland finally asked the question that most were certainly wondering: 'Rob, what will you *do* about this, then?'

After some thought, I put aside my own personal opinions and grievances and replied, 'Do? Ken was simply doing what he's paid to do by me. He believes he's right so, no, there's nothing I intend to *do* about it, Paul. I'm not pulling any rank to slide out of this because of who I am. The Chief Pilot's word is final and we're all subject to his adjudication - including me, of course. If I were to circumvent his rulings now it would make a mockery of him and undermine his position and authority.' I thought this was rather well said, although I could hardly state otherwise.

With a big smile, Paul asked, 'So, you're on stand-down now, are you? Grounded? Suspended from your own airline!' and when I nodded they all laughed to consider this unique concept. Then more mirth rocked the room when some comedian suggested we should now be called *Ground Star.*

Having the last say, I admitted, 'Now, that *was* funny. But guys, let's keep it between ourselves, please? No need for the whole damn *planet* to hear about it.' They agreed, but I shuddered as I remembered those embarrassing leaks that always seemed to *just happen*.

The very next morning, as I'd correctly guessed, a large black headline heralded:

Grant Grounded While His Airline Flies On!

Thankfully, Cynthia flew to my rescue in the media with a barrage of denials that would make any politician proud. She denied categorically that I had 'lost' my licence. She refuted allegations of 'unsafe practices' and she asserted that it was almost routine for pilots to occasionally fail a test during their careers on technical matters. It merely underlined our high safety standards, she emphasised. When asked if I would be reinstated to flying soon, she replied 'Of course. Captain Grant has more flying hours than any other Sky Star pilot – *including* the Chief Pilot.'

Her pompous optimism was promptly ignored and the scandal became an unexpected Christmas pudding for the press who revelled in my misery until another disaster came along to gazump me from the front pages: it was an earthquake in China that had killed hundreds.

24.

Disappearing from the front pages for a while provided only partial relief to me. I was gripped with an embarrassing despondency and decided to use my down-time to catch up with neglected odd jobs at home which always kept falling further behind. Grounded while my airline flew merrily on, it was an opportunity to enjoy some quality time with my children – a fatherly duty of mine that was often sadly remiss. Dave Skillen, now quite content with my decision to retire him from his position of General Manager, almost *ordered* me to take at least a fortnight off work. When he asked one day what holidays I'd taken since we'd started the company, I replied 'Never.'

'Never? You need a break. You can't afford to get sick like me,' he remonstrated. 'My doctor diagnosed me with some slight diabetes, blood pressure and cholesterol problems, so I'm only working thirty hours a week from now on, while your Amanda can take the load off me soon by absorbing much of my paper work and other office duties as she hopefully picks up the tricks of the trade. I'm winding down, Robbie, and even though I'm much older than you, I think you should also ease up and take a breather. Have some fun with those lovely girls of yours and enjoy your little farm out there. Remember, they haven't got a mother to guide them along - and you won't get them a new one either,' he winked.

He was right – about my work, of course. I hadn't taken any leave from duties since those frantic days when I'd started our one-plane charter company. Consequently, I sensed an overall weariness and quietly knew that captains should always be one hundred percent fit, not fatigued. I owed such a 'recharging of the batteries' to my passengers; and, not the least, to the company – *my* company. And perhaps Ken Tolman was partially right when he failed me on my check flight test: he may have detected some inattention or neglect on my part and used *that incident* as an excuse to stand me down for a while.

But he would surely have expected some backlash from me – perhaps even his own dismissal, and would not have anticipated my simple faxed note to him which politely said, 'Ken, I'm taking a three-week break. Whoever owns this company owes me ten years' worth of holidays. Please arrange a replacement in my absence, and set up a re-test flight check for my return on November the first. Keep up the good work. Cheers, Rob.'

I later heard on the grapevine that Ken was quite perturbed after that infamous day of my check flight, and later in the pilot's lounge, poured out his woes to whoever would listen. Another captain suggested he might be fired, and had it been wise for Ken to fail the company's *owner*? Couldn't he have simply let me do what I intended? After all, I wasn't being unsafe, reckless or illegal – was I? And any cost of the delay would surely be borne by Rob Grant himself, wouldn't it? Ken listened, then told them that I'd be angry – for sure, and therefore anything could happen. Meanwhile, he stewed in discomfort because he'd not expected our names and actions and indeed our entire airline's reputation to be splashed around the news as it was – and to our certain detriment.

So he wasn't expecting my gentle note which ended in 'Keep up the good work.' After this much-discussed incident in the company, I believed that Ken and I had developed a far greater professional respect for each other than might otherwise been achieved had it never occurred. Also, the vital warning that anyone at all can fail their check flight had travelled with urgency throughout our pilot fraternity and into other airlines where one prominent staff magazine blared: 'Are you next? If HE can fail then *you* are not immune!' Hopefully this scare raised overall piloting efficiency and competence everywhere, while generating more than a few worried brows. A stark example to be noted by all.

*

At home, I was officially on holidays, and instead of shiny black pilots' shoes, I was sloshing around our boggy farmyard in dirty gumboots;

squelching in mud and bird droppings. Near our aircraft hangar, I spied Pedro Ramez, our first Filipino staff member, helping us out on his three-day break. Pedro, who seemed to be a fine carpenter, was eagerly hammering together a wooden playhouse for my two youngest girls, Emmie and Celia. As they still enjoyed playing with dolls and toys, each day after school this week they were helping Pedro with design, construction and decoration of the large three-by-four-metre dollhouse which we'd modelled from a photo of Queen Mary's dollhouse in Windsor Castle. They hoped the replica would be almost the same size.

I'd sponsored Pedro with employment to come to Australia after meeting him in the Philippines many years ago. He was the security guard who guarded Amanda while Dave and I negotiated for those three F28 jets without any engines. Once settled here in Australia, Pedro trained as a flight steward on Sky Star and quickly became a valued employee and someone who was genuinely liked by all our staff. In flight, our passengers enjoyed Pedro's broad and winning grin, and the smile was certainly improved by his new weekly wages: a sum he could hardly believe after years of toil in a sweatbox carpenter's factory back home.

'Sixteen dollars a week, Mr Grant,' he told me earnestly while hammering a nail; not smiling this time. 'That is all they pay me in that very hard factory. Every day it was work, work, and work! For thirteen hours. Not allowed talk. Not allowed rest. Only allowed toilet two times in shift. And all for sixteen dollars!'

Pedro continued, 'Then someone tell me about security job. Fancy uniform with gun. Very good job. But I only get twenty dollars a week there. Standing in sweltering heat all day for sixty hours a week – until you give me that three hundred dollars in tip.' I asked Pedro if he enjoyed that money – not that it was any of my business – and he replied honestly that he remitted most of it home to his family in the *provinces*. I believed that he did, and now I was paying him the relative millionaire's sum of fifty dollars an hour to construct a playhouse for the girls and their numerous pets where, over the entrance way, we painted a merry sign that said:

'Ducks and geese must wipe their muddy feet before entering!'

So, the kids should soon be happy, Pedro's family should be a lot better off after this week and our web-footed pets might have clean feet. All I needed next was to pass my second flight test, because another failure and I'd be *goosed!*

25.

In the meantime I was thoroughly enjoying a whole new bonding with my family. We raced ATV bikes around the property, chased the the pets, rode *Sky* the horse and zoomed skywards for occasional joy flights in our little Gazelle. I learned to ride a skateboard. It was great fun, although I occasionally shivered at the spectre of a camera lens suddenly poking through a window of the playhouse where I was sometimes seated, surrounded by dolls.

And now, for the first time in many years, I was able to attend several parent/teacher interviews at my girls' schools. Especially important were discussions involving Amanda, who was soon leaving high school to become David Skillen's understudy at Sky Star. Several senior teachers questioned quite wisely whether she was old enough yet to be attempting such a Herculean task? I replied that at her age I already had about three thousand flying hours in my pilot's log book. I added, 'And please, I don't wish to be critical about the school curriculum in any way, but from what I've seen there's little there that she needs to know compared with what she'll learn over the next two years. I've noted with great pride that she topped the TAFE College in her Diploma of Business Studies and should soon complete her MBS.'

The teachers agreed that my Mandy was a capable and much respected student, and one who'd achieved so much without having a mother at home, (a gentle hint?). So they certainly wished her every success in the formidable responsibilities ahead of her. I thanked them, but pointedly added: 'I also had no mother.'

After the interview, Mandy asked if we could one day employ some of her girlfriends from school to become cabin stewardesses. 'Or would that be favouritism?' I answered that we possibly could – *if* they came up to our high standards and unique selection criteria. I reminded her that she'd flown on our planes often enough by now and should agree that anyone of sloppy appearance or behaviour would definitely not be needed by us. 'It could affect our reputation, Mandy, and that's the very standard you might be the chief defender of one day.'

'There are some boys who want to be pilots, too,' she added.

'We'll wait and see about that,' I laughed. 'By the way, got a nice boyfriend at the moment?'

'Yep.'

'You have? You kept that quiet, mate.'

'You haven't been around much to notice, Dad. And maybe you haven't noticed how I'm forever running around after *those three*, because if I don't, who will?'

'Gee, I'm so sorry.' I realised my absences were truly felt. 'Are the girls making much trouble?'

This inquiry started a heart-felt outpouring: 'Sometimes. I still really love those sisters of mine, but they're just normal kids who can get up to mischief when there's no adult here to control them. I've been running the whole damn house and farm while the ducks are better behaved than them sometimes. Then I have to go to school, then to TAFE . . . and everything! And they make plenty of noise and fight sometimes, and they ride off around the farm after school and talk to other kids who hang around. I can't watch them every minute because I've got to cook the dinner . . . although Olivia helps a lot.'

'Anyway, they need some more discipline, Dad. A mother - or something. It always seems that because you had no mother in your life then you think we don't need one either. But your Dad only had *you* to worry about: *one* child. There are *four* of us here.'

I reflected on her wise words. 'A very good point. I just don't seem to ever have the time for another woman, Mandy. When I married your wonderful mother I considered that to be a lifetime arrangement. I never dreamt of ever needing to find anyone else. Well, you know what happened and I never got over it. So I immersed myself in the company and my flying instead, and look how far we've come since then. But let me just say: I don't believe that I *owe* you girls another mother. You already *had* one and just because she died I wasn't about to thrash about frantically seeking someone – anyone – to walk into our home and replace her because she was simply irreplaceable.

136

Neither was I going to join some Desperate Divorcee's club because I didn't have the time or the inclination. In short, I wasn't going to buy, rent or lease a woman just to become your instant parent and free babysitter.'

She laughed. 'Buy? Rent? Lease? They're not planes, Dad.'

'I know. But seriously mate, millions of kids in the world lost their fathers in wars: the sole breadwinner of the household. Fatherless, they still had to get by somehow while whingeing solved nothing. The Russians lost twenty million in World War Two and those surviving families had to persevere in single-parent or even *no* parent atmospheres despite the unjust cruelties of fate. Anyway, the point is: we're getting there – slowly, and have done very well compared to so many others. Have I been a bad father, then?'

She sighed in exasperation. 'You're missing the whole point, Dad! No, of course you haven't been *bad* . . . '

We drove home in silence. There were no harsh feelings between us; I believed that Mandy and I had a very special relationship; one that had endured since that day when she was four and she looked up at me with her little pleading eyes: 'Are you going to be our new Daddy?' Now she was legally my step-daughter and the best any man could wish for. In essence, a real daughter and an everlasting friend for life.

Nearing home, I finally felt compelled to touch upon a taboo subject: 'I hope you haven't slept with this boy. You absolutely *can't* afford to get pregnant, you know. Ah, have you?'

Our special relationship wasn't quite *that* close and trusting, because her eyes flashed a *mind-your-own-business* look as she said, 'No, but he'd like to meet you. He wants to be a pilot.'

'Phew! He can start tomorrow – first thing.' We both had a giggle, then headed down the muddy drive to the little farmhouse below the hill where three unsupervised girls on the veranda were playing very loud music to long-suffering farm animals. 'Parental guidance' was to be my new theme song; although the angry rap music blasting across the fields at the moment was beat-boxing a theme that didn't exactly inspire patience or tolerance. As I checked my fax machine, I wondered if I should start my *Father of the Year* campaign by banning that dreadful din?

*

'Dear Captain Robert Grant' the faxed communiqué greeted me. Probably yet another pleading letter to apply as a pilot or hostie, I guessed. This was not my province at all and I usually passed these on to Marie Westcott, our Chief of Staff, for her consideration and polite refusal when necessary.

The letter continued - after I glanced at its decorative letterhead:

Shenzhen Orient Hong Kong Bank

My warmest greetings to you, Captain Robert Grant.

I hope you and your family are very well. You may remember my flight on your wonderful airline from Brisbane to Melbourne in October. I was the late passenger who urgently needed to travel to Melbourne for a most important meeting with your Reserve Bank Governors. I was accompanied by my senior executive, Mr Leung. Our limousine was delayed by the traffic in Brisbane so my driver called your airline and asked them to delay the flight. They said no: it was company policy.

When we finally arrived I saw, much to my horror, your plane out on the airport and driving away from the terminal building. This was to me a disaster as I was in the process of arranging a large financial package in which our bank was hoping to invest heavily in an Australian enterprise. The Governors were to meet me just once, as there were other determined contenders pursuing the deal, then we were flying home that night. It was therefore imperative that we got to Melbourne on your flight that morning.

It was then that I observed your plane stop and turn around, then return to the terminal to pick us up. I believed this was a blessing from Buddha Himself and I was very happy. As a consequence of your gracious actions that day, you have enabled my bank to plan for important investments for Australia. Hopefully, ones that may one day generate far-reaching benefits for us all.

138

Then later at home, my secretary showed me an Australian news report that said you were penalised for your kind actions of that day. Is this correct? If so, I am deeply sorry and regretful that such a disgrace to your good name could be attributed to myself. So, I was about to send you my apologies and suggest you protest to your management, when my good secretary explained that you are the management, and, indeed, the proprietor of Sky Star Airlines. This is somewhat confusing to me, but of course none of my business, although, dare I say, in China we would never permit such losing of face by a company owner to be publicly aired like this. The pilot who caused you such trouble would be swiftly dealt with, I can assure you.

Finally, I must apologise for the length of this letter and sincerely hope you and your fine company can resolve this delicate issue. In the meantime, for your compassionate actions I am hereby offering you and your wife and family a free holiday in Hong Kong at our expense. You will be accommodated at the Hong Kong Park Gardens six-star hotel where you will have a limousine and a helicopter at your disposal. It will be my greatest pleasure to meet you and your family. I therefore earnestly look forward to the pleasure of your company.

Please ring my secretary on HK 8861-7800-09 for all arrangements. Sincerely, Ho Lin.

Chairman,
Shenzhen Orient Hong Kong Bank. Hong Kong

26.

'Guess what kids,' I announced in the morning. 'We're all going on a holiday tomorrow.'

'Wow! Where to?' they all sang *yippee* over their breakfasts.

'Hong Kong. An important man up there has given us a free holiday. How about that?'

Instead of bubbling enthusiasm, I was hit with: 'But who'll feed the animals?' asked Emmie, remembering that we now had more pets: an additional three dogs plus a harmless carpet snake that hid in our barn. We decided that their many friends could tend to them and our horse *Sky* could be kept in our next door neighbour's yard.

'What about school?' asked little Celia.

'You're all having a week off.'

Amanda added, 'And what about my TAFE?' I told her that she should learn more about business and the world over the next week than at any college.

Finally, Olivia asked, 'Can I bring my friend Monique?'

'No, sorry. No-one else. I've been told that I should spend more time with you bunch of rascals, so I am. Now, for important business reasons, let's not tell anyone that we're going, please. There's lots of great things to do there, but if you're so keen on school work you can all write an essay on Hong Kong while we're there.'

'Oh, yuk!' they all protested – but now sold on the idea of our secret mission.

Through my private investigator's *Eagle Eyes* agency, I had determined that our Mr Lin's bank was possibly interested in acquiring either an Australian airline or a part ownership of one. We guessed he was after Ansett because of its highly vulnerable state, but it could just as easily be the much smaller Sky Star or even some non-aviation asset. But an airline purchase would give Lin a healthy walk-in slice of the local aviation scene. This partly explained his meeting with our Reserve Bank governors as our laws would never permit just *any* unknown foreigner to operate a major air service in Australia. Our Hong Kong trip therefore required a careful phone briefing with my red-haired PR manager because I could just imagine the neon headlines flashing:

Grounded Grant sells out in Asian airline coup!

'Just tell the ducks, girls. No-one else, okay. Let's go and pack. And remember: loose lips sink ships.'

This caused a puzzled Celia to screw up her face, 'Huh? Are we going by ship?'

I *hoped* she was joking.

*

I suppose it seems rather odd, but throughout my lifetime of flying, including learning with my father at twelve years old, I'd never been in a helicopter. So, as we hovered over the old Kai Tak Hong Kong airport site in our Bell Jet Ranger 206 chopper and listened to the pilot's description of the hair-raising landings that used to be everyday occurrences here, I was fascinated by our ability to remain suspended in the one spot while also seeing no wings out the window; two firsts for me.

I glanced nervously at the pilot's airspeed indicator to see it reading zero knots! – a disastrous situation in any fixed-wing plane. But after hovering for a while, he simply tilted the rotor blades and we regained forward airspeed to zoom over the spectacular Hong Kong harbour, encircled by its world famous skyline of high rises. Signatures of wealth and opulence in modern Asia. My girls were thrilled and entranced. It was wonderful to be spending time with them for a change - and, as they too had never flown in a *chopper*, this was an equally novel adventure for us all.

Before this joy flight, we'd arrived at our luxury hotel and been escorted to the penthouse apartment complex on the seventeenth floor. Mr Ho Lin hadn't previously mentioned that we'd be staying in his 'grand executive quarters' as he called them, but, open mouthed, we gulped at the marble ornamented suite of luxury rooms containing six bathrooms, five spas and sparkling fountains in three foyers. No expense was spared for us, although amidst my thorough appreciation of it all, I certainly suspected why. But my girls hadn't the time to wonder why, or even the inclination, because it was all just *so awesome!* as they declared while racing from room to room and gawking at the spectacular 360-degree views from our huge balconies.

So, at the end of our spectacular aerial tour, the smiling Mr Lin, a thin and greying man, instructed his pilot to land on the rooftop of our penthouse apartment. This was a huge surprise and thrill for us - even to me, a career pilot who'd never landed on the roof of anything! My girls were simply 'over the Moon' at this VIP gala arrival and thanked Mr Lin profusely as we stepped down from the whining Jet Ranger.

'You are most welcome, ladies,' Lin smiled and bowed deeply. Turning to me, he said, 'Robert, I am very saddened to hear that your dear wife has departed – and so long ago. I did not know this. But you are certainly blessed with four beautiful young ladies here. I am quite sure they will honour the memory of their mother.'

'They will indeed,' I agreed. The congenial Mr Lin then suggested we celebrate our visit with a few drinks on the main balcony. As the girls skipped off to explore the rest of our suite of apartments and then the whole hotel itself, a white-robed waiter appeared as if from nowhere, bowing and offering a silver tray of sparkling drinks with light refreshments.

*

Gazing over a splendid Hong Kong sunset, we sipped the finest champagne that I could imagine (not that I was any connoisseur) and got down to business – whatever that was to be.

'Mr Lin,' I started, 'firstly, I'd like to say how deeply appreciative I am of your extraordinary hospitality towards us this week. My children are quite *rapt*, they said. But I must state now that I only delayed your flight in Brisbane by about fifteen minutes, and that it cost us no more than a thousand dollars or so – a fleabite in our overall operating expenses. So I am naturally wondering why you have outlaid such lavishness and generosity towards us in return?'

Ho Lin relaxed and sipped his champagne, 'Captain Robert, in China we always do business the Chinese way. Someone might do a great favour for someone else, but then he might be repaid one day with just a small token. Eventually the larger favour might be returned in kind. If not, it is never measured in dollars or called a debt, but merely considered business as usual with trusted friends. Give and take, you might say. Of course, we can be rather upset with those who *double-cross* us – as the Americans say, but with those whom we trust we are endlessly generous and forgiving.'

I thought this convoluted answer was rather evasive, but I moved on. I related our dealings with Mr Ferdy Diego in the Philippines, and his weak attempt to sell me three jets with almost expired engines. How I offered him one-third the price after exposing his sales pitch, then threw him a fake cheque for a million dollars across the restaurant table.'

'Did he take it?' asked Mr Lin.

'He grabbed it and shoved it so fast into his wallet that I'm sure I saw sparks flying from it!' I added, however, that after all the play acting we both eventually obtained the deal that we'd originally anticipated. We chuckled together as the waiter poured more expensive French rocket fuel into my crystal glass. Unused to drinking, my eyes blurred as I gazed down at the bustling harbour thirty seven floors below us. Contented, I deciding that this was how the rich and famous lived – and although I may have been slightly rich, to the Australian media back home I was more often referred to as *infamous*.

We both concurred that the Philippines was a rather poor country and that was simply how they must conduct business to survive. Par for the course. 'But,' added Mr Lin, 'Hong Kong is a modern, wealthy and vibrant country, and a vital cornerstone of China's massive and booming economy.' Speaking of cheques, Lin suddenly narrowed his gaze and whispered, 'I do not deal in fake cheques, Captain Robert. You may rest assured.'

As the owner and chairman of a prestigious merchant bank, I certainly hoped he did not.

27.

Later when Mr Lin had gone, it was Amanda who posed the same obvious question to me: 'Dad, how come this man is just *handing* us all these luxuries? I mean, it's all quite wonderful but in my business studies no-one would lavish such gifts to people he hardly knows without a guaranteed return of some sort.'

'Exactly.' I congratulated her on 'getting the picture', then added that Mr Lin, when I asked, had skirted around an adequate answer with vague riddles. Although I'd helped him to a small extent on that occasion in Brisbane, this sumptuous holiday, although quite grand and deeply appreciated, was a disproportionate response. Therefore, I suggested that it was time for us to do some investigative work on the matter. After we went sightseeing first, of course.

After lunch, we dropped the three youngies in a supervised *Fun Zone* within our hotel, then explored the city while walking towards downtown Kowloon. After much window shopping and a few purchases by Mandy, we caught a taxi to Mr Lin's *Shenzhen Orient Bank*. It was a merchant bank; an imposing sandstone trading house for wealthy companies to borrow and invest; to trade and broker commodities in lavish privacy. Glancing around inside, there were no teller's boxes in the majestic foyer, just discrete lounges in quiet alcoves where large transactions were undoubtedly daily occurrences. Curiously, while the cavernous foyer was almost a *jungle* of huge pot plants, I spied a tiny label on one that said 'Kowloon Rent-a-Plant.'

Back on the street, we inspected the bank's facade with the detached interest of casual tourists, then wandered off to search for other merchant banks. In one such bank I greeted a particular pushy gentleman who wore a dark suit with a red carnation in the lapel, 'We are investors in aviation,' I said, answering his effusive greeting. 'Does your trading house invest in airlines and aviation in general?'

The man indicated disinterest as he replied, 'No sir. There is no profit in aviation. You wish to see a brochure about share cropping in

China? Derivatives on the Hang Seng?' I shook my head then asked if he knew of any merchant banks in Hong Kong that *did* invest in aviation. He replied that all airline investors eventually lose their money, so no-one bothers with it here. I argued that, on the contrary, Cathay Pacific, Singapore Airlines and Japan Airlines for example, had all been trading strongly for over fifty years and I hadn't heard of any great share crashes among them. He appeared not to hear me.

In another grand old establishment we enquired about airlines in Australia and were informed: 'Australia too small. Only small population. No money in air travel there. Qantas only airline in Australia.' I felt like replying that I'd personally made about thirty million dollars so far from my little Aussie airline which definitely *wasn't* called Qantas. Confidently, the assistant manager tried to interest me in a gold mine in Angola.

Outside in the humidity of the bustling midday streets, Amanda said she had an idea. 'It seems our Mr Lin might be the *only* Hong Kong banker interested in a small airline in Australia − or interested in any aviation investments at all. So, why don't we play a little gag on him?'

I asked, 'What did you have in mind?' She said to follow her, so we headed back to Mr Lin's grandiose establishment where she showily presented herself as a young American heiress wishing to invest *a* few dollars. I was introduced as her bodyguard. The mere mention of the word *heiress* was a passport and bankers' eyebrows instantly shot up. She was escorted into a plush office and seated before an eager man who, remarkably, also sported a red carnation in the lapel of his dark suit. His nameplate said Mr P. Sung. Perhaps the red flower was a designation of senior investment rank? Meanwhile, I, as the lowly bodyguard, was ushered away onto a hard bench in the foyer's *jungle* and promptly ignored.

An hour later, after we strolled outside to locate a quaint Chinese coffee house, Mandy related her exciting acting debut in Mr Sung's office. With a false *Yankee* accent, she informed him that she'd just turned eighteen and that her divorced mother had died a few years previously, leaving her a family trust that had now matured. She hailed from Texas − ah, had he ever been there? No? It didn't matter.

Anyway, she'd thought of investing the money in Texas Air, or some other American airlines, but her grandfather warned her that following the recent deregulation of US airlines, it was now a cut-throat business where no-one was getting a return on their money.'

'While Grand Pappy suggested getting involved in the new Internet technology instead, she had always loved 'airplanes' and had heard about the impending opportunities in Australian airlines involving a major carrier facing bankruptcy. So she was very excited about the possibility of a brand new player in the Down-under Aussie air scene. Could Mr Sung please tell her anything about it?

I interrupted her, 'Mandy, where the blazes did you get all this from?'

'From you!' she grinned. 'I take note of your interesting phone conversations because you talk so loud! Also, Mr Skillen tells me lots of interesting facts about airlines in the world. I looked up the rest in our TAFE library.'

'But this American heiress thing? You misrepresented yourself to a reputable Hong Kong bank? Posed as someone you aren't with a false accent? Please go on, I can't wait to hear the rest!'

Mandy smiled, 'Well, here I was; little *Miss Texas*, and I had that old Chinese man eating from my hand – almost. He eventually admitted that his bank *was* an interested player in the near future of Australian aviation, and that they hoped to step into the shoes of an airline called Ansett when it was "finally grounded." Although they could never hope to overtake the giant Qantas, if Ansett didn't become available then other smaller airlines in Australia, including the regionals, would need to be *removed* first - before Mr Richard Branson of the giant Virgin Group moves in for the final big kill. '

'After some more chatting he actually seemed to believe me. He asked just how much I might be willing to invest, should I wish to enter into a joint take-over bid for airlines operating in Australia at the moment. I said "Oh, it's not very much really. Mother left me about ten million last year when our oil shares were booming. Following outside advice, I sold them quickly and now they've plummeted, so it's lucky I struck it rich before that happened . . . " then I stuck my chest out and watched his eyes bulge!'

I laughed as she continued. 'As the dishonourable Mr Sung scribbled furiously onto his note pad, he barked rapid-fire Chinese into his phone after I told him that I'd been all around town and no-one else had shown any interest in airlines in Australia. Why was this, please?'

Excitedly, Mandy continued. 'He kept fingering his red carnation, twisting it around and around, then he said, "This is very confidential you must understand, but you are such a beautiful lady that I am most honoured to reveal some details. Ah, it is because our Chairman - his name is Mr Lin - hopes to acquire at least one of the other airlines of importance in Australia, and most of the smaller regionals as well, for approximately half price - he estimates. Then he intends to on-sell it soon afterwards to Mr Branson for the full money. In this way you might easily and rapidly double your investment money. Ah, can you follow all this so far?" '

'I told him that this was all rather complex for a young innocent gal like me, but Mother had always said how Grandpappy had taught her a great deal about the treacherous shenanigans in the oil business so hopefully I'd comprehend this very complicated *airplane* picture soon. Then, having nothing whatsoever to do with the subject, he suddenly asked if I was married. I was stunned, and answered, "No. Not yet." '

My eyebrows shot up as Mandy continued: 'Diverting his leering gaze, I said to him: "Everyone's heard of the astute Mr Branson. Would he be so silly to fall for such a ruse as this?" '

'He answered, "Only if all the other Hong Kong investment houses stay right out of it and appear to have no faith in these other Aussie air operators – which they have agreed to do. This writes the price down and is the normal Chinese way of doing business to which we are all accustomed. By the way, if I may ask, where are you dining this evening, Miss Houston?" '

Mandy said, 'I decided our Mr Sung was about as subtle as a major earthquake and let that one fly through to the wicket-keeper -

as you always say, then bravely asked him what was the name of these other Australian airlines apart from Ansett? He replied that he'd forgotten, but they had some childish names that would soon to be of little significance.'

I massaged my chin and swayed back on my chair. 'Hmm, this is quite incredible to absorb, mate. I'm just not sure what to conclude from all this. Firstly, I find it hard to believe that they disclosed their confidential investment intentions to a young person straight off the street . . . '

Mandy interrupted, 'Dad! That old guy was checking me out *big time*! I mean, he was mesmerised and never stopped fiddling with that damn flower, while his eyes were always gawking at my boobs!'

'Hey, wait on - you're only fifteen . . . '

Mandy said, 'But all my school friends say that I look eighteen. That's why it worked. Many men are lecherous old . . . *things*. Asians would be no different. He was fascinated and believed I was a spoilt little rich gal from America with far too much money to play with. But he needed to divulge some of their plans as I'd already told him that we'd been business-shopping elsewhere.'

I chewed over her wise words. 'Well, it certainly *could* happen here in Hong Kong, I guess. Not in the Sydney CBD, mind you; the plan would be far too transparent. But this city is the pulsating crossroads of international finance and trading wealth. There could be some wealthy sons and daughters roaming these streets with inheritances from time to time - maybe with millions to invest. Did you give him your real name, by the way?'

She smiled. 'Cindy Houston.'

'Why Cindy? And Houston?'

'Cindy someone was *Miss Texas* last year. And the only place I've heard of in Texas is *Houston*, as in: *We've got a problem.*'

I sighed with worry, 'Well, we might have a problem too because they'll look you up in five minutes flat! Do you know that you could be playing a dangerous game here? They won't be too pleased being duped by a smart-arse fifteen-year-old girl, Cindy . . . I mean Mandy.'

149

'Dad, you told me I had to be tough if I intended to take over your company one day. And before we left home you said that I'd learn more about airline and business management in the next week than at any college. Well, I have already. And one thing I know - even though I'm only a smart-arse fifteen-year-old, is that pretty women have gotten away with blue murder over the centuries when dealing with powerful and influential men – especially older men who haven't *had it* for years.'

'Man-deee, please!'

She smirked. 'Well sex sells, doesn't it? Everything from cars to toothpaste. We learnt that in Sociology last year. Apparently I look about eighteen so I was able to wangle trade secrets out of that old bank lecher that you would never have obtained in a *year*. You need *boobs* for that, Dad. Plus I got a free drink and you didn't. He was going to order the butler take you a cup of tea, but I said you were lazy and didn't deserve one!'

We both laughed as I digested her great story. I'd never perceived Mandy as *sexy*; although I should have been at least aware by now. But dads often continue to see their daughters as little girls for quite some time after they've grown up. I still cherished memories of my little Mandy as she played dolls and skipped with her sisters. And when she pleaded for me to be their new Daddy. Or when she angrily ran away to the park in her pyjamas. Now those early days had undeniably passed into fading images.

It was quite outrageous, but only a pretty female could have gotten away with that corny acting role in such an austere and respected Hong Kong bank. If I'd asked them myself for details of planned airline take-overs and mergers in Australia, I would have been given the Asian run-around. Or impolitely shown the door. But what a risk she'd taken! With a shiver, I decided that Mr Lin might be organising some 'friends' to join us at our breakfast banquet on the balcony tomorrow morning. Perhaps their violin cases wouldn't be for serenading us?

I was expecting our apartment door chime to *gong* like a town square clock and herald the arrival of our dear friend and host, Mr Ho Lin of the Shenzhen Orient Hong Kong Bank, but I was busy jumping on the beds with the kids, trying not to bang our heads on the crystal chandeliers that hung in opulence from every bedroom ceiling. Suitably distracted, I'd somehow been considering Mr Lin as our breakfast guest, when the opposite was correct: he owned the whole apartment complex – and probably the hotel below us as well; therefore we, rather than he, were the real guests.

Before he arrived, I'd warned my brazen Mandy that our position could be quite precarious now as who knew what the Chairman's real intentions were or what his course of retribution might be? I told her, 'If he's been made a fool of and *lost face* in his very own bank, we might be thrown from the balcony. Or worse, you could be shanghaied into marrying that sweaty Mr Sung and imprisoned forever in his dungeon somewhere.'

'Sure Dad. Whatever. But let's say they did get hold of our airline; what exactly might they do with it?'

'They might keep it going as it is. Or sell it. Or they could trash it.'

'*Trash it?*' she squawked. 'What do you mean?'

I explained, 'Lots of take-over bids are thinly disguised power plays where the shareholders' profits are the one and only concern. The wishes and interests of the customers and staff are often not considered. A take-over company would probably paint over our beautiful colour scheme and change our wonderful name. Once they own Sky Star they could completely alter our whole friendly way of doing business, then they might strip the cash and assets from the airline and bolt away into the blue yonder. Trash it: that's what I mean.'

'And me? Where would I stand then?'

'You would have collided with the glass ceiling. Those old professional board directors would dump a young female executive faster than a rap dancer's head hits the floor. It's unlikely you'd be invited to work with them for a single day. Your great ideas such as installing free on-board internet might be rubbished because it could

151

affect the shareholders' profits, for example. Traditionally, many adult women with years of experience rarely rise to be chairperson of any board or General Manager of any company. You at your age would be swiftly told to go and play with your dolls, or some such sexist remark. Sadly, it's often a chauvinistic and discriminatory world so you would need to adapt within it . . . *should* you be allowed to stay.'

'But Dad, we can still do all those great things I suggested while we remain a private company, can't we? While-ever we retain our ownership and resist going public on the stock market, we are in charge. But as soon as we sell out it's all gone, right?'

'Yes. Once on the public stock market, Lin, or anyone, could simply raid the shares anyway. With private owners he has to be far more cunning. So we could simply take any money he or someone else might offer us now and head for the hills. But how would we feel? Especially when we watch him cleverly re-sell it for maybe double soon afterwards. We might be somewhat rich, I suppose, but without jobs. At the moment we're already doing pretty damn well without selling a thing. We've got assets now of about thirty million; although they're mostly company assets.'

'Privately, I've got enough wealth to be satisfied, but why would I even consider, in my wildest dreams, leaving my creation behind at the tender age of thirty-one when I've got at least another thirty years of working life remaining? I'm not seeking any more wealth; I just love the great company which I fashioned from nothing. I want to continue being pilot number one for Sky Star while I watch you run it until I hang up my wings. What happens after that is just too far away.'

Mandy became lost in thought; pondering the savagery of the real business world as opposed to her textbook bibles from business college. It was dog-eat-dog out there, as she would soon no doubt experience for herself. I left her to sunbake alone.

Thankfully breakfast time eventually arrived and I spied no furtive characters opening violin cases outside my bay windows. This was to be our last meeting with Mr Lin, he'd said, because he was always 'very busy.'

'Burying bodies?' I wondered aloud.

'Who is?' asked Celia and Emmie as they jumped up and down my King's four-poster Royal bed. 'What bodies? Are you crazy, Daddy?'

'I think I must be, kids. Hey, how old do you think Mandy looks these days?'

On the upward bounce, Emmie guessed, 'About twenty or something.'

'No she doesn't,' argued Celia, bouncing even higher, 'she looks at least twenty five. Same as my teacher.'

'Really?' I sighed in resignation, flopping down on the bed. But she's still only fifteen, I wanted to point out. Oh, all right: sixteen next month. But she can't possibly look over twenty - can she?

Whatever the case, I hadn't realised that I was wheeling, dealing and hob-knobbing around busy Hong Kong with someone who *looked* like a grown woman. A very attractive young woman who bore a strong resemblance to my dear departed Cristina. Would all four of them end up so mature, smart and tough? Oh shudder.

'What did you say, Daddy?' chimed the girls. 'Are you talking to yourself again? What's for breakfast? We're hungry.'

'Violins,' I said, giving them a playful hug.

'Huh?'

'Kids: no wearing swimmers to the breakfast table today, please.'

'We wore them yesterday.'

'Not today. Mr Lin's coming.'

'But Amanda's wearing hers, Dad. Look out the window. See?' Near my bikinied eldest daughter, toplessly sunning herself before the whole of Hong Kong in all her abbreviated beauty, was a golden statue of a smiling Buddha gazing straight at her. I must remember to drape a towel over him.

Suddenly startled, I heard a loud jet engine whining its high pitch right above us. Accustomed to jet noises almost every day of my life, I was not, however, used to hearing one so close overhead. Of course, it was the most honourable Mr Ho Lin, Chairman of the Shenzhen Orient Hong Kong Bank, descending upon us like a god from Heaven in his private Bell Jet Ranger.

'Okay, he's here. Get dressed girls. Put some nice things on, please.' Then I yelled out the bay windows, 'Mandy, Mr Lin's here. Can you put some clothes on and pretend you're not a half-naked American heiress with ten million bucks to throw around? Quickly!'

Mandy yelled back, 'I can hear it myself, Dad! A helicopter landing right on top of us isn't exactly . . . ' but the rest of her words were drowned out by the big screaming turbine just metres away; starting to spool down from full revs. I was surprised that this time it was landing on our balcony deck beside the enormous swimming pool – not on the rooftop helipad marked "H". As we felt its massive blast of hot air and saw garden flora horizontally stiffen, I chuckled at the sight of Mandy struggling to slip on her bikini top in the whooshing downdraughts.

Growing up early, sassy, and too big for her boots – or boobs - was my parental lament. At least my three younger girls all presented their best smiles and well-dressed selves to the jolly Mr Lin as he alighted from his aerial chariot. Instantly, three white-coated waiters materialised from somewhere within the swirling dust storms to scurry around the balcony tables; unloading silver food bowls and crystal glassware.

'Mr Lin, a great pleasure yet again,' I greeted him with a firm handshake. Lin bowed deeply and respectfully, extending his bow to the girls. As the jet's howling abated at last, the girls asked if they could play inside it. Mr Lin beamed with pleasure and said 'Certainly.' He waved his pilot away as though flicking a fly, so the kids hopped gleefully inside after scrambling under the slowly-spinning rotor blades. I warned them: 'Now, don't you press any buttons, girls,' but Lin countered:

'It is not a problem. They must enjoy their holiday.'

I suppose it's not too often that anyone partakes in a sumptuous breakfast banquet whilst sitting beside a jet helicopter as they gaze over one of the world's most breathtaking skylines. As waiters fussed around me with pink champagne – a substance I couldn't abide at breakfast time – I was uncomfortably dreading the esteemed Mr Lin's undoubted knowledge, and reaction to, our silly and reckless pantomime in his bank yesterday.

Then Mandy appeared from her small balcony garden. Almost tripping over the helicopter's landing skids, she yelled through its windows to repeat my warning to her three sisters crammed into the two front seats: 'Just don't touch *anything*, you lot!'

A naughty answer came back: 'We already did and all these funny lights came on.' Luckily Mr Lin appeared politely unconcerned, although he stole a furtive glance at my big daughter, still attired – or *unattired* – in a glittering gold bikini the size of a full stop in a sentence.

After polite greetings, our banking host commenced his nine-course repast with eagerness. We joined him in respectful silence. Was he going to make me await my fate in dreadful suspense as I gulped ice cream and pavlova with cherries on top, or would the coup de grace ensue forthwith? Or maybe he simply knew nothing of yesterday's antics and we'd avoided the slippery precipice?

My trepidation was so acute that I barely noticed three voices beseeching us from the chopper: 'Can we please have our breakfast inside here? It'd be so cool and we could take photos to show everyone at school!'

Ignoring the fact that at any moment a jet helicopter with three kids at the controls might take off right beside our champagne ice bucket, Mandy decided to jump the gun and open the case for the Defence: 'Mr Lin, did your staff enjoy my American accent yesterday?' I gulped, spilling ice cream and pavlova down the front of my expensive new Hong Kong shirt, then prepared to leap from the balcony.

Without even glancing up from his food, Mr Lin replied, 'Not really. It was all rather amateurish, I'm told.'

Mandy smiled, then said, 'Mr Lin, we greatly appreciate this wonderful generosity you have given us this week, but I intend to become the General Manager of Sky Star in about two years, so I won't jeopardise my future career by immediately selling up everything my father's worked for so very hard for before I've even started. And I certainly won't watch you flog it off soon after that for double the amount. I'm sure my father will back me up when I say this.'

'He will?' my mind raced. 'Her father will? Hang on, *I'm* her father!' This flight plan was headed for disaster – if it hadn't spiralled out of control already. For me this was suddenly a make or break point; I either stood beside Mandy now or apologised profusely to our host before he lost any more face.

Ho Lin didn't look at us, but silently continued his sumptuous repast as though deep in thought. Then, just as he opened his mouth to reply, we were interrupted again with insistent voices from the Bell: 'Well, can we please? We want our breakfast in here.'

Lin glanced at his waiters with annoyance, and flicked his head towards the helicopter. They sprang into obedient action like a fleet of startled gazelles, hurrying to convey a feast fit for three royal princesses playing helicopter pilots. Then he spoke dismissively to Mandy beside him: 'Miss Grant, you are a schoolgirl. In China, schoolgirls go to school . . . *and* they wear clothes!'

But Mandy fired back a lightning riposte: 'Mr Lin: in China, do sixty-year-old men ask fifteen-year-old girls out to dinner?'

Lin nervously cleared his throat and replied, 'Mr Sung is one of my most highly respected investment managers. He has a lovely wife, four children and seven grandchildren . . . '

'So?'

I interrupted this imminent declaration of war with, 'Now everyone just cool down here, please. Mr Lin, firstly let me state clearly to you that Mandy has really caught me on the hop with her quite, ah, confronting attitude towards you today. So I apologise if she has offended you in any way, but I must also say that I agree with her about how hard I worked to create and build my little airline. I was only twenty when I started it all with one old jet. Almost at the same time, I married a wonderful woman who already had three children. Soon after we had her fourth child, she died from cancer. Instantly I became a widower with four young ones to care for, plus I had to get a new airline off the ground - in my spare time, so to speak. So I was rather concerned when our little play-acting yesterday uncovered your bank's intentions to buy up all my work so that either you - or other players could muscle into the Australian aviation scene with a minimum of effort or risk. In other words: without having contributed anything.'

I think he replied – but no-one heard him say: 'Except our money!' but instead we heard those shrill voices again:

'Aw, we didn't get any ice cream with it. It's not fair, because you all got some and we didn't!'

While I wondered if it was a crime in Hong Kong to murder your kids, Lin forced a smile through gritted teeth. 'Such . . . charming children. Nonetheless, Mr Grant, I was just about to enquire from your good self – before you all leave tomorrow . . . how much?'

I asked, 'How much what?'

He said, 'Exactly how much do you want for your small airline? What price would be satisfactory to you? Right now?'

All I could think to say was, 'Are you serious?'

'Do I look like a joker? I am prepared to give you a cheque for ten million dollars before you leave tomorrow - and this time it will be quite genuine. Remember, Mr Grant, I do not write fake cheques.'

As I contemplated this almost insulting offer – after all, it was for a *whole* airline - a little voice started to pipe up again from nearby. Lin spun and hissed sharply at a waiter. 'For Heaven's sake, get some damned ice cream to those . . . delightful children! Now!'

'Well?' Lin confronted me, completely ignoring an angry Mandy beside him whose face looked like Mount Vesuvius about to blow. 'Ten million, Mr Grant. In your hand tomorrow.'

My failure to produce any words was due to the rapid turn in events brought on, in part, by my own daughter's brazen words, but more accurately by myself. I'd been the very person pushing hard behind her to grow up faster than normal and become a company general manager while still a teenager. I almost forced her to leave school and her friends and her teenage fun days behind and enter the commercial grind of high finance, high pressure and high worries. It was me. I couldn't apportion the blame for her behaviour onto her now because it was mine. So, she'd dutifully taken my urgings on board and, with typical teenage logic, produced a full-scale onslaught of the opposition, including waving the sexual allurement flag at veteran businessmen in order to acquire secure information. Hell, now things were happening faster than a flame-out at 35,000 feet!

But what would I say? What *could* I say? Mr Lin was standing up, wiping his face with a laced napkin. The show was over. His pilot, who must have received mental telepathy signals somehow, was striding towards his chopper; his face grim and perturbed. The white-coated waiters, having finally delivered the long-awaited ice cream, again scurried towards the machine after whipping the thousand-dollar tablecloth from the marble table like a magician on stage. I half expected to see flocks of white cockatoos suddenly zoom skywards and go squawking over the balcony rail.

Then Mandy stood up abruptly, knocking over her chair. I had never seen such anger on her face before. '**NO!**' she screamed into the shocked face of Mr Lin. 'Ten million dollars for a whole bloody *airline?* No, no and **NO**!'

Ho Lin shrugged with disdain, then strode angrily towards his helicopter as he admonished me with a wagging finger. 'Robert, I do not negotiate the acquisition of companies with *children* in bikinis! What do *YOU* say, Robert?'

Decisively, I backed her up. 'WE say no!'

It was right at this historical moment that three sweet little voices chorused from the chopper's side window: 'We were just trying to say thank you so much for the lovely ice cream, Mr Lin. But could we please have chocolate flavour next time? Ah . . . is anything the matter?'

Very soon the departing chopper ascended towards a small cloud as I smiled at the three youngies: 'Well done, kids. I couldn't have scripted that better myself.'

They wrinkled their noses and said 'Huh?'

28.

We sat together, courtesy once again of the honourable Mr Ho Lin, in the first class lounge of our Cathay Pacific Boeing 747, winging our way home to Australia. With Celia sitting on my lap, we both gazed from the jumbo's small window and down at the seemingly endless lines of parallel red sand dunes that march across north-western Australia; delineating our flight track from Hong Kong to Sydney via Singapore. As Emmie and Olivia were entranced with the movies playing on the seat-backs in front of them, Amanda read fashion magazines and text books about business management. I smiled; my four young friends and I, high in the sky. And oh, what an interesting holiday we'd had; to be sure, to be sure.

'Mandy, listen up for a moment, mate,' I interrupted her. 'Just going over it again: we can't tell anyone about all this, okay? Only Cynthia - in case she's confronted with any leaks. She needs to know some details soon to thwart the Press; otherwise they'll know she's stalling. And Dave? We'll have to tell him, of course. But none of your friends, okay. It's very complicated, but we can't let gossip start flying about company mergers, take-overs, etc. The ramifications are incalculable and the pitfalls too numerous to mention.'

'What are ram stations and pit bulls, Dad,' asked Celia. 'Why do you and her use such big words all the time?'

'Oh, makes us sound important, I guess. I'm just telling Mandy to forget our talks with nice Mr Lin. Let's just remember the fun we had, okay? It was a wonderful free holiday that he paid for, so we should always be thankful to him for that.'

Celia asked, 'So will Mr Lin forget how we put our chewing gum on the pilot's red button in his helicopter, too?'

'What red button?'

'On the end of that handbrake lever thingy . . . you know, that he pulls up. Do you think he might get stuck to it?'

Yikes! The 'collective' handle. I suddenly envisaged a dreadful headline: *Sky Star boss main suspect in HK bank mogul's fiery chopper plunge!*

Mandy laughed, 'I can't believe you did that, Celie. I can't believe we did *anything* that we actually did - or said. Can you Dad? And his stingy offer: he wants to give us ten million for something worth at least twenty. What an insult!'

I said, 'It's just business, my dear Mandy . . . er, Cindy. Anyway, you must be the only teen in the world's history to knock back that sort of offer. You could write a book about that and no-one would believe it.'

'Believe what? And why did you call her Cindy?' asked Olivia. Mandy replied, 'I wasn't about to throw away my whole career and your entire business before I'd even started - for peanuts. If we'd taken that money then what the heck would we do for the rest of our lives? I've got about seventy years left to live; how would it be if I knew I'd tossed away a career like that when I was only fifteen? Anyway, we've already got more than enough money; more than most people anywhere will ever have – haven't we Dad?'

I whispered, 'Yes, but *shoosh* please! Not too loud or we mightn't have a *thing*. Mr Lin's take-over plans might be just the *first* we encounter. There's sure to be others. But, come to think of it, I wouldn't like to be a predatory raider once you take the reins. And anyway, his bank's pot plants are all plastic.'

'Are they?'

'Believe me. I spent an hour being strangled by them.'

'Why would a pot plant try to strangle you, Dad?' asked Emily.

No-one knew, and the studious one didn't care either; she'd re-buried her nose in books. Celia yawned. 'I'm tired. When do we land?'

'In a few hours,' I said. 'Then it's back to school first thing in the morning for the lot of you. Back to work for me, too.' I thought of my second check flight, due tomorrow. I'd better pass the thing or my position in the company might become laughable. Dozing off, I could see huge green tentacles encircled my neck, pulling tighter and tighter.

29.

Home, sweet home. We were back into our daily routine at sunrise the next morning. Olivia was suffering headaches while Amanda felt too unwell from Asian food to go to school. Emily reported that our horse *Sky,* being cared for next door, was also sick and needed the Vet, while Celia was fine and happy – as usual – but couldn't find her school bag *anywhere.*

Me? I was fighting cold dread as I drove to work. Today was to be the check flight to regain my captaincy. If I failed again I'd probably be flying a desk around the office and would certainly cause a few headlines on many grapevines where I'd likely be called 'Captain Laughing Stock.'

On arrival at Mascot airport, Cynthia Nilsen, my trusty PR officer, related a dozen issues that she'd neatly dealt with; and Marie Westcott needed a talk about the two staff she'd fired.

'Fired?' I gulped. 'Don't mention that word please, because I'll probably be next! Ah, what were they fired for, Marie?'

She answered, 'One was making discriminatory allegations about another person being gay; and an engineer was put off by Peter Woods for falsely certifying his time sheets.'

'Oh, for Heaven's sake,' I sighed. 'Allegations? Is this important stuff, Marie? Really? I hate the thought of anyone losing their job. And we especially don't want to lose good people. It costs a fortune to hire and train them in the first place.'

Deadpan, Marie replied, 'You authorised me to be Chief of Staff, so that's what I do.'

'All right, then. What's next?'

'Mr Tolman wants to see you soon. Oh, did you have a nice holiday?'

'It was very . . . *uplifting.* Ask Mr Tolman to grace me with his jovial presence, will you.'

Ken Tolman entered my tiny office and, without preamble, announced, 'I've arranged for Rajiv Singh from Qantas to check you

161

this afternoon. Singh's an Indian check captain from Air India on secondment to Qantas for six months. He only flies 747's but I asked to borrow him because we help them out likewise from time to time. Fair and objective testing, eh? Anyway, he wears a turban on the flight deck apparently, so nothing like a bit of variety, I suppose. Apart from that, I've never met him – so good luck.'

I felt like asking does he also play the sitar and enjoy himself whilst in-flight, but let it drop. 'Thanks Ken. And yes, we did have a good holiday – in case you were wondering. We went touring Hong Kong in a chopper. The girls stuck chewing gum onto its collective handle so it's probably crashed by now.'

Tolman laughed, then looked somewhat contrite, saying, 'Look, about all *that* business before: you've no idea the amount of flak I've copped over it. I believed I was in the right, but I guess the jury's still out on it. Anyway, you got a free holiday from that Mr Lung. Did he try to buy you out?'

'It's Mr *Lin*. It doesn't matter because he's probably dead from his chopper crash, anyway. Let's call it all quits Ken, and I'll concentrate on passing this flight test with Captain Curry.'

Ken smiled as he walked out, 'It's Captain Singh. And just remember, don't taxi back to the terminal for anything.'

'Funny, Ken. Have a nice day – if you possibly can.'

*

Rajiv Singh was a kindly gentleman of fifty-nine who planned to retire from flying airliners the next year. We shook hands on entering the 737 flight deck for our afternoon run to Brisbane and return.

Singh said, 'It's a very great pleasure to make your acquaintance, Captain Grant. I must state that, dear me, I was most perplexed to hear of your recent flight test and its subsequent uproar. This was indeed a much discussed subject over at Qantas. Meanwhile, I am sure that no Indian airline has an owner who also flies, so we have no precedent with which to judge this peculiar matter. I have decided, therefore, to simply ignore any previous events in your company and concentrate solely and objectively upon your flying competence as a captain today. Do you agree?'

'Certainly,' I sighed with relief. 'And thank you, Rajiv.'

'Robert,' Singh added as we started the twin jet engines, 'you are the number one pilot for Sky Star; therefore it is my belief that you must already be totally competent in your duties – otherwise you would never have attained and held such a position. Myself? I have not flown 737's for over three years now - only 747-200's, so I intend to sit back today and relax in your experienced hands.'

Singh continued, 'I will only interfere should I observe you taking any dangerous or reckless actions, in which case I will fail you immediately. However, I do not expect any such occurrences and am already confident of your complete success.'

Phew! And so was I. The test was a breeze; after all, I'd been flying planes since before I was a teenager, and flying jets from the age of eighteen. My logbook now boasted over eleven thousand hours' experience, making this run to Brisbane a *breeze* on a sunny day where not even the faintest ripples of turbulence nudged the airframe. We were also exactly on time.

Just prior to landing, the ever-smiling Singh enquired if I had any family; then, without waiting, commenced relating the details of his large family back home in India. I had to interrupt him: 'Rajiv, I would really love to discuss our families over coffee during the turn-around, but not now, please. I don't allow any private chit-chat inside of one hundred DME. Sorry. Company regulations.'

There is a proper time and place for private conversations on a flight deck. Cockpit voice recorders, or CVR's, always record the last thirty minutes' conversation of every flight. Therefore, should there be any incident or accident, private chats are viewed as not only distracting to both pilots, but frowned upon by accident investigators who can rightly assert that the pilots involved were obviously not concentrating as they should. DME is the slant-range distance in nautical miles from your plane to an airport or en-route beacon.

Turning onto final approach, the turbaned Captain Singh announced, 'Robert, I have already signed your flight check sheet as passed. Your flying is immaculate, as expected. But had you engaged in that private conversation with me just then, I would have changed it immediately to *Failed!* I was testing you out, Robert. My congratulations to you. Now, let's land this aircraft, shall we?'

The sly old fox!

*

Straight back to the top of the pilot's list did I merrily zoom. Not that any congratulatory comment was forthcoming from our Chief Pilot - although Dave Skillen sighed with heartfelt relief and smiled, 'Just as well, Robbie.' At last my nightmares of *Captain Laughing Stock* could evaporate.

Putting all *that* behind me, I said, 'Now Dave, let me tell you about my recent little family holiday. Well, it all started when we boarded our big jumbo jet to fly up to Asia . . . '

'How much?' asked Skillen.

'How much what? Gee, you sound like the Honourable Mr Lin, Esquire.'

'How much did he offer you?'

'Ten.'

'Holy flying Boeings! *Ten million* dollars? What did you say?'

'I didn't say anything – at first. But my daughter yelled at him: *No, no and NO!*'

'Your daughter? You mean the little one in primary school? Or the ones that talk to ducks? Or the teenager with the messy bedroom?'

'They've *all* got messy bedrooms, Dave. The biggest one who's been training with you so you can retire and go fishing.'

Dave Skillen hissed a long breath. 'Oh that one. Robbie, are you seriously telling me that you allowed a fifteen-year-old to speak on behalf of our company; and that the said fifteen-year-old refused a take-over bid of ten million dollars while you just stood there: fat, dumb and useless?'

'No, I was sitting down. And I was in partial shock. How did you know he was going to offer, Dave?'

'It wasn't hard to guess. That's why he flew you there. I think you'd better tell me the whole story, Robbie. The truth, the whole truth and nothing but the truth – so help you God.'

So that's what I attempted to do – so help me God. However, Dave didn't quite believe several chapters of my astonishing tale. Especially not the part about the rich little American heiress with her millions of oil dollars. Or me sitting in exile in the bank's foyer; posing as her bodyguard. Or the sweaty and pop-eyed Mr Sung who divulged his bank's secret take-over intentions to a young girl just off the street.

'It's all true, Dave,' I insisted. But he wasn't sure about the helicopter tale, and how it landed right beside our breakfast banquet. White-coated waiters? Maybe. And he still doubted that innocent little Amanda swaggered up to the Chairman of the Shenzhen Orient Hong Kong Bank in a bikini and yelled in his face to reject an offer of ten million dollars. Ditto for the tale about two of my girls who sabotaged the man's helicopter with chewing gum.

Dave was unsure where the real truth lay, but had some other big news for me that *was* true. It was that CASA had told him they were probably about to temporarily ground the whole of Ansett Airlines' fleet due to aircraft defects and shoddy maintenance. This would leave a gaping hole in Australia's air travel with the result that Sky Star, along with Qantas of course, would need to 'gear-up' to hurl everything they owned into the sky.

After a brief discussion, we therefore cancelled all flight crew leave and advised everyone to prepare for a massive bookings rush. In the maintenance hangars, we rescheduled non-essential work for later and spruced up our fleet of twenty-one 737's for a possible 24-hour operating schedule. 'And this might not be Ansett's only grounding,' Dave added.

Personally, this was quite an inconvenient time for me to be rostered for maximum working hours; however I could hardly shrink from it and leave others to carry the load. Yet, right now all my (motherless) girls needed me more than ever. Very soon I would have *four* teenagers to manage; a thought that gave me great reservations and fears because of my sole parent predicament. While I absolutely adored having these wonderful girls in my life, they were all nevertheless subject to the normal pitfalls and temptations of today's society. They would go through the usual teenage romances and breakups, illnesses and growing pains. The mundane grind of schoolwork, and the enjoyment of sports and dances. Triumphs and disappointments: they were all before them and they needed at least one parent who could hopefully guide and assist them.

For me: I merely had to run an airline twice as hard while another was going broke, and dodge take-over raids from smiling sharks with razor teeth. In my spare time, while being the perfect father, I hoped to get Amanda trained to run the whole shebang by the age of eighteen because my number-one man was going fishing.

30.

One night, a woman named Victoria from a neighbouring farm called on us to enlighten me in plain words that, far from being the perfect parent, I was actually a *neglectful* father who shouldn't be leaving four young girls alone on our farm for such long hours. And, while I was quite an important figure in Australian society, I 'had no rights', apparently, 'to leave a fifteen-year-old in charge of the entire household for sometimes days at a time.'

'She's sixteen now, Vicky,' I meekly corrected her.

'It doesn't matter,' the woman persisted. 'They need supervision. They're very nice kids, but are always riding around the district after school, visiting from house to house and playing in the fields until late. And who makes them come inside at dark? Their big sister, apparently. But what if Amanda's busy cooking the dinner, studying or on the phone? They're a bit too young to be out, don't you think, Mr Grant? They need parental guidance. Surely you can afford a housekeeper or somesuch if you can so easily afford all those big jets?'

Hmm, I digested these stark truisms then offered a feeble defence. 'Well, they like riding their bikes and their horse, like all the local kids do. And they're not the only ones out there. They're just having healthy fun. It's a safe community around here.' But the woman was a social worker and could possibly make trouble for us, so I agreed with her arguments and promised I'd take some action. But what? I always felt very frustrated when faced with frequent demands like these to miraculously provide our home with a wife/mother of some sort, as though I were a magician whipping rabbits from a hat.

A round-table family discussion ensued after dinner, but failed to reach any mutual conclusions. I said we needed a live-in housekeeper - like our friendly Alicia McNeil from when they were younger - but no-one wanted to risk getting some dominating house ma'am or authoritarian camp guard policing their every move. In any case, what stranger suddenly thrust amongst them could tackle four active teenagers they didn't know?

I raised my voice. 'Too bad. You're still just kids. You'll do what I say - otherwise I'll sell you off to the slave traders!'

Celia giggled that I always say that, and asked was it true? Mandy quipped, 'I hope so,' then added that soon she'd be going to full-time work with Mr Skillen at the airport, so that would leave the three youngies totally unsupervised for much of the time, plus no-one to cook their meals. This was unacceptable and couldn't be allowed. Meanwhile, the Ansett grounding could start at any moment and I might be gone for days at a time . . . again.

Our family summit meeting left me fatigued and worried. I would need an immediate solution here, but I also faced a week of mayhem in the skies. In flight, I simply used my weather radar to swerve around storms, climb above them or duck underneath, while here on the ground I had four growing humans demanding their *rights,* insisting on exploring the world and generally looking far too pretty for their own damn good. No magical radar screen could conveniently divert me around these energy-charged adolescents on roller skates, and no immediate solutions would tumble from the sky like the Red Baron's victims. At six in the morning I might be gone, yet I shouldn't be leaving them at all. As if someone could read my deep concerns, the phone call soon came: the grounding was on! We would be airborne for perhaps a week solid.

At our farm gate at sunrise, I leant from my Jaguar's window as Olivia and Emily kissed me goodbye. I didn't know when I'd be back. 'Don't worry, you silly Daddy,' vowed Livvy sincerely, 'we'll be really, really good. We promise.' No, they might *try* to behave, but would inevitably feel the urge to run free like any kids, and the endless temptations of that big world outside would inexorably pull them in other directions - unless I installed and an armed camp of SAS soldiers with a brace of snapping Rottweilers to guard my little princesses. Hmm, not a bad idea . . .

Half-way to work, I stopped at a security company near Parramatta. On the spot, I contracted for round-the-clock random security patrols of my family and property, including night patrols every hour from 5pm till 8am.

Winging from the home battlefront and into the turbulent skies, we flew into the airline storm of that week where I discovered that not all Ansett's 138 planes were grounded, but all of their Boeing 767's *were.* This left Qantas and Sky Star to somehow provide seats for an extra 29,000 stranded travellers every day. Cracks in the wings of Ansett's ageing 767's ensured we'd enjoy some golden profits until they were cleared by CASA to fly again; but we'd all have to work like demons to achieve such bounty.

I calculated the numbers and told Qantas we might manage to carry an extra 6,100 people per day while they'd have to cope with the rest. But this would only be after we flogged our twenty-one 737's for an extra two interstate flights per day each; and at all hours up until midnight while still carrying our own regular passengers.

As it was entirely impractical for me to drive fifty kilometres home to the farm each night then be back on the job at 6am, I slept on a fold-out bunk in our cramped airport headquarters behind the engineering hangars. And that left four little devils at home: safely guarded, I hoped, by patrols - plus my *Plan B.*

Amongst frantic re-arranging of our entire airline timetable and staff rostering schedules, I pleaded with Cynthia Nilsen *(Plan B)* to take up lodgings at our home for the week – or however long the Ansett groundings might last, before I was presented with the *Neglectful Father of the Year* award from our prying neighbours. Cynthia obligingly agreed, but soon after moving in she insisted I provide a proper office environment for her to remotely run her PR position; with internet, phones and fax machines – not the dingy and pokey bedroom corner I pretended was my home office.

'What a cheapskate you are,' down-to-earth Cynthia complained over the phone as I awkwardly bit into a tasteless salad roll from the airport cafeteria during brief flight breaks. I'd already flown to Cairns and back in the morning; next was Adelaide return. And always with full passenger, fuel and freight loads. We were trying to cope with surplus passenger numbers that 767's carried - planes almost twice the size of ours, plus get our own clientele to their destinations on time. By the end of this crazy week I was sure we'd have shouldered more loads than Santa Claus.

'What do you mean, *cheapskate*?' I protested in between bites. Cynthia reiterated that from her very first glimpse of my abode she'd made that conclusion. I was disorganised and needed a proper office at my farm - not my labyrinth of twisted cables, computers and assorted junk strewn around a cramped bedroom. She strongly suggested I urgently build a modern office, and that it should be a separate room as an addition to the house. It shouldn't be attached to my bedroom where kids and farm animals come wandering in and out, but joined by a covered walkway from the house. Such an office needed bookshelves, tables and numerous office fittings. And privacy.

'Not just for this week,' she added, 'but as a permanent fixture. I had no idea you called this darkened dungeon your work-from-home office.'

I protested. 'I've never had the time to arrange builders and things. By the way, how are you getting along with the kids? Have they set fire to the farm yet? Or thrown a small party for two hundred of their closest friends?'

Cynthia said, 'They're fine. We all like each other – so far. You know I'm not very good with kids, but neither am I bossy with them so they're polite in return. The youngies even say it's quite novel having a woman in the house and they like it for a change. Actually, they've been *very* well behaved so far.'

'Are you sure you've got the right address?'

'I think so. Anyway, thank goodness they're almost grown up now and not really kids anymore. And they laugh a lot, Rob. That's what I enjoy.'

'Thanks for all this, Cynth. Really appreciated. I've got to rush off for another flight. As you'd know, it's murder this week. We're all exceeding our daily duty hours and CASA says we have to reduce them. But how can we cut down if everyone wants us to fly non-stop? If the media asks you, tell them we never exceed our legal flight times but are covering the extra workload. Let them puzzle that one out.'

Cynthia said, 'I already have. They interview me every day about this Ansett grounding. Don't you read my replies in the papers?'

'Read newspapers?' I laughed. 'In my spare time, you mean? Listen Cynth, I like your idea of renovations. So let's just do it. Get that new home office built pronto, will you? Ask local builders if they can start now and have it finished in a week. Just pay whatever they quote, okay? Better still: offer them double pay for two shifts a day *each*. Plus bonuses. Tell the girls I love them and miss them. And Cynthia, where are you sleeping – by the way?'

'Where do you think, Rob? In the barn with *Sky?* Or in the hangar with that horrid little blue flying *thing* – whatever it is? I'm in your room, Rob. There's nowhere else, is there? You don't even have a spare room for guests.'

With a wry smile but some embarrassment, I realised that she was the very first woman to sleep in my bed – albeit alone – since my Cristina died over eleven years ago. Could this be a record, and would I be able, one day, to get her out? Would I even want to?

Before she hung up, I added, 'I just had another brilliant thought: design the new room, then double its size. And throw on an adjoining bedroom too – a spare guest room. I've got great plans, Cynth. Now I've really gotta fly. See you.'

'Bye. Don't forget to put your wheels down,' she laughed.

'Before or after landing?'

Miracles *can* occur, and somehow we survived that hectic week of Ansett's grounding. But not before our whole airline worked like crazy to get ours, and the extra six thousand Ansett passengers, to their numerous destinations throughout the country - and mostly on time. Meanwhile, in just one week I'd privately made such a haystack of profit from this extra trade that it easily surpassed the relatively trivial costs of my home renovations. Even better, in the following months we noted with much pleasure that quite a few regular Ansett travellers had switched over to Sky Star.

*

Bonanza or not, this frantic week's activity was not exactly what our retiring General Manager considered as fun as he stared at his last few months at the helm of Sky Star Airlines. He complained bitterly about being harassed by 'everyone on Earth,' it seemed – especially CASA officials and the media. 'I had queues of people banging on my office door every day, Robbie. Queues!' Unfortunately, Dave's unhealthy complexion and frequent red blushes had returned, and we needed this like a hole in the fuselage of a 737. For myself, I desperately needed a rest.

I attempted to spend a few restful and rewarding days at home after our frantic week, but instead we were deafened by the machine-gun hammering of builders. I eventually phoned Dave with my response to our woes. 'Listen Dave, this is how it's going to be. I've thought it all through and we're going ahead with plan *B*.'

'What's plan B?'

'*B* is the opposite of *A* where you are working yourself to death at the airport while queues of people bang on your door. They won't be banging on your door anymore because you won't be there.'

'You mean I'm fired?'

'Don't be silly, Dave. Your new office will be out here on the farm; nestled cosily and peacefully amongst the rolling fields and the quacking ducks, dogs 'n geese. I'm building a whole new quarters, semi-detached to the rear of the farm; just past the pool and gardens. It'll be an electronic delight with every conceivable state-of-the-art device, plus all the finest office furniture and fittings. We'll have more stuff than you'll ever need to work from home, as they call it.'

Dave interrupted, 'Now, wait a minute there. Firstly, I'm not driving from Middle Harbour to the Simpson Desert and back every day in the Sydney traffic. Second, I'm not into this trendy *work from home* caper - as you call it. I meet people face to face. I'm the General Manager of an *airline*, not a damn hobby farm. It's an airline which, strangely enough, is based at an *airport* which is located right here beside Botany Bay! So why would any airline GM exile himself beside the foothills of the damn Blue Mountains, for Christ's sake? Can you tell me that?'

'Because you'll be dead soon if you don't.'

'What!'

I said, 'Dave, only a few months to go, remember? Your health is obviously suffering again. Especially after the Ansett thing. I'll bet your doctor has already told you so. You don't need any new hassles, problems or worries. Think of your shiny new boat and all those happy fish just busting to be reeled in. In a week these new additions will all be completed. It'll be up and running. You will sleep here – at the farm. You don't *need* to be physically located where you are now; you can perform all your duties as the world's greatest GM from out here. *And* you can train Amanda in the job without either of you ever having to leave home.'

After a silence, he asked, 'Do I get to camp with the horse or the pigs?'

'We don't have any pigs, Dave, but my kids like to dress up as Miss Piggy sometimes. No, you'll have your own brand new room next to the office. You can live there during the week, then go home every weekend if you like. And you'll have Cynthia right next door in the other room for company.'

'Cynthia! That red-haired volcano? She'd murder me in my sleep!'

'I'll keep her on a leash in case of eruptions. She'll be living here for a while, too. She's helping to referee my kids while also working from here.'

Dave paused, then replied, 'It just doesn't seem right: this working remotely from a business's location. You need to be *on the job*, Robbie, not squatting out in the middle of the damn Simpson Desert when things go wrong.'

'Dave, it's an electronic world now. Microsoft runs a global empire from its headquarters in America, and NASA operates its Earth orbiting satellites from Houston. When things go wrong they send astronauts up on the Space Shuttle to fix them. They don't need their General Manager to personally don a spacesuit and go up there himself. Why don't you come out at take a look around our renovations? You never know, you might even like it here. You haven't even *been* here except for that once at night time.'

I heard a moan. 'Oh, all right then. I'll come out next week when it's all completed. Would I have to supervise all the kindergarten children, too?'

'Only on party days, Dave. You can be the class clown. Surely it would be better than living where you are by yourself? You'll have plenty of that soon enough. You'll be okay here for a few months; just bring your clown suit.'

'Very funny, Robbie,' Dave grumbled as he hung up.

One problem solved simply, now on to the next. Cynthia and I were getting on very well – much to my girls' giggling mirth and sly winks. She wasn't exactly a volcano, as Dave had joked, but an intelligent and tough character from a background of universities and journalism. A forceful woman who knew her path in life and generally stated exactly what she meant. If she issued an order to my troops, they mostly obeyed it. The girls never back-answered with: 'We don't have to do everything you say,' because they knew it would offend me and my new relationship with Cynthia. So far the waters were running reasonably smoothly in our extended family, and I hoped for no turbulence ahead while we eagerly waited for our new home renovations to be completed and the arrival of our honourable General Manager to complete the picture.

31.

Dave Skillen drove through our gate in his shiny Mercedes 450SL; rather a change from his dusty old Landrover of our homestead days, I noted. Builders and their equipment were everywhere, but the renovations should be completed today, they'd assured me. But just now their final hammering and banging was resonating in a raucous cacophony while the dogs' constant barking was making it worse. The girls were keeping out of the way and were somewhere in the neighbourhood celebrating their last week of school for the year. As Dave's car halted, I snickered to Cynthia. 'Listen to him have a whinge. He'll find something to complain about straight away.'

Instead, our dear Dave stepped out smiling, then ambled ostentatiously past us to inspect our farm in the daylight – for the first time. He bowed with polite exaggeration and nodded *Good Day* to the builders, then strolled on to observe the tilers on the roof. After that, he circled the property while stepping over debris; then checked the farm outhouses with their chooks and ducks and geese ponds while two Labradors scampered excitedly around his heels. Then he peered into our rusty hangar and gazed at our rough airstrip running downhill away from the front sliding doors. He pointed inside to my old two-seat Gazelle, 'Is that Sky Star's new flagship?'

'Sure is,' I laughed. 'And you're our first lucky passenger.'

Dave peered timidly through its tiny perspex window and smiled, 'Where's First Class? I always travel in First.' We eagerly followed him around the yard to watch him poke his nose into here and there. I showed him where his room and office would be – almost completed and ready for action. In all, there were more than twenty workers on the site. I explained that I'd paid them to work around the clock until Sky Star was up, up and away again from its shiny new Headquarters complex.

I asked, 'Well Dave, what do you think? I haven't heard you complain about anything yet.'

In a surprise response, Dave nodded approval, 'I actually think I like it. My sister was on the phone earlier and told me to jump at this chance. To get away from that horrible pressure at the airport and work part-time in a much more peaceful setting. She said to train that young girl to take over as soon as she can – or else, give it all away. I've got no wife to nag me, so Julie is my sole advisor these days. She said I'll be dead if I keep slaving away at Mascot, so I should spend my last months out here – in the Simpson bloody Desert.'

'Well, it's not quite the Simpson,' Cynthia laughed, 'but you can hear the crows cawing in the morning. Better than jet engines howling.'

I asked, 'Dave, do you feel comfortable with my Amanda? Can you honestly work with her for a while? It's important for me to know.'

'Of course I do,' he answered with candour. 'She reminds me of young Melanie who worked in my Dubbo office for years. A fine lass, but got married and left.'

'Do you think she'll cope with it? At her age?'

'Well, she's quite mature and level-headed, but she'll need a mind like a computer to remember everything. Luckily she's young, while my mind's old and worn. After my departure, she'll need real guts to stand up to men. Ah, did she really say all those things to our Mr Lin? If she can confront a bank Chairman like that, she can overcome anything – I hope.'

I said, 'I believe she can do it. However, Cynthia's still answering banal media questions about this *young girl* - as though Amanda's still in primary school, or something. We've been through all that with them repeatedly. But a fourteen-year-old girl recently climbed Mt. Everest - they say she almost *ran* up it, and women now fly airliners and some run corporations. So, while eighteen won't be all *that* experienced, I don't see why she can't learn to cope as I had to. Meanwhile, there'll be an advisor to ride along with her for a while.'

'Yes, who'll be doing it when I go?' Dave asked. 'Who's the interim manager?'

176

'Me.'

'What!' Dave gasped. 'You? Run this whole circus and fly as well? No way. It can't be done and you know it. It's been consuming at least fifty hours a week of my time, so how will you find time to fly another thirty hours after that, Mister Miracle Man?'

'I won't need to. I'm taking a year off flying, Dave. That's how. There's lots of young people out there hungry for a pilot's job, so we'll hire another new pilot, move someone else up the ladder to captain, then give myself a really well-earned break from flying. I've done almost twenty years of non-stop flying without even one proper holiday, except for that short week in Hong Kong. I know I often claimed that I only wanted to fly and not to manage, but things change and I must change with them. Just consider if I became sick and failed my medical test one day – and it's always possible for any pilot to suddenly have his wings clipped, then I'd hopefully be competent to assist and oversee Amanda in her office duties. But I need a rest from flying, Dave. I've worked damned hard.'

Dave added, 'And raised four kids by yourself. Hell's bells, I've never even raised *one*. But father and daughter in an office together? Running an airline? I've never had any kids, as I said, but it sure sounds like a recipe for troubled waters to me. Be careful. You need to discuss these things with her first. What if you two have a big conflict?'

'I'll fire her - or she can fire me.' We all laughed, then Cynthia sensibly suggested we don't jump ahead of ourselves when prudence suggested one cautionary step at a time.

She added, 'I agree with Dave that you take all precautions beforehand to avoid any major blow-ups with your daughter. You shouldn't ever allow any bad blood to damage the family or the company - at any cost.'

It was agreed that we all stop jumping the gun and commence work in our shiny new premises the following day; then slowly observe how it all pans out. Cynthia offered to independently arbitrate any disputes that may arise, with her rulings to be *final*. Things were shaping up nicely so far, it seemed, and our precious Dave, entering his final working stretch, seemed contented enough. I'd achieved some sort of supervision for my naughty children, I mean *active* children, and maybe even won a new lady friend. I wondered, however, if that certain lady friend, standing right beside me, was feeling likewise.

*

Perhaps in answer, Cynthia returned to the city for a few nights – not wishing to 'crowd' our house, she said. So, on our veranda that night, Mandy smirked at me. 'You're a fast worker, Dad.'

'Why?'

'It's only been eleven years and already you've had another woman in your bed!'

I said, 'Funny, Mandy. She *stayed* in my room for that week when I was away. She'll have her own room soon, or she can go back to her unit in Bondi Junction – whatever she chooses. But everyone will have their room. Mr Skillen will have his new room on week nights, then go home for weekends, and we'll all live happily ever after, amen.'

'Except me,' bawled an upset Celia. 'There's nowhere for me to sleep. Where am I supposed to go?' I quickly counted on my fingers: damn, I'd missed one room. I needed six bedrooms, not five. Even with Emmie and Olivia sharing, we were still one room short with only five because we needed one spare room for guests.

I gave her a crushing cuddle and said, 'Poor little Celie. Maybe the geese will let you camp around their pond. Or you could sleep in the hay with *Sky*; he'd like some company. Or else just stay out in the mud and rain.'

Celia smiled through tears as Mandy taunted me: 'Wants to run an airline, but can't even count how many bedrooms he needs in his own house.' This was our debut father-and-daughter clash and she'd probably won the first round on points. Then she added, 'Or you could simply let Cynthia sleep with you, Dad. Solve everything.'

Oh yes, nodded the three approving youngies. What a clever idea. That would save space. I heard another clang of a bell. Was that round two?

32.

The best laid plans of men and mice . . . often go astray, they say. The handover of the company's reins was proceeding at a reasonable rate, with Dave Skillen contentedly settled into his shiny new office and bachelor's den. Amanda was forging ahead with her Diploma of Business Studies while working as understudy to the retiring GM. Each day, Mrs Shelley White, our chief accountant, was instructing Amanda in the relationship of accounting to management systems and practices, while we sometimes enjoyed guests when my three youngest girls would, on the weekends and after school, bring their pet baby ducks and geese into the new office to show them off.

'This one's name is Horatio,' announced a proud Emily one afternoon to Dave; her pleasant smile always a ray of sunshine to him. But the frightened duck suddenly leapt from her arms and flapped onto Dave's desk where it squawked and made feathers and papers fly everywhere. Then it left a dark greeting on Dave's paperwork. 'And this one's called Adolf because he's always naughty,' smiled Celia nervously, pretending *that* didn't happen. 'Over there is Daisy, and the fat one is Amanda . . . '

Dave brushed himself clean and gasped, 'Ah, very interesting. Thankyou girls. Wonderful, in fact. But we really need to get on with our annual assessments. Perhaps another time we can say hello to Mr Adolf and his dive-bombing squadrons, eh?'

Amanda spun around, her eyes wide. She jumped up, yelling, 'Get out! Get out of here you two! Did that duck just do what I think it did on Mr Skillen's desk? Wait till Dad hears about this. I'm very sorry Mr Skillen. Celia, did you say Amanda is fat? Were you referring to me, by any chance?' The girls and birds bolted from the office to squeals of laughter and retorts of 'Amanda's a fatso! A fatso!'

'Mr Skillen, I'll clean this all up.' Amanda fussed around, and through gritted teeth, glared daggers out the doorway.

Suddenly Dave was strangely quiet, whistling softly and gazing out the window. Perhaps dreaming of his two million-dollar handout which was looming nearer with each passing day. Oh well, a humorous 'duck tale to relate at his farewell function, no doubt.

Turning to the tasks in hand, Dave asked, 'Now, where were we, Amanda? Shelley?' Shelley White replied that they were up to page 91 of the annual assessments of profit and loss from our auditing people. 'Just near that paragraph with the dark yellow stain, actually.'

But Dave didn't smile; instead he was rubbing his forehead in discomfort. 'I'm afraid this is all quite heavy going, ladies. You'll need to be right on top of this Amanda, if you're ever going to run the show. This whole business often worries me, but soon I'll be free of it all . . . Ah, I think I'll just take a quick break outside. Get some sun and fresh air. Won't be long.'

As he left, Amanda promised she'd pursue the heavy slogging, yelling out the window after him: 'Some of it worries me too. Look at all these horrendous annual fuel bills. Why can't we just fly a little slower? Dad says if we drive our cars slower we might use ten percent less petrol. And ten percent off this figure here equals . . . '

From the garden, Dave's rasping voice replied, 'We have a timetable to keep, my dear. No-one ever makes a profit by failing to keep rigidly on time. Still, you're probably right. I don't see why we all have to roar around the skies at five hundred knots - or almost full throttle - wasting excess fuel.'

'Me either,' she agreed. 'If all the airlines slowed their planes down slightly, we should all save fuel and still arrive at about the same time. That would make sense. If we took five minutes longer to fly from Sydney to Melbourne, would it matter? Who cares about five little minutes? I could put my make-up on in that time – or brush my hair. How much fuel would we save doing that, Mr Skillen? Are you still there, Mr Skillen?' She peered out the office window but the old man wasn't to be seen. He'd been looking rather pale and wearied all morning; and just now he'd seemed to be perspiring and a little short of breath. Had he wandered through the gardens and gone to lie down in his room?

Amanda re-buried herself in bookwork, reflecting on her new fuel idea. Ask Dad, was the answer. He'd know - although one would assume that Dad had considered and dismissed the idea long ago. She was suddenly startled by the sounds of birds squawking and running feet approaching the office. Oh no, not those little rats again. A total ban on them coming near the office was in order. Another item for mention to Dad when he gets home.

'Mandy!' Emmie screamed. 'Come quick! Mr Skillen's fallen over near the pool and we can't wake him up.' Racing outside, Amanda pursued her two sisters around the side of house, spying with horror the sight of David Skillen sprawled beside our swimming pool; face down and motionless.

*

'Just tell me again, please. Everything that happened this morning.' My upset girls related the shocking tale of them finding Dave's prostrate body lying beside the pool. Of Shelley White calling an ambulance and it racing down our dirt driveway; then its high-speed departure five minutes later. Amanda sobbed how Dave had seemed reasonably cheery in the morning and was quite good natured about the girls coming into the office, each with a duck in their arms. No, that didn't upset him at all. Most of the time he seemed to thoroughly enjoy the company of my three youngies, and the sinning duck's behaviour was of no relevance.

The last Amanda could recall, they'd been discussing Sky Star's high fuel bills: a perpetual dilemma in these times of soaring fuel costs in the late nineties. Then Dave seemed to be short of breath. It wasn't the first time, but now he'd suffered a stroke.

I established that he was in a stable condition in Nepean Hospital; but incapacitated, of course. As we prepared to dress for a hospital visit, my youngies had tears in their eyes; Celia crying that they'd only been having fun when visiting the office with some pets and that Mr Skillen seemed busy, but was always pleased to see them. Emily added that Dave said the pets were 'interesting and wonderful', while Amanda said, 'Just before he went outside, he told me that work worried him all the time, but he'd soon be free of it all.'

'Gee, I really hope we didn't do anything wrong.' Celia's teary face advertised her genuine concerns and devotion to the man. I suggested that their friendly office visit was sheer coincidence to what had transpired, and that Dave's last remarks were concerning work and his future escape from it through approaching retirement. Nonetheless, I laid all the blame squarely on myself: I could have asked him to retire months earlier - although I'm sure he wouldn't have gone. This was all quite disturbing as Dave had quickly become a much loved part of our family where my girls always sympathised with him having no family except a sister to phone. Here we'd all made him feel totally at home, and the youngies had naturally believed they'd be welcome in his office at any time.

Driving to the hospital, Amanda raised another subject: 'Dad, just a distraction for a while; I've been going through profit statements and all that heavy paperwork, and I'm wondering why we don't save money on our annual fuel bills. I mean, if our planes slow down in flight they use slightly less fuel, don't they? Why can't we fly everywhere five or ten percent slower and arrive a few minutes later? We might save millions.'

I said, 'Save millions? Well, we spent twenty eight million on fuel last year, so it would certainly be desirable. But it's all been thought of before, mate. We're competing with the others every day. We couldn't possibly be arriving late, departing late, and dragging the chain all the time. Five minutes late at every point would accumulate during the day, so by day's end we could find ourselves an *hour* behind – or one whole flight.'

'But Dad,' said my very bright girl, 'if we slowed down, surely the others would eventually do likewise?'

'Why should they?' I asked.

'Because, after Cynthia leaks to the press that Sky Star has just saved, oh, two or three million dollars on fuel in the current year, the others airline managements might feel compelled to copy us.'

'Hmm . . . continue.'

'The last thing Dave said this morning was "No-one ever makes a profit by failing to keep rigidly on time." 'But then he added, "I don't see why we all have to roar around the skies at five hundred knots - or almost full throttle - wasting excess fuel." 'So, if we set the example first, we'd discount our airfares instead of pocketing the fuel savings, then sooner or later they'd have to follow us - or lose business. Voila!'

Her idea certainly possessed merit, but would surely have been thoroughly researched before by clever accounting minds in many other airlines. In this vein, I'd once attempted scratching pertinent fuel figures on paper some years ago, but decided we'd simply lose business while only saving a meagre amount of fuel. However, I wasn't sure if I'd ever raised the matter with Ken Tolman or not, and needed to call him after our hospital visit anyway. There was quite a lot to discuss – apart from in-flight fuel management policies.

Looking cheerless and feeling sorry for himself in his hospital bed, gray-faced Dave Skillen feigned brightness when we arrived, but soon mumbled how he was 'terribly disheartened' by this sudden major health event. We chatted and attempted to cheer him, but he looked quite old, frail and lonely, and his voice was slurred. My girls were sad, especially the two youngies Emmie and Celia who constantly bit their lips in consternation; guilt-ridden that they had somehow contributed to this calamity. They placed four enormous bouquets of flowers on his bed, then presented him with a plastic toy goose. We could tell he loved this because a tear escaped down his cheeks.

Trying to smile, he told them not to worry about the incident with those naughty pets, assuring the kids that next time they came into his office he'd put them on the staff as secretaries. Behind them, I shook my head, silently saying, 'No, he won't be back in that office for a long while – if ever.' In fact, I was suddenly convinced: our nice Mr Skillen was finished in his career with us. Only a few months distant from his retirement anyway, this cruel setback would undoubtedly herald the death-knell of our General Manager's career at Sky Star.

In the hallway outside, I consulted a doctor. He confirmed that Dave would need recuperation for several months at least. I mentioned his approaching retirement. The doctor replied, 'In that case, he should finish up at work now. It would be against his interests to perform any work at his age and present state of health. All strokes are serious and can be life threatening. If he has no pressing financial need to return to work, then you, as the company owner, should not insist he do so – in my opinion.'

I said, no, he certainly doesn't *need* to work again, not mentioning that Dave would receive about two million dollars upon his retirement. The doctor concluded: 'Then this patient should not be managing an airline – or anything else. He needs full-time rest and recovery.'

Visiting hours were soon over and we made our farewells to the disheartened patient as nurses fussed around him. We were saddened as he tightly gripped the littlies' hands, then cuddled them goodbye with tears in his eyes. It was evident from his ghostly appearance that he doubted seeing us again. I struggled with emotion; 'See you tomorrow Dave,' I smiled. 'I've got lots of important stuff to talk about. Mandy has come up with a great new idea and I need your advice on it.'

'Do you really?'

'Of course I do, Dave. I'm just a pilot, remember? Pilots go up in the sky. We can't run this flying circus without you, so you'd best get a good night's sleep.'

'I will, Robbie. My sister Julie should be here in the morning,' he stammered, wiping his eyes. A nurse suddenly whipped the white screen around him and he was gone - just like that.

Outside in the car park, Olivia said it for us all: 'He's kind of like our grandfather, isn't he? We love him so much and don't want him to, ah, die . . . or anything.'

Amanda added, 'No, of course not. We don't have any grand-dad and David's like our only one – even if he's not really family.' Everyone agreed. Actually, the girls *did* have grandparents in New Zealand who had, for unfathomable reasons, abandoned them to me years before they'd lost their daughter Cristina. They'd since played no part in the girls' lives – particularly having never contributed to their upbringing or happiness – so they effectively did not exist in our eyes. Therefore, Dave was our hero tonight for whom we silently prayed all the way home. It was the first time I'd heard silence from my usually very chatty girls while driving.

In some turmoil, I urgently needed a drastic rethink of all our current proceedings in case our worst fears became reality. Heck, I'd forgotten to call Ken Tolman, but he would surely be ringing when I walked in the door. I decided that, of the many items in my rethink, I would need, for all managerial staff, the immediate purchase of those fancy new mobile phones that were becoming not just the rage but essential in today's business. And while Dave's old fashioned ways might not have approved them, we nonetheless needed to move on without him already.

At home, I rested my feet on Amanda's desk as I rang Ken Tolman about today's events. He seemed unmoved and concerned only about the gaping vacancy at the general manager's level. I revealed my plans to step down from flying and into management for about a year, and how such plans had now escalated to the immediate future – as in *now*.

'You don't need me on the line,' I stated to Ken. 'Paul Harland is way overdue for a captaincy. Put him up there, then the list shuffles up. Probably Jeff Slater could take Paul's spot – or Frank Phillips. It's up to you. But I need a break, Ken. I've been flying since I was a kid. I've had virtually no holidays from flying since I was seventeen and I need to avoid becoming stale.'

Ken said, 'Well, I'm just a pilot too, therefore I know hardly anything about company managerial matters. But correct me if I'm wrong: *You*, who's not qualified in the position, nevertheless intends to *act* as our GM in concert with your sixteen-year-old daughter who's also not qualified because she's only just left school?'

'I think so, Ken. Just let me work on it, okay?'

Ken argued, 'But whatever happened to your oft-repeated declaration that you were a pilot, not a manager, and your job was *up there* and not down here?'

'You manage all our pilots, don't you Ken? You recently remarked that half your time involved managing our flight crews and not actually flying yourself. A bank manager doesn't just process loans, he manages his staff too.'

Ken argued, 'Why can't you simply advertise for a new GM – or at least a temporary one – instead of assuming that you alone are the only capable person?'

'Because I just can't *afford* it as all our costs are rocketing up at the moment, Ken. That's why. We're not Qantas; we're just a little family airline where wages, operating costs and particularly fuel costs have soared in the last two years. Which reminds me . . . '

Speaking of costs, I proudly related to Ken our adventurous new fuel saving plan. I told him I was rapidly becoming convinced of the merit of throttling our jets back by five or ten percent and thereby saving, hopefully, a million dollars in Jet A-1 each year. 'But I wouldn't just pocket any savings; I'd be applying it to new all-round airfare discounts. Then, hopefully, we'll make great strides ahead in ticket sales. After that, the opposition might eventually imitate our policy and slow down with us. If not, they could lose out badly. It's hard to say how it'll go and I accept that it's a gamble but I want to try it because I'm always under regular pressure from international aviation watchdogs, the media and the public over environmental and pollution issues. While some missives I receive in the mail are hurtful, they can also be quite correct. Dave's received even more rockets.'

'So, in the air I believe we're all cruising unnecessarily too fast. That last push of the throttles over sixty-five percent thrust just makes unnecessary fuel pour through, doesn't it? A pointless luxury. You can clearly see those needles jump on the fuel-flow gauges. It's the same on most other aircraft types, as you know. Even piston engines: beyond certain power settings you're just burning extra fuel for only marginal speed gains. And it's all tearing holes in the ozone layer.'

'These days the hue and cry is all about world oil shortages and wastage, and how the world's jets are damaging the ozone layer every day with their exhaust emissions. If we could cut down our daily consumption even slightly, then we could proudly advertise our environmental responsibility while hopefully shaming other airlines into following suit.'

I was sure Ken would immediately raise loud and serious objections to my daring plan, but his silence told me he was at least considering it. Eventually he replied, 'Flight management procedures are my province to oversee, so if the company issues new throttle-back orders then I'll ensure they're complied with. At the moment, I don't see how a few minutes lost here and there can have any great effect, except that someone – well, *you*, will have to get the timetables re-written. I suggest we trial it first; say for six months, then we'll see how it goes. But if we lose money then that's your management problem.'

'Thanks Ken,' I breathed a sigh of relief. 'A good suggestion - except that we can't trial this because the public would quickly ask whatever happened to our noble sense of 'environmental responsibility' when we betray our pledge after the trial and throttle back up to full speed. But to grease the wheels a bit, I will impose slightly shorter turn-arounds at each point to make up for accumulated lost time. We mostly sit around chatting in the cabin during re-load, anyway. I don't want any more of this lounging around for half an hour, several times a day. No other places of business enjoy such regular breaks. For them, it's normally eight hours' work with just forty minutes for lunch.' Ken's lack of comments signalled agreement – so far.

I persisted. 'So that's my plan and I intend to be a leader in this new field, Ken. But I need stand-down time from flying to calculate and implement these things. And I'll be sending out a memo tomorrow concerning minimum turnaround times. Last time we turned around in Cairns, it was as though the cabin crew were having a party down the back while we waited for nothing except our departure time to arrive. I want everyone to have fun, but they can have fun during a much *shorter* turnaround. And we can all catch up on lengthy private chatting *after* duty, like every other worker has to.'

Ken finally said, 'All right, I agree. I've previously sent Dave memos about the high cost of fuel these days. They must have started him thinking. Anyway, I'll try to visit him soon. Ah, will I have to call you *Mr Grant* from now on if you become GM?'

'Just Rob will do - when you come out to visit us at the farm. It's our new Head Office, you know.'

He said, 'Yep, see you then.'

That'll be the day, I thought, when Ken Tolman ever sets foot onto our farm because I knew he simply detested the idea of my Amanda ever becoming his ultimate boss!

33.

It was quite a scramble for Mandy and I to grope our way through mountains of papers, books, manuals and documents in order to at least complement Dave Skillen's management style during his absence. Thankfully we had the assistance of Cynthia and Shelley White. Now we needed to discuss and author our exciting new fuel saving project which I had proudly christened *Blue Sky Initiatives.* These new in-flight practices were only to be discussed while our office door was firmly closed; not even the kids were to be admitted at these times (or pets), as they, or indeed anyone, might easily blab our *BSI* plan and, in a wink, I'd be hearing about Qantas's own new *BSI* on my morning news.

In the weeks of this 'mad scramble' as I called it, Mandy and I had to absorb complex management practices along with associated legal and accounting procedures. My enthusiastic trainee threw herself into the fray, while I in turn paid her an extremely generous salary for her unofficial position of *Associate Administrator.* We hadn't yet been graced with the presence of our Chief Pilot at the farm, although he'd thankfully concurred with my *BSI* and was busy writing amendments to our company Operations Manuals – in secrecy, of course. Unknowingly, he was propagating Amanda and Dave's original suggestion which was eventually to become our biggest success. This was a giggle we kept to ourselves while Ken proudly but unknowingly signed the orders as though he'd authored them himself.

Meanwhile, our Dave was languishing in his new private hospital in Windsor. His condition remained steady. No changes expected for some time. Our desire was to visit him far more than we did, but work pressures mostly prevented us. He, of all people, understood this only too well.

In January, 2000 we proudly implemented my daring plan - *BSI: Blue Skies Initiative* for our entire fleet. All our pilots were instructed by the Chief Pilot to throttle back their jets during the cruise configuration to the newly prescribed settings, with the intention of obtaining a noticeable reduction in fuel consumption. It was simply too bad if any captain refused to agree or comply with the slow-down, because at his very next top-up with the fuel tankers we would see his excess fuel usage and could penalise his wages accordingly. None of them refused.

At the subsequent press conference, Cynthia enthusiastically expounded our exciting 'climate-friendly' policy. She explained that instead of simply telling our passengers we'd be arriving at each port about five minutes late, we'd be informing them via our onboard video screens about the vital climate benefits such as a reduction in atmospheric pollutants, and the resultant savings on ticket prices from lower fuel burn-offs.

To confirm this, we'd kicked off with a ticket price war which boasted dramatic airfare discounts on all our routes. Our *BSI* was new to Australia, good for Australia and great news for Australian travellers. And we'd beaten the opposition to the punch.

At our media release, the press responded drearily with a few interested queries, but generally showed scant interest because Qantas and Ansett weren't involved and therefore it was limited news copy to them. Also, the new practices only applied on Sky Star's routes and not over the entire Australian air network.

One questioner asked, 'But isn't this all just a cheap stunt?' which Cynthia promptly ignored by addressing another reporter with:

' . . . and if you can't spare an extra five minutes in your day to help the environment, then you must indeed be a *very busy person*.' I considered this retort as slightly insulting to the public when I heard it, and later pointed it out to her. Let them make their own choices, then ignore us if they wished.

Miraculously, my top secret *BSI* project had made it through to public release day without leaks or puzzling disclosures in advance. In response later, although caught unawares, the other airlines basically pooh-poohed it as a gimmick that wouldn't work. One prominent airline spokesperson lightly dismissed it with: 'The travelling public demands fast and efficient air services, is entitled to them, and has always *had* them. We have no intentions of regressing back to Tiger Moth flying speeds here in the 21st century.'

In the office, Cynthia, Amanda and I cackled as we watched that TV news blooper. I smirked, 'Ha! The travelling public isn't *that* silly to believe that a flight which takes five minutes longer is "going back to Tiger Moth speeds." In fact, I think many will agree with us and won't mind at all if it translates into a cheaper flight on another day.'

Amanda added, 'Most women won't care less about jet speeds and all that men's guff. They'll simply brush their hair and do their make-up in the extra few minutes. Businessmen might grumble, but I bet they never object to an extra five minutes delay at a business lunch if it means sealing a deal over another beer!'

'Well said!' clapped Cynthia. 'I agree – one hundred percent.' So too, did Shelley White, applauding.

I added my two-cent's worth. 'True. And in perspective, a small delay from slowing down en-route is nothing compared to those enforced delays in the air when we are held in orbiting holding patterns by ATC. Before the construction of the runway 16 parallel runway at Sydney, we often had to hold up there for fifteen expensive minutes, and *thirty* in peak hours! Round and round we flew in racecourse-shaped patterns while complaining over the radio got us nowhere. Only air ambulances and aircraft in an emergency were exempted from landing delays, and slot times didn't always work. Interestingly though, no passengers ever complained to our company about 'holding' delays. They're like traffic jams on the road: what's the point of whingeing when we all suffer equally and nothing can be done about it anyway?'

'With our *BSI,* our smart passengers should recognise and endorse our environmental considerations. Especially after Cynth fed them that statistic I gave her about us saving two thousand litres of fuel on a typical trip from Sydney to Melbourne.'

'Do we really?' asked Mandy, the trainee General Manager who'd been the first to propose this *BSI* principle and help us make it a winner for Sky Star.

I grinned. 'I don't know, but it sure sounded good!' We all laughed then settled back to work, waiting for a ticket sales bombardment to tumble upon us at the speed of a Boeing 737 on descent.

34.

'Dad, are you going to be a TV star?' Celia asked one evening at dinner.

I was surprised, 'Not this century, my dear. Are you joking?'

Emmie piped in, 'Cynthia says you're going to be on that show *News People* at 6.30. Can we go on it too?'

'Now, just a moment girls. What the heck are you talking about?' The kids replied that I should ask Cynthia and she'd tell me all about my imminent TV stardom – of which I currently knew nothing. I promptly forgot the matter, but the following morning when Cynthia arrived at the farm, I remembered. 'Cynth, what are my girls talking about? Me on some TV show, they said. I hope you haven't . . . '

'Holy flying ducks!' whistled Cynthia, 'Sorry, I forgot to tell you last week. Mike Mayfield from Channel Ten – he's an old classmate of mine from our Uni days, asked if I could possibly wedge you out of your permanent recluse mode for a short interview on *News People*. He's their famous host and thought you'd be an interesting character on this week's line-up.'

'A person of interest, eh? So you told him *yes,* did you?' I made strangling motions with my hands around her neck.

'Well, kind of . . . I mean, he only wants to do a *positive* thing about you. There'll be nothing ah, bad of course . . . ' Cynthia weaved to avoid my clenching hands.

I declared, 'No. How's that for a precise and positive reply?'

'But Rob,' she pleaded. 'You can't avoid the media spotlight forever. You're now a sought-after item in Australian society with a highly interesting tale to tell. The public has seen plenty of me, now they want to see the real Mr Sky Star. They almost never see your face yet you ask them to travel on your airline, support your promotions and generally trust you as an honourable company proprietor and a nice guy.'

'Well I am. Nicest gentleman I know.'

'But you need to promote yourself. No point in me always espousing Sky Star's product – *you* tell them. You've used advertising extensively and even been in it once; ten years ago. But now the public wants to hear your voice, learn about your life – maybe even see your kids now they're older.'

'Now hang on Cynth. I'm not doing it at all, let alone parading my monsters on TV. Billboards are fine and rehearsed scripts that are acted for TV adverts are what we did, but no *This Is Your Life* stuff.'

She persisted. 'He wants to call you one morning soon and just talk about it. I told him you'd be reluctant but might listen to his request.'

'I might if I wasn't surveying Equatorial Africa from my Tiger Moth this very month. Look Cynth, I've always been camera shy and hesitant with the media. I gave them numerous phone interviews in the old days and somehow their editing always managed to twist or distort what I said. They either omitted pertinent points that I wished to promote, or added their own padding to suit very doubtful motives. And those journo's are all the same. You should know because you *are* one.'

'*Was* one. Mike's different. Haven't you seen any of his shows? He's nice with his guests.'

'I don't watch anything, Cynth. When do I have time to watch any TV except kids' shows when we're spending some rare family time together? I don't care if this guy *eats* his guests, he can find someone else to interview – like King Tutankhamen resurrected. Or Zombies from the Planet Zyrgon.'

'Funny Rob,' Cynthia smiled, then reached for a ringing phone.

I continued waffling, but doubted she was listening to me. 'I'm all for advertising, but not personal background stuff. For example, do those kids who advertise Vegemite also do a family exposé showing their home, their brothers and sisters and their Mums and Dads and the cat? Qantas doesn't allow personal family interviews with its directors. The boss of Holden doesn't show off his home in Melbourne. Cynth, are you listening to me?' No, she was happily chewing the phone with someone nice – as opposed to grumpy old me.

I said to her, 'If that's him, tell him you're sorry for lying your little *butt* off to him; but I'm just not available at all.' In anger, I recalled his TV colleagues in Coffs Harbour who cut Cristina off mid-sentence during her one-and-only TV appearance. First they solicited her comments, but then they chopped them off to show a pet food commercial.

Back on Earth, it was obvious I didn't even exist because Cynthia was saying, 'Yes Mike, he's right here at the moment. No, not flying these days . . . that's right . . . too busy running the company. Come out here and meet us. I'm sure he won't *really* mind. Hey Rob, where are you? Hang on Mike, he was here just a moment ago. Rob?'

This was not what I wanted at all. Cynthia was bowing to her media friends' pressures by informing them of my apparent need to provide theatre for the media, but my inability to explain the truth against twisted and pointed questions had always made me fearful of doing so. I wasn't a public debater by any measure and my only experience with talking into microphones was in my daily job as a pilot on the air/ground radio where I remained, thankfully, unseen. Cameras? Luna Park only. But Cynthia had apparently told Mayfield, 'Just keep persisting and he'll say yes.'

And I eventually did, because after several hopeful requests from Mike Mayfield, I finally relented and invited him out to our farm where I *might* discuss the matter. He would tape an interview for his 6.30pm show. Anything to keep the peace with Cynth. Hearing this news, Mandy suggested I turn it into an ad by yelling *Go Sky Star!* - or something similar. I suggested shouting *Dogswallop Dog Biscuits – for when he barks all night!*

A few days later when I was feeding some of my feathered pets, I spied a huge van belching dust as it urgently raced down our farm's driveway, scattering a few startled birds. *Channel 10* was emblazoned on its side while massive satellite dishes on its roof that seemed large enough to spy on both China and Russia simultaneously gazed reverently at the heavens above. Almost run over on my own property, I dived to one side then angrily yelled to its driver; 'It's not a speedway, guys. The gate sign says *SLOW!*' This wasn't a good start to my impending television stardom, but I noticed Mike Mayfield jump out and wag a *'you're naughty'* finger at his driver.

'You must be Rob!' beamed Mike, bounding over to wrench my hand. 'It's a great pleasure. Ah, sorry about that. Deadlines and those nasty things always pushing us. My driver forgot this is the country, not his urban rat race.'

Gazing at Mayfield, I was blinded by white light. He wore a sparkling white safari suit, spotless white shoes that reflected the clouds above, and an absurd white boater hat of straw. Even his sparkling mile-wide grin was of gleaming white teeth. It was enough to make a Great White shark jealous, but to me he looked like a white bed sheet flapping on a clothes line.

At the house, and suitably bedazzled, I accepted his apologies as Cynthia rushed to bring us coffee beside the pool. In pleasant sunshine I was soon watching, with quite some unease, frantic film crews rushing around and juggling camera equipment, boom mikes and arc lights on tall stands. Shouts and yells of 'testing, testing' reminded me of that movie *Father of the Bride.* Within moments, our peaceful little home and work community had suddenly become a mad-house film studio.

As we seated ourselves beside the lush greenery of my entertainment and poolside area, Mike was already uttering something predictable about 'peaceful life on a farm' – which I certainly wished had continued. Then I gaped at the towering stand of blinding arc lights that had risen right beside my pool, like the lights at the Sydney Cricket Ground, and which sprouted thick electrical leads dangling mere centimetres from the water. Next to it, their portable generator suddenly roared into full take-off power. Damn, if it had been my electricity I could have yanked the fuses.

'For Heaven's sake, Mike,' I whined to him. 'What's all this paraphernalia for? Are we filming *Spiderman Ten?* Can they please move those things away from the water? Obviously, one slip and it'll be *The Day Our World Ended.'* Mayfield grinned, then glanced nervously at Fangio, his moustachioed van driver who was now comically reeling out a mile-long cable around the pool's perimeter. I gasped in annoyance of it all. 'Mike, I thought we were just going to talk first. Why don't you instruct them to relax in the sun and take a breather from their rat race?'

'Everybody happy?' smiled blushing Cynthia as she placed a tray of coffee and biscuits before us. Glancing around nervously, she could see the Keystone Cops tripping over serpents of coiled leads and cables while conducting a running shouting match in some European language. She knew how much I jealously treasured peace and tranquillity around my pool – two former scenarios that had suddenly evaporated.

Over coffee, Mayfield asked Cynthia about working at our farm, then they rehashed some old university tales of mirth. I wasn't listening; I was watching Fangio & company who were now comically conducting sound tests directly in front of my bubbling fountain which always splashed and gurgled quite noisily all day: *'Can't hear you. Can't hear you. Adjust audio volumes.'* Then, right on cue, two ducks let out a raucous quacking match just below the hairy boom mikes, causing the ace van driver to glare filthy *duck soup* daggers at them.

I laughed and applauded; interrupting Mayfield. 'That one's name is Adolf. He always causes trouble. So, obviously this is a comedy show, Mike? Why didn't you tell me? Ah, are we finished yet?'

Mike Mayfield was rapidly 'getting my drift' - as Clint Eastwood would say. He could detect annoyance in my cynical attitude, but was also dismayed with his crew of bungling amateurs. He told them to 'get lost for a while' – as I'd politely suggested, then asked for a quiet talk - just the three of us.

Mayfield explained that he was under heavy managerial pressure to obtain this interview – 'at whatever cost.' Now, after such a clumsy start we still hadn't established any congenial ground at all. He could see that I wasn't impressed with any of his travelling circus and asked if I wanted to delay for a while – before a restart for a *recorded* show to be broadcast later. Recorded? Had I agreed to any other? Angrily, I sipped my café latté and silently decided I'd had enough.

Standing up, I said to him, 'To hell with it, Mike. Why does this have to be a full-scale Hollywood production? You've got seven fools over there trying to set up lights and God-knows-what. But it's already bright sunshine here today, so surely you don't need dazzling arc lights in my face? Cameras have light meters, don't they? Can't they simply adjust them accordingly?'

I continued. 'Now, when I occasionally see the TV news, interviewees are filmed just as they are; where they are. Sometimes they might be stranded in a rowboat on a flooded stream. Or maybe standing in the street? You don't have lighting props and stage managers choreographing natural disasters, or directing rehearsed road crashes, do you? So why do it here? My little home movie camera takes perfect quality videos right here at our pool, and so does our overhead pool cam which cost me about two hundred dollars. But your cameras look like they cost a million each. And this whole comical . . . *invasion* is as though a division of army tanks has rolled onto my property. So, to cut a long story short, I'm not interested in this debacle and I'm not doing any interview.'

I stormed off to the office, conveniently finding and shuffling some documents to occupy my angry self. Back on the 'set', Cynthia bolted upright from her poolside chair; shocked and dismayed. I heard her apologising profusely to her old friend, but wondered why she wasn't defending me instead: her employer? Soon she entered the office where I told her just that: her position was PR manager *for* Sky Star, not the make-up lady for media personalities.

'Cynth, they barged onto my property and adopted an instant domination of it. They almost electrocuted us with leads across the pool water. Their attitude is disgraceful while I expected you – as my PR personnel manager – to assume control of all this, not hide in the kitchen making coffee. I can get the kids to make coffee when they get home. I just find this all very annoying and offensive, so tell him to take his cowboys elsewhere because the only intelligent things I've heard around here are the ducks quacking.' I could see tears welling in her eyes as she absorbed the embarrassment of it all. Mayfield was her old friend who was now a prominent TV personality. She was desperate to impress him, but it had all quickly developed into a fiasco in which she was caught awkwardly in the middle.

Seeing her distress, I quickly softened and changed my mind out of respect for her. 'Oh, all right then. This must be all my fault. *Don't get rid of him*, then. Tell him I'll have a short friendly chat beside the pool with just him and me and one cameraman, that's all. He's not filming *Titanic* is he, so we don't need a cast of thousands milling around. Oh damn, here's the girls back home already. I thought they were out bike riding with friends?' I'd rather hoped the kids would return *after* my grand TV debut was completed.

The kids rushed over, hurling their bikes to the grass and agog with excitement after sighting the *Channel 10* News van in the drive. They'd brought a contingent of local friends with them that was large enough to form a cast for the filming of *The Ten Commandments - Part 4*. In an instant, they'd leapt into our pool like a pod of performing dolphins, causing shock waves to splash over the suddenly aghast film crew's boxes of important-looking paraphernalia. Dripping wet, Emily rushed up with a huge smile to ask if they could all be in the show too. Cynthia warned her. 'Your Dad's in a bad mood, Emm. Better not ask.'

I was even worse when Amanda swaggered up in her gold string bikini and drawled, 'Hiya Mr Mayfield. I'm the new General Manager – well, almost. Would you like to interview me?'

'Christ!' I moaned 'All we need now is Madonna swan diving off our roof.'

'Can we dive from the roof, too?' volunteered smiley Olivia. So within seconds the whole film set had transformed from a disaster epic into a fun episode of *Home and Away*. At any moment I would hear the clap-board smack: *Lights, camera, action!*

It did. As my new cast of unpaid extras romped in the pool and raced wet bicycles past where we sat, I faced Mike Mayfield, camera rolling with just one operator, as he attempted a congenial interview.

'Rob, we all love the *Sky Star* name, and simply adore its excitingly coloured aircraft with those racing stars streaking towards the tail. So would you like to tell us, please, how the name and the striking paint scheme came about?'

As I forced a smile, I decided this question sounded innocent enough. I gulped and spoke to the camera. I related how sweet little

Amanda, just eight years old, had thrown a red toy plane around our back yard. She suggested our new charter line should be named after what was written on the little toy. I picked it up and read its name in tiny print: *Sky Star*. It was bright red, and had stars streaking . . . '

From the corner of my eye I spied a smiling Amanda within camera view, parading cheekily on the diving board. She flexed her chest, then dived in. I followed the camera as it continued to capture all her ostentatious beauty and I felt like saying to its evil eye: 'And to all those viewers at home, please be advised that's she's only sixteen, so put your eyes back in their sockets!' Instead, I droned on with my boring monologue about our humble beginnings, our first old jet that we registered VH-CZG – proudly named after my late Cristina, our slow but steady progression towards today's modern fleet of over twenty jets, and finally our 'exciting' BSI fuel saving initiatives.

Mayfield obviously considered this dry waffle about as interesting as a bi-election in Botswana because he interrupted with, 'Ah, we'll probably cut some of that out later. Sorry Rob, but I only asked about the name and the colour scheme. My other prepared questions might touch on the other items when we get there. Are we ready to go again? Hey Terry, get a few more shots of the kids in the pool, will you. The family aspect, okay?' The *kids*, I murmured, not Miss Sixteen-Year-Old Beauty Queen.

Obviously Mayfield was used to dominating obedient interviewees in his live studio, but I simply wasn't going to allow him to control the *entire* proceedings. 'Rob, I understand you've been flying planes since you were quite a young boy . . . ' Don't even start, I flinched. Not on TV – not anywhere. Don't mention that I was twelve, and illegal and *up there* flying – a potential PR disaster for any airline proprietor.

I corrected quickly him. 'A teenager. I was an early starter at most things (don't mention driving cars, either.) I flew from our property herding cattle, inspecting water holes and dams, and patrolling fence lines and feed lots. We had our own Cessna that I simply worshipped. Then I became a charter pilot and eventually joined AEA - Airlines of

Eastern Australia on their fantastic F28 jet fleet. Just as rapidly, they went bankrupt, so I was out of a job before I'd turned twenty!'

Mayfield nodded. 'Rob, about your late wife Cristina, whose radiant smile we all enjoyed as it appeared on the nose of your first jet; we'd like to hear that lovely story of when you first met: how an old news footage we recently reviewed showed your Cristina describing how she *hated* those horrible noisy jets – and also despised those pilots who deafened her every time they took off. Any comments?'

I laughed and explained that she'd certainly despised me *before* we met, but not personally; just as a *driver* of the jet. Mayfield asked, 'So, how did an airline pilot from Sydney come to meet the young mother of four on the Banana Coast?'

I corrected him that she only had *three* children when we met - another one arrived after we were married. A big cheer went up from the pool audience as Celia leapt up like *Flipper* and yelped with glee: 'That was me!' All the kids waved as the cameraman panned them again. Quickly losing the limelight, sulky old me wondered if we were recording *Afternoon Playtime;* or perhaps *Poolside Pantomimes.*

But the all-seeing red eye swung back at me. I continued, 'Well, I saw her in that local TV news item. They'd canvassed her in the street. Such a pretty lady, but she was quite upset about airport noise from our *new jets,* as the locals called them. In fact, they were new just to the district, but not actually new at all. So I saw her break into tears as she sobbed about living beside the airport and trying to get children to sleep through the thunderous roar of our flights taking off. Although I used to love the enormous roar of those mighty Rolls Royce Tay engines, I felt like a real bastard when I saw this on TV.'

Someone exclaimed, 'Ooh wah! Dad swore on TV!'

Now a seasoned TV interviewee, I batted on regardless of Mayfield's constant whispering to his off-screen audio man with complete disinterest in me. He asked me questions yet had no interest in the answers. Courageously, I persisted. 'I was stuck in a motel room with nothing much to do until our departure, so I called this nice lady and asked if I could come around to apologise . . . ' Behind me, my fan club sighed: 'What a *cool* pilot man!'

'At her old house, I knocked and yelled out that I was there to fix her back fence that the planes' jet blast kept blowing over. She opened the door with squawking babies; I thought she was even lovelier than on TV – and bang, we fell in love. '

Just then, at this most romantic and touching moment, several kids on BMX bikes whizzed between Mike and I, spraying water all over us. Mike's Colgate smile evaporated in a furious flash of anger as one boy tried a posing wheel-stand on the slippery tiles and fell backwards into the pool – bike and all. This was an excellent distraction of which I heartily approved and I held up a wagging finger to the camera and warned, 'But please don't try this at home!' All the dolphins chirped agreement and clapped a noisy commotion.

Trying to help, I said to Mayfield as he hissed *Cut! Cut!* 'Mike, this is rowdier than a rock concert here. Would you like us to move into the much quieter garden area around the corner?'

Mike glanced around in annoyance. 'No, this should be okay. Let me see: young pilot struggles in life. Falls in love. Four active kids. Tragedy strikes. Succeeds in the end. Yep, it's got it all the right ingredients and a great background story line so let's keep going. We're nearly there.' Darkly, I mused, *tragedy strikes?* What a rollicking fun story that is! Should boost their ratings tremendously.

Mayfield adjusted his pocket microphone and continued the interview: 'We're talking with Rob Grant, the founder and Chief Pilot of Sky Star Airlines. Starting out with just one decrepit old plane, the young pilot . . . '

I interrupted with boring technicalities: 'Mike, I'm not actually the Chief Pilot. Captain Ken Tolman holds that position. And that plane wasn't *decrepit*, as you say. It was certified airworthy . . . ' but I could see Mike's continued disinterest and knew these remarks were probably destined to end up beside many others on their cutting room floor.

Then, as though I hadn't even spoken, he interrupted me while his head swayed slightly like a Python about to strike. Then he struck!

202

'Rob. We all remember that Ferris wheel TV ad of years ago when you acted the clown with your young daughter, Amanda. It became a highly successful TV commercial. But weren't you also acting the clown again in that notorious incident last year with another pilot – ah, was it the same Captain Tolman - when he grounded you from flying?'

I'd always known, and should have been on alert to expect, the dangerously spinning Googly ball that media interviewers apparently see as their duty to bowl at every vulnerable interviewee. It's often in the form of 'Have you stopped beating your wife yet?' - or other such unanswerable questions. Uncaring and deadly, it always intentionally strikes its victims unprepared; leaving them defenceless and appearing guilt-ridden. It's the clincher, or the money shot - as they call it, and this was the treacherous *real* reason for the interview.

I glimpsed a worried Cynthia over Mayfield's shoulder, vigorously shaking her head. *Don't go there* - her eyes were frantically signalling. The public did not need to hear me admit that I act the fool at any time. But I couldn't meekly let that one fly through to the wicket-keeper, so with great annoyance I barked at him. 'Are you honestly comparing an acted role in an amusing TV advertisement with a routine check flight many years later in which two captains had a slight disagreement over a debatable matter of policy?'

Mayfield dramatically gestured his hands in innocence. 'Well, you *were* grounded, Rob, were you not? Shouldn't the travelling public be entitled to embrace complete faith in Sky Star's number one pilot?'

As I'd suspected all along, this man had entered *my* property to ensnare *me* with banal media hysteria; not to promote my nice, friendly airline. I had a momentary flashback. I saw a camera swivel and stare at a frightened and distressed boy attending his father's funeral. Then a harsh media voice had barked questions at the boy about property ownership *before* his father had even been buried.

I shot out of my chair. I was a mere milliseconds from punching Mayfield's nose when, with heavenly timing, some wonderful and heroic girls jump-bombed the pool right behind Mike Mayfield - dressed as he was in his thousand-dollar white suit and toffed with a red bow tie under that *village idiot* boater hat!

A tsunami wave, surely a godly gift from the seas, engulfed him - and indeed us all. Thinking it part of the script, the other kids all shrieked with joy then formed a human chain and bombed the pool together. Soon it was a raging torrent as I spied an expensive-looking TV camera gurgling towards the bottom. The camera man had fallen in while trying to save his precious device. It *was* Comedy Capers.

Joining the party, I laughed, 'What the heck!' and jumped in too. Then Cynthia followed – clothes and all. Then all the kids bombed again. What a crackerjack episode of Funniest Home Tsunamis this was, decided all participants except superstar Mr Mike Mayfield.

'Come on in, Mike!' I yelled to him. 'The water's fine. You can interview the next General Manager. She's right here.' For some strange reason, our usually-smiling TV star failed to acknowledge any traces of humour in the situation, his usual Cheshire cat's grin now shrivelled to a sour pucker. He angrily shook himself like a wet Labrador on the beach, cursing and muttering oaths that were Adults-only rated. As his men rapidly packed up and headed for their van, I yelled again, 'Hey Mike! Your station said you must get this scoop at any cost. Aren't you going to finish? This tragedy's got all the right ingredients, remember?'

Olivia commented sensibly. 'Well, he said it was okay to keep filming beside the pool.'

Despite the crew's premature departure, the skylarking kids thought that this had been a wonderful scene for TV so a dozen of them posed together on the side of the pool and chorused cheekily for our overhead camera: 'This has been another episode of News People. Brought to you by Grant's Duck Food. Quack! Quack!'

Over raucous peals of laughter and copycat imitations of Mike Mayfield's plastic grin when interviewing, I heard Mandy complain: 'It's not fair, Dad. I was waiting my turn for an interview.'

'Oh well, can't please 'em all,' I laughed with the rest of them as we frolicked in the waves. 'Don't worry. Our pool cam should have caught it all. We'll send it in to *Funniest Home Videos*.'

And we did.

35.

It had certainly been an eventful day, as Cynthia commented later. 'Funny and dramatic. The kids were just great, weren't they? And who did that first big bomber?' The kids all pointed at Celia, who shrieked and hid under a pile of cushions. Our huge lounge room was full of happy youngsters because, as it was a Friday night, I'd invited them all to celebrate our victory and the end-of-school with a sleep-over party. 'Boys in this lounge room, please. And girls in the other four rooms. No visiting after lights out at ten.'

'*Ten?*' they all shrieked a protest.

'Oh all right, twelve then.' Crowding the room, we all gawked at the TV. But we weren't watching any regular shows: instead, we giggled and hooted at the video recording from our pool camera. Endless replays all produced the same howls of mirth. Especially when it was revealed that *two* girls were the real phantom bombers, not one. They were Celia and her inseparable friend, Jenny.

'No wonder the wave was so big.'

'Check out Mr Mayfield's face!'

'Look at Dad: he looks like he was about to punch him.'

'He was!'

'Oh my God, watch that cameraman trying to hold on to his camera. Look! He's falling in!'

When the youngies eventually tired of the video, Amanda asked if we'd have to pay for their waterlogged TV camera. I thought about it. 'I suppose I'll have to - although I don't see why because everyone heard when I asked him if he'd prefer to move around the corner and into the garden. And here's his answer: listen.' No, unfortunately the audio wasn't clear enough, but we could see him shake his head. So I doubted if we'd ever hear from Mr TV Star again, while poor Cynthia remained in indecision about whether to call Mayfield to apologise.

'Apologise, be damned!' I retorted after dinner. 'Didn't you hear him describe the death of my wife as a tragedy with all the right ingredients and a great background storyline?'

'He didn't really mean that, Rob. He meant the *whole* story. But now I'm quite worried about it. Many of those journo's drink at the Prince Henry Bar after work. Word will soon flash around. The reason I pushed you into it was that we need their acceptance and support, not their antagonism - now and in the future. Sky Star needs the press onside, not opposing us; and so does Qantas and every other business that aspires to succeed. If we can be at least *half* onside with them, they won't throw such dagger-like questions at me. My best advice would be to propose a peace treaty with him; a drink together somewhere. An ironing out of the facts - otherwise they could ruin you like they almost did today.'

'Aw baloney, Cynth!' I said. '*You* go and have a pow-wow with Big Chief Boater Hat. I have nothing in common with this TV personality – and vice-versa. I like him about as much as he likes me. Let's just have fun tonight with these great kids, eh?' Then I whispered, 'Are you staying the night?' She said yes, if I liked. I hissed to be quiet about it 'Cos there's twenty spies with 20:20 vision watching us.' She smiled okay, then remarked that I'd been angry with her twice today. Who, me? Oh hell . . . I slipped my arm around her . . .

Suddenly the room was full of wolf-whistles. 'Ooh, look at the two love birds over there. We bet *they're* allowed to stay up after twelve!'

'Not stay up; go to bed, you mean!' whistled another, while my innocent little Celia protested, 'They don't ever sleep in the same bed, you know.'

'Oh yes they certainly do!' blabbed Amanda as she cuddled her boyfriend Steven on the sunken lounge.

'Just like you two do!' yelled Olivia at Mandy and her beau. 'No we don't!' came a hot denial, followed by the eruption of a rowdy pillow fight. Rather than duck for cover, Cynthia and I adjourned outside to the garden to discuss the roses – anything but *shop.*

But Cynthia had prophesised correctly: shop gossip within media circles had obviously clicked into overtime over Mike Mayfield's interview debacle, because a few days later his media pals retaliated against my isolationist attitudes, casual interview attire and boring monologues with a vindictive dismissal of me as:

Hermit the Drab!

36.

On the national aviation scene, Ansett Airlines was derailing into something more akin to a train wreck than a viable, modern airline. Beset with a fleet of varying aircraft types and models, flight crews became shackled by the subsequent 'type' endorsement limitations. Worse, a strong public perception of the airline being unsafe - which followed several CASA groundings over Easter and Christmas peaks – caused the company to flounder like a wounded bird; descending lower and lower towards an eventual hard landing – or worse. As a consequence, our vicissitudes of fortune positively glowed in inverse proportion to theirs, allowing us to prosper during Ansett's difficult times simply because we harboured none of their self-defeating procedures and self-induced restrictions.

Long ago I'd made it firm policy to never wade, boots 'n all, into the fatal quicksand of operating multiple types of aircraft. Such strategy is fine for large airlines – say, British Airways or Qantas, who require numerous and varied aircraft types for their multitudes of long and short-haul flights. Also, they can comfortably afford to employ hundreds or even thousands of flight and maintenance crew to operate and service each type. Our vastly smaller business possessed no such reach or flexibility; while Ansett, I thought, should have heeded the obvious warnings and drastically tightened their game.

Needless to say, they didn't, so their entire structure of Australia-wide air services gradually became dysfunctional; a publicity nightmare no company ever seeks and from which few can survive.

While it can be a cost-saving temptation to cut corners on maintenance and hopefully evade detection, the awful ramifications when, say, cracks appear in a plane's wing mountings or tail joints, can suddenly herald horrendous losses of profit – or even doom for the whole airline. And when such disastrous misdeeds are highly publicised in the media it can be virtually impossible for the accused airline to deny such problems - even when the reports might be exaggerated.

Therefore, at Sky Star my undeviating company instructions were always: full maintenance at five-star standards - and if we went broke doing it, at least we went broke honestly.

These strict maintenance attitudes came from my perspective as a company pilot. That is: my very own life was on the line if a vital part of my plane should suffer an in-flight failure. So I certainly held a vested interest in our planes not falling out of the sky. In other airlines, unseen accountants and board directors – rarely pilots - usually direct maintenance policies without the fear of such calamitous personal penalties, while my motto has always been that while aviation in itself is not inherently dangerous, to an even greater degree than the sea it is terribly unforgiving of any carelessness, incapacity or neglect. So there should be no price on safety because it is self-evidently priceless.

To me, a dreadful headline which blared *Sky Star's Planes Unsafe!* would be indefensible; even if only one of them was unsafe - or just *part* of that plane unsafe. No matter: to the public, they would henceforth embrace the unshakable belief that all our planes were unsafe. It would be like a panic run on banks during an imminent depression: no matter how strongly you believe the bank you control to be sound, if the public perceives it otherwise you'll be stampeded in a rush of closed accounts. Therefore, I was thoroughly mystified by Ansett's dogged persistence in always sailing so close to the wind, in dodging legally required maintenance and in generally operating a mismanaged and debt-ridden company.

I was further amazed when Air New Zealand completed its purchase of Ansett and immediately injected serious funds into it. I would have thought that if the *Hindenburg* was about to burn and crash, it would be patently futile to pump it full of money when this would hardly alter the root cause of its problems nor the eventual outcome.

In this escalating embarrassment, we at Sky Star played our public cards close to the chest at all times. Neither myself, Cynthia or Amanda ever commented publicly on the plight of Ansett, nor on its foreign acquisition. Of course, while we were regularly requested to do so, we politely declined to assist the media in their inquiries. If one of our opposition wished to commit industrial suicide from which we would gain, it was neither our place to interfere, nor accepted business practice to become involved. Nor indeed would any offers of advice or assistance to Ansett be welcomed by them anyway. We just shut up and played the game.

*

With public distrust in Ansett compounding throughout the year 2000, our bookings joyfully overflowed - albeit in much smaller proportions to those of our giant rival, Qantas. We continued to observe excellent profit flows and heavy bookings that propelled me into more lease-purchases of Boeing 737's. Quickly, our fleet expanded to a very healthy thirty two aircraft; a fine and modern fleet in which there were certainly no cracks in our airframes and the whole fleet consisted of the same type and model of aircraft: Boeing 737-500's.

Any glance at our profit and loss ledgers told me that 'my cup runneth over,' and the tiny airline I'd started with just one old Fokker Fellowship flying on charter had now blossomed into a very proud mention in the prestigious aviation almanac: *Jane's All The World's Aircraft.*

So it became a pleasure to relax during my year's absence from flight duties; to hang up my wings and enjoy observing Ms Cynthia Nilsen and our Associate Director, Ms Amanda Grant, as they ran our flying circus to the best of their abilities. While another 140 staff at various airports around the country also certainly contributed to my well-deserved R & R, I often reflected upon my lengthy battle to 'get off the ground' as a young widower with four small children, using one ageing aircraft and pleasant dreams of stars in the sky.

In fact, my very favourite reflecting place was in my pleasantly serene swimming pool; floating in circles on an air mattress while gazing up at castles of clouds which, for a change, I did not have to negotiate my way around. If a black cumulo-nimbus cloud of threatening thunderstorm build-ups towered over us, I'd simply smile and enjoy another sip of iced cappuccino. But if airborne, I'd be anxiously peering ahead through the windscreen, checking my weather radar and radioing for track diversion clearance. Not anymore. Falling asleep while afloat was a habit I'd recently developed – and failed to tackle – because I sometimes rolled into the water. Luckily my vigilant daughter Mandy would see the splash on her monitor screen and run out to check on me.

37.

This is how I was found, appropriately positioned in my *Lazy Position A;* nodding off and just about to tumble into the sparkling blue water beside my fountain, when a familiar voice suddenly broke my dreams: 'So this is how our overworked leader spends his year running the corporation.'

As I squinted into the sun, my drink slipped into the water. I tried to place the voice. 'Who's that?'

'Ken and Paul. Hi Rob.' It took a while to focus, but I hadn't seen the Chief Pilot, Ken Tolman, for months - and *never* here at my farm. And amazingly, I'd never seen him out of his resplendent blue pilot's uniform. Today, he and Paul Harland wore casual jeans and t-shirts – a surprise to me. What on Earth were they doing here?

Paul smiled, 'You told us that you needed a year's break because you wouldn't cope with flying and acting as GM at the same time. Doesn't look like you're under too much pressure at the moment.'

I paddled to the side and crawled from the pool to grab a towel. 'Great screaming jets! It's the esteemed Mr Tolman himself. Well, well, well! And Mr Harland, too! Numbers two and three. Then a black thought hit me. I nervously asked, 'Don't tell me we've had a crash, boys?'

Ken assured me. 'No, thank goodness. Just came to say hello and check out Head Office and observe the workers slaving away at the coal face.'

Every airline proprietor lives in mortal dread of one day hearing that a company plane has crashed. If negligence is legally proven he can find himself in very hot water indeed. Law suits will fly. Even without deaths or injuries, the financial wranglings that follow can be bankrupting – exhausting at the least. I recalled with horror the 1979 Air New Zealand crash of their DC-10 into Mt. Erebus, Antarctica. A Royal Commission ensued from the loss of all 257 persons on board. There, instead of coming clean under oath, the company doggedly pursued a devious course of perjury and denial of their complicit role in altering the DC-10's computerised flight plan without alerting the pilots. Aghast, the Royal Commissioner subsequently castigated the company's cover-up as 'A pre-determined plan of deception, and an orchestrated litany of lies.'

These chilling words heralded a media frenzy of condemning headlines which pealed throughout the world. I often snapped awake at night, confirming my resolve to never, ever, allow myself to be strangled by any such litany of lies.

Greatly relieved that they'd brought no calamitous news, I said, 'Coal face is right. All the hard work is under the surface, guys. This pool is just a front. You've no idea what actually transpires here just to keep you lot in the air.'

For some reason they didn't believe me, and the friendly Paul Harland poked his head into the office doorway to see for himself. I heard squeals of joy from Cynthia as she gave Paul a hug, delighted that someone – anyone – had called to visit our little hive of activity. I organised refreshments by the pool for us all as Sky Star's control room bunker became temporarily abandoned. At least, I thought it had . . .

As light chatter began, I stated how pleased I was to see Ken Tolman in person; here in delightfully informal settings instead of the hectic and often tense circumstances of our work environment where screaming jet engines regularly drowned our conversations. We chatted about Dave Skillen; how he'd so far affected a reasonably good recovery from his stroke of last year, and was now buying his dream boat to fish in Sydney's Middle Harbour. Gossip about work colleagues followed, then congratulations to Paul as he was, finally, getting married. Although I knew that there would be a more important motive than staff chatter for the visit, I preferred to leave it alone for as long as possible and simply enjoy their company.

Meanwhile, I'd been wrong about one of my predictions: Ken Tolman eventually *had* set foot on my property.

I yelled towards the office, 'Mandy. Come out and have a coffee with our guests.' I saw Cynthia raise her eyebrows in apprehension, then quickly remembered that my Mandy still harboured a strong

213

grudge against Ken for grounding me on that infamous occasion. Also, Mandy was acutely aware that Ken had always viewed her as nothing but an uppity spoilt child of a rich father, and that he'd often made very clear his harsh opinions about her attaining management of the airline whilst only a teenager. This tension loomed as a potentially serious conflict for the near future - if and when Mandy took over the reins, and always hovered over me as something that I just didn't want or need.

Historically, these two adversaries had indulged in a non-communicative relationship almost since I'd started the company when Mandy was quite young. Her initial dislike of Ken began when we'd just filmed the Luna Park TV ad and were reviewing its first thirty-second segment at home. Mandy was only eight and the tall captain seemed to her unbearably arrogant and rudely unamused by our amateurish efforts to advertise our fledgling charter service. While she'd been totally thrilled by what we'd just done, he'd whipped all the pride and excitement from her with his caustic comment: 'It's bloody *ridiculous*, Rob. You absolutely *MUST* be joking!'

Now, nearly nine years later, those barbed words still stung her - along with Ken's reported grumblings at the airport about 'working under a bloody teenage girl!' So Mandy's continued non-appearance at the pool was quite uncomfortable for me - and deepening by the minute. She wasn't simply one of my daughters, but hopefully the future General Manager of the whole company. Someone who, whether they liked it or not, senior men Like Ken Tolman and Paul Harland would have to not merely tolerate, but respect and obey. And, for our business to function smoothly: to converse and co-operate congenially.

With no Mandy appearing on the horizon, I eventually excused myself and walked to the office where I said to her, 'Mandy, please come out now. If you want to run the company one day you need to be on speaking terms, at the very least, with my senior people.'

The normally pleasant Mandy spat *No!* and I knew precisely what Miss Grumpy meant when in such a stubborn mood. In fairness to all, the whole scenario was not cut and dried, so I pointed out to her that it was I who employed Ken in the first place while we were both unemployed from the lay-off of AEA, but it was Ken who held a captain's licence at the time while I didn't because of my age. So we had both benefited from this mutual arrangement, otherwise the old F28 would obviously have never left the ground without a captain on board.

Mandy swung in her chair, turning her back. 'In that case, he should be eternally grateful - captain or not. After his redundancy, he could have been washing somewhere dishes instead of getting straight back into flying with you. You don't bite the hand that feeds you, Dad.' Then, demonstrating further obstinacy as the teenager who once fiercely confronted the Chairman of a prestigious bank, she reminded me once again of 'Mr Tolman's disgraceful behaviour' when he grounded me that time. I didn't agree with *disgraceful*, and added, 'That was *years* ago.'

But she persisted. 'Don't care! He was showing off, Dad, that's what it was. It wasn't a little technical disagreement; he was showing off in front of the airline's owner just for prestige and ego. *Grandstanding*, it's called. He threw an absolute *tantrum* on the flight deck while you were concentrating on passing your check. Then the media got hold of it and you suffered much unfair public humiliation over nothing - not to mention a big loss of revenue for our company. I'll bet he wouldn't have cared less about taxying back to the terminal if he'd been checking his mate Paul - or any other pilot that day. If I'd been in charge of the company back then he'd have been selling meat pies in Central Station the very next day!'

I tried to sooth her defiance, but Mandy possessed a few fiery characteristics that I had never seen in her mother. 'We mightn't have enjoyed that wonderful free holiday in Hong Kong from Mr Lin if Ken hadn't stood me down. It all resulted from that, Mandy.'

She leapt up and stamped her foot. 'I don't damn-well care, Dad! He offered us the trip in the first place. He owns a hotel and a damn *bank*. You're too soft sometimes. You try to be nice all the time and just let people walk all over you. You always said I was a nice kid, but you never fly to my defence when he belittles me as 'that schoolgirl.'

Just like snooty Mr Lin when he snarled: *In China, schoolgirls go to school!* Remember? Our TV ad, of which I was so proud and which became wildly successful *despite* Ken, not because of him, was derided before it was even aired - just as your reputation was that day in Brisbane.'

She wasn't finished yet. 'Anyone could have guessed that Mike Mayfield was bound to throw that incident back into your face in his interview. And how much revenue did we lose from your grounding which might have caused some people to perceive our whole airline as so incompetent that its proprietor couldn't even pass his own flight check? I like Paul Harland but not that other rude and arrogant man. So I'm staying in here, Dad. I've got *work* to do, remember?'

Wow! This was a hornet's nest for me. It wasn't as though some distant uncle had popped in to say Hi; Mandy needed to develop a sound and harmonious working relationship with our chief pilot because they could be aligned together in our company for many years – perhaps another twenty or more. To suffer a total breakdown in communications at this early stage, before she'd even taken the reins, was a deeply unacceptable and unnecessary quandary for us all.

As I walked gloomily back to the pool – alone, Cynthia flashed me a nervous look of query: Is she coming out? I shook my head then lied to the men, 'Ah, Mandy's quite busy today. She might pop out for a coffee later.'

Paul and Ken exchanged rapid and awkward glances; it was obvious there was trouble brewing if *that schoolgirl* wouldn't even appear on stage for a friendly chat. Paul Harland looked particularly disappointed as he'd always liked my daughters; especially Mandy, the eldest. And from my perspective it was disharmonious and quite unacceptable that while my Chief Pilot was here, I couldn't even show him through our new remote headquarters suites because of an awkward personality clash, but I could invite Paul in there at any time.

The pregnant pause in conversation was acute, so I decided, 'Hey Ken, want to see my private jet in the hangar? It's called a Gazelle.' He said 'sure', so we ambled away to leave Cynthia with Paul.

In my rusting old hangar, we inspected the tiny blue two-seat Gazelle aircraft that I barely used these days. Its wooden prop was looking old and needed cleaning. 'I won't invite you up for a fly, Ken,' I said. 'Imagine this headline if the two of us ended up wrapped around a gum tree in that.' *Gimme a home among the gum trees –Sky Star bosses wrap it up!*

Ken forced a smile, 'I went up once in a Gazelle at Bankstown. Hated it. No flaps, no mixture, eighty knots cruise. There's more room in a bathtub. Still, everyone to their own. Do you still use it?' I said that I flew it occasionally on nice days, but always felt guilty because I had four kids to consider, and, as stated, it would be outrageously stupid and reckless for me, an airline owner, to die while flying this tiny insect of a plane.

'Speaking of kids, how's your young one, Ken. A boy, isn't it?' He scowled, then glanced away to mumble something I didn't catch. I wondered if his marriage was in trouble, but decided it wasn't my business to enquire. Nevertheless, there was certainly something troubling the man and my Mandy's boycott of him was most likely to be the number-one cause.

Getting no further response, I suggested we return to the poolside area for further chats. Then I ventured, 'There must be a reason for your visit, Ken. Something wrong at the airport? Whatever it is, it needs to be discussed soon, okay, because you can see how busy I am.' Ken didn't smile at my humorous quip, but showed quite some reluctance to return to our little gathering at all. Upon reaching poolside where the infamous TV interview *nearly* took place, I found Paul and Cynthia immersed in worried conversation.

Then, just as we sat down, I felt a shadow appear, and my dear Amanda, the future 'boss lady' of Sky Star, plonked herself down on a banana lounge between Cynthia and Paul. The atmosphere was electric like an impending thunderstorm as she angrily crossed her arms and defiantly half-smiled, 'Hello everyone.'

217

38.

The two men said hello to her, with Paul obviously very relieved to see her finally appear. Cynthia's eyes remained hidden behind sunglasses, but I knew they'd be popping halfway out in trepidation as Amanda announced, 'You asked me to come out, Dad. So here I am.'

This was clearly a rude remark that was intentionally initiating a confrontational stance. I desperately sought a brief diversionary tactic, but none flew to mind. So I nervously started, 'Looks like everyone's here now, and it's great to see you two handsome guys visiting today. Now, would you like to discuss the reason for the visit, Ken?'

Ken's distracted gaze wandered around until he unhappily whispered the following: 'It's my baby son, Aaron. They said he's got some congenital heart defect that might kill him soon. He's not even two yet, and . . . well, it's some damn disease that's so rare they can't treat it here in Australia. He needs this fancy surgeon in Germany who's too busy to come out here. He's the only one in the world who does the operation. There's no medical insurance that covers it and the whole procedure costs an absolute fortune.'

I gulped in shock and recalled the medical prognosis that destroyed my Cristina. 'That's terrible, Ken. Well, just take some time off and race over there. We'll cover you. I can go back to flying for a couple of weeks if needed, and Paul could take your position for a while. There, nothing to worry about, mate. We'll get that little guy cured.'

The others sat silently as Ken said, 'Ah, it's not quite that simple. Firstly, it's the huge costs involved. Sue and I need airfares and accommodation while we're there. Then maybe extra treatment after the operation. The list seems endless . . . and I couldn't definitely say when I'd be back at work, either.'

I assured him not to worry about these matters just now as I would certainly like to help - however possible. Hearing this, Mandy flashed me daggers: she obviously didn't agree. Staying neutral, a nervous Cynthia played a silent Piggy in the Middle. We discussed the child's plight further, then I asked what extent of expenses they were possibly facing. Ken glanced down in embarrassment, saying he and his wife couldn't even raise *one tenth* of the huge costs between them, and that it would probably come to over six hundred and twenty thousand dollars.

I whistled and glanced at the fountain, bubbling merrily away. Cynthia seemed stunned and very sympathetic, while Mandy's mouth dropped open in shock. As Ken scanned our eyes for support, Mandy displayed an explosive face; arms crossed in angry defiance and body twitching like a Cobra about to strike. After a long pause I cautiously concluded, 'Well, the thing just *has* to be done somehow, doesn't it? I can easily lend you that amount, Ken. It's not a problem to me – as you might know.'

His face flickered alarm as he glanced at Mandy, then he said, 'Well thanks anyway, Rob. But I couldn't ever hope to pay you back after borrowing that much.'

After further consideration, I decided, 'Well, I'd have to *give* it to you, then. I'll worry about the rest further down the track – ah, when he's better. What else can anyone do? I don't see alternatives . . . '

Then Mandy spoke up and my heart leapt from her angry tone. 'Mr Tolman. I'd firstly like to express how extremely sorry I am to hear about your son's plight. However, forgive me if I'm wrong, but you *are* an airline captain, are you not?'

Ken winced at *the schoolgirl* like a wounded dog; then mumbled, 'Of course.'

Mandy sharp tones stung us all as she blasted him. 'Then Mr Tolman, my father has been paying you an excellent salary for over ten years; a salary that is commensurate with the prestigious position that an airline captain occupies. So I'm just wondering how it is that you cannot even raise the one-tenth sum of sixty thousand dollars between you and your wife to save your own son's life?'

I remonstrated angrily. 'Mandy! Enough! That was completely inappropriate and plain rude in these circumstances!'

Mandy yelled back at me. 'Why should *we* have to bloody pay for it? The parents should pay. He's not on a labourer's wage. What have they done with all their money?'

Ken gritted his teeth while Paul obviously wished he was somewhere else that was very far away. Then Ken answered honestly. 'It's embarrassing. Some of it has gone on buying the house but Sue has wasted the rest on her obsession for buying clothes and gambling. I've asked her a hundred times to at least *moderate* her spending, and now when we really need money badly I've just discovered her bank account is empty.'

We all glanced around, perhaps hoping for a sudden fortuitous thunderstorm with hail and lightning to divert our attention. In answer, it remained a lovely, sunny afternoon. But meteorological event or not, Typhoon Mandy kept firing her own tempest.

'Mr Tolman,' she attacked him again, 'as a future administrator of this company, the gift of such a sum would naturally involve my approval because I will one day have a director's financial responsibility towards the company – as I've been recently studying. So I'd probably have to jointly approve any aid. But before I do, can you please explain to me why you came here today with Paul instead of with your own damned wife - who we've never met, by the way, to ask for huge charity to help your sick child? Was she too busy to join us? Out shopping again, perhaps? Or betting on the Roulette wheel?'

I was about to interrupt loudly, when Cynthia suggest we all 'cool it' while she poured more diversionary coffee. Then, as my excellent PR manager, she gave us all a brief lecture on behavioural diplomacy during this most delicate discussion. She wrapped up her address with: '. . . and perhaps his distraught wife was just too upset to come.'

'Or too rude!' quipped Mandy.

But Ken was honest: 'That's not why. It's because she's out at the club again. Drinking and playing those machines. She just won't stop. I've pleaded with her about it. I've got to pay a babysitter while she wastes the rest of our wages. So when I was at a loss what to do, Paul and I agreed we come here and talk with Rob about it.'

I was admiring Ken's honesty when, to my great horror, Mandy exploded. 'This is bloody *ridiculous*! You absolutely *MUST* be joking!'

Ken gasped in shock, exclaiming, 'What the blazes . . . ' as I angrily wagged a warning finger at Mandy. Cynthia was simply aghast.

Mandy yelled at him. 'That's what you once said to me long ago, remember? After we made our little TV ad which was eventually voted the second-best television advert for that year - despite *your* negativity. Instead of supporting our meagre efforts, you said "It's bloody *ridiculous*, Rob. You absolutely MUST be joking!" I've never forgotten those words. *We'd* just saved *your* bacon by giving *you* a job, and all *you* could say was that. So, what promotional advertising of your own did you create instead?'

I interrupted, 'That's got nothing to do with his dying baby, for Christ's sake Mandy!'

But her explosive eruptions continued. 'We've had tragedy in our family too, Mr Tolman - in case you've never noticed. The death of our own mother. Dad was left with four little brats to feed and a funeral to attend. And he wasn't even the natural father of three of us; including me. Yet he still worked fiercely to build Sky Star and employ you while raising us step-kids at the same time, and your sole contribution to repaying his generosity was "You absolutely MUST be joking!" Then you decided to publicly humiliate him with your disgraceful grandstanding in Brisbane - just to stroke your own swollen ego. Remember, Dad was stood down from flying because of you, but he still had those four brats to feed - whether he was on stand-down or not, and we still needed food, a home and a hundred other things that households require. Meanwhile, Dad's probably drunk less than two bottles of wine over the last ten years; never been on shopping sprees and never goes to gambling dens - while your wastrel wife obviously does the lot! So Mr Tolman, you absolutely *must* be joking.'

Shocked, Paul Harland interrupted bravely with pertinent comment. 'Mandy, we didn't come here begging for free charity. I merely suggested we give your Dad the facts and maybe something could be worked out. So I'm sorry if we've offended anyone. I think

221

Ken regrets some things he's done, but this awful predicament still remains . . . '

I was bereft of words; no comments I could concoct would placate all parties here. I considered Mandy to be acting very callously about this - yet at the same time she was embarrassingly right. Also, I was deeply angered that Mrs Tolman couldn't be bothered to at least *meet* us. I consulted Miss Piggy-in-the-Middle who whispered that she couldn't presume to advise anyone about six hundred thousand dollars - but would it be private or company money? Heck, I hadn't even worked that out yet - although I knew I could probably produce that kind of assistance if needed, then worry about any repayments later. While we deliberated, defiant Mandy stood up again to persist with her grand slam. I was reminded of that stubborn little girl sitting alone and angry in a park.

'Mr Tolman, I was often hungry when I was little. So were my three sisters. Were you? I doubt it. For a few years after my first father *pissed off* to North Queensland somewhere, we often went without enough food to eat because he sent us *nothing!* Do you know what it's like to be genuinely hungry or to have hardly any clothes? At one stage I had only *one* little dress before our new Dad came into our lives. One! When Mum washed it on wash day, I sometimes had to stay in bed all day because I had nothing else to wear. One Christmas, all I got was *one* nursery rhyme book as my only present. A two-dollar book! That's because Mum worked long hours cooking and washing for others so she could hopefully buy a few pathetic little presents for her hungry kids at Christmas.'

Ken's face revealed some sympathy, but it failed to prevent more salvos from her. 'I've read your staff file, however, that states you grew up in ritzy Hunters Hill in a mansion. You went to the Kings GPS Boys' College then had all your flying training funded by your wealthy father, an accountant. So everything was handed to you on a platter and life was golden - until AEA collapsed and you were out of work — for your first and only time.'

'Then someone came along and pulled you from despair - like he also pulled *us* from destitution, and your first thanks were to chastise

222

him for making humorous announcements over the plane's PA, and for encouraging the passengers to actually *have fun* on our flights instead of travelling in a flying funeral parlour and being lectured like school children.'

I said, 'Mandy, please, isn't that enough now? Ken just did the job I paid him to do.'

But she wasn't nearly finished yet. 'Dad, you've often told me that I have to be tough and strong if I'm to ever manage this large company – especially overseeing many highly professional men twice my age. So that's what I'm doing now. This person owes you the world, but instead of that he comes here – *without* his useless spendthrift wife who couldn't even be bothered turning up today, to ask for a gift of over half a million dollars! But what he *didn't* mention was why he can't seem to stop his wife throwing thousands down the throats of poker machines instead of saving her own dying son? I'm willing to bet that the amount she wastes each year would at least pay for some of this.'

Trying but failing to reply, Ken gestured his hands in hopelessness while Paul scanned the clouds until Mandy's fiery tirade continued. 'Mr Tolman, if you flew for Qantas, would you have gone to *their* CEO for this massive handout? Also, why haven't you sought a bank loan for this predicament like many other families of sick children are forced to do? You simply borrow against the equity in your home. Our governments also sympathetically treat pleas for assistance in cases like this, and often make special grants for such requests. And what about the Australian Airline Pilot's Federation? I'm sure they must help their members in need. Have you spoken to them? I've just been reading their last month's magazine where one article was entitled: "Let us help you." '

As Ken folded his arms in fury and glared at her with a sneering, seething contempt, Mandy pushed on. 'I'm wondering if you asked for help from your own wealthy family before asking ours? You haven't offered explanations towards any of these matters and I'm suspicious as to why? Also, have you sought a second opinion from other doctors? If not, why not? Mr Tolman, my first father, Tony Avey, gave us precisely *nothing* towards our apparently worthless lives while you were handed absolutely *everything* on a silver platter. A platter which somehow now seems to be empty. So where are your rich parents now?'

Ken roared at her. 'They're not bloody rich anymore!'

She ignored the flak. 'Did you know that the *BSI* fuel saving plan which has saved us millions of dollars was originally my idea and not yours? You are our Chief Pilot but you've never suggested *anything* to save us money or promote the company - have you? I'm just a trainee office chick - *that girl,* but at least I came up with *something.* So my father can't help you, Mr Tolman - unless he overrides me, I suppose.'

Paul Harland rose with Ken whose face was red with contempt and rage. Paul pleaded, 'Amanda, maybe Ken's already tried all these things. I don't know. But I'm sorry we came . . . '

'Please Mandy,' I pleaded uselessly. 'Settle down for a minute.'

But Ken snarled at her: 'I've bloody had enough of this!' The two men strode briskly away as Mandy turned and stormed back to the office, slamming the door. I raced after her and spoke through the office window:

'Gee Mandy, why didn't you just say what you really meant instead of beating around the bush like that?'

An irate yell came back. 'Not funny, Dad!'

I turned, my outstretched hands pleading to Cynthia, 'This meeting was about as successful as the *Titanic's* maiden voyage! What did I do wrong, Cynth?'

She replied that she wasn't sure – yet. She, like me, was still dismayed and in shock.

39.

Back indoors, Cynthia eventually remarked, 'I thought you always told me she was a beautiful and kind and gentle little girl? She certainly seemed like that to me when I first met her. She's nice to work with in the office and we have no trouble or hassles. But what an outburst of cyclonic proportions! What's your thoughts, Rob? I wish you wouldn't be so quiet and moderate at times like this. Some fathers would have smacked her backside for that – even if she is nearly seventeen. And I thought Ken was going to punch her!''

'He wouldn't *dare*!' I declared, then sagged onto a stool at our cedar wood-panelled bar; sighing with unhappiness. I poured myself a stiff Scotch – something I rarely did – and handed Cynthia a phone. 'Cynth, please ring *that girl* and ask her to come in here for a quiet drink while I wonder what on Earth I'm going to say to her.'

Neatly timed, Mandy's eventual entrance was just pipped by the arrival home from high school of my three little mates. I asked Cynthia to explain it all to them because they were part of the family and would also be adults before I could blink - it seemed.

When Mandy shuffled to the bar her attitude hadn't moderated but her anger had subsided. She said, 'Dad, I'm sorry if I embarrassed you in front of senior staff like them. But you did warn me very early on to "Get strong or get out." Didn't you? And just think about this, please: you know how leaks magically seem to escape from us somehow: so, if you lent or gave that kind of money to the chief pilot it'd soon get around, wouldn't it? Then how many other employees would expect a similar handout in the future? Someone else's child might get sick one day, or maybe some worker will be in trouble with the law. Another might go bankrupt. Then they might come to us pleading: "If you could so easily lend that money to Tolman, why not to us?" It could get ugly. I'm trying to protect you now, Dad, because you're sometimes too soft – like I said.'

I countered, 'But if the story is true, that baby is still sick and might die. What about that - either of you? Or you girls? Would anyone else like to have a say?'

The other three girls glanced awkwardly at each other for wisdom; then Emily, who has a heart of gold, declared honestly that we should help any poor dying baby. Celia happily nodded agreement. Olivia spoke up honestly, 'It's not as though he's a friend or anything, is he Dad? He's not nice like our wonderful Mr Skillen. He never comes here just to visit us. My friends say that some people just pretend to be friends when they want to use you.'

We prompted Cynthia who commented sensibly. 'I personally don't like the man, but it's hardly the baby's fault if his father is disagreeable and his mother useless.' So the ball bounced merrily back to my court while Mandy's raised eyebrows silently screamed: 'Well?'

I took another long pause, then finally decided, 'My vote goes with those of Emmie's and Celie's. We should certainly help any poor baby who obviously can't help itself . . . (the two girls cheered "Yay!" and gave me a high-five) and despite Mandy's volcanic objections, we'd all feel just wonderful if we heard that Ken's baby had died, wouldn't we?

Mandy argued, 'Dad. Remember when I did that school work-experience at RPA Hospital? There were maybe fifty young ones in that children's ward who might have died later – or were dying then. And all those lovely kids on the Lord Howe flight. Did any of them have some wealthy airline proprietor to come along and bail them out?'

Finally I'd had enough. 'Alright Miss General Manager, you've had your say. We heard the blistering rhetoric of your megaphone diplomacy - loud and clear! Not even politicians make speeches as long as yours today.' I poured myself another Scotch as the youngies gasped in surprise and Cynthia smiled. Then I adjourned to my bar's men-only *Captain's Corner* for self deliberations, mumbling 'It's enough to drive a man to drink!'

But the kids heard me and yelled out, 'But it's illegal to drink and drive!' This was slightly missing the point but gave us all a laugh.

*

After dinner I finally announced, 'So this is what's happening, everyone. Firstly, any money involved here is *my money* that I worked for, so it's my ultimate decision, okay? - even if you'll have liability soon, Mandy. Next: I listened carefully to all your most excellent and relevant points raised today, Miss Mandy. Nearly all of them were well said, although often as cutting as a chain-saw. I must agree that Mr Tolman should have thought through all those sensible suggestions before racing here first for help, but perhaps some people become disorientated and confused when confronted with such a family trauma. When you've just been in a massive car crash, do you always think rationally and calmly, or just open your mouth and bellow for help?'

'Now, diverging slightly. Miss Amanda: you've never told me that you girls were hungry or starving before I appeared. No-one's ever mentioned that to me before. I seem to recall that your Mum always had some food in the cupboard, and your room had that yellow box full of toys, too. Each of you older three girls had dolls and toys – including Emmie the baby.'

Celia corrected, 'I was the baby.'

'Not you, silly,' I laughed and cuddled her. 'You weren't even a little star in the sky then.'

Olivia answered for Mandy. 'Mum used to keep empty boxes of food and cereals in the cupboard for when you came. She didn't want you to know we had no food. She told us that Mrs Gorisch from next door gave us old toys from her grown-up kids. And Mum used to beg for food from the Sallies, while sometimes we had to eat dead moths off the window sills. I remember that.' They all shrieked '*Moths! Yuk!*'

Mandy confirmed, 'Well, from what I remember, most of that is right. I just remember crying from hunger while trying to get to sleep some nights. The pains really hurt. Mum used to cry too. I could hear her, so I suppose she probably went without eating more often than we did.'

I interrupted, 'But this was in modern-day Australia in the late twentieth century, for Heaven's sake. Why didn't someone track down your father and garnishee his wages? Was *Centrelink* closed down for renovations? Children starving? Bloody hell!'

'Don't swear, Daddy,' admonished Emily, who had recently arrived home from school with a warning notice that said: 'Emily Grant: Caught swearing in class.'

I said, 'Anyway, let's move on, please. Thankfully you all grew up healthy and it's the proudest moment of my life when I walked into that home. So *what* if our Mr Tolman enjoyed a fine and privileged life while we didn't? It's just tough luck: sometimes this is a very unjust and unfair world - try living in Africa. Anyway, yes I helped Ken when the chips were down and a few times since. Today, when things are dire, he sought my help again. I don't see why I can't help a senior employee once again - my very first employee. It's just petty to rehash old tales of how he wouldn't let me say funny things to the passengers. Who cares now? He's a cool, serious, and professional pilot. Would you like one of those types in charge of your flight when something goes badly wrong up *there*, or some comedian who makes you laugh but bungles it all?'

Celia laughed and said, 'The funny man.' Emmie smiled, 'The cool man,' and thoughtful Olivia said, 'You.'

I said, 'All right. Let's leave it for today, ladies. Can we continue with the next episode of *The Angry Skies* tomorrow? I might have another Scotch and then collapse into bed early tonight.' The girls chorused 'goodnight,' then skipped off to their rooms. Within seconds, a thumping beat resonated through Olivia's door. It seemed to rattle the ice cubes in my glass – or was it my hand shaking?

Amanda wandered away saying, 'I still love you, Dad. Really.' So the score at stumps for this day limped to a drawn result and tomorrow we'd need further urgent discussion. After a while I made a huge decision – then couldn't remember what it was! My head was spinning from three stiff Scotches; the most I'd drunk in as many years. While my walls continued to reverberate – either from rap music or alcohol or both - the last thing I noticed was Cynthia tripping over her shoes in the bedroom. Had she been drinking too?

40.

In the morning I sat, Buddha-like, on my floating air mattress in the pool, eating fruit compote to ease my dull whisky hangover. 'Never again,' I solemnly vowed, and probably became the world's first person to issue such a pledge. I spied Mandy, walking the curved cobblestone path around the pool towards the office.

'Mornin'!' I smiled, and she returned the greeting. Just exactly *where* had that gorgeous little sweet pea gone who once gripped my trouser leg and looked up at me with angel eyes, pleading, 'Are you going to be our new Daddy?' The person I saw now was a lovely grown woman who usually radiated a glowing smile for us all to enjoy - but woe betide anyone who upsets her. She certainly was no kid any more, and having recently dyed her blondish hair to brown, I wasn't sure if I liked it – but her boyfriend Steven certainly did, so my opinions were irrelevant and therefore not sought.

With my memory returning, I recalled my big decision and called to her, 'Hey Mandy, I've got a little research project for you.'

'What?' she turned back to dip her toes in the water.

'Just a small job. I'd like you to get on a plane to Europe, go touring around wherever you like for a few days, then do some research while you're there.'

This certainly grabbed her interest and produced another morning smile. 'Really? A trip to Europe! I've always wanted to go there and was hoping I'd get time next year. What do you want me to research?'

I explained, 'Obviously, referring back to yesterday's traumas, we need to verify the credentials of this German doctor - ah, Dr Otto Ebers, before I decide to pay out anything. I'd like you to fly to Germany, hire an interpreter, and question this doctor. Ask him everything about this medical procedure that Ken described. Assess his honesty and veracity because I'm not going to be screwed for any amount of money by some European back-alley quack. So sniff around his clinic, ask questions of staff and other people you might meet. Ask the receptionist for referrals and speak to the German Medical

Association – or whatever they may be called. And especially track down patients and their families - if you can, who have already undergone the procedure. See how they're recovering – if they are. Or did any die? Will any need the treatment again? All that stuff; you're a big girl and you can figure it out. It's just like a University assignment.'

'Wow,' she smiled. 'It's so exciting! Can I take Steven with me?'

'It's not a lover's honeymoon, it's a working assignment. Cynthia will be going with you. She's basically our company secretary now – that's where I've got her headed, and I don't need someone as talented as her wasting any more time batting away media questions – so she'll be accompanying you because I don't want you there alone. Also, she'll have tasks to complete - like you.'

'Does Cynth want to go, too?' Mandy asked.

'She doesn't know anything about it yet,' I smiled. 'But she will soon. Anyway, as our company's new secretary and therefore one of the trustees of our funds, she'll be responsible for recommending any funds I might pay out towards this young boy's operation and treatment – as recommended by you first.'

'But . . . ' my strong-willed daughter started winding up again. I'd outfoxed her and she knew it.

'No *buts*, Mandy. We heard your loud opinions yesterday, and so did everyone within a ten kilometre radius. You said I'm *soft,* but when I'm forking out over six hundred thousand dollars for this – or anything - I want to be sure it's necessary in the first place and if there aren't alternative avenues where we can obtain equivalent treatment for much less cost? You said so yourself. So that's the other aspect of your assignment: get on that internet of yours upon arrival and research this affliction, especially as it applies to infants, and hopefully find out if other doctors around the world also perform this procedure, but for a lot less.'

For a change she stayed silent, so I continued, 'Ken stated that this person was the only doctor in the world who does it, but I doubt that. I'm no medico man, but *someone* must have taught this man in the first place, so *he* knows about it; and there would have been other students present at the time, so *they* know about it, too. And no-one can tell me that no countries other than Germany are aware of this. It can't be a trade secret known only to them because international Medical Society journals report on and share these new procedures regularly. Research them, too.'

I continued, watching Mandy deep in thought. 'As you know, I buy jet planes all the time, but I never pay an extra dollar for them that I don't have to. So I'm not handing out six hundred grand to some dubious foreigner without thoroughly researching all these other avenues first. And that's because even though I might look stupid sometimes, and I even *act* stupid sometimes, I'm not actually . . . '

'*That* stupid!' she laughed.

'So my dear, if you can manage to shave even $100,000 off the medical bill, you've easily paid for your trip. Save half of it and we're way ahead if the operation succeeds. Save most of it and we're laughing. And we can hopefully claim some of it as a partial tax deduction, anyway. Then everyone wins: firstly, the baby wins with his life. Ken's family also wins. And we win through helping an employee – even if he's been difficult towards me at times - as you so vehemently lectured yesterday from your soapbox. Now it's my turn. This is a humanitarian *and* business project for me; your personal opinions of Ken were duly listened to and considered, but part three of this project is mine: I'll be seeing Ken soon and reiterating all those pertinent suggestions you made yesterday: bank loans, the Pilot's Union, family loans – all those areas. Maybe he's distraught and just never thought of any of those things, but this time he can damn-well answer lots of our questions if he still wants our help.'

'Also, I'll be insisting on seeing his wife – even if we have to drag her out of some club. She can radically change her whole lifestyle to save her baby or we're pulling out – as you inferred so strongly, because at the end of the day we can't help those who won't help themselves.'

'Finally: Ken's a highly responsible person in the air, so, if he's so fond of laying down aviation laws to me when we're flying, he can damn-well lay down laws about behavioural responsibility to his own wife. If they want our help, his wife can and will bite the bullet and start helping by not rushing stupidly to a club to drink and gamble away her baby's fading chances when they might need every last dollar. If she won't change, we can't be miracle workers and achieve the impossible. And lastly, if our workers demand the same largesse in the future, just let me worry about it then, okay?' She nodded.

'Oh, I forgot: I need you to look at some planes for sale while you're over there. Take these Aviation Trade magazines with you. Just give some of them a call, tell them my price and if they haggle or hesitate, drop it straight away. If it's a good deal, they should zip down to wherever you are and pick you up in their private jet because it's not like you're buying pineapples or lipstick. Just put on your fire-breathing dragon act and they'll be saluting and bowing in no time. I'll give you all the details later this morning. So, I'm too soft and you're too harsh. Let's declare this a compromise, okay?'

She was quite thrilled. 'Yes. Yes! When do we leave?'

'Well, today of course. The baby's life might depend on it. You've both got passports. Jump on the phone to book seats for today's flights out of Australia, then book a hotel in Europe – for the first few nights anyway. Just take a flight to any European city – wherever the first flight from here goes. Make it Business Class. If no seats there, take First Class - you'll definitely get two seats then.'

'After a few days in Europe, you hop on a high-speed train called the German *ICE* train that flies along at 290 km/h, and whizz off to where this surgeon is. I often travel this way when we go to pick up another plane. Anyway, you'll work it out. By the way, will you two ladies get along okay together for a few weeks, do you think?'

'Sure!' Mandy assured. 'I like Cynth heaps, and she seems to like me even though she's nearly twice my age. We'll be fine. I just can't wait! So, shouldn't we tell her now . . . surely.'

'Tell me what?' asked Cynthia, emerging from the sliding doors that faced onto our tropical poolside recreation and entertaining area. She wore a gold dressing gown fit for a queen – perhaps a European queen.

Mandy yelled across the pool. 'Hey Cynth, you'll never guess where we're going today!'

Cynthia curled her nose and said, 'Where? Oh, not to argue with bloody Ken again? Please.'

'Well, it's something to do with that, but a bit further away. Dad will explain 'cos I've got to pack some things, but I've got absolutely *nothing* to wear!'

'Don't worry,' I called after Mandy's retreating figure. 'Just take my Gold Visa card with you and buy what you need there. European fashions, remember. Charge it all to the card - and you must ring me regularly.'

Mandy yelled back, 'Dad, I'm not old enough to even *have* a credit card yet, let alone race around the world charging things to it.'

'Oh, I forgot. I thought you were about forty-six years old, not sixteen. At least that's how you sounded yesterday. I'll make Cynthia a signatory to the card, then. Yes, that's a safer idea. It would probably be cheaper to buy a new 737 than have a teenage girl rampaging through Europe with a free card.'

Cunningly, she asked, 'What's the limit on the card, Daddy dear?'

'I'm not telling you.'

'I'll ask Cynth.'

'She won't be told either.'

'But Daaaaaad!'

Cynthia said, 'Won't be telling me what? What's all this about Europe? Can someone please explain just what's going on here?'

I could – soon. Mandy wasn't quite as clever as she thought: by bribing her with a trip to Europe I'd managed to overcome most of her strident objections to helping Ken, and at the same time achieved a sort-of peace treaty all round. Hmm, did I win that round?

41.

In their absence, the show, of course, must go on. Later in the week, I sat with boots up on the GM's desk, a Commander-in-Chief of myself, wondering where on Earth I should start. Piles of books, mail and other frightening objects faced me; refusing to disappear. The *girls,* as I called them, had been gone three days; vanished across the globe and were probably lost amongst the great fashion houses of Europe by now. At least it certainly seemed that way because, despite my instructions to phone home, I hadn't heard a peep from them and wondered if they'd enquired about any planes for sale at all.

But first I needed help here. I called Marie Westcott, my Chief of Staff, and asked if she'd like a change of scenery for a few weeks to become my relieving GM. I offered her an extra thousand dollars a week. Yes, of course she accepted; this was a big bonus in the year 2000. 'When do I start?' she asked. Well now, please. I also needed a chief pilot to replace Ken for a while. I drove into the airport and Paul Harland accepted gladly, but I'd need to go back on the pilots' line myself to fill Paul's slot. There vanished my year away from flying. Every attempt to take a break lasted about a week or so. Most other business owners will nod and understand.

At the airport, Paul apologised for walking away from our farm that day. The fiery proceedings had rapidly become too hot for him to handle. He was stuck for any appropriate words of use, and torn between his friendship with Ken and his long-standing relationship of work and friendliness with me. He was also *very* nervous, he emphasised, about back-chatting Amanda when she was slotted to become our next General Manager very soon. *His* General Manager.

Paul explained that Ken, attempting self-defence, had recently revealed his own parents' misfortunes of years ago. His father had owned a Sydney accounting firm which, after the 1987 stock market crash, had itself crashed. His parents both fell ill shortly thereafter, and his father retired with almost no money just after paying for Ken to train as an airline pilot. Facing hard times, they downsized their home from a Hunters Hill mansion to a fibro cottage in the western suburbs. Today, they had no money left to help their son's baby.

I said to Paul, 'This only explains one small part of his dilemma and attitude. What about all those other pertinent points that Mandy raised?' Paul replied that Ken had offered few other comments on his convoluted and catastrophic predicament, and was still side-stepping his wife's puzzling role.

Reverting to the subject of Mandy, I asked him, 'Has Mandy got you worried? Don't worry, it could be worse: she could have you shot, but it's painless, I'm told.' Paul laughed, explaining that he wasn't frightened of her because he mostly agreed with everything she'd *spat out* at Ken, but he would certainly tread very carefully when near her in future. He then added that Amanda had sounded like someone much older than she actually was, and that she possessed great temerity and bravery to dress down the chief pilot as she had.

I emphasised, 'She has to, Paul. I've nagged her for months about that. Being female and young, she must at all times show a forceful front if she's ever to run a company like ours where 55 percent of the whole staff are male, but 95 percent of the *pilots* are male. The first time she breaks down into girlish tears in front of men, any credibility she had ever earned will evaporate. Then they'll walk right over her. This recent confrontation with Ken will inevitably fly around the gossip tree like sparks on a Catherine wheel, then hopefully all those tough men might consider very carefully – if they wish to retain their positions, ignoring her or making inappropriate remarks in the future. We must bear in mind that she said to me, in reference to that time Ken stood me down, that if she'd been in charge back then he'd have been selling pies at Central Station the next day. She meant that Paul, believe me.'

Paul made a valuable suggestion: 'I accept all that, but I'd strongly suggest that pilots won't easily take to a non-flyer like Amanda ordering them to obey technical instructions that pilots know are unacceptable or even dangerous. She really needs to accept her limitations here, and either go on plenty of flights in the jump seat to thoroughly familiarise herself with what they have to do each day, or else refrain from issuing any directives about tech crew matters where she plainly wouldn't know what she's talking about. It would be like an orchestra conductor instructing everyone in their tasks - but does he know how to play any instruments himself?'

'Very good point, Paul,' I said. 'I'll attend to that. By the way, old Dave wasn't a flyer so he restrained himself admirably in the technical arena. Actually, he didn't like flying at all - *terrified* would be more apt. Did you know that? On some of our flights he told the person next to him he was a deep sea fisherman.'

Paul laughed 'Why?'

'Because he shook with nerves while flying, so it would have been disastrous admitting to anyone that he was the airline's General Manager.' I reminded him that Dave gulped a pile of pills on our flight to the Philippines, then slept most of the way.

We chatted for a while longer, and neither of us raised the name of Ken Tolman again. We needed a breather from all *that*. Meanwhile, at *Leaky Airlines,* the warnings flew swiftly about when *that teenager* finally takes over: watch out! This showed that Ken had disclosed her theatrical and aggressive performance to all who'd listen.

I whistled a tune to Paul, then asked: 'What's the name of that song, Paul?'

He smiled, *'Uh oh here she comes! She's a maaan-eater!'*

42.

My musical talents approximate my skills at knitting, yet I felt like Willie Nelson and was singing *On the Road Again* as I climbed into my Superman suit - as my girls called it, and prepared to do battle in the skies yet again. The expensive blue suit with those four gleaming gold bands around the lower arms, topped with the Commander's cap and embellished with the luxurious leather briefcase – made me look just like a pilot.

Oh, I *was* a pilot - I just hadn't flown for a while. Perhaps I should have been singing *On the Wings of an Eagle;* although I wasn't too sure if my singing talents were fully appreciated around here. With a big smile, Olivia handed me a cut lunch of nice sandwiches she'd made – (I was tired of airport food, but didn't broadcast the fact in case that leaked out, too) – and I was about to head off to the airport.

I thanked her. 'By the way,' I asked, 'has anyone heard from our intrepid travellers yet? It's been six days now and I had rather expected at least one of them to report that they're still amongst the living.'

'Oh yes,' Miss Livvy chirped. 'Sorry Dad, I forgot to tell you. Mandy called last night after you went to bed. It was morning there.'

'Where?'

'I don't know.' She screeched down the hallway, 'Celie! Where did Mandy say they were?'

An answer screeched back, 'It sounded like Hungry Jacks - or something.'

'What?'

'Hungry. A country called Hungry - I think.'

'You mean Hungary?' I corrected. 'Somehow I could have sworn that I asked them to go to a place called Germany. So, did she say anything of interest, by any chance?'

'Yep, she said "Tell Dad we've found heaps of great bargain shops. Beautiful stuff at excellent prices. But it's all in Euro's, so it's a bit more in our money," she thinks.'

'Wonderful. But did they happen to mention anything slightly related to *work*? You know, that hard labour activity that some poor slaves are forced into?'

'Nope,' smiled little Celie as she, Emmie and Olivia hitched school bags onto their backs. 'We're off to school now. Bye Daddy. Love you.'

'Bye kids. Have a lovely day. See you tonight.' But my words bounced off empty walls and only a bowl of goldfish gawked back at me. They'd gone already. Zoomed away in a flash; racing up our dusty laneway on their pink bikes. Three pretty blondies, soon to be women. I stared after them and suddenly felt a chill of creeping age sweep over me. Damn, I'd forgotten to reply that I loved them too. Outside, I bade a cheery farewell to Marie and Shelley in the office - tapping away on their keyboards - then zoomed away in my shiny new Jaguar XJS.

On the way to Sydney airport, I wondered what on Earth my expeditionary force was doing in Hungary. Or had they really been calling from a Hungry Jack's somewhere? Did they even *have* Hungry Jacks in Europe? And anyway, what a stupid question to be asking oneself while driving down a motorway. Hmm, concentrate now. I'll soon have a plane load of trusting passengers awaiting my expertise to take them hurtling through the skies; safely and securely where they wish to go.

This was to be my maiden flight since voluntarily stepping down to oversee our management. *The Flight of the Phoenix* perhaps. At the airport I did a quick check with Jeff Slater in Ansett's simulator where we rented monthly hours from them, then our dispatcher told me to head for gate #6. I was off to Adelaide; but it didn't really matter where I went because all airports are very similar to pilots and it's of little interest where you go when you only spend a half hour there then you're off to the next. Unsure of my allocated First Officer today, I took a seat in the departure lounge and studied my flight plan and briefing notes among waiting passengers who read newspapers and magazines.

After some time, and passing the deadline when we pilots would need to embark, I was expectantly scanning the area for signs of my other pilot. While the captain might be vital to any flight, he certainly needs a co-pilot with him. This is a two-man job where no airliner ever gets airborne with just one pilot up front. Frustrated and angry at him, I was muttering under my breath but decided it wasn't appropriate to passengers if their captain was seen mumbling to himself.

Just as I finally rose to board the plane alone, a breathless young woman pilot rushed up and puffed, 'Captain, I'm so sorry I'm late. My name is Tania Wicks. Security wouldn't let me in.'

'Why ever not?' Puzzled, I shook her hand. 'Ah, I'm Rob Grant. Pleased to meet you, Tania. Ah, what happened back there? Tell me while we walk.' We strode briskly towards the aerobridge for gate 6. She explained that over-zealous security guards apparently decided she looked too young to be a pilot and detained her until they'd radioed somewhere for confirmation of her I.D., licences and papers. It took *ages*, she said, before they begrudgingly admitted her through to the departure lounges. Immediately I was annoyed; I'd spent years being constantly harassed about my age and young appearance – *and* my credentials to own an airline, so this touched a raw nerve.

I stopped briefly at the check-in counter and spoke to one of our ladies. I introduced myself and told her that I'd be requesting a meeting with the relevant security staff upon our return from Adelaide, and to please notify them immediately. We hurried down the aerobridge tunnel to board the waiting Boeing; then made a sharp left turn onto the flight deck.

'We're quite behind time now, Tania,' I said, hurriedly settling into the left-side captain's seat and buckling up. 'But it's certainly not your fault. We'll sort out your delay later.'

But she seemed quite unsure and almost alarmed as she sat in the F/O's seat. Her eyes swam around the cockpit. 'Yes, Captain. Thank you Captain.'

I ordered, 'Let's start whipping through these pre-start checks, please. I think we're loading already. Yes, we are. Okay, here we go: Generators on, probe heat on, anti-ice no, air-con packs yes, isolation valve auto . . . Are you with me, Tania?'

She was struggling, but whispered, 'Ah - yes sir.'

'Okay then. Cabin pressure to auto. Flaps five. APU on. Start levers to idle. All cargo doors confirmed closed . . . check? Is everything okay there?' My first officer was way behind the ball at this hurried stage, and had barely even set up her own instruments or entered any flight data into her FMS flight management System. So I told her, 'I'll drive the thing until top-of-climb then you can take over. Okay?'

Young, nervous and inexperienced. I stole a quick glance: she certainly was a pretty woman, but this was quite irrelevant. I needed a competent co-pilot, not a fashion model from the catwalk. As the purser closed the main cabin door I flicked dozens of switches on the overhead panel, then quickly started both engines as I radioed the Tower's Ground Controller. 'Good morning Sydney Ground. Sky Star one-zero-one for Adelaide at gate six. Received *Delta* and ready for push-back. Request taxi and airways clearance.'

After a tug pushed us backwards from the terminal building, we were cleared to taxi to the holding point for runway zero-seven. After take-off we'd perform a scenic departure heading towards Bondi Beach, followed by a climbing right turn over water to intercept the 195 degree radial from the Sydney VOR beacon. After that, we'd continue climbing towards Wollongong, then we'd probably receive standard ATC radar vectoring towards the south-west and on to our destination of Adelaide at a cruising speed of 510 knots – or 945 km/h. It was all quite routine to me and I'd done it countless times before.

However, to my new co-pilot it all seemed to be very rushed. I tried some light conversation by saying 'I haven't flown with you before, Tania. I knew we had three women with us now, but I must have missed you because I've actually been off for a few weeks.'

To my amazement, she answered with, 'I haven't done any flights with Sky Star yet. This is my first day. Sorry if I'm so slow.'

'Your first run? But you've checked out in the simulator okay – ah, haven't you? And you've flown other jets? I mean, you're not sim-checked only, are you?'

'Yes,' she spoke so softly on the intercom that I asked her to speak up. 'I only passed the sim last Friday with Captain Harland. He said we were desperately short of pilots and . . . '

I turned towards her. 'We're not *desperately* short. I'm sure we're not. Our Chief Pilot is on leave so that's why I've been recalled to the flight line. There's been a few other alterations . . . ah, what else did he say?'

'He said I'd be fine to do a *real* flight with a senior captain. He asked if I could start later this week and I said yes. Then I got a call at five this morning to say I was flying today! But I was out near Penrith and . . . anyway, we had five flights going out this morning and the dispatch person didn't tell me which one was mine. So when I got to security they asked my flight number and I couldn't tell them. From that very moment they seemed suspicious of everything . . . '

Heck, what a mess-up, I decided. But I had no time to hear the rest of it, and said, 'Well, on behalf of the company I apologise for all this. Little things go wrong sometimes. But tell me, what have you flown before, Tania?'

'Cessna 414's in North Queensland. Before that I did cattle mustering.'

'So you haven't flown any jets before?' It was a captain's duty to ask such a question and I didn't realise that we allowed simulator-checked people straight onto the line. They do it in the U.S. regularly, but I wasn't aware of it here. Maybe Ken, with his other worries, had forgotten to tell me. Fortunately I trusted Paul's judgement implicitly, so she must be competent.

Nevertheless, I was sitting beside someone who'd only flown twin-engined propeller planes on charter flights and single-engine types chasing cattle around properties - as I'd done long ago. Phew, I'd have to look into this later, but shivered at the thought of me suddenly keeling over the controls from a heart attack and this young person, who looked scarcely older than my eldest daughter, announcing over the P.A. 'Ladies and Gentlemen, guess what . . . '

Things were moving fast, and right now the tower was calling: 'Sky Star one-zero-one, maintain three thousand, runway zero-seven, clear for take-off, make right turn.' I asked my new co-pilot to acknowledge the radio clearance, then gently pushed the twin-coupled throttles fully forwards. The big Boeing leapt away with an enormous thrust of acceleration; an exhilaration I'd always enjoyed no matter how many times I'd done it before. 'Call the numbers please,' I said to her.

Racing down the runway, Tania soon called: 'Eighty knots, Vee-one. One hundred and ten, Vee-two . . . and rotate!' I hauled back on the control column and the 737 dutifully rose like a great bird into the blue sky – its true home. A quick glance out the windscreen revealed a delightful day across Sydney with very little air pollution. Just perfect for flying, in fact.

BANG! Just as I was ordering 'gear up' to Tania, the airframe shook badly from an intense vibration. Immediately the plane's nose yawed alarmingly to the left as the wingtip dipped dangerously close to the ground. I yelped something like: 'Hells bloody bells! The left engine's gone!' This perilous event whilst just a few metres off the ground was forcing us to swerve dangerously to our port side because of the asymmetric power of only one engine thrusting from one side. Being totally independent from each other, our powerful CFM jet engines were wonderfully designed to continue functioning through all circumstances, quite unaware if the one on the opposite side had gone on strike. So now our right-side engine was trying to yaw us (twist us) hard left when we didn't want to turn at all. We needed to track straight ahead to prevent deadly drag from our long fuselage crabbing sideways through the airstream. Of course, I could always reduce thrust on the right engine for more directional control, but then we'd lose precious altitude and have little power – or none. A disastrous crash might quickly follow.

In an instinctive reaction, I suffered a ghastly vision of a fiery crash, a smouldering wreck, then my family being fatherless. This apparition was a totally unacceptable scenario to me when my children were already motherless.

Now I needed to overcome this split-second nightmare and concentrate fiercely on the emergency at hand. Grimly, I realised that we were full: full of passengers and full of fuel - the very worst loading configuration possible. Most importantly, I had over 140 humans behind me whose very lives were now totally dependent on my immediate actions: the *right* actions, and no others. But, just in case I felt like taking a quick snooze, deafening bells rang out: *'Clang, Clang, Clang!'* meaning *Fire, Fire, Fire!* and red lights flashed before me, so I suspected our port engine had exploded.

A common saying amongst pilots having a social drink together is: you don't get paid all that big money for routine flying day after day, because it's not all *that* hard after you've learnt it. They pay you for that one possible moment in your whole career – which most never experience, when all hell breaks loose and the p.o.b. (persons on board) need your training, expertise and experience right now. Suddenly, my most dramatic moment was upon me: *Robert Grant: This is your life!*

I gulped as I thought of all those behind me. They were helpless; chained to their seats with their very lives in my hands while we were barely airborne, dangerously low and racing at 140 knots. How low? I had no time to check the altimeters, or indeed *any* instruments except the Flight Director which thankfully confirmed a small but positive rate of climb. Soon the overall predicament improved slightly with height, but we were excessively too heavy to return for a landing straight away – even though we *had* to!

With some relief, I heard an urgent female voice in my headset reeling off an emergency checklist: 'Okay, port engine failure after take-off. Gear is up, flaps coming up. Captain: fly the aircraft, (not as obvious as it seems). Max thrust on right engine - check. Emergency declared, (I hadn't even *heard* her do this). Fire warning on number one. Fuel dump in progress . . . full opposite rudder.'

Fuel dump! She was on to it already. Fortunately for us, this model 737-500 was one of the few equipped with a fuel dumping system. This would enable us to urgently reduce some excess weight for an immediate return to the airport and a hot, high-speed landing.

I heard Tania broadcast to the Tower. 'Sky Star one-oh-one. Just repeating: we've had a failure of the port engine. It's being shut down but we still have fire warning lights. Full load, so fuel dump in progress. Yawing left of the extended centreline but, ah, requesting gradual left-hand turns to return and land on runway one-six right. Our p.o.b? Ah, ask the company, please. Request full emergency services now – Sky Star one-oh-one.'

Well, that's precisely what I intended to do: return for an immediate landing on the southern-facing runway because I now had several fire warning lights which refused to extinguish. I was about to punch them a few times but she'd almost beaten me to it; so when she raised her eyebrows in question, I quickly nodded concurrence. I saw her hands racing across our glass screens, attempting to cancel emergency red lights where needed, and punching enunciator buttons. Horrible claxons and cockpit warnings barked *Whoop! Whoop! Minimums! Terrain!* - but soon stopped as we gained more height. However, we were still hearing the frightening gonging of the engine fire bells. Damn, warning lights out but bells still chiming? I didn't have time or a solution for that dire question.

This was the precise occasion when I really needed an alert First Officer and, after her tardy start, our newcomer had absolutely *vaulted* into action! Just as well. As I wiped sweat from my brow, I knew that every dramatic second counts here. Some emergency crises allow virtually no time to perform remedial actions, especially flame-outs on take-off, but must be completed anyway. The combined effects of both pilots' actions here are vital in such perilous circumstances.

I stole a fast glance down at Sydney airport as we slowly and carefully made a wide-sweeping left turn over the city. Here our altitude had finally and thankfully made its way up to one thousand feet, enabling me to reduce some thrust from the right engine and thus ease the yawing motion and rudder pressure. On the ground I saw red flashing lights everywhere – so many in fact, they seemed to cover the whole airfield.

I grinned to my F.O. 'Someone must have an emergency down there,' and she smiled briefly. Meanwhile, we continued to pump jet fuel - pure kerosene - at high pressure all over the beautiful city of Sydney, ensuring that thousands would soon be breathing our vaporised fumes. I wondered if the news headlines might yelp:

Aerial Kerosene Vandals Pollute City!

Handicapped with just one engine, albeit one *enormously* powerful engine which can produce 110,000 pounds of thrust, the aircraft maintained level flight as we gently continued our left bank over the famous Sydney Harbour Bridge with its clog of morning peak-hour traffic. Lucky motorists below might soon be wondering why their cars had become coated in a smelly, misty spray. I wished I could stream a banner out the window which said: 'Sorry everyone - we'll wash your cars later', but I was rather occupied just then. We had no choice: I had to dump fuel and couldn't do it out at sea because of the urgency of an engine fire.

Ring! Ring! Oh shut up! I ordered Tania to 'Blow the bottle. Now! And turn off that damned bell, please. We've got its message, loud and clear.' My F/O hit a red lever which activated a fire extinguishing bottle to blast retardant foam inside the left engine bay. The ringing soon stopped as we continued the engine emergency shut-down procedure for our number one power-plant.

As a recorded cabin message loudly intoned: 'FIVE HUNDRED!' we lined up for a long-final approach to runway one-six right – designated 16R – Sydney's longest runway; then rapidly ran through our pre-landing checks. What fools we'd certainly be if, after surviving this crisis on take-off, we subsequently forgot to put our undercarriage back down! But Tania firmly recited: 'Speed brakes checked. Auto pilot off. Gear down, three greens. Flaps thirty. Brakes auto. Dump valves closed.'

'TWO HUNDRED!' the voice barked. 'You know we can't go round on one engine, Tania,' I warned her. 'So tell me if I'm too high or too low.' We had one shot only at this landing.

'Yes sir.'

I asked did she brief the passengers and cabin crew for a *brace position* landing, and she quickly replied, 'Already done that.' I grinned, 'Gee, maybe I'm not needed here, then. Okay, landing checklist complete?' Yes it was.

'ONE HUNDRED!'

My F.O. reported: 'Glide path looks good. Speed good.'

We flashed over the white piano keys, which are the painted zebra stripes near the runway start, as Tania called out, 'Centralise rudder. Drifting slightly left . . . bring it back . . . that's better . . . looks okay.'

We were fast – 145 knots actually, but we had over 13,000 feet, or almost four kilometres of runway to lose any excess speed and make a touch-down, so by now I held few concerns for a safe landing.

The recorded voice intoned: 'FIFTY! FORTY! THIRTY! TWENTY! TEN! . . .

After a long, floating flare-out in which we gradually washed off speed and height, we finally and gratefully bumped to the tarmac on the left wheel bogies. Then we bounced onto the right side and lurched around somewhat as I applied only half reverse thrust to our operative right engine. With Auto-brakes previously selected, we both stomped on the brake pedals anyway – just in case, and with great relief we lurched to an abrupt halt two-thirds the way down the runway.

I wiped my brow. Well, it sure wasn't going to win me the *Landing of the Month* trophy, but at least it *was* a landing!

From all around us emerged a veritable *sea* of emergency fire engines, security vans and dozens of ambulances. Firemen jumped from their rigs to ferociously blast our halted plane with water and white foam. However, they were eventually ordered to stop as the engine was not on fire. Soon they radioed me that we were all safe, just as our alarm bells stopped ringing. The entire drama had lasted less than five minutes - but again, that's what we get paid for.

With no fire confirmed, I ordered the passengers to evacuate down the emergency slides as per standing emergency procedures. The flight crew exited next, with myself being the last lucky person to enjoy the fun run down the rubber chute. Then, after we'd inspected and gawked at the many destroyed engine fan blades from the bird strike we'd suffered, I waited till no-one was watching and snuck under the fuselage to place a kiss on the right engine's cowling; thanking it for service above and beyond the call of duty. Soon, with everyone delighted to be boarding a bus, we were all bussed back to the terminal

At the crowded terminal door we negotiated a bustle of heaving and yelling souls as media flashlights popped as though it were Academy Awards night. Knowing that I definitely didn't intend to be a news star, when a reporter yelled to me, 'Were you the pilot, sir?' I shrugged and ducked into a convenient private doorway before the hounds could get their blood. Nervously, Tania quickly squeezed through the door behind me.

43.

Delayed but not forgotten; our flight *SK101* still had to proceed to Adelaide at some point that day. Obviously our passengers had to get there by some means and we held an obligation to take them because they'd paid for it. As we had no spare aircraft to operate a replacement service, we faced a delay of more than six hours while a replacement engine was fitted to our stricken Boeing. Stripped of many turbine fan blades, the damaged CFM power plant required removal then a major reconstruction and refit at Qantas.

I changed into civvie clothes of jeans and a sports shirt, then headed for the terminal's cafeteria for coffee and a well-deserved wind-down. Heading in the same direction, I came across my new co-pilot, Tania, who had also changed into jeans. This was an occasion when we definitely didn't want to be recognised as pilots, and we both smiled innocently as a throng of jostling reporters rushed past us with cameras jiggling. It had been a wise move to get changed because they ignored us - we looked like any couple walking past; off for a nice holiday, perhaps.

I'd already rung Marie Westcott, my acting PR spokeswoman, and briefed her on the entire details of our little incident, about which she'd soon be facing the press. I warned her to give them facts, only facts, and nothing but the facts. I'm sure she complied, nevertheless TV news bulletins during the day screamed:

Passengers inches from death in fiery Sydney plummet! Woman scribbles desperate last prayers to grandchildren in Sky Star disaster!

I invited Tania for a coffee and lunch, so we strolled to a table and ordered. Here we glanced at numerous TV screens around the room that were showing endless news shots of our Boeing sitting guiltily on the apron; surrounded by rescue vehicles and swarming fluoro-jacketed personnel. Then the same few passengers were shown repeatedly, sobbing tears while clusters of cameras were thrust almost up their noses.

But the only interview I did manage to hear over the cafeteria's din was a sober business man who offhandedly stated: 'It was all over in minutes. I didn't see anyone panicking. The pilots did a great job and we soon landed safely.'

This blasé and quite un-newsworthy comment was soon yanked from the air, to be quickly replaced with an hysterical woman who allegedly had the time, in four minutes, to write goodbye notes to her grandkids on napkins. The fact that this all took place long before our food service was due to be rolled out - when there *were* no napkins - was irrelevant: it made startling news and that's all that mattered.

While I genuinely sympathised with the woman, she was obviously far better off than those unfortunate birds that had been sucked into our port-side engine. On my farm, birds were my great friends, but sadly these ones had been violently rammed at high speed through a turbine compressor where their shower of feathers had ignited and set off the fire detectors. Anyway, by tomorrow the popular news would undoubtedly have moved on to the next outrage that presented itself, and viewers would have already forgotten the victims of today's 'near disaster.'

For myself, I'd already put the whole drama behind me; filed away as good experience and nothing more. This wasn't being pretentious, merely a realisation that I'd complied successfully with years of simulated emergency training to produce an outcome expected and demanded by all. While it is always a threatening situation to suffer an engine failure as close to the ground as we were, myself and all other pilots in the world have practiced and rehearsed this precise emergency scenario countless times in our simulators. This is where an exact replication of real flying is created, and where pilots pass or fail their annual licence renewal tests. So, on this day, my *real* engine failure was barely any different at all from what I had been trained to do, paid to do, and had already coped with on numerous (simulated) occasions.

Contrary to popular public perception, when aircraft engines fail, the planes (mostly) don't *plummet* from the sky. In fact, even single-engined planes simply adopt a gliding attitude when their one and only propeller stops. Of course, they then need some safe landing ground or road to ultimately glide to, and most regularly achieve this – often without injury or damage. On large passenger jets it is easy to overlook the fact that their huge engines produce monstrous amounts of thrusting power. In fact, the mighty Boeing 767 engine generates one of the greatest power-to-weight ratios in the world, while a 747 engine will gulp more air in twenty minutes than a person's lungs will breathe in his or her entire lifetime. Our smaller 737's output is proportionally similar, so when one engine fails on any of these types it's not quite as drastic as it may appear.

When these aircraft are constructed at the Boeing factory in Seattle, their certification and licencing requirements demand that one engine on a twin be more than capable of sustaining continued fight in all situations. Otherwise they would never be allowed off the ground anywhere. Nor would Boeing have sold over ten thousand 737's worldwide. And incredibly, a British Airways 747 once *glided* for more than twenty minutes over the Indian Ocean after *all four* of its engines had stopped, making the word plummet more applicable to swooping and diving seagulls.

And to be accurate, today we hadn't plummeted at all, but actually climbed! – although slower with only one engine turning. These are facts that should be advertised but nevertheless don't receive public attention because the media often thrives on hysteria to peddle their product, not boring mundanities.

In the cafeteria we sipped cappuccinos and I asked our new pilot if she'd spoken to reporters. She assured me she hadn't. Then I said, 'Tania, I haven't flown with you before, hadn't even met you; but for your very first day on the job with us I must congratulate you on your outstanding efforts this morning. At first I was wondering if you were up to standard at all, but you certainly proved you were – and with lightning speed. So thank you.'

She smiled, then apologised again for her late arrival and poor performance prior to our emergency. She explained how traffic had delayed her bus to the airport. Then she was really panicking when the security people, for some unexplained reason, would not admit her to the terminal, even though she showed identification and was dressed in a pilot's uniform.

While they delayed her entry for over fifteen minutes she could not contact our dispatch office, so by the time we entered the flight deck it was all happening way too fast for her. She had barely minutes to familiarise herself in a real 737 cockpit before we were racing down the runway.

I asked her, 'Who rang you at five this morning for this flight? Was it Captain Harland?' No, she didn't know, but it was some man with a Kiwi accent. I couldn't think which dispatcher in our Flying Ops section would give any pilot such short notice for duty on their very first shift. Probably someone had called in sick at the last moment? Oh well, if I'm exiled out there near the foothills instead of here at the airport, things might transpire without my knowledge or approval.

I called our dispatchers on the phone. They explained how security had received a warning of another woman with the same name of Tania Wicks - several years ago - who had tried to enter the secure zone dressed as a pilot. She'd been arrested and charged with security and drug offences. Today their computers had decided that Tania was the same person and alarms had activated accordingly.

I hung up and explained it to Tania. 'Heck, what a strange co-incidence and a stupid screw-up, too. That other woman was about forty and overweight with frizzy hair - hardly you.'

She smiled, then went on to describe her previous flying days - mostly in twin-engine Cessna business-type planes, and how she'd suffered no less than three engine failures in three short years — two of them immediately after take-off. Being a single-pilot operation, she'd needed swift and exacting responses indeed to save her own neck here, let alone those of the others on board. 'And you would appreciate the asymmetric problems if you don't get the correct prop feathered quickly.' I certainly did.

'Three?' I gulped. 'I've never had a real one until today.'

Tania said she hadn't felt a moment's doubt today that I'd get us back down without any trouble. 'It was nothing like my engine-outs in the 414. That 737 has so much power it was just a breeze - obviously - to you. It was kind of dreamlike; just like another routine simulator test for me. Actually, it was only last Friday that Captain Harland and I practiced that exact same failure in the sim, so it was quite fresh in my mind. And you were so calm. You did a great job, Captain.'

'Well thanks, Tania. But it wasn't just me who pulled it off today; you certainly contributed your fifty percent.'

She said, 'Captain, I hope you don't think I'm rude, but in all that rush and drama I've actually forgotten your name. Sorry.'

'It's Rob,' I said.

'Oh. Have you been with Sky Star very long, Rob?'

I flashed a smile and replied, 'Ah quite a while, actually. Haven't you heard of me?'

'No. I'm only new — as you know.'

'Rob Grant. Ask around; someone might know who I am.' We rose to leave the coffee shop. I said to her, 'I'll no doubt see you this evening when we get going again.' Just then, we paused with others as the 'napkin grandmother' was shown on a monitor yet again; tears rolling down her cheeks. Tania and I exchanged knowing winks, then strolled on.

What an extraordinary day it had been. And what a mystery young lady Tania certainly was. I supposed she was about 21 or 22, so not a great deal older than my eldest daughter . . . I reminded myself. And she had the most incredibly big blue eyes to complement a naughty, alluring smile. But she was a fellow pilot, so it was strictly business only . . . damn it!

44.

Relaxing back in Paul's office, Cynthia rang from overseas. Instantly, sparkling blue eyes flew from my vision to be replaced by flaming red hair. 'Hiya Cynth!' I greeted her. 'Long time no hear. How's my credit card? Do I still have a daughter over there somewhere?' We chatted for some time, mostly about the intrepid adventurers' European escapades.

Cynthia related how the two adventurers had landed in Frankfurt, Germany, then spent a few days resting and sightseeing. They then took a high-speed Deutsche-Bahn *Ice Train* to Heidelberg, an historical and picturesque city in south-western Germany. It was quite exhilarating to be flashing across the green fields of Europe at a breathtaking 290 kilometres per hour. At one stage Mandy asked the conductor 'Why is it called the ICE train? We haven't seen any ice or snow yet?'

He smiled and answered blandly, 'The *I.C.E.* stands for *Inter City Express*.' They laughed - felt foolish - then laughed again. On arrival, their flight on rails seemed like just minutes.

In pretty Heidelberg, near the Baroque-style *Old City*, the girls visited the clinics of Dr Otto Ebers, an eminent paediatrician who had conducted several radical surgery procedures which were attracting great interest in world medical circles. Of interest to us were his recent innovative operations in CHD – or Congenital Heart Disease in infants. My ladies made extensive enquiries in and around this medical centre, and for some time questioned a receptionist who spoke quite reasonable English – negating the need for an interpreter at this stage. They played no deception; simply stating that they represented a two-year-old Australian boy who was suffering from a congenital defect of the right ventricle heart valve. Receiving much pertinent information, they then requested the cost of such treatment and were given some vague answers: depending on *this and that,* and with a great variation of prices from about €300,000 up to €450,000. Unfortunately, the very sought-after Dr Ebers was not available for interview; he was booked for months in advance.

That night in their medieval-era hotel which nestled just below the world renowned Heidelberg Castle, the girls decided that no operation lasting about two hours should cost those amounts. With a strong vested interest in protecting my money from unnecessary waste of this magnitude, Mandy began enthusiastically filling her laptop with reams of data from the internet before collapsing from a touch of jet lag.

Next day, in the crisp morning air, they walked to the magnificent University of Heidelberg. In its cavernous reference library, Mandy photo-copied and downloaded more vital data, then they chanced upon a young medical student named Thorsten who was proud to practice his halting English. The young man told them that medical procedures in Germany at that time were absurdly expensive because most doctors had to include crippling overheads associated with their services. Some had moved to practice medicine in Eastern Europe after the fall of the Soviet Union in 1989. Here, operating costs were considerably lower.

Helpfully, Thorsten's companion Helga suggested they head for Budapest in Hungary for the best bargains.

'In surgical procedures, you mean?' asked Cynthia. The girl smiled, 'No, silly, with zee fashion shopping! It is just vunderful. Budapest is so modern and - how you say it - vibrant? And zee shopping is half zee price of here in expensive Germany.'

This was like waving gold credit cards at a street beggar, and, quick as a speeding *ICE* train, Cynthia said, 'Let's go! I wonder how long the train takes to Budapest?'

'Probably about ten minutes at their speed!' laughed Mandy, running towards the door after thanking the two students for their invaluable knowledge. With fortunate timing, the *Hauptbahnhof* (main railway station) was right at the end of their street and an ICE train was about to leave. Icy fast indeed, but being a mostly night run they slept for much of the seven hours of rail travel which plunged through the former Iron Curtain and deep into the darkened depths of Eastern Europe on their mission of mercy to the Hungarian capital.

I remembered to ask Cynth: 'Oh yes, did Mandy locate any Boeings for sale over there – by any chance?'

'She rang two agents and they both thought she was some kid joking around.' I recalled those immortal words: "Schoolgirls should be going to school. . ."

Just as I was waiting eagerly for more, our time for news and gossip was almost up. Before hanging up, she asked 'How are you?'

'Great. Started back flying today. Filling in for Ken. Had a new co-pilot. Isn't that exciting?'

'Yep. How are those girls?'

'Riding bikes. Fighting. Laughing. Chasing boys. Driving me crazy. I love them.'

Cynthia said, 'Sounds normal. I have to go; we're off for a walk around Budapest. It's early evening here. Oh, Amanda says *Hi*.'

'Hi to her, too. Bye.' I innocently assumed they'd be pacing the cobbled alleyways of old Budapest; an ancient fortress defended countless times against marauding hordes over the last millennium. I hoped they'd be doing the regular tourist thing. But I also hoped they'd be knocking on medico's doors, researching facts and figures; marching with a fierce determination of how they were going to save Dad a fortune.

I didn't realise, however, that the fashion houses of Eastern Europe were still open and trading. Salespersons were busy brushing away the snow from their display windows, and vigorously polishing their credit card swipers in eager preparation for the evening's galloping hordes of foreign shoppers. So, into this labyrinth charged my fearless warriors, armed with nothing but a golden plastic weapon and a missionary zeal to shop till you drop!

Next, Marie rang. The press were demanding the name of the 'hero captain' from today's incident. I said that we don't have any. We only employ 'normal' pilots who do their jobs and follow instructions as per their training. Hero captains were in Hollywood. I added that crew names are never given out and we wouldn't be starting now. She enquired if I was okay. I said, 'Why? Has something happened?'

Poking my head back into Paul's office, I asked: 'Who in dispatch rang Tania at five this morning?'

He replied that it certainly wasn't him, and furthermore he was quite surprised that she'd even been in the air today. 'I only completed her final check on Friday. She was highly competent. Brilliant, I thought. But I had no idea she'd be thrust into this on her very first run. Anyway, well done, Rob. You had a real one, eh?'

I was about to explain the whole story, but my phone rang – yet again. It was Olivia calling from school. Was it my flight that had nearly crashed? And was I all right? I assured her that she wouldn't have to go scouring the countryside for a new father. 'But sshhh please; the whole high school doesn't need to hear any of this.' This plea virtually *guaranteed* that they would; and in any case it was already splashed all over TV.

'Hey Livvy,' I added. 'I forgot to say I love you little rascals this morning.'

'Better late than never,' she quipped. 'Oh, by the way: didn't you feel so sorry for that poor grandmother? It must have been terrible.'

'Um, yes. I suppose she'll get over it somehow. Bye now, sweetie. Love ya . . . '

'Awesome, Daddy. Love you.'

45.

Our flight to Adelaide which had been delayed for almost eight hours, was pleasantly and thankfully uneventful. In the dark of night, bolted to a shiny new engine and with pretty Tania Wicks beside me, I marvelled as we sailed beneath twinkling stars that glittered like tears, and floated amongst slanting moonbeams that shone down like rays through cathedral windows. Then we tiptoed over gossamer strands of ghostly strato-cumulus to finally sink down through black mists and into the City of Churches.

As in-flight entertainment, I was softly singing *'Four a.m. in the morning, carried away by a moonlight shadow . . . '* while, apart from technical exchanges, my First Officer remained politely non-committal about my singing prowess.

It wasn't quite four a.m., but a quick turn-around saw us jetting back into Sydney for the very late arrival time of eleven-thirty p.m. - after the evening curfew had commenced, but with a special dispensation from Flying Operations. Finally signing off just after midnight and with no buses to the Western suburbs, I offered Tania a lift home as I lived not too far past there. She seemed uncomfortable about it, but there were no buses or taxies waiting at that hour and she soon accepted.

As we drove out, she said, 'So much has happened on my very first day I just can't *believe* it. I found out who you were in the crew room this afternoon. They all thought I was joking when I admitted I didn't know you this morning.'

She cast her eyes around my shiny green Jaguar as I laughed, 'And that was just a *quiet* morning. Wait till it gets busy!'

We drove towards the western suburbs, engaging in light conversation. 'I've got four kids,' I volunteered. 'My wife passed away long ago.' Tania remarked that I seemed rather young for that. I replied that my eldest girl was only about fourteen years younger than me. 'We're almost the same generation.' She seemed puzzled until I quickly added *'Step* daughter.'

We soon arrived outside a dingy apartment block where she bid me goodnight. At the last moment I sang out the window, 'Come over on the weekend and have a swim in our pool – if you like. Bye now.'

She waved, 'Thank you, Captain.' Hmm, probably lurking inside was some weight-lifting boyfriend with rippling muscles. And anyway, I lectured myself, why am I interested in some junior pilot who'd be more suited to swimming with my daughters than floating around with me?

Why indeed?

*

On the home front, Ken Tolman was on leave; immersed in his family troubles. I'd recently spoken to him on the phone and he'd taken most of our lecturing into consideration; agreeing he should have initially investigated the numerous suggested avenues of assistance before simply fronting me for a massive hand-out. While I was pleased to help in any way, I pointed out that Amanda had been quite correct in taking a strong stance when government and other facilities of assistance for his young child *might* be available. Also, as she'd indicated, staff in the future might demand handouts from us if we'd readily donated largesse without question in his case. And companies are rarely obliged to assist staff in private matters that are unrelated to worker's compensation cases.

But the whole scenario was a most delicate situation; one in which there were no clear-cut solutions. Many differing opinions could be right - or all wrong, but nothing was helped by Ken's neurotic wife who had screamed at him for invoking me and my money in the whole affair. She'd called me 'That spoilt rich kid who was *given* an airline.' While nearly every single word in that sentence was wrong, I was still stung by her spiteful tone. So, while Ken was copping it from both sides, it appeared that she still didn't like me – for some reason. Puzzled, I wondered how someone who'd never met me didn't like me? Meanwhile, neither of them acknowledged that Cynthia and

259

Amanda were in Europe at my expense, seeking treatment for their child.

Personally, the whole crazy affair did not greatly trouble me as long as Ken's boy was saved. And although I'd hoped for a relaxing twelve-month's rest from flying, that could be deferred for a while. It always was, anyway.

Reasonably contented, I once again entertained visions of floating across my pool - dreamlike and nodding off. Thankfully I could do that on weekends as I'd asked Paul to roster me for flying on weekdays only. And, as a change from noisy kids, if Tania called around it should be quite pleasant to have some nice adult like her to float with.

The weekend arrived and I achieved my aim; lazily drifting around my pool in concert with the eddies from my Pool Wizard; relaxing like a floating blob of humanity in a supine surrender of sloth. Here, not a single brilliant thought flashed through my brain, nor one decibel of sound to revive me from my semi-coma, until – *SPLASH!*

It seemed that a parachuted platoon of SAS soldiers had suddenly sky-bombed my pool from thirty thousand feet above. Surfing the tidal waves in surprise, I saw not soldiers but a big bunch of naughty girls who'd been having another sleep-over party here at Grant's Free Motel. Only the most diligent record keeper would know exactly how many squatters there were, but rough estimates indicated more than twenty.

'Hi Daddy! Good morning Daddy. Hi Mr Grant!' the sky-bombers cheered as deafening music suddenly exploded around the pool and the garden foliage withered in shock. As if by magic a few eager boys soon cycled in, attracted like bees to the honey pot at a home containing four pretty sisters and their friends.

'Hello kids,' I yelled over the din. 'Surf's up, eh? Rock concert underway already?'

'When's breakfast?' asked Celia, surfacing to wrestle goggles from another girl. 'We're starving.'

'Yes, we're all starving!' chorused the Vienna Girls' Choir in perfect harmony.

I said, 'Breakfast will be when you troops make it. Do I have *Room Service* tattooed across my forehead? You can see how busy I am.'

'Your Dad's funny,' laughed one starving refugee, so I was unanimously voted the funniest man in the pool.

Then I requested, 'Emmie and Celie: first, please turn down that *alleged* music by at least ninety percent. Then get the outdoor barbie going. Wheel it over next to the pool and start a sausage sizzle for breaky. Get someone to cut up bowls of fruit, someone for salads, and someone else to fetch drinks. You know the rest. Ring a bell when mine's ready, thankyou.' Noisy chatter ensued amidst a hive of activity while I resumed my managerial position on a receding tidal surge.

'What's *alleged* music?' I heard one girl ask. 'Is that something new?' I answered - to deaf ears, that it was a dreadful noise that was purported to be music but nevertheless was not.

From near the barbecue, I heard another girl ask Celia, 'So, don't you have a Mum?'

'Nope,' came the answer. 'Never had a mother. Not that I can remember anyway.'

The girl said, 'Your Dad should get a new one, then. He's nice.'

My girl replied, 'He can't just walk into K-Mart and buy one, you know.' This was an expression I'd used from time to time to weakly justify my reluctance and chronic laziness to pursue another permanent woman. Of course, I had Cynthia here – well, some of the time. She stayed in my room on those occasions; a cosy relationship of no binding pressure. She was 'Dad's girlfriend' and my mob seemed to like her well enough – although it would be unfortunate for us all if they didn't.

Marie Westcott emerged from the office at about ten; just when the last chunks of pineapple were being hurled into the pool as Easts fought Wests in a desperate, shrieking battle. Ducking flak, I was surprised; 'Marie. I didn't even know you were here. Sorry, I would have invited you for breakfast but a locust swarm gobbled it first.'

'I heard them. I just came in for an hour's catch-up,' Marie smiled. 'And to help myself to coffee.' I asked her how she'd fared with the media about our little drama over Sydney last week. 'I gave them the facts, the whole facts and nothing but the facts,' she firmly declared.

'Marie! You're marvellous!'

She smiled a thanks, then mentioned that some woman pilot had phoned earlier. She was coming around to see me today. Might have a swim. 'She didn't sound like either of the two women pilots I know,' Marie said. 'I didn't catch her name, but I heard that Paul hired a new one recently. Was she on that flight with you? Oh well, see you on Monday, Mr Grant. When are the girls coming back from Europe?'

'Next week,' I said. 'I think they've chartered an extra jumbo jet to fly their shopping bags home. Probably cheaper than paying the excess baggage charges on a hundred tonnes or so.'

Marie laughed as she walked to her car. 'Sounds like most normal women to me.'

'Normal?' I squawked. Speaking of women, it must be Tania who rang. Surely? Who else could it be? Madonna? The Queen? No, they don't fly planes. It was a pleasant thought to envisage pretty Tania, with her short brown hair, huge blue eyes and entrancing smile. And although up to my ears in females already, *this* was one I'd truly like to see!

'Okay girls,' I trumpeted orders. 'Everyone off to the rumpus room to catch up on homework.'

'Aw Daa-ad, don't be silly. It's the weekend. We're playing.'

'Okay, play *Nuns in the Convent.* You all have to remain silent for the next fifty years.'

'Daaaad!'

'Well, go and ride your bikes round the farm, please. Also, *Sky* needs feeding and taken for a ride. Pets need feeding too. I'd like some peace for a while, please. I've got someone from work calling in for an important meeting.'

They yipped, 'Okay Dad. Let's go girls!' Just as Chamberlain once declared, 'There will be peace in our time' – suddenly there was. Time for another water nap - like a frog on a pond lily. Would she really come here? I heard a car. Was it Tania's? No, it's just Mrs Rigali our cleaning lady arriving, and I didn't think we'd have any swimmers to fit her.

I greeted her, 'Good morning, Mrs Rigali.'

She waved. 'Hello Mr Grant. I am so happy you still alive after your plane crash. I see it on TV.' Wonderful! Even my Lithuanian cleaning lady knows who was flying that plane, so there's a reasonable chance everyone else in the galaxy knows too!

*

Once again, it was sheer bliss to float under the sun, arms trailing in the warm water while drifting in slow circles. Yet the acute realisation of something missing – the chatter of excited children, had already overtaken my selfish dreams.

Staring vertically at a lone wisp of high cirrus cloud in an otherwise empty blue sky, I pondered dark images of just a few years hence when the chattering and the fun would all be gone. When empty hallways and vacated rooms would contain only dusty photographs of little smiling faces. When I might stand for hours, gazing in futile remembrance of my four finest friends as if this might magically enable them to return still young and still smiling.

Today I could foresee a time when I might soon exist in solitude; pointlessly yearning for a golden era in a loving family now grown and departed. Then, would I hear only ghostly echoes of running feet, pillow fights and pool splashes? And bikes zinging past, kids and their friends laughing and crying? In mirrors I glimpsed my sad reflections of this imminent future, and clearly saw teenagers' messy bathrooms and kitchens that would one day be permanently cleaned and vacated. I imagined once-loud TV's that had fallen silent forever, and might even yearn for that *alleged* music that had long since thumped out its final pulsing beats.

Then, the show would be over and I would be 'solitary man' - gazing sightlessly to vague horizons like an Easter Island statue.

Just *why* did I ever complain about these perceived annoyances in the first place? Had I ever really needed *four* empty bathrooms? Was all their music so unbearable after all? And wasn't it, in truth, *boring* in the swimming pool by myself? Ashamed, I reflected how only minutes ago I'd ordered my lovely girls to disappear somewhere else and leave me in peace, then lied about an important meeting. But the awful day might soon be upon me when they might vanish forever!

Overhead, my eyes followed a new strand of high clouds, lazily twirling like mares' tails, as I recalled occasionally visiting a nursing home where my ageing aunty Nina used to sit forlornly and permanently in a wheelchair, facing the distant hills. A lovely person, she'd had a son long ago who'd simply left home one day, never to return. 'He went over those hills,' she always told me, pointing to the west. 'Over the hills and far away.' In her lap she always clutched a faded photo of a smiling young man. Every year it faded a little more.

Would it be the same for me? Perhaps my girls of the future might contact me just once or twice a year on special occasions. Busy with their adult lives. Thanks for everything Dad, but see ya! Time was marching inexorably towards their adulthood. My little Mandy already *was* a woman; the others, aged between twelve and fifteen, soon to be the same. It would be a mere fleeting second in time before they'd fled the nest too; off to their futures with others. Raising their own families one day.

With no small regret, I cursed the many times I'd left them in the care of minders while I worked hard and stayed away. And it hurt to wonder how many occasions of real need did they cry for me, their only parent, in the loneliness of long nights? How often did they suffer stomach pains or toothaches, or just want to hold their Dad's hand because they had no mother? I imagine they eventually surrendered to sleep, alone with shadows and muddled dreams of a tall man in a shiny blue uniform who appeared in their lives just *some* of the time.

Spinning slowly in watery circles, my gaze saw beautiful Cristina smiling from on high. But she quickly danced away upon cirro-stratus gossamer, to be followed by an identical but younger woman together with her three sisters - all smiling and waving goodbye. My four children had been, like all children, just transient guests in my guesthouse. Somewhere to mature while growing their wings and becoming a parent's fleeting memories. A passing parade.

I heard someone singing. It could have been me . . .

Rows and flows of angel hair, ice cream castles in the air,
Feathered canyons everywhere, I've looked at clouds that way . . .

Such a beautiful song that now sounded so sad. I cursed my previous caustic comments and sergeant-major's orders to go elsewhere and play. Why had I said that? In a few short years this pool would be deserted and the paddocks devoid of chirping voices. No more knocks on my door, no bikes strewn everywhere, no piles of washing or stacks of dirty plates. The house phone wouldn't ring twenty times after school - if at all, and no longer would I stumble over shoes scattered across the floor. While forgotten boxes of pretty dolls would finally and forever be shut, no more school uniforms would flutter from the clothes-lines and no nervous young boys would politely ask if my sweet girls were home. Inevitably, they would all be gone . . . and I would be alone.

*

Alone - but just not yet. Fortunately, whoever had been singing so tunelessly just then had stopped. Had I fallen asleep and dreamt all that? I clambered from the pool to peer around the farm. Greatly relieved, I spied a bunch of happy kids playing in the distant paddocks. The girls and boys were having hay fights as our gray horse looked on. I grabbed someone's pink bike from the shed and pedalled across rough grass, then up a small incline. I came to Olivia, now fifteen and as tall as Amanda. She was gazing into a boy's eyes. . Gee, he seemed so *young* to me. She was surprised, 'Dad! . . . What? We're not doing anything wrong . . . '

'Just came to join in the fun,' I smiled. 'And to say I love you girls.'

'Dad, don't be so embarrassing in front of Ethan!'

'Sorry, Ethan,' I winked at him. 'You'll understand one day.'

But Celia wasn't coy. She grabbed my arm and shouted, 'Yay! Dad's joining in. Here's your bale, Dad. Let's smash 'em!'

We battled the enemy in our hay wars until victory was almost assured, then Emily remembered: 'A little white car drove in before. Then it went away. Wasn't someone important coming to see you?'

I stared back down the slope towards our semi-rural hacienda. 'Yes, but no-one is as important as my little monsters.' Having said that, I was promptly knocked flat on my back by a flying bale of hay. The crowd cheered. Ignoring my dead body, a girl yelled, 'Let's go swimming again!' Someone else added, 'And cook another barbie for lunch!' There was no opposition to these proposals and in an instant they'd vamoosed.

Prostrate, I remained sprawled in hay beside the pink bike as its front wheel still spun with a hum. That was when I heard a slightly familiar voice softly ask, 'Excuse me Captain Grant. Ah, is that you? Sorry if this is not the right time. I came and knocked earlier, but your place was deserted.' I squinted up into the sun. It was my new co-pilot; the important visitor.

'Hi Tania!' I grinned at her and stood the bike up. 'Hop on the back. Let's see if we can fly this thing together, shall we?' Awkwardly, we wobbled a few metres across the long grass. But then, thankfully less frightening than our maiden flight together, with a scream and a yelp we tumbled back into the hay for a crash landing.

Poolside, we sat where a dozen pairs of inquisitive little eyes followed our every move like swivelling submarine periscopes. To giggles and whispered gossip, I listened as petite Tania chatted away. Initially I'd thought she was an unusually quiet type, but today she was quite happy and chirpy. My girls had politely introduced themselves and their friends to her. Tania said, 'Nice kids.'

The girls and boys eventually stopped grinning and staring, then commenced swimming races as we watched on. Tania spoke of her apprehension in coming here today to my humble abode. People at work had certainly told her who I was, and they'd advised her to stay away – even though I'd personally invited her for a swim. Also, they'd ensured she was told that I was virtually married to a senior official in our airline who was overseas at the moment. One woman had warned her, 'You can't just barge up to Mr Grant's farm whenever you please as though you're someone important, you know.'

I said, 'Oh that's nonsense, Tania. Look around us: I've got over *twenty* visitors here already. They just barged up last night so I invited them to sleep over. We've all had fun. It's a laid-back, open house here. I can invite who I please. Anyway, are you enjoying being with us after that big first day?' I realised that without Ken's family matters and his subsequent absence I may not have met Tania for a long time - and certainly not in such spectacular circumstances where I ended up inviting her home. Those poor birds didn't die completely in vain.

Tania beamed her wide and pretty smile. She absolutely *loved* being with Sky Star; her first really big break in life. She'd originally been interviewed by another Chief Pilot but he seemed somewhat grumpy, then her final interview was with nice Captain Harland who was so pleased with her that he asked: 'How soon can you start?'

She was astonished to have won the job, then even more surprised when she'd been rushed through jet simulator training because of pilot shortages. Expecting more *real* in-flight training before her first jet trip as a qualified F/O, she was amazed when they called her at 5 a.m. for our flight last week – especially with simulator time as her sole jet experience. Then the rest had happened in such a crazy blur that she still found hard to believe.

'Ha! We always welcome our new people with a bit of fun,' I laughed.

Tania replied that her family was simply horrified when she'd rung them with the dramatic tale of our bird strike. Their TV news hadn't mentioned any pilots' names and her parents had no idea she was flying with us that day. On TV, they'd seen the weeping granny. They were old fashioned and understood nothing at all about flying. Now they were even more bewildered as to why their only child had gone into flying those 'dangerous things' in the first place.

'They're from the *old* country,' she explained. 'Our name wasn't Wicks, it was Wojciechowicz. It's Polish and no-one could ever pronounce it, let alone *spell* it. Anyway, when I worked three jobs during high school to pay for my flying lessons at Bankstown airport, they just prayed for me to win back my *sanity* – not my pilot's wings. So there I was, scrubbing tables and bars in pubs, picking up beer glasses and sometimes mopping toilets, and for each ten hours of that labour I could afford just a one-hour flying lesson. Ma and Pa gave me hell and urged me to drop all that nonsense and become a hairdresser - or a housewife, preferably. Anything but driving those awful aeroplanes.'

'Their own parents had crawled from the ruins of World War Two after constant aerial barrages throughout Poland had destroyed every home and shelter they fled to. So our family gained a permanent hatred and terror of all aircraft – especially large ones. When I told them I'd applied for Sky Star, they swore at me over the phone.'

'But we're hardly the Luftwaffe,' I smiled. 'Did you explain to them that we simply transport civilian people in passenger planes to nice destinations in peace time?'

She had, but with no effect. She'd been expecting, however, some pride from her parents upon hearing of her successful transition from general aviation into airlines. But before they would even discuss it, Tania's news of her in-flight emergency shocked them. They ordered her to 'Give it up immediately!'

'So, they're totally paranoid about flying,' Tania said. 'I think if I'd gone into stripping on the stage in Kings Cross they'd have been more approving.'

I grinned. 'If that had been my career choice instead of flying, I'd be pretty hungry by now.' Tania laughed and gripped my arm in mirth – as some people do. It was at that exact instant that a pair of beady eyes spied on us from the pool – like periscope eyes peeping from a sub. Then the eyes slid quietly back underwater; their owner submerging to the depths; no doubt to report in at Spy Kids' Headquarters.

Eventually Tania enquired about her long-term future with us. I assured her that it looked extremely rosy - especially if she kept flying as she'd done on her first day. 'I've got some rather big expansion plans coming up,' I proudly told her. 'And at the moment we're looking at Ansett stumbling towards bankruptcy and oblivion. The sky's the limit then, as they say. So you should always have a permanent position with us. You'll see.' Her eyes lit up, and she shifted ever so closer to me. I was quite enjoying Tania's company, as she apparently did mine - and she wasn't exactly ugly, either.

Feeling talkative, I touched upon my earlier unease of my 'little girls' growing up in a few years and leaving home. She added that her parents, too, still thought of her as 'their little girl.'

For the third time that day, my eager volunteers fired up our overworked barbecue, but only after I'd asked the other visiting girls to please clean it first. Fair enough, they agreed. 'My Mum yells at me if ours isn't clean,' one girl said. I thought, 'At least you've *got* a Mum.' I invited Tania to stay for a feast of barbecued pineapple, banana and avocado. She thanked me, then said she should leave after that. The girls were certainly curious and gossipy about her; especially when she'd taken a quick dip in the pool. This caused chins to wag. I failed to see what interest they could possibly have in one more person diving in, but my male reasoning was not theirs. Tania could have represented a threat; or she could perhaps appear as a prospective step-mother. To motherless kids, anything new was interesting, I supposed. To a wife-less man, well . . .

As we indulged in another delightful poolside spread, I cheekily congratulated myself on having avoided the cooking on all three occasions. Tania again laughed and touched my arm. This time I heard a whisper from the bushes behind us, 'Dad's got a new girlfriend. Whoo-hoo!'

I barked, 'Who said that?' There was a silence, to be punctuated with giggles. But I was happy – very happy.

I started singing *'Zippedy Doo-Da* . . . ' until little voices chanted, 'Don't give up your day-time job, Dad!'

And perhaps Tania agreed, because she took the hint and excused herself. 'I must go now. Thank you so very much, Mr Grant. I hope to meet your other daughter some time. See you at work soon, I suppose.'

After she left, I demanded the phantom rumour-monger own up, then said, 'Listen you lot, she's *not* my girlfriend, for Heaven's sake!'

'You always say *for Heaven's sake*,' smirked Emmie. 'Especially when you're lying.'

'I would *never* tell a lie!'

'See, you're lying now.'

'Now that's enough, thank you. And no blabbing to Cynthia or Mandy when they get back.'

'Why?'

'Because I said so, that's why. Tania is just a pilot who works for us. She came around for a swim, so get over it, for Heaven's sake.'

'There, you said it again!'

But I knew for an unfailing certainty that once our two long lost travellers approached even remotely within radar range of the farm, the bells would be pealing and the town criers would be heralding the world-shattering news of 'Dad's new girlfriend' - even if she wasn't.

Cringing, I could almost envisage fiery Amanda's attitude to someone barely older than herself gripping her father's arm. If she'd torn strips off our Chief Pilot without blinking or even once re-sharpening her sword, I could be facing the guillotine immediately upon Mandy's arrival. And that's if I was lucky. Worse, this predicament didn't yet consider the approval or otherwise of my part-time lady friend, the lovely red-haired Cynthia. Somehow I suspected the 'otherwise' verdict.

And I hadn't even *done* anything – yet. So I decided: I'll just not invite Tania any more. That was easy. And if my girls could possibly staple their lips together for the next several years, I should, with some good fortune, escape with a stern warning.

Solved. However, my dilemma was that I quite liked our new pilot. I wasn't tied down, I assured myself, and I could do whatever I pleased in life. Couldn't I? Just this very morning I'd been fearing my kids growing up and their imminent departures from home, so I had an obligation to myself to establish my future for when they've gone.

So that was that. Time to wrap up, send those other young guests marching home, and remind my little spies about school in the morning. Tidy your rooms, iron your uniforms, finish those homework assignments, forget TV for tonight and generally do what Father says, because Father knows best. Doesn't he?

About to head for my room, Celia skipped up and handed me a phone. 'It's a Mr Preston for you. I hoped it was going to be Lisa. She absolutely *promised* she'd ring today.'

I told her that they'd already had enough friends stay over this weekend to crew a large battleship, so that was enough. In response, she took no notice of my witty sarcasm and pecked me a sweet goodnight kiss.

46.

Ben Preston was a private investigator whose *Eagle Eyes* agency I paid to keep a watch over 'all things aviation.' Not as spies or agents of subterfuge; I simply enjoyed and trusted their monthly report about significant 'things happening around town,' as he had advertised to me. In a large business such as mine with millions in assets, Ben didn't patrol my planes while they were parked out on the apron at night: he surreptitiously observed the machinations of big business in the aviation world; in particular the applicable scene here in Australia.

I'd never thought of utilising investigators before he made an appointment to see me about a year ago - and failed to see why I ever should, but Ben's sharp mind soon had me considering his proposals, while his cryptic conversations made me fascinated. Eventually his tales of industrial surveillance in all avenues of business convinced me to subscribe to his regular *Eagle Eyes* bulletins, and to heed his surreptitious faxes and phone calls; sometimes whispered late at night. It was insurance, he insisted. An operating expense. 'After all, Rob, you wouldn't fly with your planes uninsured, would you?'

No, that made sense. So, Ben had explained, should rival airlines, businesses, or even governments ever plot evil deeds against me, he would likely know in advance and quickly advise me. Rising oil prices? He always knew these things first; and when I queried how, he just smiled and tapped his temple: *Smart*! True to his claims, it transpired that he, as claimed, with his brilliantly sharp mind was often aware of pertinent information that could affect me – good or bad. Occasionally he'd reveal his information sources, but most times he'd just smirk: 'It's on a need-to-know basis, and you *don't* need to know.'

I was duly fascinated and often imagined Ben snooping around in drains at night, or perhaps training micro cameras through gaps in curtains. I wondered if he sometimes dressed as a foreign operative in a business suit, exchanging rolled-up newspapers with dubious street characters who strode quickly past.

Spying antics aside: at the very least I definitely desired pertinent and timely information on Sky Star's friendly competition and their latest actions, just as they undoubtedly observed ours. Within a few months he'd already saved me some money in various matters, so it was smart insurance, as he'd stated. And, although very overweight, he seemed like a fun guy who was usually bubbling with jovial effervescence. We had a good rapport and I liked him.

I said into the phone, 'Hi Ben. What do I need to know?'

Always half out of breath, Ben puffed, 'Boss, little birdies around the place say *they're* after you again.'

'Who? Not that Chinese banker, surely? And please don't call me Boss.'

'Not him this time, Boss. People who don't want your competition – permanently.'

'But that's nothing new, Ben. You know that. I've had a dozen threats of take-over or ruin in a dozen years. It's all a big yawn to me because I simply continue providing good and friendly service, and nothing beats that. Besides, Ansett's had more sharks circling them than we'll ever have.'

'This one's just a little shark.' Ben warned. 'But a *mole* shark that could have big teeth . . . '

I said, 'Ben, can you meet me at the airport tomorrow? I'll be there after nine. Gotta fly somewhere. No more cryptics on this phone, thanks.'

'Have a nice night, Captain. Sleep tight.' Ben laughed, then rang off. Hmm, what an actor he's being today. Probably has nothing but thin air to peddle, but needs some extra income at the agency. However, he's usually an interesting and reliable source with a keen ear forever cocked skywards.

I crawled into bed, tired but quite pleased with this day. I'd had my kids to muck around with, and met many of their nice friends, too. Had a very enjoyable visit from a petite brunette First Officer, and enjoyed *three* fun barbecues and pool parties. Oh, I must remind the troops to watch our pool camera video tomorrow night after dinner. It was always fun to laugh at the re-runs of our crazy pool antics as they often screened funnier the second time and third times around.

But shark? A pool shark? What on Earth was a *mole* shark? Who cares, it's off to sleep for me.

*

Ben Preston was a large man – too large, as I often reminded him, and for no unfounded reasons did I call him Big Ben. An ageing hippie from the 1960's *Flower Power* era, his slender years of youth had long departed – or rather *expanded*, while the sole remnants of hippiedom was his shoulder-length straggly hair and sloppy clothing. For Ben, the flowers had truly wilted.

At his suggestion, we were meeting in an unused paddock just near the old Qantas base. Feeling rather exposed and uncomfortable in this open paddock, I asked him if we were in the CIA and was the Cold War still on? And what was wrong with my little 'dog box' office behind the hangar? The man of few words puffed, 'Some little birdies have big ears.' Although I'd never seen birds with big ears – or indeed any ears at all, I wasn't about to challenge his expertise.

Before my spy vs. spy briefing began, I politely reminded him again of the risks of obesity; in his case, *extreme* obesity. 'Ben, you're not losing any weight as you promised me last month. Instead of sleuthing around back alleys as in those detective novels, you might like to research obesity and its direct links to diabetes, heart disease, and a host of other nasties.' Ben replied, as he always did, that he'd be losing weight 'soon.' I told him that no pilot of ours would ever pass their annual medical check-up at his weight and condition. He countered by saying he had no intention of ever becoming a pilot, so I retorted that no plane of ours could ever lift him into the air at his current maximum gross weight. He laughed. It was all in jest, he thought. I was serious.

Feeling quite conspicuous in the middle of this paddock, we sat in his rusty red Mercedes to talk. With the light banter over, I said, 'Now, let's get into it, please. I have to fly in an upwardly direction in sixty minutes.'

Never one to dally, Ben kicked off with: 'Okay, here we go: I spy with my little eye, something beginning with *B*.' I asked him was this a quiz show and could I ask the audience - or maybe phone a friend? He shook his head. So I guessed, 'Ah, banana? Band-Aid? Bozo? I don't know, Ben. Why don't you enlighten me?'

He whispered, 'Boss, *they've* got a plan. *They* see huge changes coming in Aussie aviation real soon. In their crystal ball they see a billion dollar bonanza coming up for grabs.'

I interrupted - without asking who *they* were. 'So it's *B* for bonanza, is it? Or ball? Or billion?'

'None of the above. Anyway, this little birdie told me that Uncle Reg's airline (Ansett) was being bought up simply to strip it of its assets, then bankrupt it.'

'Not the first time that's happened in the commercial world, mate,' I assured him. 'And it won't be the last. So is it *B* for birdie, for Heaven's sake? The suspense is killing me, Ben. I just love these childish games, especially when I haven't a moment to spare. Anyway, what's all this got to do with Sky Star – which I have to propel into the atmosphere very shortly?'

Ben whispered, '*They* aren't going to let you grab the extra ninety thousand seats a month that come on the market once Uncle Reg flies off the radar.'

'Who the Christ are *they*, Ben? And he's already *off* the radar; Reg Ansett is dead!'

White Man who speaks in riddles said, '*They!* Listen Boss, Reg is gone and so is his airline very soon – hook, line and sinker. It might be still flying today - yep - there goes one now, but soon, probably by the end of 2001, *they* intend to have it.'

I said, 'I don't even *want* ninety thousand extra seats! Where the hell would I put that many additional passengers? Sticky-taped to the wings? *Six* thousand a month would be quite enough for us – that's only about two hundred a day. Then I'll buy one or two new planes and let Qantas carry the remainder. We coped with it once before when they were grounded for a few days, so what's the problem here?'

Ben smirked. 'You're not going to get *any* seats at all – unless you slip *them* quite a few bucks now to stay out of it. If not, they've already got a plant inside your bunker. To ferret out your whole operating position – eventually. They'll access your accounts and books; your computers and especially your personal life. That's the rough plan so far, to derail your show just at the right time. After that, they'll run you out of town because they'll be too big for little 'ole you. Then they might go after Qantas, too.'

'Well bloody good luck with that project!' I grinned with much amusement while imagining an ant chasing an elephant. 'Wait a minute. A *plant*? You mean like a pot plant? Or a machinery plant? That doesn't start with *B*, Ben. No-one's ferreting out my operation. Your little birdie sure has got a vivid imagination in his bird brain. My office is just metres from my bedroom bay-windows. It's one of the reasons I moved it way off the airport: to be directly under my control at all times. My staff there are impeccable. One of them is my own daughter, as you know. Another is my lady friend and companion. Our computers and records are locked and secured at all times. Any break-in sets off a flashing light and buzzer near my bed. I'm highly security conscious, Ben. I've told you all this before. I think you even installed some of this yourself. It's Fort Knox. I'm well aware of the possibilities of industrial espionage and I've got staff that I totally trust. No-one else can get in.'

'They will easily if you *let* them in,' argued cryptic Ben.

'I won't! And now that you've warned me, I will be extra vigilant in future about any lurking saboteurs wearing dark raincoats and hearing aids. Okay?'

'Forget in the future. Forget raincoats. I told you before: they already have a mole with one foot in your bunker. *They* hold the cards; you are naked.'

I sighed with annoyance, 'Ben. Is this like one of those cryptic crossword questions: 'The mole in the bunker was having sex with the ferret, but was it on a Wednesday?'

'Something like that,' he grinned.

I said, 'All right. I give up. Spill the beans. What starts with *B* that could possibly be of any interest to me or Sky Star, Sherlock?'

Big Ben chimed, 'I spied, with my little eye, a *B* for *bikini.'*

'Whaaaat!' I yelped. 'Are you mad? Bikini, for Christ's sake? What's that supposed to mean? I don't even wear a bikini!'

Ben laughed and assured me, 'Not you. Who else wears a bikini, Rob?'

'Only half the world. All the women on all our beaches all summer long. I don't wear one personally, but they sure do.' Suddenly I was jabbed with a dark thought: I'd only seen one person in a bikini recently: my new pilot, Tania. 'Are you by any chance referring to Tania Wicks, Ben? What do you mean you spied her bikini? At my place? You haven't been to my place for months. Er, have you?'

Ben whispered, perhaps for dramatic effect, 'We got a hot tip, okay? A trusted source recently told our operative that a certain young lady had entered your bunker as a new employee. *Someone* had manipulated your computers so she'd fly with you. They'd been hoping she'd be rostered with you eventually then she could commence her work, but they hit the jackpot on her very first day – due to a bit of expertise thrown in. It worked like a charm - especially with that unplanned emergency occurring. Then you quickly became attracted to her and invited her home, right? So I went there to observe her that weekend.'

I held up a hand: 'Now Ben, whoa! Tania is a genuine pilot and a genuine employee. She's not a spy from Eastern Russia. She's no fake pilot. No imposter. No *agent provocateur.* She can fly. Believe me; I was astonished how well she reacted in our crisis. Couldn't have done much better myself. In any case, Paul Harland employed her, not me. He checked her out in the simulator. He interviewed her and investigated her résumé and flying experience. He verified her integrity. It's all legitimate, Ben. She's a pilot, not a spy.'

Ben smirked, 'I don't care if she's a butcher, a baker or a candlestick maker. Or a pilot, an astronaut or a check-out chick. *They* altered the flight rosters on *your* computers. It's called hacking and it's easy. I do it all the time. She's working for them and now she's made such incredible early progress that they had to quickly revise all their plans.'

I didn't like the sound of that word 'hacking.' Although it was still early days on computers for most of us, apparently some smarties (and him) already knew how to breach the system. 'What damn plans?' I protested. 'How could she possibly affect Sky Star Airlines by simply coming for a barbecue and a swim at my place? And just what is all this bikini rubbish anyway, Ben?

Big Ben whispered: 'Listen: inside knowledge is power. Power is money. It was hard work - plus good fortune that I got such a lucky, early-warning tip-off. And then I found out she was wired, so now we're one step ahead of *them*.'

'Wired!' I yelped. 'You mean with a hidden microphone? At my place? My guest at a barbecue had a hidden wire? How stupid! What was she hoping to record? The avocado's slicing open? The sausages sizzling? Kids squealing and splashing? And where was this evil wire, anyway? I sat right beside her for two hours and saw nothing.'

'Inside her bikini. *B* is for bikini, Boss. You're a wealthy man. For big money people will go to any lengths. Just a few of your recorded words could be quite valuable to certain vested interests in the future.'

Sceptical and wary at first, I was also becoming quite alarmed that this might just possibly be true. It was shocking to consider that anyone might intrude on my private life in such an outlandish manner, and especially to record my words about 'big expansion plans' – or anything else I may have uttered in casual conversation.

Still, I acted blasé and asked him, 'Are you sure you haven't been watching too many James Bond movies, Ben?'

'No time for movies. Reality is scary enough. Remember how you drove her home late that night because she has no car? And there was no bus, she said. But last Sunday she arrived at your farm in a small white car; a BMW. She claimed that security held her up at the terminal door last week, yet now they've got no record of it. We checked. I think *they* hacked the system to slot her in with you, then

278

they concocted that delay in their haste because it was all taking too long to find out which flight you were on.'

I said, 'Wait. This is absurd. I called my dispatcher that afternoon and he explained that entry delay. They thought Tania was some woman who impersonated a pilot some years ago - it happens from time to time – drunks, usually – and I can't remember the rest of it just now because I was racing to take a flight.'

Ben continued, 'Exactly. I told you: these people *hack* things. Whatever occurred at the checkpoint was quite beside the point: it was long enough to delay her. So anyway, that night you dropped her home in a dark street out near Penrith somewhere. But she lives at Punchbowl, Rob. A long way from Penrith. Your staff records will reveal that – just as they showed me.'

'Well, maybe she was staying at a friend's place. A boyfriend? An Olympic weightlifter who owns a BMW. Who knows?'

Ben smirked. 'I bet she thought it was Christmas. Gets magically slotted to fly with you on her very first shift, then gets dropped home that night by none other than the Big Boss Man himself. A few days later she's diving in your pool – after you spilled your heart out. Did you hand her the deeds to your planes, too? Plenty of men have hurled their fortunes to a pretty woman. So, just exactly what did you say to the lady, lover boy?'

'Ah, "Pass the tomato sauce?" I can't remember now, Ben. But I'll tell you what, whatever I did tell her it's all recorded on our own wire. With video pictures, too. We've got our own pool cam, as you should know. It was right above our heads the whole time. If her bikini was stacked with something extra, our little birdie might have caught it. Do you mean that your paparazzi telephoto lenses failed to notice my little pool cam? You may have even installed it originally. It once recorded Mike Mayfield's cameraman falling into the pool – camera and all.'

Ben looked slightly worried. Was it possible that Mr Super Sleuth had forgotten about our own camera? He stroked his chin, 'Hmm, we might just beat them at their own game . . . '

I asked him, 'And Ben, were you *really* at my property that day? Spying something beginning with *B*?' He pleaded guilty so I said, 'I never saw you and you're not exactly a *small* target. So where did you hide?'

'Behind the horse, Boss. He didn't like me much, though.'

I laughed, then gulped at the power of his lens to see us clearly from that far. Or could it? 'Behind the damned horse? And who'd blame it for not liking you? Poor thing probably thought you were holding an enormous weapon, or something. And tell me this, if Tania carried some sort of recorder, wouldn't it get wet when she swam?'

'Might, but probably waterproof. We bought waterproof cameras recently for under two hundred dollars each. Same thing.'

'I wouldn't dare ask what they were for. Maybe you're snooping on illicit fish orgies now? '

'Could be. Anyway, my urgent advice is that you've got to be rid of that one. She's dangerous. How many women did James Bond have who double-crossed him?' I rubbed my chin in thought, but 007 had probably lost count. And a licence to kill? That might come in handy one day. But was that Bond or his women? I couldn't remember now; I'd been too busy running an airline with thirty two jets to ever attend movies – except *Snow White* with the kids.

I was angry. 'Get rid of her? You mean *fire* her? After just one shift? That might be a world record. Gee, what planet do you come from? Even better than that Ben, instead of flying into a rage and sacking her – which instantly gives the whole game away, why don't I simply invite her over again sometime and do what all self-respecting double-agents do: plant bogus or misleading information to see what transpires? I might even enjoy being the new James Bond. I hear they're looking for another replacement.'

Ben grinned. 'Shaken but not stirred, eh Boss? But you don't own an Aston Martin – yet. Look Boss, we aren't playing with fools here. Double-Oh-Seven you are not.'

I concluded, 'You're right. If I had a gun I'd probably shoot my foot off. Well, you and your little birdies are veritable founts of riveting information and I thank you. But before you go, can you just tell me how you managed to hide behind a horse – given your, ah, largish size? Wouldn't a horse be more successful hiding behind *you*?'

'Funny, Boss. Were you ever a stand-up comedian before taking to the air? And by the way, I come from the planet Earth – like you.'

This was rather hard to believe, and despite our usual light banter I was starting to consider that our Ben was hardly a jovial joker; far more likely an insidious threat. Nevertheless, I decided we should part on a humorous note – for now.

We shook hands. 'Anyway, very interesting advice, thankyou Ben. Please send me your bill. But just before I go, would you like me to sing you that old hit song: 'She wore an itsy-bitsy teeny-weenie yellow polka-dot bikini?'

He must have heard my great singing before. 'Ah, no thanks Boss. My other piece of advice is that you don't give up your daytime job.'

47.

In the evening, with three of my best friends, we watched our pool video replay. I pretended to show little interest and thankfully the girls soon tired of it - mostly because we'd all seen so many pool videos before and many others from when they were younger had been funnier than this one. I was relieved when they soon adjourned to their rooms so I could watch it over again – in slow motion.

Alas, even in slow-mo, the video displayed no world-shattering revelations, nor any spicy Spy-vs-Spy titbits. And most of the audio, at any speed, was distorted by the chattering and splashing of so many kids around us. Even when listening extra-carefully, my voice seemed to drone away with barely a decipherable word, while occasional comments from Tania were hardly headline-grabbing stuff. After sundown, the tape showed a monotonous picture of my bedroom sliding doors. I watched it for a short while in fast forward, then tossed it into a drawer to join all the others.

Thinking deeply, I reasoned that most of Ben Preston's warnings could be like someone firing blanks: lots of noise but nothing of substance. Tania may have lied about her reason for running late that day because she was terrified of the consequences - it being her very first shift. If so, certainly not a very honest start with our company. But she obviously wouldn't have foreseen that she'd be flying with the company's founder and owner. She didn't even know me. The dramatic emergency soon to follow was totally co-incidental to anything - unless those hapless Kamikaze birds were also part of the plot?

But seriously, Tania may well borrow a white BMW car but simply prefers to travel by bus into the airport - as thousands of commuters do every day. Many people dislike driving to work in city traffic. She never claimed that her residence was where I dropped her; it might have been her parents' place, her friend's, or her boyfriend's? And if she did in fact carry a small recording device onto my property, how on Earth did she benefit from taking such risk? What did she hope to hear me say? Did she assume I was blatantly reckless enough to disclose crucial details of our company's operations to someone I'd known for less than a week? And would any young person anywhere, having just commenced employment in a well-paid and prestigious position, risk losing the lot, and perhaps prosecution, to surreptitiously obtain a few meagre morsels of business information which would be unlikely to possess much worth, if any?

Upon deep reflection, it seemed that Ben's investigative work and subsequent warnings could have easily originated from rumour, gossip or other such mischievous misinformation - that is: blanks.

Or perhaps not? The more I speculated, the more complex it all became. For example: someone might whisper to Tania how incredibly rich I am — even if that's an exaggeration, and how could I deny it when a recent cover photo of *Business Review Weekly* showed me posing proudly in front of nine of our jets? Seeing it on a news stand, perhaps Tania boasted to someone — a girlfriend, possibly — that now she's a Sky Star pilot she'll probably fly with the wealthy Rob Grant one day, the rich owner of Sky Star, and if she can she'll try to seduce him - or at least burrow her way into his life and affairs to obtain advantage one day. Such tactics were hardly revolutionary new strategies in human relationships, but went back to Cleopatra and Antony and long before them. The Cold War was awash with glamorous Russian spies who slept their way through to blueprinted missile diagrams. In fiction, trading sex for national secrets was not only expected, but *de rigueur* in all Cold War novels.

So our Tania, armed with a few juicy paperback novels and a copy of *BRW*, may have decided on such a course of tactics and her companion — whoever it was, confided her boasts to someone with keen vested interests - i.e. *THEY*.

Mired in indecision, yet sharply aware that I'd always made it a habit to make at least one important decision before retiring to bed, this time I mentally tossed a coin and finally decided that no, this quaint event was scarcely worth devoting much more of my time or attention. Yet, trying to sleep, I recalled that this hiccup wasn't exactly new and, as company head, I'd endured a few threats over time —

some specific and some vague, from unknown writers disgruntled over perceived injustices. And several angry voices on the phone had blasted unprintable, and often unintelligible, tirades in my ear.

None of these onslaughts were worth the effort of informing the police, but I kept some letters for amusement. One received note warned: 'Your flites cr*p cold food and cofee plane bumpy to.' I enjoyed this master-crafted manuscript of eloquent English as apparently en-route turbulence was actually being caused by cold food and our pilots; not the swirling ambient atmosphere after all. Perhaps I should have issued urgent warnings to our caterers and pilots - or posted a free dictionary to the author? But alas, he'd omitted to pen his name or address.

My other favourite noise complaint letter proclaimed: 'Yore jets so noisy here we got dogs barkin all bloody nite. Cows lost milk so no thanks to youse barstuds!' Slightly flattered, I'd never realised I was a bar stud and hardly ever ventured into bars to practice as one, but I wondered why he couldn't simply erect signs asking the dogs to please tone it down, or his cows to produce milk as expected?

Before lights out my intercom buzzed and, just like the Walton's little farmhouse on the prairie, tired voices wished me 'Goodnight' - as I did to them. Dousing my table lamp, I concluded 'nah, this is just another silly threat.' But, just in case, I could easily afford a much better quality pool camera for the future because the old one was an el cheapo. In fact, I could afford the very best. So in the morning I'd ask Marie to purchase all-new video surveillance security systems for our office, home and property. For twenty thousand or so, I might save much more than that in a future attack against our little company.

Also, I had four teenagers living here and they deserved upgraded protection all round. Should I re-employ that security company? Perhaps I could hire *Men in Black* to patrol the premises? Ah, the dilemmas of the rich and famous . . .

As for our cheeky Tania, she was indeed a very naughty person if she'd been tempted into spying on us. Not to mention exceptionally foolish. But on overall balance, I was convinced this bizarre affair belonged with those missives of the aggrieved farmer and his mate the turbulence expert: in the bottom drawer.

And maybe *B* simply stood for bullshit.

48.

But in the morning, indecision struck me again and I'd still made no firm resolutions about *that* subject. My jury was still out. Seeking a convenient diversion, I told the girls to take a few days off school because we were going away on a short break for some quality family time together. 'Where?' they chirped – but anywhere would be fine if it meant an excuse from attending school.

'Well,' I explained while giving young Emily an arm-wrestle on the kitchen bench top. 'I've been thinking . .'

'Did it hurt, Dad?' smiled Celia, looking on.

'Yep. Anyway, Mandy and Cynth are having a nice European holiday for nearly three weeks while we've all been slaving away here in the salt mines. They'll be home soon, but we should slip away for our own short break while all these people are here updating the office security and cameras and gizmo's that I've just ordered on the phone. It'll be a mess, but Marie can supervise them. Probably much easier if we're all not around, though.'

Olivia asked, 'But where are we going? Hope it's not driving up to the boring Blue Mountains again.'

I said, 'No. I've got a flight down to Tasmania this morning. So, I'll take a spare captain, plonk you three on the flight, then we'll stay in Hobart for two nights. On Wednesday morning, bright and early, we'll fly SK127 back to Sydney. You lot can go from there straight to school by taxi. Simple.'

Smiley Celia leapt up. 'Yay! We've never been to Tasmania. Can I sit up the front?' 'Me too?' repeated Emmie. 'Me three?' said the inevitable last one.

'You can take turns,' I said. 'There's only one jump seat, so one at a time.'

'Will we see some Tasmanian devils?' Emmie wanted to know. 'I want to cuddle one. Hey, I beat you again!' She was a strong little person and had quickly slammed my arm backwards when I wasn't paying attention. For years these girls had been beating me at arm wrestles, so I must be a fairly easy conquest - or else I let them win occasionally . . .

'A Tassie devil? We might see one; you never know. But they like eating people so watch out! Now, let's go, girls. We've got one hour to get ready, then it's outa here! Just take one backpack each, please. There's no need for suitcases the size of removal vans for only two nights away.'

'But where will we stay?' they asked.

'In the wild somewhere. With the devils. They've got tiny, beady, pink eyes. They can see you in the dark − long before you see them. Then they attack! The first thing you see is those evil pink eyes - but it's already too late . . . your last, petrifying moments!'

'You're lying, Dad!' squealed two of them, but Celia was uneasily chewing her nails and deliberating if I was or I wasn't.

Then she asked: "What about Tasmanian tigers? Do they eat people too?'

'They're extinct,' declared Olivia.

'Why do they stink?'

'Not stink, *extinct*! - like you'll be if you ask any more dumb questions! Won't she Dad?'

But Dad was on the phone to Air Services weather briefing office. I was more interested in the 500 hectopascal winds and the holding fuel requirements for Hobart this morning. You never know, it often gets socked in down there without warning. If we arrived overhead without enough fuel to enter a holding pattern, we might also become *extinct* like the tigers.

*

We departed off runway 07 at Sydney, just as I had done on that recent dramatic morning. This time, both big CFM engines dutifully sang their whirring notes right up to 37,000 feet. Happily, statistics declared that the chances of me having another flame-out just after lift-off were more than a million to one.

For the take-off, Emily was sitting in the jump seat between myself and First Officer Frank Phillips; excitedly curious and amazed. She gazed around at the banks of switches, dials, glass screens and instruments bunched around us. 'Dad,' she whispered over the intercom, 'this is so awesome, but how do you know what all these *things* are?'

'Haven't got a clue,' I stated, deadpan. 'I was kind of hoping that *you* would know what they're for . . . or maybe Mr Phillips knows?'

Frank smiled as he turned around to her. 'Me? I'm still looking for that red button that says *Ejection Seat.* Just in case, you know.'

Emmie squealed, 'Does it really do that? Ah, you're just joking - aren't you?'

I turned around to her, 'This is much the same flight deck as the F28 when we went to Ayers Rock. Have you forgotten that?' Perhaps she had, but wasn't sure. 'Wasn't that you who made the radio broadcast on our way in?' That was Celia, she said – and she'd never stopped boasting about it since. I said to Frank, 'Hey Frank, would you mind swapping seats with Emily for a few minutes? Thank you. Actually, you might like to bring us some drinks and save our ladies some work. Lemonade for Missy, please.'

Emily squeezed into the co-pilot's right-hand seat after Frank exited the flight deck. (I should explain here that family and other visitors on the flight decks of airliners were a routine occurrence in those days.) Mesmerised, Emmie fired off a dozen questions which I attempted to answer through my oxygen mask, then I gave her some very basic instructions as we flashed along in the cruise mode at 945 km/h. Every guest always wants to know how fast we are flying, but Emmie couldn't grasp how, while glancing out the window and spying the ground so far below, the Earth seemed to be scarcely moving beneath us.

I spoke to her over the intercom. 'Okay Emm, we've only been going for five minutes and already we're past Wollongong. Now see that wide bay down there? It's called Jervis Bay. That's the Nowra

Naval Air Station just near it. Soon we'll be over Moruya; then Merimbula, Mallacoota and out over Bass Straight. After that, Tasmania should appear on the horizon. If it doesn't, then we're probably lost and will continue on towards Antarctica.'

'You're a crazy pilot, Dad!' she squeaked. 'I want that other man to fly us.'

I said, 'Take hold of your wheel, Emm. Now steer us along and don't let us go upside down, okay?' She gripped the control wheel fiercely while staring blankly out the windscreen, but we now had cloud layers passing below us so she stared at nothing but white and misty strands of cirrus. I started to sing: 'I've looked at clouds from both sides now, from up and down and still somehow . . . '

Luckily, Frank returned to the deck carrying a tray of drinks. He saw my girl clenching the wheel and happily believing she was controlling the plane. I noticed his eyes quickly flicker to the auto-pilot master switch. Force of habit.

Emmie turned to him. 'My Dad said we might miss Tasmania and fly right to Antarctica.'

Frank whistled and agreed. 'Well, Dad's the captain so he should know.'

Soon I announced 'Time's up!' and Emmie went back to send another fearless aviator forward. With Olivia taking her turn at the wheel, things were quite different. She was white-faced and barely enjoying it. Soon she claimed airsickness and left to get Celia.

My little baby Celia, now twelve years old, was my main hope for a pilot-daughter one day. Once seated, she appeared to easily grasp the concept of what she was doing, so I confessed that the auto-pilot was actually 'steering' us along; not her.

'I know that,' she asserted cleverly while pointing at the green enunciator lights. 'It says *A/P Master ON*. And *A/P ON*. Right there.'

I asked, 'Frank, should she do the landing then?'

Diplomatic Frank replied, 'In ten years she might be doing just that.'

I gazed wistfully over at my youngest girl, wishing I had a crystal ball. 'I certainly hope so. That would be wonderful. I've got four girls, so I'll be content if just one of them becomes a pilot.'

Alarmingly, Frank sighed, 'My son is on drugs. He won't be becoming anything.' I gulped, then apologised to him. Life is often cruel. I had four wonderful children of whom I thought the world. So far none had stumbled into the numerous pitfalls of today's society. It was mostly a lottery of luck, but often avoided with a good upbringing - I liked to believe. Nevertheless, many parents - probably my co-pilot included, had given it their very best only to observe their worst nightmares descend upon their beloved child. And what a nice fellow Frank Phillips certainly was. He deserved much better. Many people deserve better. I glanced at smiling Celia: had she taken note? No, she was too busy flying an airliner.

Soon afterwards, Frank made a perfectly smooth touchdown on Hobart's wet and windy runway 12; the snapping crosswind testing his professional expertise. Crosswind landings are always a precise and delicate balancing act performed at about 130 knots (240 km/h) where the plane is skewed at an angle through the air like a racing crab; floating just a metre or so over the runway with its upwind wing lowered slightly. The pilot then applies an equivalent amount of opposite rudder to force the aircraft to track straight above the painted runway centreline.

Flight SK126 was safely down, and with our wipers still on high speed we closed the roaring thrust reversers and halted near the south-eastern runway end. Selecting flaps up, we about-faced at the turning node to backtrack and exit to the arrivals terminal via taxiway *Delta*. Upon disembarkation we left Frank with Captain Alex Hill. They'd shortly be returning to Sydney.

It was bitingly cold and rainy as we dashed across the car park to our rented eight-seat Tarago. The girls were thrilled to be visiting Tasmania for the first time, but were stunned by the dramatic crash in weather from the warm Sydney we'd left behind just a few hours ago.

'It's still supposed to be summer here, isn't it?' shivered Olivia. 'But it's so cold, it feels like winter. Brrr!' They all giggled *brrr* together.

We travelled the highway to Hobart's suburbs, then motored over the graceful arch of the Tasman Bridge. Reaching the city, we gawked up at lofty Mt. Wellington towering nearby; partially shrouded in ghostly clouds. After checking in to Hadley's Hotel and hurling our backpacks onto beds, I assembled a family round-table conference before we left to explore the local sights.

'Okay troops, listen up. A few quick words then we're off. In a few days, Cynthia and your big ugly sister Mandy will be back . . . '

'She's not ugly,' protested Emmie. 'She's beautiful.'

'Oh, sorry. I hadn't noticed. Anyway, my little mates, I just wanted us to have some special family time together before they're back – and without the intrusions of work, school, friends, phones, and workmen - all those distractions. Now, to me it seems that you're all growing up much too fast, and in just a few years might be leaving home to find your own ways in the world. They'll be exciting times for you all, but also sad times for me. You see, I'm going to miss the world out of all your noisy chattering, crashing and banging around. And even your music. Well . . . maybe not that.'

'Hurry up, Dad,' urged Olivia. 'We want to check out Hobart dock and all the shops and historical things.'

'But we already are,' I declared. 'This hotel, *Hadley's,* is the historical hotel where Roald Amundsen stayed on his return from the South Pole ninety years ago. Has anyone heard of him?' Emmie said they'd recently learned about him at school. He was the first man to reach the South Pole; just beating Scott of the Antarctic.

'Correct. And guess what: this is the actual room he stayed in for two weeks. That's why all these historical pictures are on the walls, and in the halls and foyers outside.' They gazed around with keen interest, then I returned to my speech: 'Well, what I'm trying to say is this: from the time I first met you three little rascals until right now, that quick decade seems to have passed in a flash. Zoom! So, for now – ah, just a big thankyou for being such good kids most of the time. Thank you for helping and supporting me so much when you didn't have a mum and I didn't have a wife.'

'I hope I've given you all some decent examples to help you in life, some paths you may wish to follow, and some enlightenment on how to, one day, maybe run a family of your very own. When you're grown up and gone, I'll miss the heck out of you terrors. But I'll be brave, I hope . . . like Mr Amundsen.' The girls gasped as I let a few tears escape.

'What's the matter, Dad?' I got a cuddle from Celia. 'I'm not going anywhere for a long time. And you're the best Dad in the world.' I told them that nothing was wrong; let's just go out and have some fun. Leaving the girls perplexed as to the purpose of my mini-speech, I realised I'd probably messed it all up. I hadn't said what I'd intended at all – because I couldn't. So, although none of them had grasped what the heck *that* was all about, they just knew we shouldn't waste a moment of our very brief two-and-a-half-day holiday.

As we briskly strode Hobart's grand streets, Celia skipped excitedly beside me while the other two ran ahead, exploring every single shop front. We all delighted in discovering this modern but historical city that was resplendent with yachts and spinnakers, gardens and galleries, sandstone cottages and stately Georgian homes.

'It's like being in another country,' Emmie yelled back at me. 'I love it!' Hobart certainly was quite pleasantly different and I regretted never having previously explored it because, although I'd spent many nights in Hobart airport motels, I'd never ventured out. Fast turnarounds had prevented those ambitions.

After exploring Constitution Dock, the Marina and the trendy Salamanca Place markets with its famous seafood outlets, we motored up the steep winding road to the lookout near the peak of Mt. Wellington; towering 1,270 metres above the city. Incidentally, while this elevation figure is of scant interest to most tourists, it is vital data to arriving pilots conducting instrument let-downs into Hobart through low clouds, because no other Australian cities have such high ground to negotiate before landing, nor any adjacent mountain over 4,000 feet high to stay well clear.

At the summit lookout we all gasped in the icy air, laughing as we blew vapour breaths at each other. We took funny photos – they with their tongues poking out, of course - then gazed down at the picturesque city far below. And what a magnificent harbour Hobart surely has. Grander than San Francisco's harbour, even superior to Sydney's: it is an Australian wonder of which many are unaware.

We'd rented three bikes to bring up the mountain in the van. Now it was time for the girls to pedal them downhill - a particularly popular activity for locals and tourists of all ages. I couldn't join them because I had to drive the van back down; following closely behind. At least that was the plan, but before I could say *downhill racer* they'd hopped on and bolted away! Fearless – as young people are.

Oh how easily we forget. *Me*, who'd flown aeroplanes at just thirteen years of age, was yelling after *them*: 'Hey, hold on you lot! Not so fast! Slow down on those tight curves; they might be icy. There'll be traffic coming!'

My futile shouts into a twenty-five knot icy wind were lost as I gulped at three fast disappearing pony-tails, swishing behind them. As I cursed myself for not inspecting their bikes' brakes, I leapt into the Tarago and pursued their crazy antics of whooping and screeching to the very bottom. In doing so, I probably became the hundredth anxious parent to chase his kids down the mountain that day. But I never actually caught up with them till the end; the long descent with its dozens of hairpin bends left me far behind those three elusive angels who boldly negotiated every twist and turn of the descent with glee.

Finally reaching the bottom, they yelled 'What kept you, Dad?' Gee, how I loved them so much!

*

In the morning we jogged to the picturesque dockside again. Fortunately the showers had left us and it was mostly a sunny and clear day, so we took a seaplane joyride over the stunning harbour and city. I sat in the back, shrieking and pretending to be terrified. Up front, when an embarrassed Emily told the pilot that I was an airline captain, he glanced around and shook his head in doubt, saying, 'Yeah . . . whatever.'

After thirty minutes, we asked him to land on the Derwent River right outside the Cadbury Chocolate factory and were thrilled as waves of spray gushed past our windows when we splashed down. This was our first landing on water for all of us. Here the girls did a quick tour of the factory and received free chocolate samples while I chatted near the pontoon with the bright young pilot.

When I flipped out my Sky Star ID and showed him my name, his earlier scepticism became an astonished delight. His name was Simon and I was quite impressed by him. He'd recently applied for a pilot's position with Qantas, but hadn't heard back from them yet.

I offered him the chance of a lifetime. 'Simon, if you're free, come back to Sydney on Wednesday with me in the jump seat. You can do a check-out in our simulator up there with our acting Chief Pilot. You never know, we might just have a vacancy for a new starter at Sky Star very soon.' It is hard to describe the extent of his enthusiastic response, but you can be assured that when he arrived back at his waterside Flight Office, he said something like: 'You'll never guess who was in the back seat pretending to be scared out of his wits . . . '

We nibbled free chocolates for lunch, sitting on manicured lawns beside the gently flowing Derwent. Then, after waving goodbye to Simon as he lurched skywards with spray flying from his Cessna 206 float-plane, we boarded a majestic yacht for a three-hour sailing cruise. Shivering in a rather biting breeze that whipped across the deck, all three girls took turns to cuddle their Dad as our captain sailed us lazily around the choppy waters, gazing at harbour-side mansions and the many others sprinkled up the mountain's sides.

Our last day was a scenic expedition of driving south to historic Port Arthur and its old convict settlement, before travelling to a wildlife park to see a few Tasmanian devils. Far from cuddling them, the girls were afraid to even touch them because of their rather ferocious looks, so we took careful photos from as close to them as we dared.

Our final night found me in the girls' room handing out a short quiz of questions like a schoolmaster on pertinent aspects of Tasmania and the fun places we'd explored. They were surprised, and flashed each other 'this is boring' looks. Emmie lodged an official protest: 'Aw Dad, you never told us this was an exam or something.'

I replied, 'Life's one big test, mate. And there's an essay to be written, too. Anyway, that's why people write travel books: so their journeys are recorded in writing – not in fragile memories which will often fade. Listen, my little friends, what is the point of doing anything in your life or going anywhere if you've forgotten it all by the time you get home? Or soon after?'

'We've taken a few photos, but will they ever tell anyone how you really *felt* at the top of Mt. Wellington? Or what you all said up there? Will photos remember how cold it was? Will they depict everything you saw in descriptive words? What was it like to rush down the mountainside on your bikes? There's no photos of that – obviously. Or to fly over the harbour, land on its water, then sail upon it?

'When you're old grannies and your grandkids sit on your lap and say, 'Grandma, tell me some stories from when you were a little girl,' you might answer: "I went down to Tasmania in the year 2000. Here are some old photos." But then, how will you reply when they ask, "But what was it really like, Grandma? How did it feel pedalling right down that steep mountain with your sisters way back then?" Are you going to answer: "I can't remember. It was too long ago." '

They started to understand. 'So here are a few questions I'd like answered first, please. Essay writing tomorrow. It's much less work than if you'd been at school these past few days, but will cover far more than you might have learned there in the same time. Some of the questions are dead easy: like, what State is this? You only get one point for dumb ones like that. How high was Mt. Wellington is worth five points. Four points for the name of the bridge over the Derwent.' They glanced at each other and rolled their eyes, 'Ah – umm ... '

But they were interested. 'And what country was Mr Amundsen from? Ten points for that! Others questions ask you to remember what we all ate for dinner in that beautiful seafood restaurant on the Dock . . . ' Emily shot her hand up: "Lobster!"

'Shoosh! Write it down. And this one asks what is the name of that dock where the Sydney to Hobart Yacht Race finishes?'

Celia interrupted eagerly with, 'I know, it's Constipation Dock.' The other two fell over backwards, rocking on their beds and howling with laughter. 'What's funny?' Celia yelled in embarrassment, her face cherry-red. 'What's so *damn* funny? Oh, shut up you two!'

'Nice try, mate' I consoled her, suppressing a smile. 'You see? That's something else you can tell those grandkids of yours one day. Oh, anyone who remembered to check their bike's brakes before they rode down the mountain gets an extra ten points.' No-one did.

'So let's all finish the tests tonight, then I want you to write a small two-page essay about this short trip while we're flying back. I'll have someone else in the jump seat so you'll be passengers this time. And no moaning about it please because it's only an hour's work and a small price to pay for getting a few days off school and experiencing all these fun things.'

After goodnight kisses I walked to my adjacent room. Just before entering, I heard more screams of hysterical mirth through their door, followed by Celia yelling, 'I *hate* you two!'

But she didn't really because in the morning they all wore smiles of happiness and enjoyed quite a few giggles in the breakfast restaurant when I joined them. They'd completed part-one of their homework assignments and handed them in, cheekily chanting: 'Good morning, Mr Grant!'

What nice kids. They would become lovely women, I felt assured.

49.

What I had meant to say to three-quarters of my family whilst in Tasmania– and what I *should* have said, was that despite their fondest wishes and their constant nudging hints that I should marry Cynthia one day, it would unfortunately not be happening. For most of their lives my girls had desperately wanted me to find another lady – a replacement mother for them – to complete a family structure. This was a perfectly reasonable expectation and one I thoroughly understood, but Cynthia and I had recently arrived at the conclusion that the required magic just wasn't there – despite anyone's most fervent wishes.

Cynthia was a wonderful person and we'd spent many an enjoyable time together, but mostly it was a working relationship between two different people. She was a headstrong former journalist and now my trainee company secretary, while I was very different. Privately, we clashed over many ideals. Domestically, Cynthia had little interest in becoming anyone's Mum, while romantically, it was me who let the side down. It had been more than a decade since my beautiful Cristina had departed our world and I'd honestly sought no replacement spouse.

As my daughters grew up fast, I saw less need than ever to obtain a substitute mother figure for them because she wouldn't be needed for long. Or, while she may become a good wife to me, she might have no intrinsic interest in other people's kids. I wasn't going to obtain a Rent-a-Mum: just anyone to sleep with me and do the housework for a few short years until they'd grown up. My kids would be adults soon enough and the pressing need for a new mother was rapidly receding with each passing year.

As a result of my obstinacy, this predicament isolated me into a lonely cocoon of bachelorhood as I passed through my thirties; a self-imposed social barricade over which, I fretted, I may never hurdle.

So, great disappointment would probably have ensued in Hobart had I disclosed this news – which I failed miserably to do. And this naturally leads to my recent interest in young Tania Wicks – or whatever her true name was and motives were. I certainly felt some attraction to Tania which merely proves that I'm human, but under these convoluted and distasteful circumstances I'd be wise to quickly forget her. Leaving aside for a moment any peculiar questions of espionage, the entrance of Tania into our household at this stage would be dynamite in many ways. Amanda would loudly and totally reject her, and Cynthia would . . . who knows what? But doesn't a single man of my age have any choices here? It's rather complicated, but 'no' is probably the correct answer.

*

Upon our arrival home from Tassie, a solution arrived in the form of a sealed and registered document that was delivered to me. My pondering, worrying, and occasional gnashing of teeth over Tania was suddenly all over. It read:

"Ferret told everyone she had wild romps with you – and many others too! Says you ordered her to come back to the farm after your mob went nighty-nites. Says you crazy in love. Says she resisted, but you rich powerful boss and threatened to fire her. I think she wants money. Watch out, or bang! From: Man behind horse."

Sickened to the stomach, I faced several urgent options. Step one: I could simply laugh off these horrid allegations and say to everyone 'What a joke. Who'd believe that?' But plenty *might* believe it, and Cynthia would undoubtedly repeat her customary statement: 'If the mud flies, some will always stick.' Second choice: immediately contact Paul Harland to fire Tania on the spot. Or *backfire* might be the operative word when she *reveals all.* Third: confront this person myself and resolve the matter once and for all – even though I simply couldn't believe she'd do this.

Otherwise, the last alternative that I'd once considered: play her little game and plant misinformation that would eventually discredit her – then we'd certainly fire her. But I simply didn't have time for all this dangerous tomfoolery and needed instead to schedule an urgent meeting with *Man behind Horse*.

But before that, and speaking of horses, I had an urgent appointment with a *real* horse in a real paddock for a re-enactment of certain recent events. It's not as though I had anything much else to do, apart from running a medium-sized airline and a large-sized family, so how better to fill in a morning before flying across the continent to Perth and back?

In turmoil, I tromped off in gumboots, squelching across sodden fields. It was with nagging trepidation and no small coincidence that I sank deeper into the mud when I realised that our globe-trotting gals would be back home tomorrow. And when the mud flies . . .

50.

We all stood, spread evenly around the pool's pebbled edge, where the only sound to be heard was the merry gurgling of the pool fountain. It could have been the famous showdown from *High Noon,* or the lynching in *Hang 'em High,* but it was just poor old me facing off against five females and I wasn't sure whether to draw first or head for the hills.

Amanda stood angrily with hands on hips – her favourite aggro pose - and demanded: 'She did *WHAT*, Dad?'

I glanced at Cynthia who was valiantly trying to look neutral but failing, then ordered the three younger girls to 'Go away please. Go to your rooms. This is private business.' I watched them slink sideways behind bushes and outdoor furniture, ears cocked for any morsel of gossip; then they squeezed behind sliding doors – leaving one slightly ajar. 'Girls!' I roared. 'Shut that damned door!' It slammed shut.

My bossy Amanda, recently returned from the romantic clutches of leering European men, was about to repeat her demands for *me* to account for *my* actions in her absence.

'Wait on, please Mandy.' I waved an arm at her. 'Just listen for a moment. You've been home for half a day and I still haven't heard anything about your trip. Cynth hasn't been able to get a word in sideways, and you're accusing me of this, that, and everything else. Let me start by saying this: I've been managing, somehow, to successfully run this company since you were about five years old. I realise you're training to take over, but I think I might know a few things about the business we're in.'

'So just listen carefully: Tania flew with me and it happened to be her first day. No big deal: a few other pilots have done likewise. After our little drama in the morning, we didn't clock off till after midnight. Because she had bussed in to work, I offered to drive her home. She lived out this way – that's what she told me, anyway. I've given a lift home to many of our staff before, and I will in the future. Also, I'm over thirty years old and I'll drive whoever I want to wherever I want, okay?'

Mandy re-crossed her arms, pouted, and replied insolently, 'You're telling the story.'

I continued. 'Yes, I am. Anyway, as I was leaving I invited Tania to come here for a swim one day - just like I've invited many of our company's women and their families to the farm before. Marie and her little ones swim here often, as do entire battalions of you and your sisters' school friends from this neighbourhood. So, Tania turned up on the weekend, we sat beside the pool along with lots of kids and had a barbecue, then she went home. Now, just what part of that story is so hard to understand?'

Mandy shot back, 'The part about swimming with a microphone in her bikini. Strange, but I've never bought a bikini that was tagged "*Microphone included.*" '

I gasped in exasperation. 'I just don't know how the youngies found all this out and told you. I wish they'd minded their own damn business!' At an angle, I glimpsed a bedroom curtain raked quickly closed.

Cynthia finally joined the fray. 'Rob, Ben Preston claims this fanciful plot exists against you. You say nothing at all happened to compromise yourself but he hints of schemes of possible extortion. And you still haven't revealed what this Tania person says for herself. What did she say when you asked her about all this?'

Embarrassed, I searched for excuses but found none. 'Ah, I haven't had the time to call her yet - or the inclination. I chose to take the kids down to Tassie instead – to give us all a break. We had three wonderful days there and I'll tell you about it one day - if you don't lynch me first. I didn't want to even think about this *other* business because I didn't believe it.'

Mandy spoke up, 'So, just exactly what did the police say when you told them you might be facing blackmail – maybe for a huge amount?'

Obviously I was guilty until proven innocent. Vaguely, I replied 'Ah, the police?'

'Yes. The police.'

'I, ah, haven't contacted them either, Mandy. It's just ridiculous: imagine me tittle-tatting to the police about someone who came to a barbecue *after* I'd invited her. Oh yes Sergeant, it was like this, you see: She sat beside me. She ate. She had a swim. She went home. And the cops would say: So? Then I'd tell them my P.I. claims she had a hidden wire inside her bikini. The cops would ask if I saw it? Did I feel it? Did I remove her bikini? And precisely just what information did you reveal to her, Mr Grant, which would warrant recording anyway? Nothing? You mean nothing at all? And exactly how much is this ransom demand so far? Nothing?' I sighed, 'Then they'd probably lock me up as a public nuisance!'

'Not funny Dad,' Mandy said. 'So, did she come back later that night or not?'

'No, she did not. And it's absolutely none of your business, Miss Amanda, if packs of howling werewolves came prowling around that night, or tribes of jungle pygmies beating tom-toms. Or if I ever have late night visitors to this house at all. You're not seventeen yet, and you've had your Steven calling around at night. I've heard him. And I can do the same . . . '

I immediately regretted saying that because I glimpsed the quick hurt in Cynthia's eyes. Hell, this was a situation where I could either lose, lose - or lose. Oh what fun! Who'd want to be anywhere else?

Cynthia suggested, 'Surely if she sneaked back later we would see it on the pool cam tapes?' No, I'd viewed it and thrown the old tape in question into a drawer. We went inside just after I caught another glimpse of rustling curtains. Six inquisitive ears were obviously perked up at full antenna height; their owners having no intentions whatsoever of sleeping tonight amidst this exciting inquisition of the damned.

I relented and called out: 'Okay girls, come here you big snoops. Who told you lot about all this mess?'

When a guilty-looking Olivia walked out in pyjamas, she said 'That man.'

'What man?' demanded Mandy.

'I don't know. A big fat man.' My eyebrows shot up; to be followed just micro-seconds later by Mandy's then Cynthia's.

While the other kids rummaged through the rumpus room drawers on an urgent tape-seeking mission, whispering secretly among themselves, I asked, 'When did you see this man, Liv?' Olivia explained that a big man was in our laneway when she rode home yesterday. She asked him what he was doing. He explained that he worked for me and was conducting investigations for me about the woman named Tania. The one who was trying to blackmail me.

Puzzled, Olivia queried him. 'What? Who?' and the man replied, 'Don't you know? Your father should have told you all about this new pilot. She could be dangerous. She was spying at this farm recently. She had a recording device in her swimmers.'

'Olivia,' I squawked. 'You didn't tell me this before!' Olivia explained that I was away on the Perth run at the time – as I am so often away from them. Man on the run.

She continued, 'He works for you, so I just thought you'd know all about it. Anyway, then Mandy and Cynthia's taxi pulled up right behind my bike – just after I'd spoken with the man. It was so exciting to see them again that I forgot about him.'

In total exasperation I flung my hands into the air and beseeched Mandy, 'Then why on Earth didn't you two notice this man when you arrived . . . this Ben Preston?'

'I don't know,' replied Mandy. 'He must have gone. Disappeared. Did you see anyone, Cynth?' No, she hadn't either. Man Mountain had become the Invisible Man.

'Did you look behind the horse?' I asked, and they all looked at me strangely. As the others continued burrowing with frustration through the rumpus room drawers for the tape that showed nothing, I thought quietly, 'For a very large man, our Ben can certainly be quite invisible when he chooses. It's a trick of his trade, I suppose. Perhaps he can just snap his fingers and . . . *poof*! he's gone.

Eventually, the girls gave up on the missing tape. 'It's not here.'

I demanded, 'How can it *not* be here, for Heaven's sake? I put it in the drawer myself. It doesn't reveal anything, anyway.'

'Someone might have taken it?' suggested Celia, looking slightly suspicious.

Amanda levelled an accusing finger at me, 'Unless . . . unless Dad has accidentally on purpose lost it?'

'Give me a break please, people,' I gasped. 'So it's me who's blackmailing myself here? Oh now I get it: I invented all this so I can extort millions out of myself. Then I destroyed the only piece of evidence. Is that it? But will I pay up before the dastardly villain – *me*, shoots myself?' I pointed a finger at my temple and went *Bang*!

Amanda shrugged, 'Well, I give up.' Cynthia agreed, 'Me too.' Then I cheered, 'Hooray for that!' as the littlies laughed then ran around in circles going *Bang! Bang!*

So, with precisely nothing resolved at Sky Star farm we agreed to adjourn this summit meeting until evening around the pool when, with the grace of fortune, we would hear all about the ladies' epic journey; their medical mission of mercy to save a stricken baby, and the recently depleted stocks in Europe's top fashion houses. Discussions about Tania would simply have to wait – thankfully.

At the dinner table, Emmie smiled and asked: 'Dad, do you really have werewolves come around some nights?' I replied, 'Yes, something's got to control you lot.' So the three of them started howling like wolves while Livvy dressed like a jungle pygmy and beat our bongo drum. When Emmie ran past with a karaoke microphone tucked into her pyjama waistband, we all howled laughing.

I loved it.

51.

I'd awarded myself a few days away from flying. We'd hired two new pilots: one was a woman and the other was Simon, our eager float-plane pilot from Tasmania. Ken Tolman was due back shortly, so I proudly gave myself with another rest as I had many things to do: cards to lay on the table, issues to decide, and the irresolvable to be resolved. Incidentally, our new female pilot was not exactly what some might deem as *sexy*. Nor was she young or slim. So when Paul Harland described her to me, I told him she was *precisely* what we needed!

It was a starlit evening around the Sky Star ranch pool; a delightfully pleasant enjoyment we'd all treasured over many years. With the youngies sworn to silence, not a ripple kissed the water's glassy surface, not a girlish shriek or squeal pierced the sound barrier and no *thumps* from the rumpus room beat box rattled our bones.

So, first things first. I commenced the proceedings with, 'Amanda, would you like to deliver the opening address about the main reason you went to Europe, and the results of the research and targets I gave you? After that, I'm sure you both have many fun tales to relate, but the health and welfare of Mr Tolman's baby obviously comes first.'

Mandy stood to reply and spoke from a sheaf of notes from within a manila folder. Listening were myself, Cynthia Nilsen and Marie Westcott. Also present was our legal team; represented by solicitor Bill McFarlane and his secretary, Coralie Eastman. They'd been invited to legally advise on the distribution, if any, of funds allocated overseas towards any medical procedures for Ken's little boy.

Disturbingly, I'd had just one conversation with Ken Tolman during the last month. We'd sipped coffee near the Nepean River banks as he, downcast and hangdog in appearance, only once thanked me for my offer of assistance; merely repeating that he still needed it. He could obtain some government and union financing but it was all dependent on filing reams of paperwork, waiting months, and enduring official delays while his child became more endangered each day. His wife Sue had heeded his and my advice to quit escaping reality by exiling herself in the gambling rooms of clubs, but now moped around the house all day in a permanent fog of depression and neurosis. Strangely, I had never met her because she still didn't like me, so I decided that she wasn't a person I wanted to know anyway. I asked Ken if they'd sought other doctors' opinions and he assured me the surgery was not done here in Australia yet – which wasn't exactly answering the question. Then I asked if he'd be fit to fly again soon and, while he replied 'sure', I was anything *but* sure.

With this background, Mandy began, 'Sorry for my occasional bitchiness everybody, but we all have problems from time to time, don't we?' While I pondered what problems she could possibly have – especially after just having scored a wonderful free trip around the world – she continued:

'We went to Germany as instructed by my dear father . . . ' I stood to take a bow as she flashed me a naughty wink, 'and there I compiled this dossier about the operation to save Captain Tolman's two-year-old boy Aaron, a procedure that they don't do here in Australia yet.'

'Caretakers of Dad's money, Cynthia and I decided that the German quotes for this operation were quite outrageous - especially after we received a tip-off that it might be done in Eastern Europe for half or less. I'm keen for Dad not to waste large sums if it isn't absolutely necessary because I'm training to take over administration of the company in the near future and therefore should be adopting a responsible attitude and obligation towards our company's funds and assets now.'

Bill McFarlane nodded assent, saying 'I thoroughly agree,' as his secretary scribbled shorthand notes on a pad and I wondered: Gee, where does my daughter get all these big fancy words from? From me, I silently admitted to myself, as Mandy continued:

'So, we *trained* it to Eastern Europe and located three surgeries in Budapest, Hungary, where the procedure can be carried out for about one-third of the $625,000 originally quoted to us by the child's father. A substantial savings, obviously. This is due to not only medical and surgical expenses being much lower in Eastern Europe these days, but also general living expenses like wages, rents, etcetera. From there we travelled to beautiful Prague in the Czech Republic where we discovered one further medical centre willing to perform this operation for a similar cost.' She added a short description of historical Prague – or *Praha* – a distinctive 1,100-year-old city with its wonderful theatres of music and opera majestically sited on the Vltava River.

She took a sip of iced tea, then continued. 'However, not being a medical practitioner, I have to honestly conclude that I have no idea if these alternate surgeons' quotes are accurate or otherwise. Nor can I be certain if these doctors are properly qualified or even if the procedures are correctly and safely carried out. Also, we didn't always have the luxury of interpreters so we often struggled to take accurate notes. This made it difficult to arrive at correct conclusions in this matter. But I've compiled a huge amount of positive data on my laptop here - if anyone wants to access it. My conclusion is: I can't be positively sure what to recommend so I'll have to leave it up to my father who, after all, will ultimately foot the bills.'

Cynthia added, 'One doctor stressed that he could perform the operation and it *still* might fail; the baby could die. Although true, I understand this can happen anywhere, and in the most routine of operations."

I interrupted, 'Yes, but we still have to try, don't we? I'm the one who might have to go to bed one night after this young boy's funeral, knowing I didn't fund this procedure just because it cost a lot. Or because it might have failed anyway. Or because I might have wasted some money . . . '

'But life itself is a waste of money, sometimes. People could easily assert that buying aeroplanes is a waste of money when I already own over thirty. Or that buying mountains of clothes is a waste when we can only wear one outfit at a time.' I winked across at Mandy, '. . . or dining out is an extravagance when we could easily eat baked beans at home. So where does it all stop? In perspective, this proposed expense is probably no more than the cost of fuel that our planes burned yesterday while zooming around Australia. One day's fuel. So, Mandy is right: let's just leave the cheque signing deliberations to me, please.'

The company solicitor agreed. 'I'm no medico either, just a lawyer. Legally, it's up to you Robert, of course. But it's a gamble, and seeking recompense later from some European who might run off with your money might be nigh-on impossible. We might wait years for tribunals to even look into the matter. I will read through Amanda's reports thoroughly; especially the cases she documented about similar operations previously performed by these people. Initially, it seems the ladies have done a remarkable job and I congratulate her and Cynthia.'

The 'ladies' were still smirking and whispering together over my barbed 'clothing' remarks, when Marie jumped into the pause with: 'I'd like to go through the report too, please. If I'm to join senior management, I intend to be fully conversant with all relevant matters.'

Then Bill McFarlane rubbed his chin and stood to speak. A seasoned courtroom lawyer, I sensed an imminent dressing down for me. 'Now Robert and ladies, we need to, with some urgency, address this rather distasteful matter of possible blackmail threats against you and our company. Coralie has briefed me several times, but I'm afraid to admit that I still don't quite follow it all. Can you enlighten me?'

As my three youngsters' ears pricked up and their eyes bulged, I informed everyone that, after constant deliberation and much indecision, I regarded most of this affair as mere silliness and scurrilous nonsense. I added that I now harboured strong reservations about my own investigator's advice and held a general suspicion of the whole affair. 'Do you know that he claimed he was observing this woman from our fields while hiding behind our horse? But I recently went over to where the horse was standing that day and I couldn't see this swimming pool from there because the barn and the dollhouse were in the way. How about that?' Everyone glanced that way but saw only a darkened barn and stars twinkling in the night sky.

My lawyer was quite perplexed, and scratched his head in bemusement. 'Horse? Pool? Barn? Members of the jury, I beseech you, has anyone ever heard such crazy tales?' Olivia shot her hand up. 'I did at school once . . . ' then remembered she was under orders of silence.

I continued the pantomime with relish, 'So I put it to the court: how could the alleged observer – even with telescopic lenses – observe the alleged offender operating her secreted recording devices if his view was obstructed?'

Everyone laughed, and we all started playing court room games. Cynthia laughed, 'If you were sitting right next to her the whole time and even *you* couldn't see what she was doing, how could Ben Preston watch her from a distance - even through paparazzi lenses? And through a horse?'

As the littlies galloped around the pool snorting horse noises, someone suggested: 'A transparent horse, maybe?' Then Marie asked had anyone interviewed the horse yet?

We all laughed as Mandy again suggested I report this possible extortion to the police. But what could I tell them? They'd laugh me out of the station.

I heard a motion-detecting buzzer sound, then a night courier appeared at our poolside gathering and handed an envelope to Coralie. She passed it to me as the others kept playing *Famous Courtroom Dramas.* I receive dozens of such items each day, so I just played with the envelope in my hands for a while as the chatting continued. After a while, I slit it open and glanced down with little interest as the others kept talking eagerly. However, after a few words, I gripped the letter with alarm as I read the rough grammar:

'Hello Robert Grant, its sure been a long time, but I'm hopping you and the girls are keping well. Elsie and me always think about our own little gran-daughters who I suppose are all growed up now. We hope their doing well at school. We are coming over from NZ soon so are hopping to meet up with all 3 of them. Maybe take them out to Micdonalds or somewere. Its been hard but we will soon be part of their lives again. Our familys regards, Fred Parsons.'

Fred Parsons? *Fred bloody Parsons!* I cursed silently. 'What's the matter?' asked Mandy with concern. 'You look upset. Is it trouble?' I deliberated for a short while, then handed her the letter which she scrutinised with a scowl that deepened with each sentence scanned. For once, Mandy was wordless. She stared at me for answers. I asked her to pass the letter around.

After they'd all perused it, I explained: 'Now let me tell you about this wonderful man, ladies and gentlemen. Mr Fred Parsons and his charming wife Elsie are my deceased wife's parents who live in New Zealand. Not only do they *reside* in New Zealand, but the said Mrs Parsons *remained* in New Zealand during her own daughter's funeral because she was otherwise 'indisposed'. Likewise was my wife's sister, who merrily continued backpacking around Europe at the time and was also similarly indisposed.'

'Now, during the whole course of Cristina's battle with breast cancer, these devoted parents visited their dying daughter just once. Apparently it was just too inconvenient for them to come over more often, especially after they'd had so much *trouble* raising Cristina.'

I wasn't finished yet. 'But the alleged trouble was, in fact, the parents themselves – as Cristina often told me. They were cruel and heartless. They favoured the younger sister and always called Cris a 'tart' – simply because she was so pretty. They boozed and popped pills and gambled every day, thus ensuring their two kids almost starved. It's a very long story, but one desperate day Cris hurriedly packed a backpack and rushed out of home at the age of sixteen. She fled to Australia because in those days no passport was required. Her sister eventually followed suit and fled to Europe.'

'Being so attractive, Cris quickly met men on our NSW north coast, but unfortunately fell for the worst one – as many desperate girls often do. They married when she was seventeen and had three daughters in quick succession. Almost as rapidly, the man soon bolted to the wild blue yonder of far North Queensland – his silence thereafter being his only contribution to his own little children who then faced extreme food and other essential deprivations while he languished in chronic laziness and unemployment.'

Mandy listened to this tale of history with sad eyes; it was painful to recall her mother's brief and distressed life. Bill McFarlane interrupted with: 'Excuse me Robert, but is this relevant to Coralie and I? If it's difficult family stuff we don't mind leaving.'

I said, 'No. Stay please, Bill. I think this might become *very* pertinent soon. Now, even though I have *four* daughters and not three, charming Fred, true to form, fails to mention young Celia - let alone enquire if she's even *alive*. This is because she's not one of his so-called 'three' grand-daughters and obviously he couldn't give a damn. Anyway, in the dozen years since Fred's most reluctant and token twenty-minute appearance at his daughter's funeral service, we have received precisely *nil* dollars in support for Cristina's children.'

'And Christmas presents? Birthdays? Toys? Dolls? Mandy, tell everyone how many presents have ever arrived in the post for you *three* girls – forgetting Celia, because she apparently doesn't even exist.'

Cynthia gave me a cuddle, 'Please Rob, try not to get so upset and angry. In all fairness, they know you own this airline so they'd be well aware that you are rather wealthy. They most likely think there's nothing they could ever buy to compete with someone who owns an airline. Right? Perhaps they're just getting older, are well-intentioned, and feel like making contact again? And he only wants to take them to *Mick Donalds*, as he calls it.'

I conceded, 'Maybe. Mandy?' I glanced around. Fortunately the youngies were inside listening to music.

Mandy sniffed a few tears, then replied, 'They're bastards! Dad didn't have *any* airline when we were little and could have used some help. He struggled to start it up with just one old mortgaged plane. We lived in a dilapidated rented house where Dad might have gone without food himself some nights just so we could eat.'

'When Celie came along it was even harder. Me and Olivia sometimes ate dead moths off the window sills when Mum was struggling. Then she died, so sometimes we did it again when Mrs McNeil was minding us. But we never told Dad. Anyway, the answer is: once or twice in my whole life I received a cheap doll or trinket from them at Christmas. The rest of the time? Just a card and no gifts. Can't remember if the others ever got anything. Certainly not baby Celia.

311

Bastards! They knew very well that our first Dad had deserted us and we were their only grandkids. Deserted by our father, then by them. What did we ever do to deserve all that? I wasn't even five years old!'

'This is so sad,' sniffed Marie Westcott. 'My children have never had to go through this.'

I took over again. 'So, there we all were: our struggling little family consisting of myself and *four* hungry children. After paying out ninety percent of my week's paltry profits from one charter plane for food, power, and essentials like nappies, for instance, and as I had no parents to call upon because even my adoptive-Dad had passed away, I wishfully dreamt that the girls' own grandparents might contribute something occasionally. While I certainly don't need or want a cent from them these days, the kids could have benefited way back then. It was a pitiful and futile hope.'

Bill McFarlane said, 'Sorry, but I need to ask: couldn't you have sold your rural property out west to alleviate matters, Rob?'

I answered, 'I had already borrowed to the hilt against its equity to buy our first jet, plus I sold my lovely Cessna three-ten. All at a time when the drought began severely depressing the rural land market. Like the drought, I'd wrung my borrowing abilities dry just as the *Wundala* estate became unsaleable for years - as did most others. Then everything changed some years later. It's the way of Australia: a sunburnt country; a land of droughts and flooding plains.'

'Anyway, the letter says: "We will soon be part of their lives again." So, poor Fred's broke. Runs out of beer money and thinks: why not go over to Australia and extort maybe a million out of that rich airline owner who married his terrible daughter – you know, that one who was just *so difficult* to raise?'

'Wait on,' interrupted Mandy. As the other poolsiders gazed at the backlit water while lost in intense thought, she asked, 'How could this Tania have anything to do with him . . . or any of this crazy maze?'

I answered, 'I don't know – yet. But I *do* know is this: I smell sharks circling. Or is it a big fat rat? And the rat's a Kiwi because Ben Preston has a New Zealand accent and he once told me he originally came from there. From around Wellington, actually, which is on the southern tip of the North island. Amazingly, this is just where our Grandfather of the Year, Fred Parsons, also happens to live. Hmm, what a remarkable coincidence, don't you think, everyone?'

Bill said, 'Hmm, not really. Lots of people come from Melbourne but they don't know each other.'

Cynthia was thinking aloud, 'So, if Fred takes his *three* girls out to McDonald's – or somewhere which might cost him a whole twenty dollars, then he might keep them and blackmail you for a million? Then we'll all go to war with New Zealand and live happily ever after?'

'Would you like fries with that?' smiled Coralie.

We all enjoyed a well-needed laugh; then I added, 'I know what Celia would say: "Aw, it's not fair. They all get to go to Maccas and I don't. Boo hoo!" Seriously folks, I don't know for sure how any of this unravels - believe me, but Cynth was right. I'd suggest that old conniving Fred and Elsie live over there in some rented shack without a cent to their names. Then they see me in magazines buying more new jet airliners and think: Hmm, look at him: he's got zillions these days, so here's our one-and-only golden opportunity.'

'Meanwhile, they may have met our *Super Snooper* Ben Preston because they're about the same age and possibly even went to the same school . . . I don't know. But if they did, maybe one day Big Ben goes back home for a holiday. Walks down the streets of suburban Wellington and spies his old drinking buddy and former school mate, the Right Dishonourable Fred Parsons. "Hiya Fred, whatcha doing? Got no money, eh? Well, I'm doing really well. I'm the security advisor to that rich Aussie airline guy, Rob Grant. What? He married your *daughter,* you say? Oh really? How incredibly convenient!" '

'So, over a beer or six, they devise a plan to extract an amount of money from me. Ben would surely have enthused with great interest when he heard that Fred was the legal grandfather of my daughters, and undoubtedly paid for all the drinks. So, while Ben concocts these 'allegations' about me, they arrange for old Fred to fly over here one day then write me an introductory letter about getting to know the kids better and becoming part of their lives again. Then, when he takes them out somewhere he either keeps them and bargains for some kind of ransom for them, or if that won't work, he proceeds to manipulate the girls against me with these scandalous 'Tania' allegations.'

Mandy laughed. 'Ransom? Kidnap us? I'd like to see him try! Anyway, who'd pay anything for us mob?'

'Not me,' I laughed. 'No, wait: I'd pay ten bucks for each of you - but no more.' Jokes aside, I briefly reflected that it would be a brave kidnapper indeed who ever tried to abduct our Amanda.

I glanced around nervously – again, hoping the youngies weren't listening, then continued: 'So one day they strike. They threaten me with these wild sex romp allegations that, in my powerful position, I supposedly forced upon a defenceless young pilot when she'd just started working with us. Next, they ask me for a kind donation of a million dollars or so, or else they'll reveal to those sweet innocent girls of mine exactly how evil their Daddy really is - and reveal it to Cynthia. Then they'll leak it to the press who'll undoubtedly rejoice to the high heavens a trumpeting headline which will probably screech:

Flying High! Grant's daughters horrified by Daddy's nude romps!

'It's blackmail. My planes will be empty from that day on. I'll have lost my whole airline. Farfetched, ladies and gentlemen of the jury? I doubt it. I rest my case, Your Honour.'

Bill McFarlane offered his opinion. 'In that event it mightn't be classed as blackmail. Extortion, more likely.'

I said, 'Gee that's a relief, Bill. I'd feel much happier being *extorted* out of a million dollars than blackmailed out of a million.'

Mandy joined the general mirth, then said, 'Dad loves to mix sarcasm with his humour. Sometimes it's straight sarcasm, though.'

Coralie Eastman smiled, "Maybe they could make a new movie called *Flying Low!*' This produced more laughter all round.

*

Later, after much clinking of glasses and pleasant chit-chat, we sought a relieving diversion, so our reunited family recounted their exhilarating European escapades while the ladies and youngies oohed and aahed over the acres of new fashion wear displayed around the rumpus room. I politely inquired if they managed to squeeze it all into one jumbo jet, but was either ignored or designated a 'typical boring male.' However, it did make sense for our company's top ladies to be stylishly attired; I quietly admitted to myself.

Leaving the fashion talk, Bill and I fled back outside to flop onto poolside banana lounges. After some time, the chattering females emerged to conduct a poolside fashion parade; a glittering affair displaying the very latest European ensembles. I switched on the flashing overhead disco lights, then, as the youngies were excitedly parading their own new apparel along the catwalk, followed by Mandy and Cynthia, I snuck away to crouch in the shadows of tall hedges.

When Drama Queen Mandy came strutting along the pool's edge, accompanied by whistles and cheers and echoing music, she was announcing: ' . . . and this one cost about a thousand, but you can see how beautiful it is . . . '

I rushed out and shoved her into the pool – thousand-dollar dress and all! Just as quickly, I vanished like *The Phantom* – around the back and into my shed; listening to the screams, curses and splashing.

52.

Revenge was a certainty, of course, but would bide its evil time until an opportune moment. So, hiding in the shed with *Sky* for a while, my mind drifted from *Maison de Fashionne* to Place of Reality.

I'd considered replying to Fred's pathetic letter with just one line: 'Yes, it certainly **has** been a long time since you saw your **three** grandkids,' but decided against dignifying his behaviour with any response at all. He was probably just testing the waters and might soon lose interest. Hoping for a peaceful resolution, I hoped that if he'd successfully ignored us for the past decade or so, we would act likewise for the next. I wanted him to wait for an answer that would never come, and I wanted that to make him feel uncomfortable. He may never attempt any subterfuge against me, but he still deserved our steeled silence as penalty for their years of neglect and mistreatment of my lovely Cristina.

While I doubted that he'd ever ring me, Bill McFarlane had warned me earlier that old Fred Parsons could just as easily turn up at our door any day – or attempt to. After all, everyone at Sydney airport knew that I lived out here near the lazy Nepean River; on a farm where all and sundry were usually welcome. Fred only needed to enquire around the airport, or simply ask any locals here for directions.

I returned cautiously to the pool area where soaking wet Mandy was ranting that Famous Fred had better not knock on our door any day – or else! I reminded her that, harsh as it may be, grandparents aren't obliged by law to give anything to their grandkids. Nor to look after them or even *visit* them. But if he called in here it was hardly against the law. Mandy stamped her foot and yelled, 'Don't care! Bet *they* had plenty to eat all their lives. Bet Mum's sister got whatever *she* wanted most of the time, too!'

Yes, the mysterious sister? We knew nothing of her life except that she'd wisely vamoosed from that entirely dysfunctional family.

I watched Mandy attempt to struggle from the sodden dress. "That expensive dress looks rather inspiring when wet, don't you think, dear? Did you slip in?'

'You know I'll get you back,' she threatened.

Bravely, I continued the earlier discussion. 'You know, I never really appreciated that you littlies were genuinely hungry those times. Kids are always saying they're hungry; they want this and they want that. What did I say to you back then?'

'You used to say to wait for dinner – or something like that. But we always swooped on those airline meals you put in the fridge - especially the chocolate puddings.'

I said, 'I feel so bad, looking back. I sometimes existed on those plastic meals and puddings myself. For a while we had no income from the old F28 – just horrific outgoings. Some weeks I couldn't afford groceries for us, so I always ordered a few extra meals for our flight and hoped a few passengers didn't turn up. We got there eventually, but I'm so sorry for those empty tummies, mate.'

'Forget it, Dad. Some kids endure far worse in other places. We all grew up healthy and that's the main thing.'

As everyone needed a breather from *that* subject, Mandy diverged to a tale about a handsome Italian named Nicky who studied in Bulgaria and holidayed in Hungary. While her three sisters were enthused with this exciting tale of romance, I tried to follow this complex navigation exercise and maybe guess what happened next. Nicky had spied her in a Budapest street and rushed up to chat. She smiled but couldn't understand him as he tried Hungarian first, then Italian - then German. Gesturing her non-comprehension, she said, 'Only English. Sorry.' I should have guessed: the Italian Romeo conveniently spoke fluent English as well, and invited them to a riverside Pizza café for lunch.

Then it became an exciting and romantic tale, and I was pleased that she'd quickly fallen for this young man who'd vowed to pursue her to Australia one day. By then she probably wouldn't need me: her silly old Dad. Looking at her, I briefly reminisced over a delightful little girl; a motherless child in a torn dress who never seemed to let go of my hand; who always cried when I had to leave then whooped for joy each time I returned. The child who always smiled when I read her goodnight stories as she slowly closed her eyes.

I laughed one night when she whispered, 'You read me such nice stories, but when you sing those lullabies they sound really bad!'

Back to this (almost) grown woman, I asked, 'Ah, speaking of this lecherous Latvian Lothario from Lithuania who holidays in Lichtenstein – or whatever you said - what happened to Steven, then? He's only around the corner.' It turned out that poor Steven was suddenly boring. Even worse, he wasn't European so he had no chance.

Diverting somewhat, I told my love-struck daughter that there was plenty of work coming her way, and that the office would be humming again very soon. I needed to discuss our new renovations with her and Cynthia; especially the greatly updated computers and security procedures with all-new CCTV surveillance monitors and a new high-tech poolside camera. Then I asked what she meant earlier by her *bitchiness.* 'Well, I'm here and he's over there,' she sighed, summing it up neatly. I reminded her she was not seventeen yet, so there was plenty of time for *all that.*

I was shocked when she replied: 'Mum was the same age as I am now when she was pregnant with me, and she only had six years of life left. You don't know for sure if there's plenty of time for "all that" Dad.' Tragically, she was quite correct and, thoughtlessly, I hadn't considered this angle.

Slightly altering the subject, I asked what Nicky the Romeo did for a living – if at all. She smiled and replied, 'Student. His interests are art, soccer and pretty girls.'

'So he just needs a pretty soccer-playing nude art model?'

'I could be two of those things,' my naughty daughter smirked. 'Not too good at soccer, though. Oh, and you'll never guess what his father used to do - it's really funny, although he's retired now.'

I thought aloud: 'Ah, Court Jester in the Vatican? Gondola driver? Spaghetti baron? I give up.'

She grinned, 'He used to be in the Italian Mafia for many years. Isn't that amazing, Dad?'

I had one of my instant, brilliant flashes. 'Does he still do hit jobs? I could use a handyman like him right now. I know a very large target that he couldn't miss . . . '

Mandy smiled, 'You're so funny sometimes, Dad. Not very often, mind you, but sometimes.'

I gave her a quick kiss, then said, 'Don't tell Romeo that another man kissed you. And especially don't tell the Godfather.'

'It's *Nicky,* Dad.'

'That's what I said. See you in the office soon. I'm having a swim first. And speaking of large targets: I'm expecting *him* today. You know what to do, don't you?'

'We're coming in, too!' chorused the Three Musketeers who'd been very patiently listening in. The women were already chatting in the pool so we conducted a combined bombing raid, splashing down right beside them. They disappeared beneath a blue wave; cocktails and all.

53.

Later, with Mandy locked in the office and everyone else cleared from the scene, I waited for Mr Super Sleuth, Ben Preston, to arrive at our infamous poolside. Unknown to him, however, would be the fact that we'd totally revamped our home security system to the extent that lots of undetectable surveillance was now in place. Our old and obvious pool cam had gone, to be replaced with a hidden camera secreted inside a large *black-boy* palm frond. It was an expensive, high definition, wide-screen device which was lodged in a basket half-way up a wall. Here, the basket itself blended in perfect symmetry with the veritable nursery of vegetation that adorned the brick walls of our house, office complex and gardens.

I'd asked the installers and builders to provide me with a system that not even security experts themselves might find – not mentioning anyone in particular, of course. After their work was completed, it took Marie and I nearly half an hour to locate the new camera. Perhaps an expert like Ben might spot it straight away, but hopefully not if I ensured he concentrate on my conversation and not be gazing around.

Further to this little surprise, another four hidden microphones and two smaller cameras were nestled in the foliage, together with laser trip beams to thwart intruders and direct alarms to our nearest security office. We now had more listening and watching devices than a Test Cricket ground, and though Ben had overseen the old installations, this time they had been done without him.

Eventually our eagle-eyed electronics wizard detected a visitor arriving. I heard an office buzzer go off and cancelled it with a hidden switch under my pool chair. Then a puffing and sweating man of, shall we say, rather *generous* proportions, stumbled around the corner. The image of Kermit the Frog leapt to mind. Attired in unwashed jeans and well-worn sneakers, Ben Preston was, as usual, *not* a veritable picture of sartorial elegance.

'Ah!' I forced a false smile and extended a hand. 'Wonderful to see you again. How's the snooping business, Ben?'

We shook hands as Puffing Ben immediately fired off his machine-gun staccato: 'Clandestine, Boss. By its very nature. You made some changes, I see. Going into nurseries, are we? Botanical gardens? No more flying?' Ben always spoke in these abbreviated sentences. No formal preambles for him; economy of words being his verbal signature. Alas, he'd never make a politician.

I said, 'Now Ben, me old mate, let's not waste your valuable time with me giving you a comprehensive tour of my new botanical gardens – as you call them. Even though I must admit it all looks rather lovely and *greenish*, I'm quite sure your time is far too precious.'

Abbreviated Ben said, 'You just uttered about fifty words but didn't say a thing!'

'Maybe,' I replied. 'Now let's play that funny stratagem game of yours. Ready? I spy with my little eye, something beginning with L.'

Humorous Ben shrugged. 'Ah, Lamborghini? Don't tell me you bought me a Lambo, Boss! You really shouldn't have bothered, but thanks anyway.'

'No, L is for *liar,* Ben. I spy a liar.' He shrugged again, causing dandruff to shower from his long hair. I continued, 'A liar who said he could observe my pool area when he actually couldn't because the barn and the kids' dollhouse were in the way.'

Quick-thinking Ben replied, 'The horse moved. Horses move. I moved along behind it. Got a few peeks that way, Boss.'

'It's always tethered.'

'But on a long tether.'

'Sure, Ben. And just why would anyone need a few peeks at our Tania anyway if she was wired in the first place?'

'For confirmation of suspect in the target area, Boss. No use just her testimony claiming she was here; I needed my own proof. Standard operating procedure.'

I conceded. 'I see. Well, just testing you with *my* standard operating procedures. I was angry when I recently stood out in that paddock near the horse's water trough and couldn't see our pool. *Liar* is what I instantly thought. Sorry Ben. Now, has she made any more demands or threats? You can't blame me for being very suspicious and paranoid.'

'Not yet. But it's been whispered that she'll probably hit you for a big amount very soon. If you won't pay she could go to the press with some *sex romp* scandal and that'll cost you even more, Mister Airline Man.'

'So bloody what? I can invite anyone I wish to my place. I'm free, white and over twenty-one.'

He argued: 'No you can't, Boss. Other people can, but not you. What about drag queens? Orgies? Bondage? Midgets? Doesn't matter if it's all lies or not. There are lots of allegations she could fabricate and some people will believe at least *some* of them. Mud flies: some of it sticks. Headlines will be murder. Business will be real bad. Old grannies won't fly with you. Nor will majority of the rest. This scurrilous *goss* doesn't matter to most, but to a person in your prominent public position . . . you could lose your whole airline if this ever gets out. To ignore it is a dangerous spin of the wheel . . . '

Frightfully, it was mostly quite true, but I was still puzzling somewhat over *midgets.* Flippantly, I asked, 'Is that all? What about swinging from the chandeliers? Seriously Ben, wouldn't it be just so much easier for Tania to simply sit back and enjoy flying planes with us for her whole career instead of taking this massive risk for such a short-term gain? She'd probably earn far more money working with us over forty years than any amount she might extort now.'

Clever Ben said, 'That's the whole point. People are greedy. She wants some moolah now while she's in her early twenties and young, not when she's a 65-year-old granny. Times have changed. She might be feeding a drug habit and needs money badly. Could have stand-over men pointing nasty things at her. That's what I'm hearing anyway, but who knows how the cards might fall? We've gotta keep this real quiet Boss, 'cos you can probably see the headlines right now . . . '

In fear I yelped, 'I can! I can! But times sure have changed from people working for a living to people *stealing* for a living, haven't they, Ben?'

Ben rubbed his chin in thought. 'Hmm, not too sure about that . . . but you must always remember that it was *you* who invited her to *your* property. She didn't turn up here uninvited.'

Yes, it *was* me. Stupid me. I felt foolish. I already had a lovely lady friend in Cynthia and as soon as she went away for a few weeks I was inviting a pretty young pilot around. Innocent at first, it now seemed to be the nastiest error I'd ever made. Worried, I asked, 'So you're sure that Tania will be going through with all this one day soon? That she's probably on drugs and involved with crime gangs who have guns? If so, she's a most unique pilot in the aviation fraternity, wouldn't you say, Ben? And why haven't I heard a peep from her about any of this?'

He gestured his hands to the Heavens. 'I said "who knows?" But a little birdie says to definitely expect a call soon. Easier to play along now than mess with these types, eh? Just give them what they ask and stay alive.'

'What about involving the police when it happens? Or now?' I asked.

'Just told you about keeping quiet. Squeal to the police and face trouble from these boys forever, or pay up now and it's all over. My advice, anyway. Gotta go. I'll send ya the bill. Bye.' He rose, and just before turning the corner, glanced up and asked: 'What happened to your pool cam?'

I said, 'I threw it out. It was old, had a dirty lens and its opacity was of concern − like yours. The sound was terrible, too. Oh, by the way: can you do me a favour one day? Look up a man called Fred Parsons?' Finally, I'd sprung the trap.

'Never heard of him, Boss.' This rather too-quick reply saw Big Ben's bushy eyebrows displaying a guilty flicker of alarm, then he shrugged and departed in the same manner as his grand entrance: sweaty rolls of fat tromping through my beautiful developing shrubs that I'd just planted between the pebbled paths.

But I hadn't asked him if he'd ever *heard* of Fred; I'd merely requested he research the name. Hmm. Once again the buzzer went *bzzzz!* I cancelled it then attempted to salvage some flattened flowers while deciding that, for all our jovial repartee, we now shared a strong mutual aversion because happy-go-lucky Big Ben was probably about as friendly and trustworthy as a large hand grenade.

A hidden lens recorded Ben wobbling back to his rusting Mercedes and driving away. Then Mandy ran out and whooped, 'Got it all. Loud and clear. You played that really well, Dad. Drugs, orgies, guns, gangs . . . what a load of bull. It's him – and maybe her too. They're probably in it together.'

I replied, 'Maybe. Anyway, I didn't want him to think I'm so naive that I trusted him implicitly. But I needed to test him to the extent that he revealed information he doesn't realise I know about. Do you follow that?'

'No.'

'Neither do I. Let's just play a waiting game now and see what transpires. Hope you backed up that conversation on disc. I'm going for a run then a swim. Cancel Ben's contract and call the police if he ever shows up again, please.'

Jogging across my hay-strewn paddocks, I worried deeply about some of Ben's words: 'You could lose your whole airline . . . ' Despite his lies, this frightening spectre was possibly quite imminent. No matter how guilty I may or may not be, such a scandal could become a horror movie for my family and I, while the public, not knowing, would forever speculate with great suspicion.

And then he'd said: 'Spin of the wheel . . . fall of the cards . . . ' Hmm. More Big Ben games? Was High Rolling Ben a gambler because the stakes were certainly getting higher . . . ?

54.

With affirmative action my most desired course, no more could I simply laze back and float upon false sanctuary because my home and head office had slowly turned into a security fortress. Apart from concealed surveillance equipment planted around our farm like land mines in a war zone, I now had regular manned patrols raking through our estate up to four times a day. At night, they combed through our gardens, scaled fences and rummaged through the barn and adjacent hangar with flashing torches. I often woke to slanting beams of LED lights slicing through my curtains, and heard whispered voices and hissing radios. Irritated, this seemed to be my unjust penalty for simply trying to provide a nice air transport service to the public. Welcome to real life.

Although my security patrol officers were all very nice types whom we'd vetted thoroughly when hiring, it was impossible for them to adequately perform their assigned tasks without causing at least some inconvenient disruptions to our lives and creating a feeling that our home was not a home any more. Regretfully, I could foresee no relief from this armed camp atmosphere where we might magically skip back into the good old normal days, because this now *was* normal.

Consequently, my girls had lost some interest in swimming after being occasionally confronted by uniformed personnel who often carried guns, and school friends had become wary of visiting us. Hardly conducive to having fun was a welcome mat with guns.

With much lamenting, I despaired at the death of our past privacy and the cherished memories of an innocent, idyllic lifestyle of days gone by; although sometimes I tried to see the funny side: perhaps I should erect a neon sign over our gate?

Welcome to Paranoia Park. Please bring your darkest fears with you!

*

My good friend Paul Harland often called in for a poolside coffee. Together we ran the flying side of Sky Star Airlines while Ken was away. One morning, while gazing at an unfriendly warning sign marked *SECURITY ZONE* on a wall that had formerly announced: *Welcome to the Grant girls' Fun Farm*, we discussed my woes of a vanished private life. Paul reminded me that the rich and famous of Hollywood endure this fortress-like scenario for much of their lives, while many other wealthy people in the world suffer to some extent.

'Exactly. This is not where I want to be, Paul.' I exclaimed. 'But thinking back, I seem to have been rather naïve about many matters. I always believed I could build a greater company by simply buying more and more planes and we would suffer no detrimental effects at all. It never once crossed my mind that anyone would make *demands* of me one day - especially criminal threats. Our lives have changed substantially over the last year, yet – until I recently hired armed guards - I'd done little to protect us against those changes or to increase safety for my children.'

'Paul, our farm has always been one big open house where everyone from neighbours to half the local high school are offered open invitations to drop in at any time. But, while I always played Mr Nice Guy, there are some people out there who are obviously not quite so nice. Could I have been irresponsible, do you think? Especially to my family?'

Paul rubbed his chin in deep thought. 'Irresponsible? It's hardly my place to comment on that, Rob – even though you asked me. I'm not a parent – yet. But yes, perhaps a touch naive. In this world you can't be rich without putting iron bars on your windows and guard dogs in your yard. Rich means *target.* Airline owner means *big target!'*

He added, 'I'm not suggesting abductions here, but your four daughters are all quite pretty – in case you haven't noticed - and could easily become the future target of any dubious persons sniffing money in the air - if not already.'

I interrupted with 'See? It's not fun anymore, Paul. We could leap this hurdle then another threat appears down the track. I've lost my fundamental interest. I'm just a pilot, basically - like you. I only ever wanted to fly. It was all an exciting challenge but now that seems to have gone. I don't like being backed into corners in intractable situations like this.'

Paul nodded in agreement, but without solutions we needed to move on. 'Ah, speaking of pilots, Rob. We have to discuss other big issues now. Firstly, Ken Tolman wants another month off to take his baby to Europe for this operation. I understand you've approved this?' I confirmed that I certainly had. I told Paul that Mrs Westcott would arrange the extra month's leave, and that he, Paul, would continue as acting Chief Pilot.

Paul cleared his throat and said, 'Thankyou. Now, I received your lengthy and very disturbing fax about First Officer Tania Wicks. I shouldn't have to point out that I was astonished that you hadn't advised me earlier, instead of general hearsay and 'shop' talk, about this whole situation which is of extreme concern and relevance to our flight operations.'

I reacted. 'Hang on, Paul. I've merely informed you of *an* early situation. I don't know that she's done anything wrong at all, yet. She came here for a swim at my invitation. She swam, she ate, she left. The most riotous thing we've ever done together is enjoy a barbecue. I haven't seen her or heard from her since then. But then Ben Preston started hitting me with all this . . . weirdo, cryptic stuff . . . then said things like: "Just a few of your recorded words could be quite valuable in the future to certain vested interests . . . "

'My problem is, Paul: I just can't remember exactly *what* words I said her. Not being a courtroom stenographer, I'm not obliged to remember my every casual conversation around my pool.'

Paul held his hand up like a traffic cop halting cars. 'Well Rob, the list of allegations that our investigator has made is quite horrendous - if true. And our solicitors should have commenced legal and police proceedings against her days ago. So am I guessing correctly that you have, or *had*, a certain interest in Tania and this prevented you from believing the worst about her? If so, you should have asked others to make in-depth third-party inquiries about her - primarily to clear her name if you believe she's innocent. But firstly you should have informed myself and Mrs Westcott, as Chief Pilot and Chief of Staff.'

'Yes, you're quite right, Paul. I suppose I simply hoped it'd just go away, so I flashed down to Tassie with my kids and hid my head in the sand for three days of peace. But back here, I wasn't about to hire even *more* investigators when I was already paying the steep fees of Preston's *Eagle Eyes* agency. So I asked him to explain his so-called 'tip-offs' which rapidly became more outrageous, and now he's warning about criminal gangs with guns and drugs. I just haven't had the time or inclination to dwell upon this drama all day long while I'm trying to operate an airline. Anyway Paul, did you call Tania in to your office? I'm very eager to hear her side of it all. So far it's been one big magical mystery tour for me, and a guessing game of increasingly mystical proportions.'

Paul folded his arms in serious officialdom. 'I interviewed her yesterday after a Melbourne trip.'

'And?'

'Tania claims she knows absolutely *nothing* about any of this. She was astonished and outraged. She denies every single allegation and rejects as ludicrous this claim about her wearing concealed recording devices. She was very angry at you, and asks how you - or anyone at all - could possibly know what was inside her swimwear? She then became quite upset and related a lengthy tale about her immense difficulties growing up in a backwards family who resisted her every effort in learning to fly, who believe in religious quackery and arranged marriages and who live in some kind of *other world* after the traumas of war. Then, when she finally succeeded in aviation despite fierce parental opposition, her world spun upside down.'

'In summary, she denies sneaking back to your property after the barbecue. She also denies ever knowing anyone called Benjamin Preston. Further, she says she's sorry she ever met you and regrets that she ever applied to work at Sky Star. Then she even stormed out hating *me* – for some reason. In summary, I wouldn't be surprised to receive her resignation at any moment and I currently have her on stand-down because of her state of anger. Lastly, I believe you compromised yourself when you just *shouldn't*.'

I shook my head in despair. 'See, this is exactly what I was referring to before, Paul. We give a young woman a lucky break and her first shift was nothing but a damn nightmare. No-one I've ever heard of has suffered a take-off flame-out on their very first flight. Let alone the rest of this . . . *war*. And now I can't even invite any female home for a few hours . . . '

As Paul shrugged without answers, I referred again to Tania's first day: 'Before her flight – as you know - she couldn't gain admittance to the terminal because of some ridiculous security bungle - even though she was in uniform and showed I.D. Because of this, she got to the departure lounge quite late. When she arrived she was thrown to the wolves with me – the airline's owner. She didn't know me at first, but must have wondered why I slipped out of sight after the incident.'

'So her first grand day lasted for over twelve hours on duty. Then she had no means of transport home apart from an unaffordable taxi. I offered her a lift as I go right past her exit. Anyway, I thought Tania was pretty and invited her home for an innocent swim sometime, thus making me the first man in history to ever ask a pretty female to his home - so shoot me! And by the way, did you sign her out with only simulator time?'

Paul confirmed that he did. He explained that Ken had introduced new licencing rules that allowed new pilots with exceptional abilities to go straight into the F/O's seat without a route check. He added that although it was a slight gamble that many other airlines also take, he was confident of her outstanding proficiency.

At that particular moment, Mandy walked from the office and settled on a banana chair. She and Paul exchanged friendly greetings, then Mandy asked why was I being shot, and was it because I'd recently pushed her into the pool, because I should be. Thankful for small mercies, I reflected that at least there was strong mutual admiration between these two; unlike the poisoned cloud that always hung between Mandy and the infamous Captain Tolman. Incidentally,

Mandy had recently lamented that it was a pity Paul was now taken, because she'd always had eyes for him.

Paul cleared his throat, then started to reiterate Tania's lengthy denials to Mandy, who interrupted with: 'Paul, I've already listened in to everything that was said out here just then. And it's recorded in excellent clarity. I think we should just file police charges against Ben Preston now and clear this whole mess up.'

Paul said, 'Hmm, but your Dad's right. They'd want suitable evidence first.'

'You bet they will,' I agreed. 'He's one smart and shifty character and will have all his bases covered, you can bank on that. And remember his words: "We hack things. I do it all the time." Hacking Ben is no slouch with computers, as he often boasted to me. So, in my lofty position I can't go wildly roaring into police stations with unsubstantiated allegations that could leave me looking foolish and the press rejoicing.'

Mandy said, 'Speaking of computers, Paul: we've also got that last visit of his recorded on our computer hard-drive. He clearly states that Tania is probably on drugs and involved with crime gangs and guns. Then he threatens Dad that "it's easier to play along than to mess with these types." He advises Dad to part with a large sum – probably a million dollars or so – and not report it to any authorities. But what sort of investigating agency supposedly working for us recommends concealing such crimes?'

Paul answered correctly. 'A guilty one. By the way: I sprung a routine drugs and alcohol test on Tania at yesterday's interview. She was clear.'

I leapt up from my seat. 'See! There goes the first of Lying Ben's allegations right out the window! He's all lies. She's not on drugs and has no need to blackmail me. This jumbo juggernaut has assessed my wealthy situation and devised an extortion plan that's infinitely more rewarding than the monthly invoices I pay him. But he can't just march up to me and demand a million bucks: he needs some inducement or threat. Then he hears of a new pilot who's pretty, so he decides on the oldest inducement in the world. With short notice, he tries to hack our computers so she's rostered to fly with me, but for some reason it takes a little while to achieve this on Tania's very first shift – thus the delay. Then later I carelessly invite her to my place. No self-respecting extortionist ever stumbled upon such a golden opportunity.'

Paul asked, 'But hang on, everyone. Why on Earth does he – or *they* – need to delay Tania at security at all? Apart from irritating you by being late, what the hell did *that* ever achieve? This is the big question.'

Mandy declared, 'Probably because when we consider that we have five flights out of Sydney each morning and Dad was the captain of just *one* of them, *they* urgently needed to manufacture some short delay to determine which one it was. Obviously Tania couldn't go rushing from gate to gate asking Security: "I'm a pilot. Which one is my flight?" Remembering that it was also Dad's first day back at work because Ken was away, and that Dad was supposed to be at home in our office, it certainly must have surprised them when *they* saw that Dad was coming back and taking a flight that very morning. They needed to jump quickly otherwise it could be weeks or months till Tania's roster put her with Dad – if ever.'

'So they probably leapt for joy when they saw that they might be able to slot Tania in with you on her very first flight. But as it's confidential information which pilots take what flights, the big question was: which flight out of the five was Dad going to take? We know now that it was SK101 to Adelaide, but how could *they* find this out?'

'It was approaching departure time and Tania would surely be arriving any moment – *should have* arrived already, actually. By hacking our computers and inserting that malicious data about another woman with the same name, they bought themselves brief but valuable time - maybe fifteen minutes. They were probably still hacked into our system when Tania arrived at the airport, already late from traffic. Then, while security puzzled over this strange alert which had suddenly been uploaded to their screens, our hacking friends were frantically trying to find which gate they should shepherd her towards. Luckily for them, at the last moment they eventually saw that Dad's flight, SK101 to Adelaide was at gate six. Then they quickly shuffled the rostered F/O from there to another gate and . . . bingo! Game over.'

This was an astute assessment. Paul asked Mandy if her real name was Mrs Sherlock Holmes? Then I posed the question: 'How on Earth do you *know* all this stuff, Mandy? And what about that forty-year-old woman pilot; overweight with frizzy hair? And why did Ben insist that I fire Tania?'

She smiled, 'The only photo of a female pilot they could find in a hurry, I suppose. The rest was probably educated guessing. Anyway there's more. Fortunately, Tania's late arrival at the departure gate makes Dad feel sorry for her straight away. They establish a brief rapport. But then, their big win: the take-off emergency and subsequent arrival back home after midnight. She lives out Dad's way so he gives her a lift. This would never have happened if the flight had been routine. And why fire her? Because that was his ploy: he could hardly suggest you retain a spy on the staff . . . '

Paul added, 'I checked that Punchbowl address. Her parents live there but she recently rented a unit near Penrith. She told me her parents hated her moving out and she's still in transit between places while she argues with them about it. Also, she sometimes borrows her mother's white BMW'

I sighed. 'Hey, enough folks. What a hole we're in with this entire matter. We can't legally prove any of this . . . weak surmise. She could be lying, or Lying Ben could be lying - or both. We can't lodge serious charges against anyone with flimsy evidence such as: "I gave her a lift home so that proves she's a spy." Paul, what are our Terminal security people saying about this?' He answered that they keep no records of delays at the door and can't quite remember it because they have thousands of people pass through the doors every week. So they didn't even realise they were hacked in the first place, and now there's no trace of it.

I rubbed my aching brow. 'Computers. Hacking. Security. This is all giving me a damned headache. It'd be much more simple and peaceful if I just flew around a farm somewhere out west, mustering cattle in my lovely little Gazelle, and gave all this up.'

55.

An unknown voice suddenly interrupted: 'Howdy everyone! Is this Rob Grant's place? Lovely day, eh?'

Greatly worsening my headache, I spun around to spy a dishevelled man standing right behind us in our garden; holding an object. 'What the hell?' I yelped, thoroughly astounded. And why didn't the buzzers go off? Where on Earth were my security people? Do we have no privacy anymore? Maybe I should get guard dogs? And just who the hell is *this*?

I pressed a pager's button in my pocket. My phone rang back immediately. I said into it: 'Our seats are full for today's flight to Norfolk Island.' Paul said, 'Huh?' and Mandy looked at me oddly because we have no flights to Norfolk Island – ever. My security crew were at our local sandwich shop. They'd be here at high speed - in five minutes or less – while we stared at the hobo in our garden.

I stood up to confront this surprise visitor who'd miraculously just *appeared*. Mandy showed a shocked face. Paul was amazed. I was infuriated! Cynthia and Marie ran from the office saying: 'It's showing a red *Pool Area Breach*! There's alarms going off everywhere . . . ah, who's this man?'

I was about to introduce our uninvited guest. He was draped in baggy and torn clothes. His gray hair and straggly beard was dirty and matted. Several of his front teeth were missing and the remaining ones were darkly stained. A rolled cigarette dangled from his cracked lips. Then, with terror, I noticed he clutched something in his hands. Was it a bomb? My eyes widened in fright . . . Jumping Jesus! All my nightmares had become real!

Before I could react, the man said, 'Wow. Nice place you've got here, Rob. Now, where's me three beautiful girls, eh? I'll bet they're all nearly growed up by now, that's fer sure. Home time soon, I s'pose, but I don't mind waitin' till they get here. They'll be thrilled to see their old Grand-Daddy again.'

Perfectly timed for maximum effect, school had just finished so his invasion had literally *vacuumed* any proposed words from my mouth. Paul stepped forward to say something, but Mandy exploded angrily from her chair. 'You BASTARD!' she screamed, frothing with nearly seventeen years of pent-up vehemence. Both Cynthia and Marie grabbed their mouths in fright while I bowed and swept my arm in an introductory arc.

'Ladies and Gentlemen, please let me introduce the devoted grandfather of my children. The proud and loving father of my deceased wife, and my greatly cherished father-in-law: The Right Dishonourable Fred Parsons, graciously visiting us today, albeit without invitation, from lovely New Zealand.'

But before anyone could utter another word, and luckily before Amanda could murder him, I glimpsed a flash of two racing black uniforms as they swept past us with banana chairs, pool floats, tables and glasses all crashing aside. With a sickening thump, the two uniformed guards crash-tackled our distinguished guest in mid-air and pole-drove him backwards into the pool. Following the almighty splash which engulfed half our new gardens, Mandy, purple-faced, turned and barged towards the office, screaming 'I'll bloody *kill* 'im!'

When the three of them surfaced with Fred spluttering and choking, I smiled and said, 'Welcome to friendly Australia, Fred. Feel free to have a swim. The water's fine.'

Behind me, I heard Cynthia whisper, 'Wow, that should make the best video ever!'

Speaking of kids: like the synchronisation of the finest Swiss watch, I suddenly glimpsed three bicycles zipping down our lane; their gleeful riders pedalling with an after-school zeal that announced: 'We're home! We want afternoon tea. Who's that jumping in our pool? We wanna join in!' Noisily, more beeps and bells chimed from inside our security bunker. Our roadside movement sensors, now switched to *ALERT*, were simply doing their job after being triggered from the security car, then activated again by the three bikes. But how did Fred just wander in at will?

And just in case Fred didn't notice them, the girls all gleefully rang their bikes' bells, adding to the general cacophony. 'Christ!' I cursed. Normally I was delighted when my little friends came biking home - even though it usually heralded the end of peace and tranquillity. But today was decidedly different.

Making a fast decision, I raced to the office. 'Mandy, quick! The girls are riding in. Pack some bags. I'll get Cynth to drive you all to our favourite motel in Windsor for the night. Call me when you're there. Cynthia, take them out for a nice dinner somewhere - and the movies, if they want. You'll know what to do. I don't intend for *him* to ever lay eyes on any of my girls.'

Except that it was too late: he'd already seen Mandy and she'd sworn at him. Then the sudden ringing and chirping of the other three girls made his head turn as he struggled in the pool.

Called into duty, Mandy leapt into swift action. She used the rear walkway to access the house, then to hurriedly pack bags for a lightning exodus. By mere seconds, our smart manoeuvring had managed to avert a disastrous confrontation with a drowned rat.

Racing out a side door and shepherding the girls before her in a confused melee, Cynthia asked, 'What should I tell them, Rob? The truth? Or what?'

'Ah, just say there's a crazy old drunk in our garden — well, there is! And he was holding something . . . ah no, don't tell them that.' Cynthia scurried towards her car behind the puzzled girls, shepherding her flock. Forced suddenly from their home, the girls protested briefly then were happy when Cynthia announced that it was a surprise motel, dinner and movie night. And with no school tomorrow thrown in as an added bonus, who could complain about that? Phew, one crisis temporarily averted; now for the next one.

Back outside, we observed the swishing, splashing and cursing as three soaked figures emerged from the pool. Or, to be more correct, as two young, wet and muscled security guards hauled a bedraggled man from the pool by his feet. I said, 'Thanks very much guys. Much appreciated. Do you need to get changed somewhere? I have spare clothes here – jeans and things?'

The men said no thanks; they'd stay right here because they were still on duty and obliged to guard our surprise guest. Cynthia fetched them towels while Fred was roughly manhandled to a poolside chair, coughing and blaspheming by not only taking the name of The Lord in vain, but mine even more strenuously. Puffing, he was held down vice-like while I tossed him a towel; the very least I could do for a long-lost family gold digger such as himself.

Paul Harland said, 'Wow! I haven't had this much fun since my twenty-first.' But we weren't free from danger. Who knows? – as Big Ben would say. Fred might have accomplices hiding nearby? His crazy wife Elsie, perhaps?

After regaining his breath and bravado, old Fred fired off a salvo at us all. 'Jesus' teeth! Australia sure has changed, hasn't it? Used to be, in the good old days, a bloke could come over here and the first thing he'd hear would be Gidday mate. Wanna beer? Not anymore. I turn up for a friendly visit to my own family – after politely writing first, mind you – and get assaulted by these *bozo's*!' Thumbs tightened into his shoulders and he gasped; then continued: 'I should report this to the damn police, I should. Whatever happened to friendly Trans-Tasman relations?'

A guard interrupted, shaking him. 'You had something in your hands, sir. That's why you were tackled. What was it? A weapon?'

Fred sneered. 'A little present for me girls, that's what. Me own family. I bought 'em a doll. Least I could do. Now it's at the bottom of the pool. Waste of thirty damn bucks!'

Wow, I thought: a *whole* thirty dollars expended on three kids. If you add on the proposed feast at *Mick Donald's*, it might amount to a total of fifty dollars outlaid over a dozen years. Was Fred a registered charity? His generosity was boundless.

I levelled my gaze directly into his face and said softly, 'Fred, speaking of Trans-Tasman cordiality, do you happen to know a Kiwi by the name of Ben Preston?'

I caught a flicker of surprise, then a sneer as he quickly denied, 'Never heard of him. Anyway, where's me grandkids? I travelled two thousand kays to see 'em, only to get tossed into your stinkin' pool!'

I persisted, 'A whole two thousand, eh? But it's only a three-hour flight, Fred. It's not as though you had to swim here doing the dog-paddle. So I'll ask you again: Ben Preston is his name. A huge guy. Long hair. Sleazy; just like you. Comes from your district around Wellington.'

'You're just a smart-arse, Robert Grant,' he sneered. 'Never did like you. Too hoity-toity for our lowly family, eh?'

'Hardly,' I countered. 'I married your daughter, remember? The eldest one that was just so difficult to raise.'

Fred grunted, 'I mean, too high and mighty to speak to us now. I'm no fancy *fly boy* like you – born with a silver spoon. I was a boot maker when I left school . . . '

'And a child beater later. What did you conquer next, Fred? Strangling kittens? Bank robbery?'

'Me and Elsie worked damned hard on farms. We lived in shacks and struggled for food.'

To his shock, I violently kicked the chair out from under him. He crashed heavily to the ground. 'You mean, *Cristina* struggled for food, don't you Fred? Not you or your low-life wife who was too lazy to attend her own daughter's funeral! Cris told me all about her disgraceful family, don't worry. I heard how you and Elsie and Suzie were always eating well while little Cristina had to *beg* for food while she watched on. You evil pig!'

'So before you go to *our* police, we might alert your own police to your child beating of years ago. It can be back-dated, you know. They should be very interested to hear about the regular beatings you gave Cristina for no reason at all – and the deprivation of food and liberty you forced on her. And how, as soon as she was old enough, she was forced to flee her country because of your violent behaviour and threats.'

He stuck his craggy nose in the air and pretended he wasn't listening. But I wasn't finished. 'There's lots more too, Fred. Unfortunately for you, Cristina wrote it all down before she died. She loved writing, so she scribbled her whole life story into school notebooks. I kept them Fred. I've still got them right here in this house. It's written evidence. Sworn testimony. Dozens of pages.

Would you like me to show you some now? You should recognise the handwriting.'

Now the old man really *was* worried - and so was I, because there *were* no such notebooks as proof of his mistreatment - although the tales themselves were entirely true. The bluff worked and he clammed up; finally devoid of even minor blasphemies.

Then a guard who'd been talking on his phone took me aside to whisper, 'My mates in the Federal police looked up this Benjamin Preston person again this morning. Seems he needed to urgently fly to Singapore yesterday on business.'

'Well, that could be right, Gary. He *is* in business, after all.'

'But for ninety days? He had a ninety-day visa. Now they're checking with NZ police about him. When he returns from Asia - *if* he returns from Asia, they're going to detain and question him. Also, it seems that Preston has huge gambling debts all over town. I thought he was supposed to be smart?' I thanked him kindly, then reflected with no small relief how matters now seemed to be turning strongly in our favour.

Then I asked, 'Gary, just as a matter of interest: how come this trespassing man just waltzed onto our property unnoticed when we've got more security gizmo's here than Fort Knox?'

He was embarrassed. 'Very sorry, Mr Grant. We took the outside garden security number five circuit off-line for one hour's maintenance while we got our lunch. The rest was all still active. We decided that we'd visually watch the road to your property from Faretti's shop nearby. It was only to be a brief outage and we expected nothing to happen in that very hour. No cars went up your way so I guess he walked across the paddocks from Nepean Valley Lane right at that very period, then blundered through the only off-line sector in the whole system.'

I threw up my hands in surrender and decided to let it pass; nothing was one hundred percent secure, yet Fred could easily have carried a real weapon. He could have lain in wait for my children, and he could have attempted to kidnap them with the weapon. Anything could have occurred – but it didn't. I shook my head then bent back down to old Fred, sitting miserably on the hard and wet pebble stones.

I fiercely gripped his shirt front: 'Fred. Do you know that Cristina wrote that you evil bastards used to disappear for days at a time, leaving her locked alone in that cabin? And when the few scraps of food ran out she ate dead moths off the dirty window sill? She eventually told her own children that and sometimes, being so young, they copied her in sympathy. Those strange chalk marks on your stone walls were the number of days you left her imprisoned. Remember those terrible marks? Eighteen chalk scratches over three different periods. And do you remember how old she was then? No? I'll tell you. She was five. Five bloody years old, the first time! And even when you *were* home she was malnourished for years, so maybe she eventually became sick because of all your ill-treatment. Maybe her weakened immune system encouraged her cancer to develop; and now we'll never know. You should be in jail, Fred – forever.'

And then, into the several surrounding microphones hidden by greenery, our Fred abruptly shouted. 'That's damn lies and you know it! She wasn't five years old. She was at least seven . . . or even eight. We left her food but we didn't realise she couldn't reach the top pantry shelf. We only ever went fruit pickin' for a week at the most and she was always alive when we got back. Anyway, you're the sick one, not me. You have sex orgies here. Gang parties, bondage queens, midgets . . . it's disgusting! I know all about it. That's why I came over here: to get those kids away from all this *filth* forever. This . . . den of depravity! And to make you pay – fancy *fly boy*!'

I laughed, 'Gee, that little checklist of entertainment sounds quite familiar. Seems like I heard those very words just recently from someone else. Should go well in court with all the other recordings we already have; don't you think so, guys?' The 'guys' agreed enthusiastically.

However, apparently our waterlogged Fred hadn't heard me properly, because he growled a string of double and triple negatives that would make a linguistics professor resign: 'You can't prove nothin' 'cause you ain't got no s**t on me. I ain't admittin' nothin' to no damn cops about no bulls**t child beatin' neither!'

'But you already *have* admitted it, Fred,' I assured our esteemed and eloquent guest. 'Be warned. We're recording all this. There are microphones all around you and you just stated that you often left a child of seven or eight locked up alone for a week at a time with insufficient food. That's a crime!' I turned to my security men. 'Gary, take him to your police mates at Windsor, please. Ask them to charge him with illegal trespass – for starters.'

'Anything else, Rob?'

'Ah, how about: 'Enter Australia with intent to abduct minors? And/or to commit extortion' - as admitted on recorded hard drive. By the way Fred, where's your charming wife . . . your accomplice?'

'In a car. Down that back lane.'

'The getaway driver, eh? How about you boys pay her a visit on the way, please?' The two men smiled, then dragged soggy Fred away.

Marie appeared bewildered at these dramatic events, while Paul smiled, 'Wow! That was more exciting than flying a boring old jet plane.'

But I wasn't excited, and mumbled through gritted teeth: '*K* is for Kermit the Frog. He's next. Croak! Croak!'

Later, I dived to the bottom of the pool and retrieved an old wrinkled and soggy doll which had probably come from a garbage dump. I dried it out and painted its face with a gray beard, then stuck Fred's crumpled hat on it and plonked it beside the duck pond. With a bit of luck the ducks would take the appropriate action in due course. But just in case, I fed them extra bread as an advance performance bonus.

56.

In the morning, the kids were back home from exile and we related the entire saga of dramas to them – warts 'n all. When I mentioned Fat Ben and Old Fred hailing from the same district, then showed the kids our recent HD images of both, Olivia spoke up: 'You know, even though this man Preston has got a really fat face and yucky hair, his wicked smile still looks the same in that old school photograph I've got.'

'What photo, Liv?' asked Cynthia, while I was instantly intrigued.

Olivia said, 'That photo Mum left us. Along with the cards and notes she wrote before she died. I'll show you. I've had them under my bed ever since. My only memories of Mummy. Her goodbye notes. It's just a few little things - but really sad.'

She raced to her room then returned with an old, dusty shoulder sack. I'd never seen it before. It seemed to be the only miserable item of belongings, apart from a backpack, long since gone, with which Cristina had fled New Zealand so very long ago. Inside were a few handwritten notes to her beloved girls, a faded card from a boy at school saying he liked her, and a few grainy, black-and-white photos. I grabbed them with fascination, gawking at an old image of a smiling girl of about fifteen - although painfully thin. Smiling - despite existing in a life of turmoil and pain. I cried: her innocent face was oblivious to the few remaining years she had to live.

'Livvy,' I fought tears. 'You've never shown me these things. This is incredible!' Olivia explained that her mother had passed these things to her at the hospital where she died soon after. A shaky scrawl on a card said: "To my four beautiful little angels. Remember me. Your loving mother, Cristina."

And finally there was a tattered school photograph from the past; probably taken in the late 1950's although the exact year was hard to read. About thirty teenage students grinned at the camera.

Along the front row, just above *Mauriki High School* and the list of pupils' names, leapt three unmistakable faces out at me.

'Holy guacamole!' I squawked; eyes popped wide. 'Read this!' The caption said: "Elsie McVeigh. Frederick Parsons. Benjamin Preston."

There were now no doubts in the world: Cristina's parents were sitting side-by-side in high school, right next to a long-haired but skinny Ben Preston whose broad grin was probably contemplating a lengthy and fruitful career in extortion and computer hacking.

I exclaimed, 'You're quite right, Livvy. That's the same man you spoke to when you rode home the other week. That fat man in our laneway who told you all those scary things, then disappeared when Mandy's taxi arrived. Look at this: he's sitting right next to your grandfather!'

She stared for a while, then said, 'I know it's him now. It's the same bad man's face.'

Mandy grabbed the photo and spouted, 'So they *did* all know each other after all. Bloody class mates! They've been setting this up for ages.'

They had. Their conspiracy took its roots from way back then. My mind reeled as the items were passed around. Celia took one look and sobbed as she grasped the evil plot. Cynthia gulped and turned away. Mandy performed her usual act of stomping away to the office again, while Emily just stared silently at her mother's faded and tragic image. The three youngest girls had seen these items and the class photo before, but had never thought to show me. And they'd probably never even glanced at the teenager seated next to their grandfather: the grinning hippie who was supposed to be so clever but apparently now owed more than a million dollars in gambling debts to various casinos.

Just as Ben the loser had certainly lost, we had definitely won, because if this dirtied old shoulder sack was Cristina's only legacy of memories from a stormy and deprived youth and her desperate escape from her home and country, then right here before me were her finest achievements: four beautiful human beings in the very image of her, proving our Lady Cristina, star of the skies, had been ultimately triumphant.

Despite our hard-fought and tragic victory, I glared daggers at the faded school photograph and, just before ripping it to shreds, I growled between gritted teeth:

I spy, with my little eye, something . . .

57.

Sometimes the years seem to fly fast. Fast as a jet plane. Now it was the year 2001 and we were well and truly into the twenty-first century.

On the Australian airline scene, Ansett Airlines teetered on the very verge of bankruptcy and a final grounding, while new owners Air New Zealand bizarrely continued to prop it up and reassure us all of the company's on-going viability. Amidst all this, even though Sky Star continued to be a strong player in these turbulent times, I still wasn't sure where we'd eventually fit in – if at all. But it was obvious that a sudden grab for Australia's skies would soon occur and Qantas would be handed a golden gift on a platter when their main rival folded up. They would then rejoice in running rampant and almost unchallenged around the country – except for little Sky Star. While robust, we only flew less than twenty percent of Australia's air travellers and it would pose no impediment for the government-backed Qantas to simply gobble us up if they so desired.

Thus far I'd resisted most offers to dispose of our little outfit – my creation, but often lay awake wondering if I even wanted to reject them? Did I plan to spend my entire working life enslaved in the harsh cut and thrust of worrisome aviation management? I'd been there and done that but still wasn't an office/management type of person. My Amanda was now seventeen and both of us were shying away from the idea of directing our airline where we had no taste for endlessly fighting predators in take-over bids. Further, I would not endure any more criminal demands such as we'd suffered in the past. We'd been shaken *and* stirred.

And neither of us particularly relished any more critical staff problems like Ken's sick child who was now well again, thank goodness. Nor of raging and skyrocketing fuel prices now that the days of fuel hedging had tightened. Lastly, we'd tired of constantly competing with others for our slice of the market, and we dragged our feet to awkward media conferences where our spin often matched theirs.

In essence, I was simply a pilot. That's all I'd ever aspired to be. But when AEA went down just after my career had commenced, I stubbornly refused to accept that the whole show was already over so soon. When no-one else offered employment to us redundant pilots, I barged in to start my own air company at just twenty years old. Socially, I married an extraordinary and beautiful woman who had three terrific kids. We had another - then the very worst happened.

I stuck it out through thick and thin, persisting with my airline dreams until they finally and thankfully came to fruition – but only after many years of battling to feed four little mouths, plus my own. After a decade of steady progress through struggle, I'd eventually made an obscene amount of money and owned over thirty jets. I was King of our little mountain; a second Reg Ansett – although years younger than he'd been at this stage.

But along with such victories had come the sour taste of others angling for our wealth. Even from our own relatives.

Happily, our Fred Parsons and his plotting wife had eventually been deported back to New Zealand for planning extortion, although they avoided jail in Australia because they had never actually extorted money from anyone. The abduction allegations were dismissed here – despite my taped recordings. We heard that authorities in New Zealand might be investigating the thirty-year-old abuse allegations concerning my Cristina, but, as she was now deceased it was a futile hope indeed for anyone to expect them to expend much time on it when current cases of a similar nature would surely deserve priority. So I asked them to drop it. The incriminating school photo had been strong enough evidence to me, but it no longer existed and would not have flown in a court anyway because it's hardly a crime to sit next to someone in a forty-year-old school photograph. Goodbye dear Cristina; I tried to defend you, my darling.

Now all of us, especially me, needed to let it go, while finally I must state that I hold no grudges against the nation of New Zealand because my beautiful wife came from there!

Ben Preston remained untraceable in Asia; as are many other wanted businessmen from Australia. When police raided his *Eagle Eyes* Burwood office they found it empty. At his Strathfield home unit they found just a few computer files in the trash that the master hacker had thought he'd deleted but hadn't. There were three draft letters of extortion threats: two demanding the modest sums of $500,000 each, and the other asking an adventurous five million dollars - an absurd amount of money that I could never raise in cash. I was a business owner with my money lodged in our assets like most businesses; so perhaps another flamboyant playboy billionaire might possess such merry lucre on hand, but not me.

These days Ben has faded into, as the police succinctly put it, 'a person of interest.' So I'm sure our Ben is still in Asia somewhere; investigating, conning and hacking to the best of his ability - wherever he may roam. But he shouldn't be too hard to find: on a continent of three billion slender Asians, Big Ben must stand out somewhat. With a sly smile, I often doubt if he's lost any weight in that sultry tropical heat?

Could *H* stand for heart attack?

58.

And now I felt a powerful weariness. We had new managers and pilots, new maintenance crews and cabin crews - and even a few more female pilots. But I felt strong yearnings to be elsewhere. I'd achieved what I'd set out to do long ago – and much more. It hadn't been at all easy, but is any worthwhile battle in life trouble-free? Who makes millions effortlessly apart from a few lucky rock and sports stars?

At home, the kids were still there and I wasn't quite rid of them yet. But these days I saw *women* in our rumpus room - not kids. Young women chatting to other young adults, and the eldest ones driving cars in and out while the youngest two raced cars around the farm - just as I once had. Now on the threshold of adulthood, was Amanda (intelligent, bossy) aged 17, Olivia (quiet, studious and learning to drive) 16, Emily (smart, talented) 14, and Celia (loving, funny) aged 13. Adult life, with all its joys and pitfalls, eagerly awaited them now.

Our family's theme had always been to ensure we made up for Cristina's many lost decades of life and her decidedly miserable early years. Unable to bring her back, we could hopefully *pay* her back. Four lovely grown women in her likeness would be a wonderful token of our eternal gratitude.

And so, just before the fax arrived in our office, my undecided future plans had almost ratified into what we pilots call *a command decision*. Just like being hit with a sudden engine failure, my time had finally come to burst into action. No use sitting around in a daze while your fan's on fire: it's command decision time and it's here right now!

I'd actually picked up my phone to call Zhiran Jacobs at Qantas when the fax came beeping in. Zhiran had always stated, without much enthusiasm, that if I ever considered selling Sky Star, Qantas would probably snap it up for perhaps fifteen million - just to be rid of us, most likely. But I hoped they would at least proudly utilise our superbly-maintained planes and equipment – not to mention hiring our fantastic staff. Whatever transpired, they'd never offer what I'd ask for and expect - that was certain. While a mere fifteen million dollars would be of little inconvenience to them, I wanted about thirty million if I ever sold out. Then again, who would cry poor if someone handed them a neat little cheque for fifteen million dollars?

I told my newly qualified company secretary Cynthia, that I was calling Qantas about something very big. She knew what that meant, and shivered. Mandy, still studying company management, stared at me but remained silent – for once. I started punching numbers on the keypad, when Cynthia said, 'Oh Rob, here's another fax just in. It looks important.'

I told her, 'Not now, please. Show me later.'

Just then, a phone rang and Amanda spun around, 'Dad! You'll never ever guess who's on the other line . . . '

Uninterested, I took a guess. 'Ah, Santa Claus? Elvis?'

Grinning and shaking her head, she handed me the phone. A familiar voice with an Asian accent said, 'Greetings Mister Robert Grant. This is Mr Ho Lin of the Shenzhen Orient Hong Kong Bank. We found that chewing gum in our helicopter. Those naughty little girls! But I will be very brief: we have re-valued our old offer to you and now I wish to pay you the sum of thirty million dollars for Sky Star. What do you say, Mister Robert?'

Thirty? I'd just decided that I'd ask thirty million from Qantas while knowing they'd offer only about half that. So here was my golden opportunity to bail out in grand style. A firm offer. Let Ho Lin have the whole damn thing. He could strip it or sell it or do whatever he pleased because I hadn't the incentive or energy to fight anymore. We'd noisily refused his previous offer of ten million years ago, but times had changed and our fleet had doubled while I'd wearied.

And right here in our office, Mandy had already hinted she sought other directions, because if my interest was waning then so was hers. She no longer relished the prospect of administering so many men without me as the company's owner. The fire-breathing dragon was slightly tamed. My lovely Cynthia, with no intrinsic interest in airlines, also desired to leave us and write books while pursuing other industries with her new managerial qualifications.

And with great alarm, I'd recently read a European magazine article about the large number of wealthy people in Italy and elsewhere whose children had been kidnapped for ransoms. Some of them were never returned. We'd already brushed against this nastiness first-hand and I simply could not live with myself if this happened to us; thus my resolve to divest us of the company was now complete. I'd achieved my aims and so it was now or never.

Softly, I started to sing that song: *It's now or never,* but the womens' smirking glances indicated disapproval.

Ignoring their unkindness, I opened my mouth to say, 'You've got it, Mr Lin!', but before I could speak, Cynthia tugged forcefully at my shirt and stressed, 'Read this first!' She shoved the fax in my face and made me read it.

I was saying, 'But . . . but . . . Cynthia, please. I'm busy!'

And Amanda was yelling over the din, 'Is Mr Lin offering again? Take it this time. Please! Take it!'

There sometimes comes a unique moment in a person's life when they make such a monumental decision that it permanently alters the entire course of their existence. *THIS* was to be my finest hour when I said into the phone, 'Please hold for one moment, Mr Lin. Thank you.' This historic statement made me chuckle as I dared to imagine our honourable Asian friend's demeanour at being put on hold after making *that* offer!

Cynthia breathed relief, 'Thank God! Read this.' I took the wrinkled fax from where it had been unceremoniously rammed in my face. It was headed: *Virgin Airways. Virgin Atlantic Group.*

I mumbled, 'Oh okay, it's from Virgin. But I can't think of anything exciting they'd want us for.' From time to time we had minor correspondence from Richard Branson's giant Virgin group of companies – these days a global conglomeration of over 3,000 companies, while back then it was a mere few hundred. With us both being airlines, we traded occasional information concerning technical flight and engineering matters. Ensuring Mr Lin's call was still on hold, I strolled outside to be seated in my delightful garden; a venue of enduring pleasure and stark memories.

Settling on Mandy's favourite banana lounge, I stared at the fax page and commenced to read this astonishing letter. It was from Richard Branson himself.

Dear Robert,

Firstly, please accept my humble apologies for failing to have never made your acquaintance. I could claim that I'm a busy man, but then again, so are you - I'm told.

I'm in Australia again next week and was hoping you could pop around to see me. I'd love to shake your hand, as I've always admired your wonderful aviation achievements which together we've often paralleled.

With the big grab for the Aussie skies upon us very soon, I'll be up-front and tell you now that I am starting up an Australian arm of Virgin to be called Virgin Blue. It will very soon replace the doomed Ansett. I don't foresee, however, all of us squeezing comfortably into bed together, so was wondering if you'd ever contemplated flogging your fantastic Sky Star?

If so, I might be in a position to offer you a few dollars for the whole show. Don't want to give you false hope however, so I couldn't possibly make it more than forty.

I'd appreciate your answer soonest, and will call you next week from Sydney. Kindest regards for now, Richard.

I scribbled my one-word reply to him. It was undoubtedly the quickest and shortest letter I'd ever written. It simply said: 'Sold!' Without hesitation I ran back to the office and rammed it into the fax machine, punched buttons and sent it away before I could change my mind.

Looking over my shoulder, my startled office ladies asked why I had such an insane grin on my face. I said, 'Oh, nothing important, really. I just sold the airline.'

Mandy squawked, 'You *sold* the airline? Our airline? The *whole* bloody airline? But to Mr Lin? Or to Qantas? Or Virgin? Dad, you finally did it!' I told them that Mr Branson, one of the world's most admired businessmen and my role model since the very start of my aviating dreams, wanted to buy Sky Star and had made me an offer I couldn't refuse – just like that!

In our little office, this monumental event was surely the equivalent of the Moon landings, and Mandy sat with arms hanging down, mouth agape and blowing air like a beached whale. It was all over. Cynthia said nothing – probably contemplating her imminent future. Finally, Mandy asked 'How much?'

After a thoughtful pause, I said, 'Well, it's all rather amusing, actually. If you read the fax again, it says he *might* offer me a *few dollars*. Later he says "no more than forty." I just sent off my reply saying 'Sold!' so it's entirely possible that I've just sold Sky Star for the princely sum of forty dollars! Branson isn't the world's smartest businessman for nothing, you know. Oh well, win some lose some, I suppose. I'm going for a swim.'

Then Cynthia yelped, 'Wait on. What about Mr Lin? He's still on hold. How much did *he* offer?' I just grinned wickedly, and they both deduced what that meant. I ran to the pool and dived in. In just one dramatic minute I'd picked up an extra ten million dollars!

Mandy shot after me faster than a tin hare at the greyhounds. As I surfaced she yelped, 'Dad! Dad! Mr Lin hung up. I heard him swearing. Now, you really *are* joking - aren't you? Mr Branson obviously meant forty *million* dollars – didn't he? Surely you're not *that* . . . er, stupid. Are you?'

I floated on my back. 'Well, if you already look stupid . . . It's in writing, Mandy. Too late now. Sorry.'

'Very funny, Dad. And just what, precisely, would we do with *forty damn dollars*?'

'Well, it certainly wouldn't even buy you one pair of shoes. I've seen those price tags. No, I'll tell you what: take a well deserved holiday and get over to Europe and find that Nicky. And don't leave till you're his new art model.' For once, my daughter heartily agreed.

Gazing skywards, I sighed, 'Well, we might have got even more if we'd held out. But I don't see any better offers floating down from the heavens just now and that's the way of business. So it's time to bail out Mandy - my little Drill Sergeant.'

She asked, 'What on Earth will you do for the rest of your life, Dad?' Again I gazed to the clouds for answers. As usual, there were none.

Mandy suddenly remembered: 'Do you think I should call Mr Lin back?'

'Ah, maybe not. I don't think he likes schoolgirls very much . . . '

59.

Sky Star considers Virgin offer from Branson

This headline was the most accurate I'd read about us for years. Well, I'd certainly considered Richard's offer of just forty dollars for at least half a minute - then replied 'Sold!' This was a joke, of course, and Mr Richard Branson always appreciates good jokes. But my intent to sell was there when I fired off that fax, and I persisted with my decision to bail out and leave the operation of an airline to a real professional with massive resources behind him. Branson wanted my planes, air routes, slot times and terminal space to help get his *Virgin Blue* up and flying. Eventually he'd replace my planes with his own new Boeing 737-800 models. But in the meantime, for someone who can't sing, I'd just sold out to him for a song!

In due course the historic day arrived. At our Sydney meeting, the very busy Richard Branson broke the distressing news to me that my beloved *Sky Star* name would no longer exist; it would henceforth become part of the Virgin Group and operate as *Virgin Blue*. My striking red, white and blue colours, although slightly similar to the Virgin colour scheme, would also vanish forever, along with the flying stars and Cristina's smiling face on our flagship plane.

As I scratched my final signatures onto the relevant paperwork, a team of Virgin lawyers and mine (Bill McFarlane) peered over my shoulder; then scrutinised every dot, mark and crossed *t*. I hung my head low, hoping no-one would notice the few tears escaping down my cheek. Then we stood to shake hands as I faced banks of cameras with a forced smile while Richard's famous grin was definitely genuine.

Later, over a private coffee, Richard promised to employ Amanda in a senior managerial position upon turning eighteen – if she chose. I warned him, 'She eats razor blades for breakfast, you know,' and described her chewing out our Chief Pilot and a Chinese bank Chairman.

'A potent woman of leadership. That's exactly what I'm looking for,' laughed one of the richest men in the world who some call Mr Deep Pockets.

I told him how Mandy had originally suggested the name *Sky Star*. 'I would never have thought of it if she hadn't shown me that little toy plane. I'd considered many different names for it, but they were all rather ordinary . . . ' My beautiful airline, my dream, had just died. Richard Branson politely didn't comment. He'd bought other airlines before and had undoubtedly witnessed similar scenes.

We shook hands again as he grinned and handed me the historic cheque, then several photographers took a few more snaps of us. For a moment I wondered why our lawyers were laughing behind their hands, and then, faster than a departing jet plane, it was all over.

Fighting a few tears, I eventually glanced down at the cheque: it said, 'Please pay the sum of . . . forty dollars.' Richard noticed my raised eyebrows, then we both laughed, arm-in-arm. Always the joker, Richard grinned, 'Don't worry, Rob. I heard all about your little story. The *real* cheque is in the mail.'

It was.

*

In September 2001, Ansett Airlines finally came to its inevitable end. Immediately, Richard Branson's *Virgin Blue,* together with Qantas, filled the yawning gap in Australian air transport while Sky Star vanished forever. Somewhat sadly, I watched TV news of the official receivers' final carve-up of Reg Ansett's empire; reminiscent of AEA's scenario a decade before.

Then, over the following years, I sometimes spied my old planes taking off in their new colours; a lump firmly wedged in my throat. I'd been offered a pilot's position with Virgin but couldn't bear the thought of fighting my memories while flying for someone else. And I said 'no thanks' to a management position simply because I wasn't a manager. Besides, I had no need for more selfish income; my energies could be far better employed by giving free joy flights to sick and disadvantaged children.

Meanwhile, some of our loyal staff went to Virgin and Qantas, some went overseas and some seemed to vanish. For a while I thought Tania was one of those. My great friends Paul Harland went into flying 747's for Qantas, and Frank Phillips became a Virgin captain. And lovely Cynthia finally wrote her novel: it was cheekily called "High Altitude Adventures with a Flamboyant Billionaire." How embarrassing! Thank goodness I never read novels.

In 2003 I received a card from Aaron Tolman, now attending private schooling in Singapore. He thanked us for our previous assistance when he'd been a baby with a defective heart. His father Ken Tolman had long since left Australia to fly in Asia, and had made a feeble vow to track down Ben Preston for me - if he could. His mysterious mother remained afflicted with alcoholism.

We all went our separate ways, but I'm sure none will forget the grand and golden days of Sky Star. A saga where we were, for a while, a shining star in the sky. For myself, my corporate days were now long gone. My thrilling years at the helm had flown over the hills and far away.

These days, on our private Barrier Reef island that I'd renamed *Cristina Island,* I had ducks, geese, dogs, turtles and chickens to feed, and exotic birds to observe while our regular house guests swam amongst frolicking tropical fish in our own mini lagoon.

This week's esteemed guests at the beachside bungalow were Mr Ho Lin and family of the historical Shenzhen Orient Hong Kong Bank. Upon his arrival I'd presented him with a packet of chewing gum for his newest helicopter. Mr Lin smiled graciously, then thanked me profusely for my reciprocal hospitality - which was surely the very least I could do. He then spent the week playing golf on my mini one-hole golf course with his once arch enemy Mandy as his occasional caddy – although this time suitably attired. He expressed interest in buying our island, but we lied and told him the sand flies would drive him crazy.

Now it was 2010. My long-held dreams had come to fruition and we sat on a sparkling beach together; four beautiful ladies plus my lovely second wife. And nearby sat my sleek and sexy new toy. I had flown them all to my small private island in the Whitsunday group in my private Citation 750 jet: a gorgeous multi-million-dollar plane with ten luxurious leather seats of rich bone-white matched to gleaming walnut woodwork. This was *Cristina Island* and for once I harboured no adventurous future plans. I already had everything and more – including my lovely second wife Tania whom I'd married in 2004.

I'd pursued her after the demise of Sky Star. After a year of trying, she'd been accepted into Virgin as a pilot. In dogged pursuit, I found her and we very quickly overcame our huge disagreements and misunderstandings. We fell in love simultaneously after realising that others had once marred our paths in life – not us. (And to think that I'd once considered firing her!) Tania was almost ten years younger than me and not that much older than Amanda, but this mattered little as my daughters had quickly become firm friends with their long-awaited step-mum.

'Better late than never!' quipped Amanda at our wedding reception. "We thought the next *Ice Age* would arrive before Dad ever got married again!'

These days Tania revelled in flying for Virgin, and at the moment we were looking forward to her annual holidays when we'd be zooming the skies together again – perhaps to Bali this time in our sleek Citation jet. Sometimes, before take-off, we held brief debates over who'd be the captain, but most times she won.

And I finally met her strict Polish parents. They caught a bus from Sydney to our wedding and it was wonderful to meet them at last – although they politely declined a free joy flight in our jet.

*

On our private beach which we'd renamed *Smugglers Cove*, Tania sat contentedly on the white sand as she joined with my family surrounding me on this, my special day: my 40th birthday. She asked if I was okay. I said yes. She asked why I had tears in my eyes. I said it was the wind and sand.

Before me was beautiful Olivia, now 24, married, and with husband Tom and their three children. She was a happy mum with her two little boys and a girl who all called me *Poppa.* 'I mustn't waste time, Dad,' Olivia smiled, as the kids dug sand holes with plastic spades. 'We might even have some more one day.' I knew what she was referring to: Cristina's short and tragic life was prominent in our thoughts this day. You just never know . . .

My sweet Emily was 22 and living with a nice man in Port Douglas. She had one son, Bobby, who they'd named after me. She'd become a dancing teacher and now owned her own dance school where they taught hip hop, jazz funk and ballet. I'd picked them up in Cairns the previous day where cheerful little Bobby probably thought that everyone's grandad owned a gleaming white jet.

My baby Celia was now 21 and learning to fly light planes in Brisbane. With Tania, she had co-piloted our jet from there back to Cristina Island while I lazed up the back; chauffeured to my own island! My precious Celia would hopefully become an airline pilot one day; although I wished her every good fortune and success in whatever she eventually chose - should she ever change her mind. This was a policy thoroughly endorsed by my wife who had fought tooth and nail with her parents over her learning to fly.

And finally my sometimes fiery Amanda, now 25 and my greatest friend, had worked in management with Virgin Blue for two years then took an excellent position in marketing with *Air France* based in Paris - where 'the shopping is grand!' she assured me. Marketing was more her forte, she explained, rather than management itself. Once in Europe she'd pursued her European Lothario, Nicky, from all those years ago, and married. They had no children as yet. On holidays from France, my lovely Amanda was sitting beside me right now on the pure white sand of our private beach. How could I be happier?

I had a sudden thought: 'Hey girls, remember long ago at the farm when we tried to find that video tape to prove that Tania didn't sneak back to my room that infamous night? I know I put it away in a rumpus room drawer, but it just disappeared. I always wondered about that, and have been meaning to ask one day . . . '

Emily and Celia laughed. 'We stole it, Dad. Put it away where no-one would ever discover it. In case everything went bad for you one day, we could produce that tape to the courts and the public which proved their allegations and the whole case were all lies. It showed your bedroom sliding doors in the moonlight, and only a few ducks waddled past your room . . . apart from . . . '

'I know. I fast-forwarded it years ago. But why did you hide it?'

'Because you only fast-forwarded it for twenty minutes, silly! Later it showed two boys sneaking round the back towards our bedrooms. They only threw pebbles at our windows . . . honest. '

I feigned horror as Tania laughed, 'Well, I know that I didn't go back that night - although I would have liked to . . . ' Reflecting, I wondered if perhaps Tania was the only one who *didn't* come sneaking around that night?

Wisely, Amanda quickly changed *that* subject and stood up to make a speech. I recalled how, unlike me, she possessed quite some talent in this.

'Since the age of thirteen, our Dad has been a cloud dancer. Can't sing, can't dance, but he sure can fly a mean aeroplane and has waltzed them through the skies in the grandest elegance. Now it's his fortieth birthday and we're all gathered on our beach here today to be a family together once again. But we girls couldn't even *imagine* what present we could possibly buy for someone who has his own private island and a jet – plus a few other assets as well! So we finally decided on the ideal gift. Something unique and precious to only you and us. You'll never guess in a thousand years what it is . . . '

My quartet of girls smiled knowingly as little Bobby toddled forward. He was nearly two years old and learning to talk. There was something in his hands: a small gift for my birthday which he clutched ever so tightly.

I said, 'Aw heck, kids. I don't want anything for my silly birthday, for Heaven's sake. There's nothing I need. Birthday presents are for the young and deserving, and I'm neither. *Yesterday* I was young. So let him keep it, please.'

Despite my pleas, Emily held out Bobby's little hand and said, 'Dad, do you remember this?' She unfolded his tiny fingers and I gasped in unbridled astonishment! It was a small toy. An old red, white and blue toy. It was faded and worn, but still recognisable as that original plastic plane! I gripped it fiercely and fought back tears. Peering closely, I spied a few remaining painted stars flying towards the rear. With difficulty, and with my reading glasses perched on my nose, I could just make out the faded writing along one side: it said *Sky Star*.

I reminded everyone that it was Mandy who, out of the blue, came up with the unique name for our great airline when she was only eight years old. In a survey we conducted in 1999, a majority of those polled said they flew with us because of our catchy name: it was different, exciting, sexy. If this was in fact true, then Mandy's creation may have generated millions in income for us because where the humdrum name *Ansett* was simply the name of its founder, and *Qantas* is an awkward acronym, *Sky Star* attracted many travellers seeking a fresh carrier with a stirring new name. Conversely, I shuddered to consider how *Grant Airlines* may have fared. Or my other absurd idea: *Oz Air*.

Filled with pride, Emmie explained, 'We kept the toy all these years in Mum's little bag with our most treasured possessions. We never told you and wanted to wait for the right moment. See Dad, you haven't lost your great dream after all. Do you still love it?' My girls cuddled me as I hung my head, turning the precious toy over in my hands.

Little Bobby smiled as he said, 'Happy birthday, Poppa.'

I couldn't answer him for tears, so Amanda, that little princess whose tiny pleading eyes had once helped to persuade me to marry her wonderful mother, took it from me and smiled. 'Acts tough, but he's really just an old softie. Let's see if it still flies, everyone!'

She hurled the tiny toy skywards and it flew like an angel! Laughing, we adults pursued my tribe of grandkids as we chased the soaring toy along the beach beside small breaking waves.

But then, for one amazing moment, I seemed to be watching four young girls running with their pony tails flying in the tropical breeze. In overwhelming happiness, we all glanced up at my tiny birthday present as it looped the loop and again become a star of the sky – a place from where my Cristina was surely watching.

Embracing Tania, I managed to say, 'Look! Sky Star flies once more. Should I do it all again, girls?'

They all turned around and beamed their best smiles as Amanda grinned, 'Funny, Dad!'

Then, from nowhere, I seemed to hear some of the hauntingly beautiful words of my favourite song: *'Yesterday, when I was young, the taste of life was sweet as rain upon my tongue . . . '*

'Oh dear,' warned Tania. 'Your dad is singing again.' My girls giggled – I wonder why - then I ran, singing, towards the little ones who were making sand castles near the water's edge. On the way, I leapt up to catch the little toy plane again and hurl it higher - just as a camera flashed its light at me. I was framed, off the ground, with a crazy grin on my face and pretty clouds behind me.

With my gray and shaggy beachcomber's hair and beard, for one worrying moment I hoped that photo would never be published because I could just *imagine* the headlines:

ECCENTRIC WITH OWN ISLAND AND JET, DANCES WITH THE CLOUDS!

www.ingramcontent.com/pod-product-compliance
Lightning Source LLC
Chambersburg PA
CBHW071156020726
47502CB00002B/439